Destiny
of
HEROES

Destiny

of

HEROES

Lt. Dan Marcou

Thunder Bay Press

Holt, Michigan

Destiny of Heroes
A Novel by Lt. Dan Marcou

Published by
Thunder Bay Press
Holt, Michigan 48842

First Printing September 2013

17 16 15 14 13   1 2 3 4 5

ISBN: 978-1-933272-42-9
LCCN: 2013948597

This is a work of fiction.

Book design by Amelia Turkette.
Cover design by Julie Taylor.

Printed in the United States of America
by Versa Press — East Peoria, Illinois

Killed in the Line of Duty

They always knew they could be,
They never thought they would be
God knows none ever should be
Killed in the line of duty.

Some made their final stand,
Their profession's last demand,
They fell with gun in hand,
Killed in the line duty.

A routine to many a cop
Some made one final stop
Someone's Mom or Pop
Killed in the line of duty.

Others answered one last call
To a robbery, theft, or brawl
They arrived only to fall
Killed in the line of duty.

Some were dressed in brown some blue,
Some in gray and plain clothes too,
Some dressed like me and you,
Killed in the line of duty.

May their souls be forever blessed,
For now they are at rest
They died doing what they loved best,
Killed in the line of duty.

Forgotten they never could be,
Forgotten they never should be
They never thought they would be
Killed in the line of duty.

God bless all those who fell,
They are missed and loved so well,
Let us pray and toll the bell
For those killed in the line of duty.

—Dan Marcou

ONE MILLION SOULS LIE SLEEPING

They lived, they loved, they laughed, they cried,
One million souls lie sleeping.

They stood and fought, then fell and died,
One million souls lie sleeping.

They did all we asked of them and more,
One million souls lie sleeping.

Some eighteen, as they marched to war,
One million souls lie sleeping.

Remember them as you bow your head,
One million souls lie sleeping.

For freedom they all fought and bled,
One million souls lie sleeping.

America is the land of the free,
One million souls lie sleeping

A debt is owed by you and me,
One million souls lie sleeping

It is not too much to, once a year,
One million souls lie sleeping

To remember them and shed a tear,
One million souls lie sleeping.

—*Dan Marcou*

Since 1776 more than 1,000,000 American soldiers have died in combat. This book is dedicated to those souls and the men and women who fought beside them who continue to courageously risk all by going once more unto the breach.

Table of Contents

CHAPTER ONE

Ambushed by the Queen of Hearts

As John Savage squinted through the stinging sweat in his eyes to see what potential dangers lay ahead, he pondered. In Iraq, the heat was just like the enemy. You sensed its heavy presence, but it surrounded you unseen. If you weren't careful the heat could kill you as certainly as the blast from an undetected IED. John reached into the small pocket of his vest and grabbed a piece of Bazooka Bubble Gum, unwrapped it, popped the gum in his mouth, and started chewing it soft as he read the comic. He smiled and carefully folded the comic, tucking it back into his vest pocket.

The heat was bearable only because he was a soldier at war and had no choice but to endure the 118 degree temperature. Anyone born and raised in Wisconsin grows accustomed to cold winters. During the summer when a day reaches into the 90s, "Cheeseheads" will all praise themselves for being able to tolerate a Wisconsin summer. They bear the burden of the humidity, longing for the higher temperatures of an arid climate because it is a "dry heat."

John day-dreamed himself back home listening to his mother complain about "the humidity," as she longed for that "dry heat." The thought inspired him to shout up to his gunner, Balduzzi. "Dry, wet, or covered in shit, 118 degrees is hot," shouted John.

"I can't even catch a breeze up here," shouted down Balduzzi, who was top side of the Humvee manning the 249 SAW.

John hydrated himself as he always did whenever he thought about the heat. He knew that if he was thinking about heat he was losing focus. A sip of water always brought him back to the business at hand. At this moment John rode shotgun in the lightly armored Humvee, which was the last vehicle in a three vehicle reconnaissance. His unit lumbered along route Irish. The road was a heavily traveled supply artery which languished through the desert outside Baghdad.

The mission today was to clear the route for the convoys which would follow. John scanned the roadside for something out of place, like a child with a cell phone standing alone waving and smiling, freshly disturbed soil, or construction materials scattered about in a manner that was too random to be accidental. So far nothing looked out of the ordinary in this environment that had been home to him and his squad since the 3rd Infantry took Baghdad.

He felt his stomach turn again as it did every time they approached the curve up ahead. It was a perfect spot for an ambush, but they had passed it fifty times before, and even though he would always get on the radio and give a quick "heads up here on the left," nothing ever happened. On the left was an escarpment that curved perfectly as if it was man-made instead of natural. Below it was an irrigation ditch running along between the road and the escarpment. Either spot would be a perfect place to set up an ambush.

Before John could give his "heads up," Chase cut in over the radio, barking," Heads up on the left!" Chase was the best friend John ever had and they, along with Balduzzi, were referred to as, "The Three Amigos," by other members of the unit.

John was already looking left and saw a movement in the irrigation canal. The insurgent blended perfectly into his surroundings but had done nothing to alter the black detonator, which stood out to John like a distributor in a V-8 engine. "Balduzzi, 2:00! 2:00! 2:00! Take him out now!"

Balduzzi shouted, "I see him!" He racked the SAW and spun it toward the black detonator, which to Balduzzi seemed to be hovering in mid-air. Then the box jerked as the bomber hit the detonator's trigger just as Balduzzi's opened up with the SAW. The rounds from Balduzzi's weapon ripped through the dry heat of the desert and into the bomber. They arrived a moment too late to prevent the explosion triggered by the camouflaged bomber. It belched a ball of flame from the right side of the road, seeming to swallow up Chase's lead vehicle. Simultaneously the area from the left and above the escarpment seemed to come alive as a contingent of hidden enemy opened up, and the ambush John Savage had seen in his day-dreams and nightmares was happening right in front of him.

John shouted, "Cut right off the road. The incline will give us some cover!" Haldane, the driver, was already moving.

"Balduzzi concentrate your fire on that ridge. Boots, cover the irrigation canal. You could conceal an oversized company in there. I am going to make my way around the left and flank them." John had not only pictured the ambush, he had mapped out his response. He had given these commands fifty times before in his daydreams and nightmares. His dream, which to some would be considered a premonition had prepared him well for this day.

As the Humvee rolled to a stop, John secured his M4, spit out his gum, and rolled out of the Humvee, staying low so that he could not be seen by the enemy. He ran fifty yards parallel to the road, following the ditch line to a small bridge. Reaching the bridge, he cautiously approached but paused at the embankment adjacent to the bridge with his M4 at the ready. As the battle raged to his rear, he leaned slightly out to clear the area under the bridge, and there they were. There were three of them. The leader was turned to the two that followed him, and he was giggling as if they had just succeeded in leaving a bag of burning feces on the neighbor's doorstep and watched him stomp it out.

The two that followed the leader were also joyous at the apparent success of their surprise attack. There was the abrupt change when the two realized they had celebrated their victory too soon. John sent a burst in their direction, trying to conserve his ammunition for the fight ahead. All three went down.

As John moved past the three ambushers, he quickly checked to make certain of the effectiveness of his fire when he noticed the red triangle patch on their uniforms. It was the patch of Saddam Hussein's vaunted Republican Guard. The faces of the three in death took on the appearance of masks. Two of the dead had a look of horror frozen in place as if John had hit a pause button on a remote rather than the trigger on his weapon. The leader, who never perceived his imminent demise, was still smiling a garish smile. So passed eleven seconds of John Savage's life, from which every sound, sight, and smell would be forever emblazoned in his brain's hard drive. There would be time to dwell on it all later. Now was not the time, for John Savage was on the move.

As John approached the enemy's right flank, he could see that all of the fire was coming from the ridge along the top of the escarpment. As he climbed the path leading up the escarpment, he could see the lone bomber in the canal. He was clearly visible now that the camouflage was compromised because the bomber had been nearly cut in half by Balduzzi's accurate fire. Because of the curve in the road, John could only see the smoke of the lead Humvee, but it was clear from the rate of fire that someone had survived the explosion and was "truly pissed."

John had scouted out the escarpment months earlier, and he headed quickly up the path stopping just short of the top. As he eased up, he used the muzzle of his weapon as if it was his third eye, and he saw he was twenty feet from two guardsmen desperately firing back toward Balduzzi, Haldane, and Boots. There was no celebration going on here for there was a third guardsman who would be sending no more letters home. He had obviously been hit in the head by Balduzzi's SAW and lay dead. John took aim carefully, but quickly, and "Pop-Pop, Pop-Pop." Both guardsmen, who were already prone, dropped their heads as if they had simultaneously dozed off. John was on the move again as he continued to work his way up the Iraqi line.

The path snaked its way along the back side of the ridge, which took the shape of a strung archer's bow. The Humvees were caught in the sights of the bow. John was working his way from the lower limb of the bow to its tip. The rocks and scrub brush allowed him to move from position to position without being seen by the Iraqis, who were all heavily focused on the Humvees below.

As John came upon the next position, he saw three insurgents firing toward his buddies, but a fourth was on his knees facing John with his head down. He was frantically reloading his weapon; when he looked up and saw John he screamed, "EEEiiiiii!" As the panicked Iraqi tried to put his replacement magazine into the weapon backward, John fired at the three, taking them out of the fight and then hit the screaming Iraqi who had dropped his weapon to pick up a grenade. He managed to pull the pin as he was hit, and John ducked behind a rock and waited for the explosion.

After the loud, but dull "Whump!" he was on the move again. As John passed the scene of his work, he saw the screaming Iraqi must have slumped forward on his own grenade when he was shot. The aftermath of this encounter caused John to slow down, trying to interpret its meaning, as if the scene were a Picasso painting. Once he realized he was slowing down, he whispered to himself, "Get your ass moving, no time to dawdle." John sped up as he switched out the magazine in his M4 and slipped the old magazine into his side pocket. It still had rounds in it which he might need later.

While John worked his way toward the middle of the ridge, he came upon a heavily prepared position. Flat rocks were carefully chosen and piled to give the occupants cover from the front and both sides. They had prepared gun ports in their position, but all faced forward. John could not see anything of his adversaries but their muzzles and an occasional helmet top popping above the white rock wall. He scanned the area and could see no one guarding their flank.

"I can't believe this is the Republican Guard. I heard they were supposed to be the best, and as of yet no one is covering their six," John said quietly to himself as he slung his M4 and took two grenades out. He moved quickly, pulling the pin out of one as he held the grenade and the striker lever tightly in place with his right hand, preventing the grenade's detonation. John efficiently went about multi-tasking in a manner which the person who invented the word could never have envisioned. He pulled the pin on the second grenade with his right hand as he held the striker lever on the second grenade with his left hand. He moved quickly forward, hugging the white rock wall of the prepared position. All the occupants were heavily engaged in trying to kill every member of his unit, and members of his unit were all vigorously returning the favor.

Got to wait for the last second, thought John, *I am too close to let them have the opportunity to throw these back.* He took a deep breath and let it out. He released both striker levers simultaneously, and they sprung clear of the grenades. John held the grenades longer than he had ever held live grenades before in either training or in combat, and at what proved to be the last possible moment, he tossed them both over the rock wall. He turtled up, making himself as small as possible as he plugged his ears. Instantly, there was one loud explosion as the grenades went off in unison. He found the Iraqi position to be well fortified because the metal particles of death from his grenades were all either held within the bodies of John's enemies or contained by the hastily built, but well-constructed, rock wall.

John swung his M4 about, quickly peeking around the back side of the wall. He discovered that the two grenades had turned this deadly location into a messy but now peaceful scenic overlook. Enjoying the view, however, would be for someone else at another time. John was moving again.

Ahmed's plan was working. The position he had chosen and prepared for this attack was perfect. Since Saddam and his generals had gone into hiding, Al-Qaeda had taken a leadership role. Ahmed had no rank, but he was the de facto commander of this small contingent of Republican Guard, which would have melted away long ago if not for Ahmed's inspiration and his ready supply of cash. He watched with great satisfaction as the improvised explosive device detonated and engulfed the lead Humvee. He shouted, "Allahu Akbar! Allahu Akbar!"

His initial joy gave way to shock to see the Americans somehow roll out of the burning Humvee and return fire at an alarming rate.

Ahmed fired back with his two companions. As the battle was joined, Ahmed realized that the heights provided a position of advantage over two of the American Humvees, but he could see neither the rest of his line nor one of the Humvees in the American Squad. "Damned it! Abdullah set off the charge too soon!" he shouted to Hussein, who was next to him firing at the Americans. Hussein did not even react since he was engaged in firing his AK-47 wildly at everything but hitting nothing.

"Hussein. Take careful aim. At this distance you will hit nothing unless you aim," shouted Ahmed, but Hussein was "praying and spraying" as was Tariq next to him. Ahmed listened and could hear the entire line of Republican Guards he had personally positioned engaging the Americans. He smiled and shook his head thinking, "We will win this glorious fight."

Ahmed had wondered if his unit would stand and fight with him. Since the fall of Baghdad, even the Republican Guard had lost its zealous loyalty to Saddam, who was hiding in a hole somewhere. Saddam Hussein occupied himself moving from place to place and sending out communiqués occasionally telling non-existent loyalists units to, "Fight to the death against the American devils and make their blood flow like rivers."

Ahmed and many like him had stepped in to fill the void. His orders were simple. He was to cajole, bribe, or threaten Iraqi's into inflicting a continuous flow of casualties on the Americans and their allies until their "weak leadership" ordered the military to withdraw as they had in Somalia. Ahmed had been only fourteen when he went to Somalia to join the Jihad. He had fought in the battle of the Bakaara Market in Mogadishu. He had been in the battle of Kandahar and with Bin Laden at Tora Bora. Ahmed thought himself to be America's worst nightmare. To him, Islam was not "the religion of peace" but a sacred call for a violent Jihad. He refused to die needlessly for Allah but instead felt better suited to kill for Allah.

As Ahmed watched the battle develop, he noticed one American soldier fighting from behind some rubble on the opposite side of the road. When he had escaped the burning Humvee, he appeared to be moving too fast to be injured. The soldier would expose himself occasionally to take a shot from behind a discarded chunk of concrete he was using for cover.

Ahmed shouldered his rifle and took careful aim. He began taking deep breaths, letting each one seep out slowly like life's last whisper. He was patient. He would wait for a kill shot. "Come to me, come, come, come, Allahu Akbar," Ahmed whispered as he squeezed the trigger. "Bam!" The soldier crumpled to the ground. After Ahmed fired the one round, his rifle jammed.

Ahmed locked the action open and yanked the magazine out, but the casing had failed to eject after he had fired. He sat up and began working the action forward and backward repeatedly trying to free the casing. He blew hard on the sand covered rounds in the magazine and slipped out his knife to pry the empty brass from the chamber. "Goat Fuck!" Ahmed shouted as he pried the brass loose enough to take hold of the rim and pull it the rest of the way out. "This ammunition is shit!" Ahmed shouted to the heavens.

⸺⧽●⧼⸺

Just before John rounded the bend in the line to reach the last position, he press checked the chamber on the M4 and saw the round glint in the sun. His ever-faithful and ever-present companion in war was waiting patiently for its opportunity to continue the fight. John never failed to take care of his weapon and, in turn, it never failed to take care of him.

John took a deep breath through his nose and blew it out through his mouth as if he was on the range preparing for his qualification course. He peered up over the ridge and saw his friends were holding their own. He had maneuvered to a point where he could see all three Humvees and the fighting positions his friends had taken. They had chosen well. Even from these heights the available terrain appeared to be providing good cover. As John counted the puffs of smoke, he could see everyone was fighting, and it did not look like they had suffered any casualties. This position, chosen by the enemy, provided great defensibility if properly manned, but the distance to the road was a long shot for an average soldier to make under battle conditions. The enemy's attack was proving to be a wasted effort. He smiled with pride, admiring the fighting spirit of his unit.

John woke himself from his ill-timed reverie and was just about to move as his buddy Chase rose up to fire. Before Chase could take his next shot, there appeared a puff of pink mist from just below his helmet and Chase slumped to the ground, motionless. One of the best friends John had ever had was gone in an instant.

"Chase!" John cried out painfully to the blue Iraqi sky as he went on the move again. The last position was built in the same configuration as the position he had just taken out with grenades, but its occupants had only piled the rocks about a foot and a half high. Two were on one knee firing down toward the patrol, both oblivious to John's arrival. One was sitting up and trying to clear a malfunction in his rifle with his knife. John opened fire, killing the one closest to him first. The man never saw what hit him.

The second soldier reacted quickly and swung his rifle toward him, and John, whose blood was up for the fight, fired four times at the guardsman before he could get a shot off. John could see his rounds hit the man in the throat and head, and the one-time member of Saddam's personal guard toppled clumsily over backwards falling into the lap of the third man. The last living ambusher's eyes and mouth opened wide and he dropped his knife and rifle abandoning his effort to clear his weapon. As he did this, he thrust his hands high into the air.

"Please don't shoot. Don't shoot. I love America. Fuck Saddam!" Ahmed turned and spit at the mention of the name. "My name is Ahmed. I am not your enemy. God Bless America. God Bless You. You have saved Me!" whimpered Ahmed. "Please don't shoot."

John Savage was frozen with his weapon trained on the athletically muscled, dark-haired man with light olive-colored skin, which appeared to be turning an ashen gray. The man spoke excellent English with a slight Julio Iglesias-type accent but not as pronounced. Up until this moment, Previously John had surprised his foes at each position, but this encounter took him by surprise. He was ill-prepared for this particular situation.

Before John could say a word, the man rolled his dead comrade out of his lap and slowly got up. Ahmed began unbuttoning his uniform shirt as he loudly cried, "I hate Saddam!" He ripped the shirt off, spit on it, and then offered it to John, "You can have this. I love America. I studied in America. God Bless America!" When John made no move, Ahmed threw the uniform shirt to the ground, and he ground it into the dirt with his boot. He looked into John's eyes and could see the confusion. Ahmed thrust up his hands again to feign the dutiful prisoner.

"You are our liberators. You have freed us from the pig, Saddam. I now can go home to my family. Please let me go home. I will never raise my hand against an American again." Then Ahmed conjured up a look of glorious love and while his eyes were locked on the eyes of John Savage he said, "You have not captured me, you have rescued me. God bless you, my young American friend. Thank you."

"You're welcome?" said John instinctively, an out-of-place courtesy ingrained in John, the result of living a lifetime in Wisconsin. Cheese Heads were known far and wide to be congenitally friendly. This fact is proven by their willingness to tolerate a moniker like Cheese Head without punching someone in the nose. This amiable nature, however felt out of place on the battlefield, even to John.

Ahmed could see in the eyes of the soldier that the American had succumbed to the ruse emotionally, but not tactically. The muzzle was staring unwaveringly at Ahmed. He could see but one option before him. Surrender would be unacceptable because he would eventually be discovered as a member of Al-Qaeda. He had made a name for himself. He had earned such a reputation his heavily whiskered face was emblazoned on a deck of cards. Surrender would mean he would be sent to Guantanamo Bay and would never see home again.

Ahmed deduced attacking this American would be suicide, and throwing his life away without reason or reward, even for the cause of Jihad, was ridiculous for a man of Ahmed's talents. Now that he stood eye to eye with the enemy before him, he assessed that this man was a warrior, by his actions, trappings, and bearings. The warrior's eyes told Ahmed that this American possessed something Ahmed did not possess. Ahmed deemed this trait a weakness with no place in the pantheon of modern Jihadists… mercy.

Ahmed put on the most tragic facial expression he could muster as he explained, "I hate Saddam. I will wear his uniform not one moment longer. Please do not shoot me." He dropped his hands and sat in the dirt pulling off his pants.

"What? W-W-Wait," stuttered John.

Ahmed ignored John's half-hearted words of caution. He had judged this American correctly. John would not shoot. He continued to roughly rip at his pants and pulled them over his boots.

Ahmed kicked free of the last vestige of his uniform and thought, *I was willing to sacrifice all of the soldiers I led to this hilltop to kill one American soldier and I have done it. Now I must live to fight another day.*

Ahmed popped up to his feet and said, "Thank you, GI. I am free now, just like in America. I can go home now to my wife and children. I love America. My war is over. Thank you. God Bless America," and with that Ahmed turned and ran down the back side of the hill yelling, "God Bless America! God Bless America!"

"Stop or I'll Shoot!" shouted John, and it was not an idle threat. He took careful aim at the man running away from him in his underwear screaming, "God Bless America." It would be an easy shot to make, but John found it a difficult shot to take. This man running nearly naked down the side of the hill was either exactly the type of person he came here to kill, or exactly the type of person he came here to liberate. There was no way for John to know which one was the case. John found himself here in the middle of the desert, swimming in the unfamiliar waters of indecisiveness.

"WOOMP!" John recognized the unmistakable sound of a 40 mm MK-19 grenade leaving the muzzle of its launcher fired from below toward his position. John's friends were obviously unaware that he had cleared the position.

Instinctively, John ran back in the direction he had come from, toppled over a boulder and skidded to a stop as he tried to avoid the imminent spray of killing fragmentation, "BOOOM!" Rocks and shrapnel ripped through the dessert air around him just inches over his head.

After John emerged from the mental and physical haze created by the near miss, he regained his equilibrium. John keyed his mic and radioed, "Road

Dog Three to Road Dog Leader, Cease Fire! I am on the ridge. The ridge has been cleared and is secured. Cease Fire! Repeat, Cease Fire!"

"10-4 Road Dog Three," crackled the response followed by the command, "All Road Dog Units Cease Fire! Cease Fire!"

After a brief pause there was a cluster of frenzied communications. "Road Dog One to Road Dog Leader we have one KIA."

"10-4 Road Dog One, who is your KIA?" came a voice sounding concerned.

"Chase is down. He's gone," followed the response from a voice reflecting the realization that a good friend would not be going home.

John came up with his weapon at the ready, but Ahmed was nowhere in sight. "Well, bad guy or not I guess you are now officially liberated, Ahmed. Peace out," said John kissing two fingers and flashing a peace sign toward the area he had last seen Ahmed hightailing.

———⟫●⟪———

Two days later as John played five card draw at Camp Victory, he discarded a six of clubs, hoping to fill an ace high inside straight with a queen. The dealer with one hand adeptly flicked a card across the table, causing it to slide face down neatly in front of John's chips. John tried to look emotionless as he slid the queen into his hand and managed to conceal his joy after his wish was granted.

Then his poker face fled the battlefield as the emotion of joy was replaced by the sinking feeling of depression. He laid down his cards face up and said, "I'm out guys," as he pushed himself away from the table.

Not believing his eyes, Balduzzi spread out John's cards and bit down hard on the tip of his cigar, causing it to stand at attention. Balduzzi managed to talk out of one side of his mouth, gripping his cigar tightly between his teeth. He displayed John's cards in disbelief. "That's OK if you want, partner. I'll always back your move, but that's an ace high straight you are walking away from, Johnny."

The rest of the players hooted in approval. Boots declared, "Out is out! He's out!" He sat straight up realizing his aces and eights may take the rather sweet pot. John had been the big winner up to this point. Boots was not the type of poker player who would ever question why another player with a winning hand was folding. "No guts no glory, he's out!"

Balduzzi was a friend first, poker player second, and it was disconcerting to see such an uncharacteristic mood shift in the rock solid John Savage. "Whadaya doin', Johnny? What da fuck?" Balduzzi sputtered.

"The face on the card. That's the guy. The guy in his underwear God blessin' America that ran away from the ambush," explained John. The deck that was being used in the game was one of the decks passed out to the coalition soldiers with photos of the most wanted war criminals in Iraq. It was a coalition strategy that proved very successful.

Balduzzi shifted his cigar to the other side of his mouth as the smoke drifted into his left eye. He picked up John's cards, "Are you sure, Johnny. I thought we got most of these peckerwoods. Which one is it?" asked Balduzzi as he fanned the hand out and closely scrutinized each face on each card as if he looked hard enough he might be able to recognize someone he had never seen before.

John walked back and pointed as if he was picking him out in a police line-up, "It's him. I'm certain."

"Are you sure of it. Looks like just another Ahmed Abdullah Bin-Asshole to me," said Balduzzi with a tone of incredulity.

"I'm sure it's him. This was him. Ahmed Abdullah Rahim. He even used the name Ahmed; besides I'll never forget those eyes. I had my sights on an Al-Qaeda commander, and I let him get away. I'm telling you that's the guy! The son of a bitch! We were ambushed by the Queen of Hearts."

Chapter Two

OOO-AHHHH!

John Savage sat calmly in the chair centered before a long table at which four distinguished local luminaries sat dispassionately. He had been before this group once previously, and they had approved his hiring by the La Crosse Police Department. Before he was hired, 9-11 happened and John Savage enlisted. The only thing that had changed since then was John was a little bit older and he had served his country in two wars, after which he had left the regular army and joined the reserves.

John thought he had reached the end of the interview, when the tall, thin balding man in the center of the table queried, "I have one more question for you. Are you any relation to an Ernie Savage? I served with him in the 7th Cavalry at la Drang, Republic of Vietnam."

John answered, "I got that question a lot in the service, so I checked and discovered that he is a distant relation, but I never had the honor of meeting the man. I am honored to meet someone who was with him at Ia Drang." John instinctively began to salute the soldier who had been part of the famous "Lost Patrol of Ia Drang," but he stopped as soon as he started, concerned about violating the protocol of a civilian interview.

"Thank you for that young man, and I would like to thank you for your answers. That will be all…"

"Excuse me," interrupted the woman to the bald man's left. "We have asked the prepared questions, but I am allowed to ask some unprepared questions if I have concerns," said the angry looking woman.

"Concerns?" asked the balding man, who was the police and fire commission's chairman. "'What kind of concerns would you…" and then the man looked at the handsome young man in the coal grey suit seated in front of them and realized any discussion about the interruption better be had outside the presence of the candidate. He bowed to the harsh woman and said, "Proceed Ms. Thomason."

"Indeed I will," she said glaring indignantly at the chairman.

Jane Thomason was a 60-ish old former state legislator who still wore her straw blonde hair long and straight in the same style she wore at Woodstock in 1969. The only variation of this standard look was when she expected trouble in those days of rage. When she was one of the instigators during an anti-war riot, she braided it. It was braided when the Madison Wisconsin Police tear-gassed her and her fellow radicals on Bascom Hill at the University of Madison in May 1970. It was a time when some professors gave credit in classes for students who attended demonstrations. She was, as she described herself to her close friends, "An unrepentant pot-smoking-hippie-radical; a leftover bi-product of the tumultuous '60s." She still held a special disdain for anyone who would wear the uniform and carry a weapon and kill for the advancement of American Imperialism.

Now, Jane Thomason had a veteran of "one of America's wars of colonization," and he was in her sights.

"Savage? That's quite a name. What kind of name is that?" asked Thomason in a tone of an inquisitor rather than interviewer.

John Savage had been asked this question many times before. He had no answer for it the first time it was asked, but John had made it a point since he was a child to never be unprepared for the same situation twice. He answered smoothly, trying not to sound as if he had memorized the answer even though he had. "Savage is old English and possibly Gallic. It is an example of one of the original surnames that survived from the times when a man's name was derived from a certain attribute. It dates to a time prior to William the Conqueror when surnames were first developed. My family emigrated from England in the early 1600s. You might say I come from a long line of Savages," John answered with a smile, noticing that the answer caused the whole panel to smile except the angry woman who had asked the question.

"Very interesting, Mr. Savage. I see that you were offered the position of police officer in 2001 and declined the city's offer. Can you explain why you would turn down the position and yet ask us to consider you again now?" asked Jane.

"Well, ma'am, I am glad you asked that question. I was offered the position the afternoon of September 11, 2001, but had been so moved by the images of those attacks I felt compelled to enlist. It seemed to me that I had witnessed my generation's Pearl Harbor and thought it my duty to enlist as my father did during the Vietnam War and my grandfather did in 1941. I explained this to the chief at the time and told him I would reapply upon my return," explained John. "He encouraged me to do so. He said he could make no guarantees, but I would receive fair consideration if I re-applied."

"Yes, very admirable... admirable, indeed, fair consideration," said Thomason whose tone sounded as if she could have expressed her sentiments more accurately and efficiently by just saying, "Whatever." She opened and perused the manila file on the desk. "I see you are a combat veteran," said Thomason looking through a document in front of her and acting as if she had just made the discovery.

"Yes, ma'am," answered John. *Enough said...*

"Have you ever killed anyone?" asked Thomason without looking up from the file, "I see you have won the Silver Star. They do not give those out to conscientious objectors, although I truly wish they would."

"Ms. Thomason, where are you going with... What are you..." sputtered the commissioner, who was stifled in mid-sentenced by Thomason who snapped her hand up like a traffic cop stopping a speeding Porsche approaching her intersection.

"Yes, ma'am, I have been humbled to have received that particular decoration for actions in combat," answered John hoping that by throwing out that small bit of meat he would satisfy the bizarre cravings of this snapping dog.

Not the least bit satisfied, Thomason snapped again, "You did not answer the question, Mr. Savage. Have you ever killed another human being?"

"Jane," beckoned the portly man with a round head and red face on the opposite end of the table. He was quieted with a look that would have killed him if a look could ever have such a result.

"Yes, ma'am," answered John Savage with an honest, matter-of-fact directness. He sat bolt upright as if at attention and now looked the openly-angry woman in the eyes.

"Have you ever sought out counseling since those troubling events?" asked Thomason trying to muster an empathetic but obviously insincere resonance.

"No, ma'am, I have not," answered John, telling the truth knowing full well he was now in the realm of, "Damned if he did and damned if he didn't," with this woman.

"I have long held the belief that war is so destructive and so damaging to the psyche that everyone who has experienced it should seek and receive counseling for a considerable length of time—maybe even a lifetime. I also believe that after suffering such a trauma that the career of police officer, which is fraught with unique dangers and requires a cool head, is not the best profession for combat veterans who may be hyper-vigilant or susceptible to the temptation to… let's say overreact," said Thomason, who then cocked her head toward her left shoulder and waited for a response.

After thirty seconds of quiet, she straightened her head and looked puzzled and asked, "Do you have an answer, Mr. Savage?"

"Do you have a question, ma'am?" asked John.

The bald man glared at Thomason, clearly frustrated by her, leaned forward, clenched both fists and growled, "Jane, you made a statement. You did not ask the young man a question. Please, if you wish to continue with this, dispense with the editorializing and ask this young man questions."

Thomason tightened her jaw, put on her glasses that were on a chain around her neck, and looked at the file once again. After spending a few moments shuffling papers, she took off her glasses and asked, "Do you feel at all psychologically traumatized after the killing you personally did?"

"No, ma'am. I did what I had to do, and if I wouldn't have, I would not be here right now and some of my buddies would not have made it home. My country was at war, and I was doing what I was trained to do and sent there to do. I did not seek counseling, because I felt then as now that I am at peace with what I was called upon to do. It is what soldiers sometimes have to do, and I am as proud now as I was then to be an American soldier," answered John with a clear and unfaltering voice.

"I see that you are actually still in the service and required to return when called upon?" Jane asked.

"Yes, ma'am. I am a Reserve. I will be required to attend a monthly drill and yearly training. I may be asked to return to active duty for specialized training and/or redeployment," answered John.

"Where will your loyalties lie, with the city or the military?" asked Jane, her voice rising as she leaned forward and slapped the palms of her hands down on the table in front of her as if she were Joseph McCarthy and had just discovered a card-carrying communist in their midst.

"That will be all!" said the bald man with insistence, cutting off Thomason and making a point not to look at her while he tried to salvage the professionalism of the interview. "Thank you, young man, for your time and we will be in touch."

"Thank you for the opportunity," John nodded to each member of the commission and he turned and exited the room.

As soon as the door closed behind him, the chairman looked straight down at the table in front of him, avoiding eye contact with Thomason. He said with disgust, "That was disgraceful. We not only should offer that young man a position, but we *must* offer that man a position."

"What!?" blurted out Jane Thomason indignantly.

"These interviews have to be conducted in a fair manner. That interview showed a distinct bias against that young man, whose only crime was to answer the call of his country. You asked him about his loyalties in reference to his Reserve status. That is clearly prohibited in this venue. An employer must yield to and accommodate the schedules of Reservists and National Guard members. Employers are allowed to give extra consideration to veterans, but they are not allowed to discriminate against them, which is what you just did. It was even done in our presence. For God's sakes woman, have you no shame?" The chairman continued, "Don't answer that question; it was rhetorical. In addition to that, you reminded me of how I was treated when I returned from Vietnam," said the commissioner now turning red.

"I did not know you were a Vietnam era veteran. You never said anything...," said Jane.

"I was not a Vietnam era vet, I was a Vietnam Combat Veteran, and because of the way I was treated upon my return, I was guarded about who I divulged that information to back then and even now. Because of the attitude about the Vietnam War from what I call the 'vocal minority' at the time, I ultimately told no one except those closest to me. I can tell you that this young man deserved better than what he received today from you."

"But I only...," chimed in Jane.

The commissioner mimicked her traffic-cop move and continued, "If we do not hire that young man who, by the way, is the best candidate I have seen by far up to this point, he will have legitimate grounds for a federal law suit against the city for discrimination against a veteran, and I for one would testify on his behalf. Are we all agreed on this?" Everyone nodded except Jane Thomason, who looked shell-shocked.

"I am sorry to have offended you. I did not know you were a soldier, Jim" said Jane in an appeasing tone.

"Ma'am, I was not just a soldier. I was 7th Cavalry. I was Air Cav from 1962 through 1966. I re-enlisted and served again from 1967 through 1971, and I will not stand by and have another generation of returning veterans treated badly. I was spit upon at the airport when I returned from a tour in 1971. By the way, did you ever spit on any soldiers, Jane?"

"I w-w-well uh w-w-why," stuttered the old hippy.

"Don't even think about answering honestly," interrupted the old soldier, "Although that time was and is still troublesome to me, no one tried to steal my dreams as punishment for my service as you have attempted in the case of this young man."

"I am a Marine who fought in the first Tet Offensive, Battle of Hue'
City, and I will not idly stand by while this young man is treated in
this manner either," added the round-headed man on the far end of the
table, and he ended by pounding his fist on the table and barking out
an enthusiastic, "Semper-Fi!"

The commissioner turned to the old Marine, his eyes twinkling with
remembered youth and the reawakened heart of an old warrior. He
answered as if the two old privates were on opposite ends of the bar
in Saigon. He was once again the army grunt trying to exceed the
enthusiasm of the jar head. He replied, *"Air Cavalry, OOO-AHHH!"*

Chapter Three

A Hero of Jihad

hmed sat patiently on the hard Louis XVI style couch in the waiting room of the mansion. He had no idea either who owned the home or where it was located. He had come to the SWAT Valley to be reassigned after his efforts in Iraq had delayed but did not prevent an American victory.

When he arrived in the valley, he was roughly picked up in the dark of night, hooded and driven for hours without a hint as to the purpose of his abduction or whether he would survive it or not. As he sat hooded in the back of the truck, his thoughts leaped through his memories of the bombings, decapitations, and killings he had participated in, wondering which one of these acts of terror crossed the line and may have raised the ire of his commanders.

He was certain all of his actions fell in line with the long-range plans of the upper echelon of Al-Qaeda. There was one act which, if it had been discovered, may have been looked upon with disdain by others who could not understand his reasons and motives for doing it. That was his ignoble and inglorious retreat from the muzzle of the American soldier at the battle that had come to be known as Martyrs' Ridge. As it was, he was the only survivor of the fight, and in his telling of the battle, he had left out certain unflattering details.

In his reports, the ambush had killed many more than one, and the American assault that killed his entire contingent had involved many more than one. Ahmed also painted his escape from the ridge in a considerably more heroic light than the nearly naked head-long flight of reality. In retrospect, he still judged his ploy to be brilliant, but this could be the cause of his brusque abduction. He reasoned that others made privy to the true facts might judge his tactical escape as the act of a coward. He thought, *they know the truth of the matter. I shall not survive this night. I pray to Allah, who knows my heart, that the end is quick and merciful.*

After countless hours of humming along smooth highways and bumping, rocking and swaying down mountainous roads, the body jarring jerk of the squeaking brakes told Ahmed they had arrived. *Where have we arrived at and for what purpose?* he wondered.

Ahmed was rudely yanked from the truck and with a man on each arm was led through doors, around corners, up steps, and down hallways, where each step echoed as if he was in a large, endless cavern rather than a building. The floor that he was walking on felt smooth and polished. Without a word, he was sat down as abruptly as he was taken. His bindings were removed and the hood was jerked from his head. As his eyes adjusted to the light, he expected to see a firing squad in front of him. There was none. Ahmed breathed a temporary sigh of relief.

"Stay! Do not move from this room!" said one man in a harsh tone.

The other man, sensing Ahmed's trepidation, smiled and with the voice of a diplomatic envoy as smooth and as soothing as the caress of a velvet-gloved hand said, "Ahmed, my comrade, please make yourself comfortable. You have no reason to fear. I must assure you that you are here as a servant of Allah and as our honored guest." He then nodded sternly to first man who turned and left quickly while the diplomat followed, turned, and smiled as he exited through a double, elaborately-carved door.

The room he found himself in was less of a room and more of a great hall. As he tried to take it all in, he was interrupted by a man carrying an AK-47 and, quite oddly, a silver tea service. The contrast was disturbing and, at the same time, puzzling to Ahmed.

"Tea?" The gunman asked.

"Yes, thank you," said Ahmed, who found it difficult to turn down the offer of tea from a heavily armed waiter. He dared not turn the man down and most certainly was not about to ask what the alternative was.

Ahmed assessed the attendant as he returned with the tea. He was a lean, dark man with a heavy dark beard like Ahmed and wearing the kufiya in the manner of a proud soldier of Allah. The tea was just as Ahmed liked it, hot and sweet. It had been a long time since such a sweet flavor had graced Ahmed's palate. Conditions had been harsh in Iraq, especially after what the Americans had called "The Surge." Ahmed thought it should have been called "The Purge," for he was one of the few Al-Qaeda operatives left still operating after the Americans began their focus and aggressive push.

"Thank you. May I ask where I am?" asked Ahmed tentatively.

"I can't tell you where this room is, but I can tell you what this room is. The room is to be dedicated as the 'Hall of the Heroes of Jihad.' That dedication will take place when he finishes." The attendant gestured toward a man in his fifties painting passionately at the far end of the opposite wall. "He has been painting for three years now," explained the servant/warrior as he left the room.

The room was filled with a flourish of murals, which were elaborately painted in the classical style. Ahmed decided he did not know what lay in store for him but felt relief nonetheless. He was calmed not only because of the words of the diplomat but also because this place did not have the flavor of the bleak destiny of one who faced execution.

As Ahmed sipped his tea, he watched the man painting for a bit, and as his courage returned, he stood and began to wander about the room like a tourist on vacation. He perused in amazement at the depictions of the great moments of Islam. It reminded him of the cyclorama he had seen at the Gettysburg Battlefield, which he had visited when he was assigned to the United States. He had pretended to be a college student while gathering intelligence and identifying targets for future attacks. The large all-encompassing painting of the battle had left a lasting impression on him.

One portion of the mural in the Hall of Heroes showed the venerated Mohammed entering Mecca. Ahmed gazed in amazement at another painting. The lifelike action swirling about on the wall before him represented the battle of Tours, where Abdul Rahman Al Gahfiqi nearly conquered the infidels in the high tide of Islam's jihad. *Sadly, he was defeated,* Ahmed thought. *If he had won, we would not be fighting this war today.*

The paintings took him through the history of the unending Jihad. As he strolled to another scene, he gazed admiringly at the painful expressions on the faces of the Crusaders as they fell to the sword of Saladin on the walls of Jerusalem.

In the next sections, the battle of Constantinople raged. The historical perspective continued chronologically right up to the assassination of the American presidential candidate named "Bobby" falling to the gunfire of Sihran Sihran right next to Anwar Sadat above the caption, "Death to the Appeasers of our Zionist Enemies."

His wander led him to the September 11 painting. Ahmed admired at length the portrayal of the second plane angling into the second of the twin towers as another plane careened out of a brilliantly blue sky into the pentagon. Ahmed could not help but notice that flight 93 was left out of the image. He had lost a good friend on that flight. A necessary omission, he thought. He remembered dancing in his camp in Afghanistan when the towers went down. "What a day of joy was this," Ahmed said to the painter. The man fastidiously continued with his work, but took the time to nod and smile.

Ahmed tried to take in every detail of the wondrously painted "Mural of the Jihad." He meandered and sipped his delicious tea as he moved closer, leaning into the paintings so he could actually see the individual strokes which would stand as a testament for all time to the arduous work this painter had put into his masterpiece. Ahmed was overwhelmed that he was here to see it being done. He said to the painter, "This is more magnificent than any of the paintings in the cathedrals of the infidels. You are indeed one of the world's great painters."

The painter paused and bowed in a reverent manner as he responded, "Thank you. I am honored and humbled to receive such praise from a hero of the jihad." He then added, "Come and see. Please. Tell me if you approve."

Ahmed strolled over to the image the painter was currently adding to the sprawling mural and was shell-shocked as a sense of recognition came over him. Ahmed was then engulfed by a flood of emotion.

"Did I capture the moment? It must be difficult for you to relive. Now that I see you, I am quite satisfied with the likeness. I used a photo of you, others, and of the battlefield which were provided to me. I hope you approve. You are the first of my subjects that I have been privileged to meet." He bowed again even more lowly and reverently.

There before him was a painting of himself standing with a warrior's persona raining death from the heights of the ridge upon the American soldiers below. It was an excellent rendition of the battlefield he had chosen himself as well as an idealized image of his own version of the events. He was painted carrying on the fight alone as his comrades lay fallen all about him. He and his fellow soldiers were wearing the red and white kufiya along with the black uniform of Al-Qaeda warriors rather than the uniform of the Republican Guard, but Ahmed found that deviation flattering. He wielded an AK-47 rifle in each hand as he was dealing death to the Americans below. Written below the painting was the name his engagement had been given. It had been so ordained, "The Battle of Martyrs' Ridge."

Ahmed felt as faint and flushed as he had when he looked down the American's muzzle. Ahmed wondered to himself, "Except for the mercy of that American I could be one of the martyrs on that ridge. Instead of dying, I dropped my weapon, stripped off my clothes, praised the infidels, and fled nearly naked from the battlefield." Ahmed eventually was reduced to lie shivering in a culvert until the Americans had left so that he could return to the battlefield for his uniform.

"Was this an act of cleverness or the ultimate act of cowardice?" he asked himself for the thousandth time since the battle. That would not have made such a wonderful painting as this, he thought.

This painting proved that if his act was one of inglorious cowardice it had been performed in historical darkness and unknown to all but Allah himself. He would tell no one of the act or its justifications… ever!

"Well? Do you approve of the likeness?" asked the painter beaming with pride.

"You have captured the intensity of the moment and do honor to those brothers who fell on that ridge. But if I may be so bold to ask, why is this mural being painted? Is it not forbidden by the Quran to idolize men in paintings?"

The painter explained, "This palace is owned by a member of the secular government, who has commissioned it as a historical rendition." The painter then covered his mouth and fear swept across his demeanor, for he had knew he had just revealed too much, "I must say no more."

Ahmed nodded. He had grown accustomed to such convenient rationalizations of deviations from religious doctrines. Ahmed calmed the painter's fears as he patted the man holding the brush and easel on the back and added, "Praise to Allah for sending you to us to tell the story of our struggle in such a glorious manner."

"Thank you. Thank you. Oh, thank you," said the painter as he bowed repeatedly, clearly moved by the praise of one of the "Heroes of the Jihad."

"Ahmed, please come; he will see you now," came a voice from behind.

Ahmed turned and saw the diplomat with an AK-47 still slung on his shoulder, gesturing urgently.

Ahmed looked for a place to set his tea cup, but the diplomat said, "Keep your cup. We shall refill it during your meeting."

Ahmed followed the diplomat through a set the double doors into a large office with no windows but more traditional Islamic paintings. Near the far wall in the middle of the room was a large desk, like that of a Chief Executive Officer of a major corporation. Behind the desk was the man he was to meet. It was the current ranking "most wanted man in the world." Ahmed had met him in the camps of Afghanistan before they had awakened the sleeping giant on September 11th.

Since that time Al Qaeda had been diminished considerably. The lower echelon was being eliminated either on the battlefield or by suicide attacks. The upper echelon was delivered sudden death in their cozy abodes by American drone strikes and Seal Teams.

The Commander spoke as Ahmed approached, "Ahmed, Allah has kept you safe for a reason. Please sit," the great man said graciously.

Ahmed was led by the diplomat to a lone chair in front of the desk. As Ahmed sat more sweet tea was brought to him and poured by one of the four armed men in the room.

"I live to serve Allah. All praise to Allah," said Ahmed bowing to the commander.

"Your instructions from me will be simple. You will go to the United States and strike a devastating blow against the Great Satan. You will be given specifics of your travels when you leave here, but the target will not be known to you until you are in a position to strike. If you are captured on the journey, you will not be able to give them any information about your target because you will have none. Do not let yourself be captured, my son. Do you understand?" asked the tall bearded man.

"Yes. I understand," answered Ahmed.

"You shall not return, my son. Allah has spared you for this mission. Like so many before, you have the honor of being chosen to die a hero of the Jihad. That will be all, Allahu Akbar!"

"Allahu Akbar," replied Ahmed.

Ahmed was led without fanfare or ceremony from the room. His meeting with the commander had lasted less than three minutes, and his mind was reeling. His knees were weak and felt like buckling underneath the weight of the words of the great man. Ahmed was to, "die a hero of the Jihad."

After Ahmed was led from the room, the bag was replaced over his head for the first leg of the journey to a destination unknown to him. As Ahmed sat bag-headed in the back of a truck, which once again bounced along the mountain roads of Pakistan, he wondered if there was room for discussion about any of this or if the decision was final. He wondered *Who would I have such a discussion with?* He wanted desperately to suggest that there may be many advantages to allowing Ahmed to remain a living hero of the Jihad.

Chapter Four

Stella

It was a moonless Monday night on a residential street in La Crosse, heavily populated by University of Wisconsin students. Blake woke up at 3:00 in the morning with an incredibly full bladder which was screaming to be relieved. He was known to some as a diligent college student, to others a reliable pizza delivery man, and still others a party animal. To meet the demands of these identities required a great deal of his time and left him only 4 to 6 hours of sleep each night, tops.

Blake had fallen into bed on this night dead tired and without taking the time to practice proper bladder maintenance. Now his bladder woke him up as certainly as a cock crowing at sunrise in a rural farm yard.

Blake maneuvered through the debris on the floor of his room, the result of his relentless schedule. Upon reaching his destination, Blake stood hovering over his porcelain target and relieved his glutted bladder, adding to the authentic bouquet of his collegiate habitat.

Being a tad more alert upon returning to his bed, Blake was jolted awake as if reveille had been played in his ear. He rubbed his eyes to make certain he was not walking about in a dream. When he opened his eyes, Blake was unsure if he was in heaven or still among the living on earth.

There was Stella, his beautiful Viterbo College art major-neighbor, who lived in the brown Victorian-style mansion next door. The house had been built and owned in the nineteenth century by one of the many lumber barons who once called La Crosse their home. Now the house was showing its age and had been cobbled into eight small apartments rented exclusively to college students.

Stella's ground-level apartment was located straight across from Blake's bedroom separated by a sidewalk and narrow strip of yard. Blake could see at a glance that Stella had set up a studio in the room adjacent to and straight across from his bedroom. Stella, with brush in one hand and her palette in the other, was painting, and the nude model she was using was breathtakingly beautiful, for Stella was painting a self-portrait.

Apparently not satisfied to paint from memory, Stella had set up a full length mirror to her right, and she stood before her canvas in front of her mirror in all her naked splendor. Blake stood, stilled by her beauty.

Blake thought, like Halley's Comet, an opportunity like this may come but once in a lifetime. Although he would not sacrifice sleep over a body in the heavens, he would miss a whole night's sleep to gaze longingly at Stella's naked heavenly body. Blake had been smitten by the beauty the day he introduced himself to her when she had moved into the long-faded mansion next door.

Blake positioned himself at the bottom of his bed in his darkened room watching Stella swirl the brush into the paints on her palette and then ever-so-gently place the brush upon the canvas. Her movements were so exquisite there was something beyond the sexual to this experience. Even so, Blake felt compelled to mimic Stella, stroke for stroke. He convinced himself he was righteous in his voyeurism because it was she who brought her naked elegance to him; he had not gone to her.

What elegance it was. Stella was tall, sleek, and her skin was the color of a light toffee. Her hair was a dark brown, and although it was long, Stella had it tightly swirled, collected, and somehow secured atop her head giving her a Halle Berry-like mystique

Blake continued his strokes also, but he was startled out of his sexual self-reverie by a dark figure, which crept stealthily up to Stella's window. The man, dressed in all black, paused at the lower right corner of the window and stood motionless, watching, watching, watching. Now Blake was watching a complete stranger watching the naked Stella paint… the naked Stella. Blake instantaneously felt overwhelmed with guilt about his own behavior out of fear for Stella.

Stella set her brush and palette down. She picked up a rag and wiped her hands as she critically assessed her latest progress. After nodding in approval, she looked about and picked up a pair of gray sweat shorts. She steadied herself and stepped into them. She turned again and picked up a maroon and white UW La Crosse football jersey and slipped it over her head. As she popped her face out of the jersey, she looked directly out the window, causing the dark figure to duck and drop to his knees.

Blake watched the figure instantly become a motionless shadow in the darkness. If Blake did not know the figure was there, he would not have been able to see him. Stella looked into the mirror and touched up her hair, turned and walked back into her apartment, disappearing from view. After a moment, the light went out signaling the end of this night's session.

Blake watched the dark figure remain motionless. Blake's eyes strained against the darkness to see, wondering if this man was actually still there. Blake's mind pondered the man's motivations, his intent, and finally his next move. During the first few minutes as Blake watched the darkness, he conjured in his mind an image of the man to be just like Blake, a harmless voyeur, just a bit bolder. Blake thought, he may just be a college student on his way home from the bars. Maybe he just happened by chance upon this nude beauty painting a self-portrait in the dark of the night. What college age heterosexual man could resist the urge to stop and gaze upon such a beauty as this? Blake reasoned, even some gays and lesbians would be drawn to look at Stella. She's a… masterpiece.

The longer the man stayed hidden, the more Blake leaned toward the belief that this man might not be a college student who found the place by chance. Instead he began to conclude the man in black was a "Peeping Tom," who had developed his stealth and skill after years of prowling in the night. As the minutes continued to tick by, Blake's imagination once again morphed the man's persona into that of a dangerous serial killer. Blake was certain the man would wait until Stella slept, and then he would enter, rape, and kill her. He's waiting for her to fall asleep and he is going to rape her or worse, thought Blake. Blake's heart pounded in absolute agreement.

Blake spun adroitly in his bed and reached for the phone on his cluttered bed-stand. He dialed 911 and then cupped his hand over the phone to conceal the pale greenish-yellow light of the phone's display, which seemed to him to light up the entire room.

"Hello La Crosse Police 911, what is your emergency?" the voice on the line asked with calm professionalism.

Blake wondered how anyone could sound so calm at a time like this. "I'd like to report a prowler. He is hiding in the dark along-side the house next door to mine, and he is dressed in black. I think he means harm to my neighbor…" reported Blake in an adrenalized chatter.

———>●<———

The night had been a quiet one for John Savage. He had been out of the service for eleven months, and in the meantime he had completed the academy a second time since he had lost his police certification while serving his country in Iraq and Afghanistan. He got himself hired in spite of the concerns of Jane Thomason and made it through Field Training. Now he was out on his own, and after a busy weekend it was rather nice to have a quiet night.

John Savage loved being a cop, and even though he had only been on his own for a month, he knew this was the life for him. John was assigned tonight to third shift, and he was working the college area. It was a dark, moonless night. He had not heard anything on the radio for at least fifteen minutes so it almost startled him when the dispatcher called, "236."

John reached for the mic and keyed it, "236, go ahead."

"I have sent you the address via the computer. There is a prowler on the east side of that location. A caller on the line says the suspect is lying motionless in the shadows and is dressed in black pants, black sweat shirt, and a black watch cap. He had been a Peeping Tom, but when the lights went out he stayed. The complainant says he will stay on the phone and give us updates."

John shifted the screen on his squad's laptop to cut the glare and looked at the address. He was, by chance, just coming up on the neighborhood. "I am arriving and will be approaching on foot from the southeast."

"235 my ETA (estimated time of arrival) is thirty seconds, and I will be coming in from the northwest," answered Ryan Chen, who was working the adjacent beat. The house's location just happened to be along the border between the beats, and both officers were close.

John pulled up to the curb around the corner from the address. He slid silently out of the squad car and shut the door slowly and carefully, making a barely-perceptible click which, even then, seemed to echo through the night air announcing his arrival. The neighborhood was dark and quiet as John slipped through the shadows.

As John reached Blake's home, he left the sidewalk and crossed in front of the residence buckling his knees and cushioning his steps to avoid any noise in what cops called "doing the Groucho." As he reached the corner of the house adjacent to the location of the suspect, he stopped and leaned out to look between the houses. There he was, just as described except the prowler was no longer engaged as a simple voyeur. The suspect had a knife in his right hand and he slipped it between the screen and the frame of the window. As he popped the screen out, the man in black deftly caught the screen and lowered it to the ground, operating in his own professional stealth mode.

John thought, *His hands are occupied with the screen, now is the time.* John drew his weapon and hit his flashlight as he shouted, "Police! Don't Move! Drop The Knife Now!"

Without hesitation, the man in black dropped the screen, threw the knife at John's light, turned, and fled at a dead run. The suspect's immediate reaction caught John off guard, but John was still able to instinctively pivot back behind the corner of the house as the knife ricocheted off the siding, and fell harmlessly to the ground behind John, missing him by inches.

"He's running north!" shouted John as he holstered his weapon and keyed his shoulder mic, all while following at a dead sprint. It was dark, but he could make out the silhouette of the suspect clearly as he headed toward the lighted alley. The suspect had the physique of a sleek competitive runner except for something bouncing against his left side as he ran. Damn! A fanny pack, thought John. The prowler reached the end of the yard and tripped over a shin-high, wire garden border, fell flat, skidded, and bounced back up undeterred. John was able to gain ground but still had twenty feet to make up as the suspect began pumping his arms like a sprinter coming out of his crouch. John managed to stay with him.

John Savage considered his military service and law enforcement position very much like a professional athlete would consider his next competition. He trained hard to win. He was driven to train because he realized that losing wasn't an option in either arena. Once when a fellow recruit asked why he trained so hard, John explained, "Athletes could lose and there would always be another game next week. If we lose, there might not even be a next week because what we do is not a game."

John was not thinking at this moment about his conditioning. All he could think was, *I have to catch this guy. He's dressed like a pro. He's done this before, and if I don't catch him he'll do it again.*

When he reached the alley, the man in black cut east, "He's running east in the alley now," radioed John, whose transmission was breathy but more controlled. He was in the groove of the pursuit now.

"I'm coming around," Chen was heard to shout from somewhere behind and to the left of John.

John looked over his shoulder and saw Chen in the alley about forty feet back. The man in black had guessed right. If he had cut west instead of east, he would have run right into Chen—a cop built for such a collision since he was a muscular, former-collegiate linebacker who looked like he could get back into the game tomorrow.

The man in black continued down the middle of the alley and crossed the street without even turning his head, continuing his escape into and through the next alley. As the man in black ran, John noticed the suspect's right hand stop pumping and drop, then reach across his body, causing the suspect's sprint to turn into a modified gallop. John began to gain ground because the awkward gallop diminished the suspect's speed considerably.

"He's reaching for his fanny pack," shouted John back to Chen.

John did not consciously think to do it, but his Glock 40 caliber duty weapon found its way back into his hand.

As the suspect's hand reached the fanny pack, John heard the Velcro separating as the man ripped open the concealed gun compartment of the fanny pack. John's focus was on the hand. He now was not chasing a man; he was chasing one hand that had disappeared into a fanny pack. The hand came out with a black semi-automatic hand gun, and with one practiced movement the prowler began what John perceived as a slow deadly swing about. John shouted, "GUN!" as he reacted to the movement and John cut right as Ryan Chen cut wide left. Ryan was fifty feet back and out of position.

As the suspect began the swing with weapon in hand, John fired and kept firing until the suspect fell, sliding roughly over the asphalt surface of the alley sprawling face down. As the man in black slid to a stop there was growl, then a whimper, followed by the gasp of air billowing out of his lungs; then... silence. The gun was still in the prowler's hand but rendered safe by the death of the would-be cop-killer.

After a time this former serial rapist and failed cop killer's DNA would later be matched to twenty-five sexual assaults and one homicide throughout the Midwest. Blake had been correct in his fear that he was watching a serial killer, for that was this man's intent, so aroused had he become during his first murder.

The man's string of killings stopped at one because of his fateful meeting with John Savage. From this day forward, his death meant countless nameless victims were spared the horror of being raped, injured, maimed, and even killed at the hand of this animal.

At least one victim, a beautiful young budding painter, did have a name. She avoided a terrible fate thanks to the full bladder of Blake as well as the timely arrival of John Savage. There would be neither the rape, nor the murder, of this beautiful nocturnal artist, Stella.

CHAPTER FIVE

A Man on a Mission

Ahmed's eyes were stinging from the sweat rolling off his forehead. The sweat was blurring his aim. He found a dry spot on the sleeve of his uniform and wiped the salty liquid from his eye. He aimed carefully at the spot the American's helmet had last appeared and waited. It appeared again; Ahmed fired.

The puff gave notice to Ahmed that he had killed the American soldier. As he went to fire again, there was nothing. He tipped the weapon to the side and checked the chamber and could see his fired round which had failed to eject. His weapon was jammed, and as he tried to clear it, his joy turned to terror as another American appeared suddenly on his right flank, killing everything in sight. Ahmed thought of the painting in the Hall of Heroes. He would not flee again. He picked up the weapons of his two dead comrades and swung them toward the American, who opened fire and as the rounds began smashing into Ahmed's chest the American screamed, "Die Ahmed! Ahmed! Ahmed…"

"Ahmed! Ahmed, wake up! Wake Up!"

Ahmed sat bolt upright gasping for a breath in the stifling heat. "Who are… what is going on?" he blurted out in a startled and confused rambling.

"Ahmed, you were screaming in your sleep. I woke you up before you brought the border patrol down upon us," replied Jorge Sanchez, the guide Ahmed had hired to personally get him across the border from Mexico into the United States.

Ahmed's consciousness quickly came back to him. He realized that he had just completed the border crossing from Mexico to the United States. He was in a desert, which felt like home to him, in the state of Arizona. He had been directed by his commander to cross into Arizona to complete phase one of his plan. He was to mark his passing so that all would know Al-Qaeda had returned to wage war on American soil. "Thank you for waking me, Jorge," said Ahmed, rubbing his stinging eyes awake.

"Ahmed, you have paid me well for this special crossing. I have made hundreds of crossings. So many I can't count. It is a good living even though it is a hard life." Jorge sat down on his bedroll and took a long drag off a marijuana cigarette he was smoking, held it, and blew out the left corner of his mouth.

Jorge looked at Ahmed, squinting one eye and opening the other as if he had some deeply troubling unanswered question about Ahmed that he desperately needed answered. Then Jorge looked down at his marijuana cigarette and said, "Hombre, this is some good shit. You must try it."

He offered it to Ahmed, and Ahmed took it, inhaled it deeply, and blew out the bluish gray smoke into the night air.

"I am so happy you took a hit from my roach, man," said Jorge with relief.

"Why is that?" asked Ahmed.

"Well, with a name like Ahmed and all, I thought maybe you were some terrorist or something, but I know Muslim's don't drink or do drugs, man. I just was worried, you know," said Jorge, taking another long drag from his product. He tipped his head back and blew the smoke straight up into the sky. He gazed at the stars wistfully. The rich grade of Mexican marijuana taking hold and relaxing him, mind and body, may have even relaxed his soul if he had not sold that to the devil years ago.

"You know," said Jorge, "I have guided many a Juan, Juanita, Jose, Alberto, Norberto, Luis, and Lupe, but you have been my first Ahmed. I was afraid because of the money you had that you might be a terrorist or something," laughed Jorge.

"Jorge, what if I was?" replied Ahmed matter-of-factly.

Jorge took his gaze off the Northern Star, slowly, and brought it back toward Ahmed, who had somehow acquired a gun and had it pointed right between his eyes. Jorge saw a flash like a photograph and then he saw, as Poe's *Raven* would say, "Never more."

Ahmed pulled Jorge by the legs out of the brush they had been concealed in and laid him out on his back spread eagled. He went through Jorge's gear and found the cash that he had been paid to guide Ahmed and returned it to his own backpack. Ahmed then opened a pocket of the pack and removed a neatly folded white scarf. Displayed on it was a smaller version of the painting portraying the attack on the World Trade Center. He tied the scarf around Jorge's ankle. Written in Arabic on the scarf were the words "To the hero of Martyrs' Ridge." Ahmed stood up, paused, admired his display and said, "Yes. This will do."

Ahmed changed the magazine that was in his Beretta so that he would be fully loaded and slipped it back into his pancake holster tucked inside his waist band. He rifled through Jorge's belongings and found three kilos of a white powder he deduced to be cocaine and threw it in his own back pack. "I can use it for barter. It is better than cash in some places in the land of Satan."

The only other thing he took was water. He would need it for the rest of the trek. Ahmed felt a rush as surely as if he had taken a snort of the cocaine he had in his backpack. He was on an incredible high. Ahmed had just successfully crossed the border into the United States and already had struck a blow to let everyone know Al-Qaeda had returned. He wanted for nothing in this world for he was a "Warrior of Allah" who had a weapon, ammunition, a map, a GPS, water, cash, and a destination. Best of all, he was a man on a mission.

CHAPTER SIX

He Likes the Look

"The doctor will see you now," said the receptionist in the front office of Dr. Rhonda Sistek at Gunderson Lutheran Medical Center.

Four days had passed since John Savage's encounter with the serial rapist, the late Robert Smythe. John, having been involved in a fatal shooting was required to see the doctor to, according to policy, "maintain his mental well-being and assess the emotional impact of the incident." John had been on paid leave since the shooting, also required by policy. This was all new to John, the consequences of his first officer-involved shooting.

John returned the receptionist's smile as he walked passed her. He entered the doctor's office, which was decorated in soft colors. There was an aquarium built into one wall with two large matching fish—both looked like Nemo—swimming about the bubbling aquarium. The large tank was complete with a deep sea diver and a sunken ship. "Have a seat, please," said Doctor Sistek, dressed in beige to match the colors of her office walls, drapes, wall hangings and carpets. "So nice to meet you," she said motioning to the chair in front of her desk but not offering a hand shake.

John had instinctively brought his hand up, but as she looked away he brought it down to his side and sat in the chair, which was deep, but oh-so-comfortable. John said as he sat down, "I could sleep through a super bowl party in a chair like this."

The Doctor answered, "Indeed," and continued passing up the opportunity for small talk, "You are here today, I see, because you were involved in a fatal shooting. I read about it in the paper and it has been all over the news; how are you doing?" asked the doctor brushing back the hair from her eyes. She was an attractive woman in her early fifties, thin with blonde hair. John surmised it was probably naturally blonde at one time, but now was colored to hide the gray. She had a concerned look on her face that gave the inference to John that she truly believed that something must be terribly wrong with him.

"I'm fine," said John with sincerity.

"How can that be after such a close brush with death?" asked the doctor.

"If anything I am finer because of it. The man would have killed me if he could have. He couldn't so I am alive. I am breathing, the sun is shining, and it's a wonderful day. I might not just feel fine, I feel great!" John said, convinced his perspective was not only healthy but appropriate under the circumstances.

"Are you having trouble sleeping at all?" asked the doctor.

"A little, because my schedule is off. I normally work the night shift and now because I have to be off for a bit, my sleeping schedule is a little screwed up," answered John.

"How are you… coping with the fact that you have taken a human life?" asked the doctor.

"I don't look at it that way. I saved my life, my partner's life, and maybe the intended victim's life. There is nothing to cope with. A bad man was doing bad things, and now he will not do them to anyone anymore. I am glad of that," answered John.

"So you feel that this incident has had no impact on you psychologically at all?" asked the doctor.

"I am here because I was able to do what I did. I am having no trouble coping with that at all, Doctor," said John leaning back in the chair and turning to look at the clown fish, which were facing each other and looking like they were about to kiss. He chuckled when they did.

"Why are you laughing?" asked the doctor in a concerned tone.

"Oh, sorry, I wasn't laughing at you, Doctor. Your Nemo fishes, um I mean fish just kissed. Well it probably wasn't a kiss. It was probably some other fish thing they were doing, but it looked like they kissed. It was kind of funny," said John reaching into his pocket and removing a piece of Bazooka Bubble Gum. He took a second one out and offered it to the doctor, "Gum?"

"No thank you," she said as she began busily writing on a notepad lying on the desk in front of her.

"Have you ever experienced any trauma like this in the past?" asked the doctor, still writing.

"You call it trauma, but I call it my job and the answer is yes. I am a combat veteran," said John reading the comic from the gum. Then he carefully folded it and tucked it back into his pocket.

"Iraq?… Afghanistan?" asked the doctor, looking up from her notes.

"Yes," said John, "both."

"Have you had to kill before?" asked the doctor.

"Yes," answered John.

"How did that make you feel after those killings?" asked the doctor.

"The men I killed were the same men that danced in the street on September 11 when the towers went down. They were my enemy and I was their enemy. They tried to kill me and my friends, and I was luckier, faster, better, or in a superior position, so I got to come home and they…" John suddenly was nearly overcome with emotion trying to rush out like kids heading for the exit on the last day of school. He was not thinking of the killing of his enemy, however. Instead he pictured himself on that ridge in Iraq pausing for just a moment as he watched Chase's head rise up and then in a puff he was gone. He took a breath, recovered, and finished his answer, "some didn't."

"Please explain your feelings. Something just touched you deeply," said the doctor excited by the fact that she had struck an emotional pressure point.

His composure had completely returned and John explained, "I had and still have no issues about those lives I had to take in the war. I just remembered one circumstance that if I could undo I would, but never can," said John "There was one time when we were ambushed and under attack. I was able to move to flank the enemy."

"Flank? What does that mean exactly? I am not a military person," said the doctor.

"Flank means I was able to come up on their blind side and then, yes, I killed them. I did not have any issues with the killing of any of them for they were pouring fire down on my friends. I was troubled because during my move I stopped for less than a minute before continuing on to finish the job, and during that minute," John looked down and rubbed his eyes, then looked up again and said, "my best friend was killed. I paused for a moment and someone I loved died. If I would have kept moving and finished the job, my friend would be alive today," said John looking straight into the doctor's eyes. John's eyes projected a loss along with a dark determination when he said, "I decided from that day forward that I would never hesitate again when lives depended on it."

"What if there are other options?" asked the doctor looking stunned.

"If there are any other viable options, of course I would take those first, and my training and experience has prepared me to make those decisions. The other night with Smythe, well, doctor, there were no other options and so I am okay with that," said John.

"Our time is up here," said the doctor, "I would you like to schedule another appointment?"

"Is it mandatory?" asked John.

"Well, no, but don't you think it would be helpful to talk? We could certainly schedule you in as often and regularly as needed," she assured as she continued writing feverishly.

"No. I would just like to get back to work as soon as possible. I do not mind taking time off, but not under the term suspension. I would like to get back."

"It is an administrative suspension. There is no suggestion you have done anything wrong," explained the doctor.

"I realize that, but it is still a suspension, and I would like to be unsuspended and back at work. I am told that you can authorize that.

I would like to ask you to do that, Doctor. Please," said John with a gamely smile.

"Well, I see nothing right now that would prevent me from doing that. I must admit that I do not have what it takes to do what you do without being forever traumatized," said the doctor. "It is hard for me to believe that you have not been emotionally traumatized at least in some small way."

"The feeling is mutual, Doctor. I can honestly say I am comfortable with what I've had to do, but I will say I don't have what it takes to do what *you do* without being forever traumatized. Isn't it great God gave us the gift to help others in our own special way?" John Savage said in a manner that beguiled the doctor and belied the name Savage.

John then reached into his pocket and pulled out the Bazooka Joe comic and said, "This was kind of ironic. I like Bazooka Bubble Gum and have saved comics since I was a kid. Some are worth as much as $20 a piece now. Anyway, I just opened this one and it, as I said, was ironic." He then handed the doctor the comic.

The doctor read the comic out loud, "The teacher says 'All salmon swim upstream,' and Bazooka Joe says, 'Not all of them do.' The teacher then asks 'Which ones don't?' and Bazooka Joe says…" and the Doctor paused for a moment and handed the comic back to John.

"The dead ones," answered John. "It is ironic, because you have been asking me if I am traumatized by having to take the life of this rapist or the enemy I have killed in Iraq and Afghanistan. I have to say the comic explains it all. I know what I did in service and what I do now makes my life more difficult than it has to be. It's kind of like I have chosen a life of swimming upstream. But just like the salmon, I firmly believe I am hard-wired to do what I do and even though it's not the norm and at times is tough, I know it is what I am meant to do. I also know what happens to the salmon unwilling or unable to swim upstream. It is the same thing which happens to cops and soldiers who are unable to take that shot when it is necessary. I reject the alternative. I love my life and choose to continue to swim upstream."

"Officer Savage, I think we need to get you back to work," said the doctor as she signed a slip on the desk in front of her, ripped off a pink copy and a yellow copy. "Take the yellow one into work and give it to the Assistant Chief. You can keep the pink copy for your files. They may not put you back on the schedule immediately, but that is not because of me." She stood up and extended her hand to John, who accepted it. "It was nice to meet you, Officer Savage, and if you ever need help, please feel free to ask for me."

John shook the doctor's hand, "Thanks, Doc, and if *you* ever need help, feel free to ask for me."

"Say, John," asked the doctor," I always wondered when I was a little girl how Bazooka Joe lost his eye? Do you know?"

"He never lost it. He just wears the patch because..." said John pausing in the door way of the office, "You know, he's a kid and it's a patch. What kid doesn't think a patch is cool? Well he's Bazooka Joe; he knows what he likes, and he likes the look."

CHAPTER SEVEN

Destiny

"No further questions," said the District Attorney.

"You're excused, Officer Savage," said the Judge to the witness, and John Savage nodded his head, stepped down from the witness-stand, and made his way out of the hearing room at the Law Enforcement Center in downtown La Crosse.

John Savage had just completed three hours of testimony describing the events leading up to the shooting of Robert Smythe. The point eliciting the most intense scrutiny was, "How could the rounds John fired have struck Smythe in the back if he was a lethal threat. The line of questioning was understandably necessary to John, but he still found it troubling.

There is a fine line between exoneration and prosecution, and John realized that line would be drawn by justification. John could see while he was on the stand that the Hollywood image of the "dirty little coward that shot Mr. Howard in the back," was an impediment to understanding for anyone not at the scene.

John left the hearing believing his accurate re-telling of the events leading up to and including the killing of Robert Smythe would lead anyone present to conclude the shooting justifiable. As John was leaving the hearing room, the prosecutor, in a raised voice, called out, "I would like to call Officer Ryan Chen to the stand." As Ryan reached the door of the hearing room, John stepped aside, held the door, and smiled at his friend, who nervously smiled back as he entered the room. They had been sequestered so that one's testimony would not taint the other.

John stepped out of the hearing room, found a seat and sat down. He was sitting alone in his thoughts when the voice of a young woman lifted him out of his mental daze, "Officer Savage?"

He looked up, and his heart leapt as if triggered with adrenaline at the sight of the woman next to him. There was no denying the beauty that inspired his response. "Y-Y-Yes, ma'am," said John standing up quickly. He was startled by her undetected approach as well as her exquisite loveliness. The combination of the two made the usually calm professional appear to be quite the awkward school boy. "How can I help you?"

John felt his attraction was on display for the whole world to see. He looked about to see who else was witnessing his loss of composure. John was relieved to see they were alone in the waiting area at the time. He tried to take an undetected deep breath to bring himself under control, but as he gazed into her oh-so-brown eyes, there was no stopping the freight train in his chest. "I am John Savage," he finally said.

"I have something for you, John," she declared opening a portfolio containing a large sketch pad. She slipped a sheet from the pad. "I have it right here. I made it myself as a small token of my appreciation." She produced sheet from the pad, which was covered by another light sheet of tissue.

She called me John. He didn't know why that should make him so happy, but it did. Now an unexplainable joy coupled with whatever else in God's name he was feeling, made his knees weak. He cleverly covered for his wavering legs by saying, "Care to have a seat, ma'am?" John sat down and motioned for her to have a seat next to him and she did. She smelled of lilacs and peaches, and the exquisite bouquet made him even more faint. *God, I fought battles in the desert and never felt faint. What's going on here?* He thought to himself.

She sat next to John and put her portfolio down on the seat next to her. "Please, enough with the ma'am. You, of all people, may call me Stella. My name is Stella Moreno," she said as she extended her hand.

John immediately recognized the name. She had been the woman whose apartment Smythe was about to enter when John arrived on the scene. After the shooting, other officers continued the follow-up investigation. He never had the opportunity to speak to the intended victim. This was their first meeting.

"I recognize your name. It is so nice to meet you," he said as he took her hand and marveled at the warm inviting texture of it, wondering if there was anything about this woman which wasn't perfect. John held the hand longer than a mere handshake, and she did not pull away.

Her eyes did not calm his heart but somehow assured him she was feeling something too. They both felt a connection; neither could resist it. John had been with women before but neither sought nor accepted overtures of relationships. He had been a soldier experiencing long dangerous deployments. He did not want to subject a woman to the worries and sacrifices required of the young wife of a soldier. Things were different now. He had a career, a home, stability. He never had that before. He never felt this particular feeling before either.

Stella took a breath, which brought them back to the moment and they each released the other's hand. Stella said, "I made this for you myself. I would have baked cookies, but I don't bake," she laughed and continued, "I hope you like it." She handed him the 22" by 20"sheet lightly wrapped in tissue and John accepted the gift.

He unwrapped the light covering of tissue and he looked at an amazing likeness of himself on the witness stand with the American flag behind him. On the top of the sheet were the words "John Savage, My American Hero," In the right corner was the name Stella Moreno in a script that was as artistic as the charcoal drawing itself. John looked up and said, "Thank you. You are…"

Their eyes met again, and John found his mental train derailed. He felt intoxicated by her eyes and looked away for fear of becoming addicted but knew he was already hooked. He looked back at her drawing, consciously regaining his composure, and finished, "…an incredible artist. You must be a professional."

"How kind you are to say that. I am a graduate student in art at Viterbo University. I hope to someday become an artist," she said, buoyed by the fact that John seemed to sincerely love her gift.

"No, you are an artist. I love art and have seen art all over the world, and although I am not an expert I know great art when I see it and this is great! Thank you. This is the best 'thank you' I have ever received since becoming an officer," said John as he lightly traced the lines of the art, without actually touching the paper.

"It's such a small gesture of appreciation. You arrived in the nick of time for me. I can't believe I slept through it all while you were out there risking your life to save me from…" she suddenly clasped her hands over her mouth and her eyes started to well up as she looked at John. A tear escaped down her cheek, and she just looked at him without speaking, saying everything with her eyes.

John put his arm around her and she leaned against him. Stella put her head on his shoulder and she began to quietly cry. John gently patted her shoulder. His own emotions were back in check as he comforted Stella. *No criminal has ever served enough time to account for the fear they leave with their victims in the wake of their barbaric acts*, John thought.

This was not a groundless fear in Stella's case. She had indeed been saved from a terrible fate but had come so close to the event that she nightly conjured up the horror of what might have been. Being an artist, she had been able to visually paint the terrible scene in her mind as she lay down to sleep. Every howl of the wind, every rustle of the leaves, and every skittering animal in the night was another Robert Smythe coming for her. Even during the day on a crowded street, she found herself sensing an evil presence somewhere blended into the street scene like a jungle cat in the rain forest ready to pounce.

Now for the first time since that night as she leaned against John Savage, she felt herself melting into the safety of his powerful arms. She felt like lying down and sleeping for days, safe in his embrace. She wanted this moment to last forever. Other than her parents, she had never felt this comfortable next to anyone before in her whole life, and she had just met this man.

She never wanted to leave his side again. Without moving she asked in a whisper, "John, do you feel it?" Stella said nothing to explain what "it" was. If he felt it he would know.

John returned her whisper, "Yes."

Stella stayed on John's shoulder, now curling her feet up on her chair as if they were in front of a blazing fireplace. Her tears had begun to dry on her cheek. Her pain chased away by a caring touch. "John, I've never felt so instantly connected to someone before."

Gone were John's initial nervous stutterings. Words flowed like sweet Wisconsin maple in the spring, "I feel the same way. I feel like we've known each other forever and yet we've just met. This feels like…"

Then, as lovers have done throughout the ages in moments when their hearts are inexplicably connected, Stella finished John's sentence for him whispering, "Destiny."

Chapter Eight

Redemption

Ahmed reached into the post office box at the Madison, Wisconsin, post office for the three envelopes and single package that waited for him. It had been a busy ten days since he had killed Jorge in the desert of Arizona. He had checked on the internet and discovered the body had been found, but there was no mention of the message he had left to mark his arrival. "No worries," Ahmed concluded after he discovered that his warning had gone unreported. The fact that no mention was made of such a serious threat as he had left is proof of the fact that they are taking the threat seriously. *The American Government deals more urgently with informing its people about a diet drink that may kill them in 50 years than a foreign adversary who might kill them tomorrow,* Ahmed thought. *This is a strange phenomenon which I do not understand, but I know it to be the case.*

Ahmed had bought a car, a used gray Chevrolet Impala. He had sold all of his stolen cocaine in only three stops along the way. Even though he offered the buyers a bargain-basement deal on the street poison, he was still able to add $25,000 to the credit column of this operation. He was also able to barter for a Beretta 92-F, Glock 26, and a Glock 17 as well as a Remington 308 rifle. He still did not know exactly what he was expected to do, but a variety of weapons would give him a variety of options when he received his orders.

Ahmed had arrived in Madison two days earlier and was able to find a furnished apartment on Mifflin Street near the University of Wisconsin Campus. His commander in Pakistan had researched this mission meticulously. He told Ahmed that Madison was a distinctly favorable location to operate out of. He would blend into the diverse campus community. It had a history of anti-American activity, and some members of the community still relished its own flag-burning, building-bombing past.

Ahmed's mission commander, Abu-Masab had told Ahmed during their last meeting, "You will blend in among them. Offer them only a smile and a warm hand, but embrace no one. You will be given your target when you arrive in Madison. The passage will be the most difficult part of your mission. There is an advantage though. The southern border is wide open to stealth crossings, and the Americans are so arrogant in their strength they fail to see the need to protect themselves there. You will be given further information via the post office box when you arrive in Madison."

Ahmed collected his package and envelopes. As he shut the post office box, he paused and smiled at the package as if it was an expected gift from home. He was careful not to look nervous because he knew he was being watched by a security camera. His commander had said, "American police are brave about their profiling when done from an office with a security camera on a remote. They are less inclined to approach a young Arab male in person who does not show outward signs of guilt and ill intent. They are more afraid of being called a racist than they are of the death we shall bring to them. This weakness will lead to our ultimate victory." These words made Ahmed feel secure in the success of this mission.

He hoped the target would be an important one because the road he had traveled had been long and perilous. The last words Abu-Masab had said were, "Ahmed, death will be your reward. All praise goes to Allah!" Ahmed wondered if death was such a reward why all of his leaders had chosen to run, hide, and live, while he and others were expected to gloriously choose to fight and die. This thought troubled him often.

As Ahmed lifted his head, his eyes met a woman opening a box near him. He held up his package and grinned largely saying, "From Mama. I am so happy," he exaggerated his accent for her benefit.

The brunette looked at what she thought must certainly be a student, longing for home. She returned the smile and warmly replied, "How very nice for you. Have a great day." She then turned and left.

Ahmed strolled out of the post office and drove directly home. He quickly sat on his couch and laid the envelope on the table and gently set the package down in front of him. He went to the kitchen and poured himself a tall glass of Jim Beam. He had convinced himself that this unholy indulgence was not an acquired taste, but one of the sacrifices he must make to blend into his surroundings. He dropped three ice cubes into the whiskey and then took a long drink and opened the envelope.

As he read, his heart leapt with great joy. He could not believe he had been entrusted with this mission. They had given him a mission that even Ahmed would be happy to die for if he managed to complete it. He read the words out loud. "The lion has passed. You're assignment is to kill the lamb. He will die for their sins. He has betrayed his Muslim roots by rejecting the Quran and picking up the book. Choose the time, location, and manner. We have sent you a package containing some things that might assist you in your mission."

Ahmed opened the package and in it was the uniform and beret of an American Soldier. The name tag on the uniform said Margolis. There was a note written in Arabic which said, "Remember our brother Hasan from Fort Hood! All praise to Allah."

Ahmed unfolded the uniform, went over to a mirror on the bedroom door, and held it against his chest like a young girl with her new prom dress. "Yes this will do. How fitting it is that I die in uniform, for I am a soldier, not a terrorist, and I have been given the honor of killing the lamb," he said out loud to himself, for the lamb was code name for his target. "I will be wearing their own uniform while I kill the President of the United States, their Commander in Chief. For such a great deed I will be long remembered on earth and will be met in heaven with great reward."

As Ahmed smiled at himself in the mirror at the thought, his mind took him back to "Martyrs' Ridge," and his inglorious flight down the hill in only his boots and underwear. His demeanor grew sodden at the thought. His face transitioned to a look of relief as he said to himself, "Allah has sent me this opportunity so that I might achieve redemption."

CHAPTER NINE

Bad Guys Better Be Careful

s John Savage's eyes opened, he heard the gentle music of her breathing and felt the rhythm of her soft breast rising and falling with each breath as she lay pressed against him. The sweet taste of their love making was still on his lips and he said a silent prayer congratulating the Lord on his fine effort when he created Stella and thanked Him for sending this beauty to him.

It had been three months since they met, and their lives became one immediately. After just a few weeks of dating, Stella moved in with John, who had bought a three-bedroom split-level on Milson Court located at the entrance to Hixon Forest. Hixon Forest was a large forest preserve within the City of La Crosse, which had been donated to the city by the 19th century wife of a lumber baron. Mrs. Hixon's only request as part of this huge land deal was that the City of La Crosse forever use the land for recreation. It contained a golf course, a nature center, a scout center, hiking trails, cross country ski trails, and acres upon acres so pristine that it still could be recognizable to the native Ho-Chunk, who hunted the land for centuries before the white man came.

John had hiked and climbed the bluffs in the forest his whole life and jumped at the opportunity to buy a home bordering Hixon Forest. John benefited from a lifetime of frugality, the G.I. Bill, and a buyer's market. Mrs. Hixon's deal insured that John's forest home would never fall victim to urban sprawl.

John felt La Crosse was a great town to live in and a fun town to police. It was situated on the Mississippi River and a line of beautifully scenic bluffs. The population was generally friendly, but it was home to its share of the criminally inclined and socially maladjusted. Enough, at least, to insure the life of a police officer would be busy and interesting. It also was the home of a brewery that touted ownership of the world's largest six-pack. It stood near a lively bar district, which was nationally known for its raucousness. This area was frequented by students of three colleges, who thought it to be their play-ground and themselves to be immortal. Many of these students hadn't developed the practice of maintaining moderation in drink or deed. More often, they practiced the Forrest Gump's philosophy of "Stupid is as stupid does." To beat cops this translated into job security.

John had been back to work for some time since the shooting of Smythe, and although he had received an opportunity to move to second shift, he stayed on nights. He liked the action as well as the people he worked with. His schedule also worked out well socially because Stella liked to paint at night. Her nude project was completed, and if she ever was assigned a similar project, she was ready, for John's windows were equipped with drapes.

On his nights off John would stay up, slip in his ear plugs, play his music, and read while Stella painted. Stella had a Greta Garbo-like intensity about her when she worked. John loved to peek up from his book occasionally, watch Stella work for a few moments and then contentedly return to his reading. Between war and his life as a cop, he had experienced enough raw excitement. He thrived on his quiet nights at home with Stella.

On nights when John worked, he would hit the sack after his morning supper and catch a few hours of sleep while Stella was at school. Many times, Stella, smelling of lilacs and peaches, would return to slip in beside him, and even Shakespeare would be powerless to describe the intimacy they shared.

John and Stella both had been brought up on fairy tales and realized their real-life circumstances made Stella John's "Damsel in distress" and John her "Knight in shining armor." What was unspoken between them was the concern that their love might be a shooting star that lights up the night so brightly to leave one in awe but is just as quickly extinguished and forgotten. They wondered if love discovered in the midst of such adversity which burned so intensely could survive the severe test of a day to day mundane existence.

Laying in bed before the sounding of his alarm, John contemplated their relationship. He shrugged and whispered to himself, "So far so good." Glancing at the clock he realized he had just four minutes to lie next to her warmth, feel her softness moving against him, listen to her breathing, and enjoy her fragrance. It took every ounce of his discipline not to make love to her again, but he did not want to rob himself of these minutes of bliss. At the one minute mark he slipped his arm out and slid quietly out of bed. He turned off the alarm, shaved, showered and dressed. Quiet as a night breeze, he returned to kiss her softly before slipping away to his duties.

Tonight, as usual, he thought he had made it without waking her, but as John reached the door Stella called out, "I love you, John. Please be careful out there tonight."

Laughing, John shook his head and called out, "Good night, Stella, I love you too." Turning, his demeanor changed from lover to warrior as he prepared his mind to go where the night would take him. He mentally shifted gears and said to himself, "Bad guys better be careful."

CHAPTER TEN

Shit Magnet

"You going to marry her?" asked Ryan Chen as they walked down 3rd Street from the Law Enforcement Center, where they had just booked a suspect who made the mistake of causing a disturbance when he had an outstanding "Body Only Felony Warrant." Ryan and John Savage were assigned to walk the 3rd Street bar district on this night.

"I can't imagine marrying anyone else right now, and I can't imagine her married to someone else. We've slowed down a bit though. I am hesitant to take it that far yet. I'm concerned it may just be a survivor's infatuation thing going on," said John.

"Taking it slow? Meeting someone and a few weeks later moving in together is your idea of taking it slow? Man that's taking it fast in dog years or even rabbit years. It may be slow for May Flies, but I'm not sure about that. I'll have to get back to you on it," said Ryan as he stepped into the doorway at Wettstein's appliances and he gave the door handle a tug, finding it secure.

"It is," answered John.

"What is?" asked Ryan.

"It is slow for May Flies. Once they rise out of the river they only live for about 24 hours. It is slow for May Flies, so don't waste your valuable time on the Google search," said John. "Anyway, right now all I can say is 'it's all good.' I'm already trying to work up a way to ask her. I want it to be special. I figure if we are still together when I think up a way to ask her that no one else has used in the history of the world, then I will pop the question." John then popped a Bazooka Bubble Gum into his mouth, read the comic, carefully folded it, and put it in his pocket as he walked.

As Ryan and John crossed the street at 3rd and State Street, John spotted two guys cutting into a parking lot a quarter of a block up on the left. "Those two don't fit together. I think someone's buying and someone's selling," said John.

"Good eye," agreed Ryan as the two officers picked up their pace just shy of breaking into a run.

John reached the alley first, peered around the corner of the building, and could see the two men standing between two parked cars. One was taller and had long unkempt brown hair with a sky-high forehead. The shorter and younger of the two had a shaved head. Both were smoking and their manner along with the odor that drifted in the air, ever so lightly, caused John to whisper, "I smell probable cause."

"No doubt about it," whispered Ryan.

Just then Big Forehead removed something from his pocket, palmed it, and slipped it to Shaved Head. Shaved Head in turn handed some folded bills to Big Forehead, who put the roach in his mouth while he counted the money. He shook his big forehead as he refolded the bills and slipped them into the opposite pocket he had removed the palmed item from, as smoothly as if he had done it one thousand times before.

"That's probable cause on steroids," said John.

"Bracket 'em! We don't want them to run. Let's move," said Ryan.

The two druggies had been more concerned about the other setting up a rip-off and neither had been paying attention to the two cops walking right up on their exchange. Both Big Forehead and Shaved Head were startled when they heard "Good evening gentleman, I am Officer John Savage of the La Crosse Police Department. You are both under arrest. Please put your hands out at your side like an air plane…"

The two men were stunned into cooperation. John handcuffed Big Forehead, who still had the doobie hanging from his lips. When John searched him, he found six small jewelry bags of crack cocaine on him along with two baggies of Marijuana and a pocket scale. He also had $2020.00 in cash and was the proud owner of a long history of "priors."

Shaved Head had one jewelry bag with one rock of crack cocaine on him. He admitted that he had just bought it from Big Forehead and claimed that was all he had on him.

Ryan answered, "No way!" He was certain Shaved Head had the mother-lode concealed down his crotch after he conducted a visual scan alone. Ryan had handcuffed the young man and then asked him, "What do you have concealed down the front of your pants, sir?"

"Nothing, man. I ain't got nothing," said Shaved Head nervously.

"256, we need transport for two to the Law Enforcement Center," said John calling for a car to transport themselves and their prisoners to the County Jail, as he watched Ryan's progress with interest. "We will be 10-95 (suspect under arrest) two times."

"Come on. I am going to have to look. I want to know what you have hidden down your pants. I am not going to get stuck with a needle or something, am I? I know you are crotching something," insisted Ryan, certain beyond a doubt, that the young man was concealing a major stash.

"Honest. I swear to God that one rock is all I had on me. You got it all!" insisted the young man.

"Whatever. Spread your feet and look to the left," said Ryan as he began an invasive probe of the area to verify his suspicions. After a brief but conclusive digital search of the area, Ryan straightened up, turned toward John with a startled look on his face, and then turned to the young man and said, "Well um, ah, I don't know what to say except…Hey you should be proud," after discovering the large package concealed in Shaved Head's pants was absolute proof to the world that all men are not created equal.

"Thanks. I guess," said Shaved Head sheepishly.

Two and a half hours later after getting statements, booking the suspects, testing, weighing, packaging, and securing the drugs as well as writing the reports, John and Ryan were back downtown on foot. The crowd was gone, the radio was quiet, and the night was still.

"Ryan, what would happen to those guys in China if they were caught doing what we just caught them doing?" asked John.

Ryan Chen was born in Hong Kong while it was a British protectorate. As the clock ticked down for the thriving capitalist city of millions to be turned over to Communist China, Ryan's parents fled with him to the United States. Ryan spoke English, Mandarin, Cantonese Chinese as well as Hmong and Japanese. John was particularly fascinated by his history.

"I can tell you that before the Communist Chinese came to Hong Kong, the system was much like ours here. The adjudication would be faster. There was no such thing as the exclusionary rule in Hong Kong though," This is a uniquely American rule that prohibits evidence from being used against a criminal when officers make mistakes in the obtaining of the evidence.

Ryan continued, "I understand things have changed since the Communists took over. If you are caught dealing drugs in Communist China today, your trial would be tomorrow and the day after that they will wake you up early, give you a good breakfast, and take you outside. They say, "Please to kneel down, thank you. Bang! One round in the back of your head," said Ryan firing his finger like it was a gun and blowing the smoke from the imaginary muzzle.

"Three days, two nights and lights out. No shit?" asked John in disbelief.

"No shit," answered Ryan. "They would harvest him though."

"Harvest him. What's that?" asked John.

"They would try to shoot him with a caliber that did as little damage as possible and in a spot that would kill him instantly. Then they would harvest his eyes, kidneys, heart, lungs, skin and whatever else they could use or sell—women too."

"You mean like donating the body to science in China?" said John as they reached the downtown area. The bars were now closed and they began pulling the doors of the businesses as they walked, checking windows and locks for tampering.

"Well, some, but there is also a business where China sells parts to other countries. There is one group that actually pays for entire bodies and turns them into art," explained Ryan.

"I heard of that. Are those bodies from..."

"China, man—most of them are prisoners sentenced to death. One of them is probably that brave dude who stood in front of that tank in Tiananmen Square," answered Ryan. "Drug dealers, murderers and dangerous dissidents get the same treatment. Three days, two nights, and Bam!"

"What makes a dissident dangerous?" asked John.

"They tell the truth. Totalitarian governments and others en route toward totalitarianism are afraid of the truth. A dissident tells the truth, then… bam! It insures the silence of others less brave." Ryan acted out another feigned execution. "No appeal. I am so glad to be here in La Crosse, Wisconsin, United States of America." said Ryan.

"I'm glad you're here too, partner," agreed John as they bumped fists.

After the two partners split and checked the front and back doors of everything on 3rd Street, they eventually met on Cass near the twin blue spans of the Mississippi River Bridge. "You hungry?" Ryan asked.

"I could grab a bite, yeah. What's your idea?" asked John.

"I'm hungry for a Kwik Trip Bratwurst and Kraut," said Ryan as he gazed east toward the bright lights of the Kwik Trip at 5th and Cass just two blocks away.

"Brats, huh?" asked John with a chuckle, "Boy Mister, 'You should be proud' really must have made an impression on you. Now you're hungry for a Brat."

"Fuck you, asshole. You ruined my appetite for Brats now. I think I will make it Cheeseburgers and Zingers," said Ryan. "Let's go."

"I'm in. I'm having a Brat though if they are on special, two for two dollars," said John following.

As they reached the Kwik Trip, they walked through the lot, sweeping it, looking for ne'er-do-wells and drunks but failed to find any candidates. That being done they cautiously entered, since night businesses are frequent havens not just for cops but also criminals, who often target them. Satisfied the store was clear both officers entered the bathroom and washed their hands.

As they exited the bathroom a big man in a leather coat entered the store and went straight to the soda area. He had a distant look on his face and did not seem to notice the two officers in the far back corner of the store. Ryan cut right and headed to the front in the far aisle, while John stopped and held his ground and peered over the shelving to watch the man, who caught both officers' attention. Their shared concern was unspoken but somehow communicated telepathically as partners are able to do.

The entrance door suddenly burst open and a second man, who was skinny as a rail but much shorter, wearing a leather coat, and armed with a shot-gun, began shouting at the attendant, "This is a robbery. Give me all the cash or you die!"

Ryan drew his weapon and ducked behind the shelving in the first aisle and shouted "Police! Drop the weapon!"

John was in the far aisle and could not see the man with the shot gun but drew his weapon, crouched, and began to work his way to the front of the store. The large man by the soda fountain had his back to John and still had not seen him. His hands went quickly into his coat and as he turned he brought up a stainless steel four inch revolver with one hand while he pulled on a face mask with the other.

Big Man moved quickly toward the front counter to help Skinny Man and still didn't see John.

Ryan hoped his words would be enough, but Skinny Man spun with the shot gun and fired down the aisle toward Ryan with neither hesitation nor aim. The nine 32 caliber pellets in the double ought buck round smashed into the twelve packs of Bud Light to the left of Ryan. The beer cartons began to spray their contents from the wounded cans onto the floor of the first aisle. The attendants did not have to be told what to do. They hit the floor immediately and frantically belly crawled toward the emergency exit, opting to live and watch the gun fight at a later time via the tapes of the security camera.

Ryan fired, hitting Skinny Man, who yelled, "Fuck!" as he spun and ducked behind the shelving at the opposite end of the aisle from Ryan.

John continued to move forward, since he had not been seen by either robber. As he reached the end of his aisle, he saw both men crouching side by side using the shelves for cover and the Big Man was asking, "Did you see a fucking cop car outside?"

"Fuck no. I think he's by himself," said the Skinny Man, "What should we do."

"Kill the mother-fucker," answered Big Man without hesitation.

John aimed carefully and said calmly as possible, "Police behind you, do not move or I will shoot you. Drop your guns Do it…"

As he formed those words both armed robbers began a quick, aggressive spin toward John's voice. As John fired, Skinny Man instinctively stepped away from him, forgetting the aisle was covered by Ryan. Like a "Threat Target" on the range, Skinny Man appeared in Ryan's line of sight, weapon in hand. Instantly, Ryan shot him, but Skinny Man wasn't done yet.

Big Man fired once, the round burying itself harmlessly in a large mountain of bananas before John put him down with one round to the forehead. Skinny Man fired one last 12 gauge shotgun round after he was hit, but his round chewed heavily into the right buttocks of Big Man, who was already beyond caring. Ryan and John fired within milliseconds of each other, ending the gun fight. They stood in its smoky aftermath, the victors of this encounter.

As both suspects appeared motionless on the floor John shouted, "You OK, Partner?"

"I'm OK, are you OK?" replied Ryan.

"I'm good! I'm calling it in," John radioed, "256."

"256 go ahead," said the dispatcher.

"We broke up a robbery in progress at the Kwik Trip at 5th and Cass. We have shots fired with two suspects down. We need back up, a supervisor, and first responders. We are both OK."

After calling in the shooting, John called to his partner, "Ryan, cover these two, I am going to clear the area."

"Got it!" shouted Ryan.

As John moved through the store and his normal pre-gun fight faculties returned, he realized the emergency exit buzzer was sounding as a result of the store employees making their escape. John swept through the store and found there was no one else left in the store. When he checked the lot outside, he could hear the sirens approaching but still at a distance.

While scanning the lot to see what had changed since their approach, he noticed a white Ford van at the pumps, but no one was pumping gas and the engine was still running. He quickly acquired another magazine, stripped the one he had in his weapon and slammed the full magazine hard into the magazine port. The partial magazine clattered to the pavement as John squinted to see a man in a leather jacket behind the wheel.

John moved to the side of a mail box just to his right and took cover, but the driver decided John's reload was a bad sign for this hastily planned robbery. The leather jacketed accomplice accelerated sliding and squealing around the pumps and bounced out of the lot onto 5th Street, choosing to ignore the flashing red light as he careened his van West onto Cass Street trying to make good his escape in the direction of Minnesota.

"256 to dispatch," radioed John.

"256 go ahead," responded the dispatcher.

"A white Ford van just tore out of the lot westbound on Cass Street toward Minnesota. The driver was dressed in a leather jacket, similar to the ones the suspects were wearing."

"256, 10-4. We will notify Houston County. Are there any units in position to intercept that vehicle?" asked the dispatcher.

"236 I am coming in from the East and am about two minutes out."

"235 I am coming from the North and am about a minute and a half out. I will head West on Cass and try to locate that vehicle."

John noticed the lot was empty except for a bakery truck and a paper delivery man just pulling in.

John re-entered the store as Ryan was checking the vitals on Skinny Man. "No need covering or handcuffing these two John. They are both 10-100 (deceased). Let's secure the scene. "

John turned and secured the front doors of the store as he asked, "Ryan, what's going on here. Three people have tried to kill us in almost as many months. Is it you, or me? What's this all about?"

Ryan suggested, "This is new to me, John. You could write it off as luck, chance, great police work, but I would venture a guess saying that you better get used to it. I think that you are one of those phenomena in law enforcement we call a 'shit magnet.'"

CHAPTER ELEVEN

Bad Dreams but a Good Life

"Are you troubled by your dreams?" asked Doctor Sistek.

"I would say… no," said John fifteen minutes into his second mandatory session with Doctor Sistek required by policy after surviving the gun fight with Big Man and Skinny Man.

"I could not help but notice there was some hesitation in your answer. Can you explain that?" asked the doctor.

John crossed his ankles as he spread out on the couch and crossed his hands behind his head while asking, "Is it all right for me to get comfortable?"

"Please do," said Dr. Sistek gesturing with her hand as if the couch was a prize on *The Price is Right*, and she was one of the show models.

"What was the question again, Doc?" asked John.

"You hesitated when I asked you if you were troubled by your dreams. Could you explain to me why you hesitated when you answered 'no,'" the doctor repeated.

"How do I explain that?" John Savage pondered out loud to himself. "Balduzzi taught me to tame my dreams. Is that good enough or would you like an explanation of the explanation?"

"We have time. I would prefer an explanation of the explanation," said the doctor, her interest piqued.

"Did you ever have a bad dream when you were child, Doc?" began John.

"Yes, we all do," answered Doctor Sistek as she leaned forward, uncrossed and re-crossed her legs, then sat back again while pushing her glasses up her nose.

"Well that's when dreams frightened me and were, as you said, troubling. There was neither rhyme nor reason to them. The dreams contained monsters and things that went bump in the night. They had no context to them. They came out of the blue. You know, you played ball, won your game, and then went over to your buddy's boat house and went swimming. You had a great day and you went to sleep and 'Bam' out of nowhere something is chasing you, or you're falling off a cliff. You woke up sweating with the Beegeezuz scared out of you," John explained sitting up, planting both feet on the floor and looking straight at the doctor.

"Well, one time in Iraq after I had been in the shit for a while…sorry, ma'am," said John.

"No, no, it's quite alright for you to use whatever vernacular feels right for you to frame what it is that you are feeling," said Dr. Sistek.

"After I had been in some heavy combat, I apparently was thrashing about one night and I woke up scared from a dream, and my buddy Balduzzi in the next bunk woke up too. He'd been through the same sh— combat I had been through and knew I had been dreaming. His dad had seen a lot of action in Vietnam. When Balduzzi went into action, his dad warned him about the dreams and taught him how to tame them…" said John, smiling and becoming rather animated.

"Tame them?" asked the doctor of psychiatry, who had never heard such a term in conjunction with dreams. Bad dreams are psychiatrist's job security.

"Yes, tame them. Balduzzi's dad taught him and then Balduzzi taught me, and then I was able to tame them. Balduzzi said his dad told him, 'there is no dream the mind can conjure up that is so wild-ass scary it can compare to what a warrior has lived through. So when you wake up, sit up immediately put your feet on the carpet, scrunch it up with your toes and tell yourself 'I'm home. I'm not in the bush, I'm not in the Mog, I'm not in the desert. I am home. I lived through that shit and it made me better, stronger. That shit didn't kill me then and it sure as hell can't hurt me now.' Then kiss the person you're sleeping with, lay back down, and sleep like a baby."

"Balduzzi's dad said it is easier for a warrior to tame dreams than a child, because children haven't had the opportunity to face what they fear the most in real life. Warriors have faced real nightmares and survived."

"You keep using the term warrior and not soldier, why is that?" asked the doctor.

"Balduzzi's dad told his son we're all warriors after Balduzzi came back from the Mog..."

"Excuse me once again. You've used that term twice...the Mog," observed the doctor. "What exactly is the Mog?"

"The Mog is Mogadishu, Somalia. Balduzzi was one of the Rangers pinned down all night in Mogadishu in the middle of the Bakaara Market. They made a movie about it called, "Black Hawk Down. Balduzzi was the guy...did you see the movie?"

The Doctor looked back a few pages in her notes as if the answer was written there and said, "No. I um, don't watch war movies."

John continued, "Never mind then. The city of Mogadishu, Somalia, was called, 'The Mog' by the Rangers and the Navy Seals that were in that fight."

"Thank you, I remember that. Now you were saying about warriors?" asked the doctor now writing feverishly on her pad.

"Balduzzi's dad said priests, rabbis, and reverends were God's shepherds sent to protect His flock spiritually, and warriors were sent to protect God's flock physically. He said there is something hard-wired in us to protect and no matter how we are raised, when the flock is endangered we step forward. He says warriors gravitate toward the military and law enforcement careers."

"Why create wars then?" asked the doctor.

"God gave us free will to choose to live in peace. God created man, man created war. Honorable warriors protect the flock. That's what we do.

Are you supposed to be curing me of my faith here, Doctor? Because if you are…" John added in a defensive tone.

"Sorry, no. I was just getting a little philosophical," interrupted Doctor Sistek. "Go on."

"Anyway, Balduzzi's dad said that bad dreams went hand-in-hand with being a warrior. There is no avoiding them, but you can learn to contain them and tame them. You tame them by realizing they are dreams and can't hurt you like the war that seared them into your brain forever. You contain them by not letting them impact your life. You own the memories that spawn the dreams. You are the warrior that survived and must always remember and therefore dream for the sake of those that didn't come home.

He explained that warriors must strive to make a good life for themselves and live it for their buddies that didn't make it. So that's what I did. I tamed my dreams. They are the baggage of a warrior. I have dreams, sleeping memories I call them, but they do not trouble me anymore because I have tamed them. I lived them for real and survived, and they can't hurt me now. Warriors that have tamed their dreams can have bad dreams and still have a good life."

Doctor Sistek had stopped writing and she was now sitting up straight with both feet on the floor. After a long silence she said, "Well our time is up here. Would you like to make another appointment with me?" asked the doctor.

"No, ma'am, unless you can't clear me to return to work right now." asked John.

The doctor walked to her desk, filled out the paper work, and handed the copies to John. "If that is what you want, that is what I will do," she said as she scribbled words on a form and then separated two copies, handing them to John. "I must say, though I have enjoyed our talks," said Dr. Sistek.

"I have too," said John truthfully. "Yellow to the Assistant Chief and I keep the pink one," said John as he read the sheet and smiled when he saw she had cleared him for return to duty.

She walked John to the door and held it open for him. "Stay safe, John. I hope we don't have to keep meeting like this,"

"Me too, Doc, but I can't guarantee it," said John with concern. "They say I am a shit magnet."

"Shit Magnet? " The doctor said.

John stopped and said, "You see, Doc, that's when…"

"That's all right, John. I think I figured that one out myself," said the doctor stepping aside to make room for John to pass.

John continued on past the doctor and offered her a Bazooka Bubble Gum. She took it and said, "Thank you, John."

As John quickly made his exit, the doctor turned to her receptionist. "Hold my calls for 30 minutes, please." She shut the door and walked to the chair behind the desk. Dr. Sistek un-wrapped the gum and popped it in her mouth. The doctor unfolded the comic, read it, and smiled. Then she nervously looked around and, satisfied she was alone, licked the gum taste off the comic as she had done when she was a little girl.

She softened the gum with some bubble-prep-chewing. As she chewed, Doctor Sistek kicked off her shoes and put her feet flat on the floor. She slowly began digging her silk-stocking covered toes into the carpet. It felt cool, relaxing, and she said out loud, "Tame the dreams. What an interesting concept." She closed her eyes as she continued to roll the carpet between her toes. After a few minutes she began to chant repeatedly mantra-style, "I can tame the dreams. I have bad dreams but a good life… I have bad dreams, but a good life… I have bad dreams, but a good life…."

CHAPTER TWELVE

Their Special Place in Hell

Ahmed put his car into park, leaned forward, found the trunk release lever, and popped the trunk. He walked around the car to the trunk as he looked about to find the woodpecker he could hear tapping its way through a dead tree trunk toward its lunch. When he finally located the small bird making the big noise he laughed and observed out loud, "What a strange bird is this peckerwood."

There was no one at the range today, which was why Ahmed picked Tuesday and Wednesday mornings to train. Ahmed reached the trunk, pulled out his hockey bag, and threw it over his shoulder. He walked down the trail through the woods to the small arms range, set his bag down on a bench, and unzipped it. He liked using a hockey bag because he could carry his weapons around downtown Madison without anyone raising an eye brow. He pulled out three targets and the stapler and walked down range and stapled each target to the backing on the target stands. He had purchased realistic targets for training to become mentally prepared for what he must do. One target was a police officer, another was a SWAT Officer in full gear, and the third he had posted today was a mother holding a child.

These targets were originally designed to be used as "No Shoot Targets," for police training, but for Ahmed they represented his adversary and his prey. He would have purchased a target with his intended victim on it, but individuals named Ahmed purchasing target images of the President of the United States would raise the eyebrows of even the most lackadaisical Americans. Ahmed's alias for his last name varied, but his first name was always his given name. He found that doing so avoided confusion, and it was best to lie as close to the truth as possible to be believable. Ahmed was too common a name to trigger alarms on its own merit.

Ahmed returned to the bench, loaded a magazine into his weapon, jacked a round into the chamber and holstered his weapon. Ahmed immediately dropped and did fifty push-ups, sprung up, and ran down range. When he reached the targets, he turned about sharply and raced back to the bench. At the bench he dropped and did 25 push-ups as slowly and correctly as possible. When he finished, he was up again and sprinted down range, turned sharply, and quickly ran back. He dropped and did 50 sit-ups and ran down range, stopping at the 7 yard line. He slowly turned away and then suddenly spun, shouted "Allahu Akbar!" while he drew his weapon, and fired three rounds into the uniformed police officer, one round into the face of the SWAT Officer, another into the face of the mother and paused. He took a breath shouted "Allahu Akbar!" once again and shot the baby.

Akbar repeated the entire cycle four times. When he finished, his arms felt like lead poles as he stood examining the hits on his targets. He admired the tight groupings and said to the still tapping woodpecker "This is excellent shooting, but paper targets do not shoot back my peckerwood friend."

Ahmed ran his fingertips over the cluster of holes in the head of the baby and pondered, *my bombs have killed men, women, and children, and this has never bothered me. I wonder if I can point a weapon at a child, even the child of an American and pull the trigger.*

As Ahmed mentally debated with himself about what would justify the shooting of a small child, a line of sweat trickled into his eye, setting it to stinging. He thought of his painting in the Hall of Heroes. "I am a hero of the Jihad. I must do what is expected of me without such sentimental concerns," he said out loud as if he was trying to placate mother and child he had just shot in the "No Shoot Target."

Ahmed rubbed the sweat from his eye with the sleeve of his Nike "Just Do It!" t-shirt and took three steps back from the target and shouted, "Tears for tears, and blood for blood, Allahu Akbar!" With that he drew his weapon and emptied his magazine, ripped the empty magazine out of the magazine port, reached for another, slammed it into the port, charged the weapon, and fired until the second magazine was also empty, firing every round into the mother and child. He hit the thumb release on his weapon, which had locked open on the empty chamber, and the action slammed closed. Ahmed holstered his weapon and whispered to the Mother and Child targets, "I am a warrior of Allah. You are my enemy." Ahmed found little inner peace after this reconciliation he made with the targets.

His training completed, Ahmed turned to the East and folded his hands, laying them perfectly positioned to the side of his face as he prayed the Fatihah. He bowed, bent, knelt, and prostrated himself for a ritual that he completed five times each day. As he ended the ritual, he solemnly recited, "Allahumma salli 'ala Muhammad."

He stood up, looked about the range, and found himself still alone and still troubled by the thought of killing defenseless children. He always hoped that prayer would give him the sense of clarity that others seemed to possess. As he rose from his most devout prayer, he found he still possessed doubts about the killing of innocents.

He gave up once again on clarity of conscience and settled for clarity of purpose. He drew his weapon and fired it again and again at the targets as he shouted in near perfect English, "Damn all Americans; Allah Be Praised!"

———————>•●•<———————

Logan Tyree was the night shift Lieutenant. As far as John Savage was concerned Tyree was a great leader, a great commander, a great cop, and ideal role model. John had written a letter to his buddy Balduzzi and he had this to say about Logan Tyree, "You have to meet my shift commander someday. I'd go into battle with this guy."

Since Logan had grown up on the north side of La Crosse and graduated from Logan High, most people assumed he had been named after Logan High School. The reality was that he was the fourth Logan in a line of Logan Tyrees, each named in honor of his great-great-grandfather's commander in the Civil War. The commander led from the front lines throughout the war and cut a striking figure riding into battle upon his black thoroughbred stallion. His troops called him Black Jack Logan and loved him because he brought them courage and victories.

Although Logan Tyree was not kin of the swashbuckling general, he inspired the same enthusiasm for the mission that Black Jack Logan had and shared the same coal black hair and moustache. The only critique Logan Tyree ever received from his supervisors throughout his career was,

"Logan. Your hair needs to be cut shorter and more often." Since he was now the ranking officer on third shift, he could pretend his hair was a beer tapper during the half-time of a Packer game and let it flow. He did.

It was Tuesday morning, and each Tuesday Logan Tyree would meet for his Kei Satsu Jitsu Class. Kei Satsu Jitsu is a little-known martial art that literally translated means, "The Police Way of Combat." Its origin was the La Crosse Police Department, during the 1970s.

Practitioners met once a week to train in preparation for the inevitable combat that lay in store for them as police officers. Today there were fifteen officers seated on the mat in the La Crosse Police Department training room.

Lt. Tyree said, "I am honored as always that you come here on your own time, without pay or compensation, to prepare for the challenges that lie ahead for you. You prepare for the most honorable of combat. Your combat is the most honorable of all because you enter it knowing that your opponent will not play by rules, in fact they will break all the rules of honorable combat. You, on the other hand, have taken an oath to follow the rules even during a life-and-death struggle. This does not mean that we can't strike, kick, pepper spray, TASE, and/or shoot our adversary. It just means we will do it with proper justification, and make no mistake about it, when it is reasonable and necessary to strike them, the practitioner of Kei Satsu Jitsu is expected to 'strike like thunderbolts from the nine layered heavens,' as Sun Tzu would say. Let's train. Ones have the blue bags, twos are striking. Line up!"

Seven bag holders faced seven officers and John was the odd man out. Tyree picked up a bag and motioned John Savage over to him. "Ready!" shouted Tyree and all of the officers facing the bag snapped quickly into a defensive stance shouting, "Back!"

"Forearms, Strike!" shouted Tyree and with every count of "Strike," the officers snapped a forearm deep into the blue bags, trying to drive the bag holder back. After several impacts Tyree shouted, "Stand down,"

"You guys look really good, except I want you scary good." He tossed the blue bag to John Savage and said, "You are all doing well, except you are striking to the target instead of through the target. You do not want to make contact with the suspect, you want to strike him and drive through him. You want all of his internal organs to feel the impact. In fact if it wasn't for the bad guy's spine you would cut him in half. On each and every impact you want to increase your power by driving off your back foot and make noise. Noise lowers your inhibitions, lets the air out of your abdomen, and startles your opponent. It also sends a message to onlookers and, most of all, causes an involuntary flexing of your muscles at impact."

Tyree then looked to John and said, "Get ready, John. Don't let me move you. Are you ready?"

John Savage brought the bag into his body as tight as he could and set his stance. He dug in and took a breath, determined to be an immovable object. "Ready," said John blowing out a long breath of air.

Tyree exploded out of his stance and drove his forearm and elbow into the bag and John felt it through the bag. The force of the impact seemed to rattle John's teeth and moved him back a foot as Logan Tyree barked, "Back!"

Logan Tyree never showed off his talent, without reason. He would only do it to demonstrate proper technique, and occasionally in the classroom officers would get a glimpse of how good Tyree was. It was all for one reason. To prepare these officers for the inevitable, which he said was, "To survive physically, legally, and emotionally every challenge this career throws at you." Every person in the class tried to fine tune their technique, using Lt. Tyree's example as their goal.

John Savage, while shaking his head as if his eyes had gone blurry and he needed them refocused, said, "I wonder if anyone hit by that much power on the street would still be standing?"

"I hope not, but if they are and they still want to fight I will just hit them again," said Tyree. "If they don't wish to continue the fight I will happily accept their surrender."

"Question answered, problem solved," said John subconsciously rubbing the impact area of his body as he handed the bag back to Tyree. The class continued through all of their empty hand impacts, called counter measures, and had an incredible sweat going when they finished their last set of impacts.

Those that worked with Logan Tyree on a nightly basis knew what he was capable of. When he laid hands on people, they went to jail even when they didn't want to. They would go voluntarily, handcuffed at a normal walk, or he would apply any number of holds on his suspects that would put them instantly on their tip toes singing out instinctively, "Ow! Ow! Ow! Ow! Ow!"

Logan Tyree was extensively trained in the martial arts and held all the tactical instructor certifications offered by the State of Wisconsin. He was an empty hands control expert and shared those skills with everyone in his Kei Satsu Jitsu class. Tyree taught that the TASER was an excellent tool, but the night shift devotees of Kei Satsu Jitsu would say in their best Frito Bandito accent, "We don't need no steeeenking TASER."

Tyree would laugh at their youthful confidence and say, "Everything works some of the time, and everything fails some of the time. It is important to keep all your options open. Never say never and always avoid using the word always in the world of law enforcement."

Today the class was scheduled an extra hour because Tyree had reserved the eight station in-door range at the police department. During the last break in the class Tyree said, "Take fifteen minutes and meet me in the range in full uniform with your vests and duty belts. Your weapons should be holstered and cleared along with your magazines."

After everyone was gathered in the range, Tyree said, "Load your magazines to capacity and do not charge them." Ammunition was out and everyone went about loading three magazines for their Glock 40 calibers. The laughing and camaraderie made the scene seem more like a light practice of a football team the night before Homecoming rather than a firearms class. This group was a team—partners, pals, buddies, any word which meant humans working together like a fine oiled machine while having fun.

"I'll bet you lunch that my group is tighter than yours," Ryan said to John.

"Not just lunch, lunch at Coney Island," said John as he slapped the side of his full magazine, causing the bullets rattle into alignment. They had a tendency to bunch up in the magazine as if they all were anxiously pushing to the front of the line impatient to be the first to go "Bang!"

"Coney Island it is. They say hot dogs are bad for you, so if I live long enough to be killed by a lifetime diet of hot dogs, let them be Coney Island's Dogs. I will die happy. Is the five dog limit the bet, like usual?" asked Ryan as he rapped the side of his last magazine, flipped it, caught it, and slipped it into his pouch.

"You're on; five dog limit it is," agreed John, "Mustard. Chili, onions, and hold the salt," he added.

"Everyone, listen up!" shouted Lt. Tyree. The laughing and talking stopped on the proverbial dime.

"We will not charge the weapon, so your first round fired will be a malfunction. Leave your weapons holstered, and as a team we will run the length of the basement hallway and then climb the stairs eight floors to the top and eight floors down. We will run back to the range and you will do as many push-ups as you can do up to 75. Then we will go in two groups as partners. I am calling this the Hasan exercise. That's after Nidal Malik Hasan, who killed twelve American soldiers. Two of the dead were Amy Krueger and Russell Seager of Wisconsin. Let's have a moment of silence in their memory," said Tyree. "Dear God, bless their souls, and sorry, Lord, you'll have to wait for ours. We aren't going without a fight. Thank you for giving us the will and the skill to protect others who can't defend themselves. Amen," said Tyree.

You will notice the target down range is either Osama Bin Laden or Saddam Hussein. I got a bargain-basement, dead-bad-guy price on the targets since they are both old news. One was hung high and the other was sunk low, thanks to the most honorable military in the history of the world," said Logan Tyree.

John Savage, Ryan Chen, and two other young veterans in the group instinctively barked, "OOOAAH!"

"Make no mistake about it, Muslims are not our enemy. In fact, we seek to protect Muslim and Christian alike. Terrorists, who have dishonored the faith of Islam by hijacking it for their evil mission are our enemy. Now, Team one will be at the line first and team two will be behind them. At every command you will fire two, three, four, or five rounds. It will be your choice. When your magazines are empty, drop to a knee and shout 'reloading' and your partner will step in and continue until they have to reload, and then they will drop to a knee to reload and ones will be back at it until we all run dry. Are there any questions?" No one answered. "OK, let's go!"

The group, with Logan Tyree at the lead, lined up and he shouted, "Moving!" Down the hall and up the stairs they ran at a jog.

The run was taxing for all, grueling for some. Everyone in this class acquitted themselves well since they had been inspired by Tyree to be like Tyree. At forty years old Logan Tyree could outlast, out-distance, and out-fight any suspect the street had to offer. He firmly believed in what he taught: You have to be better because there is no second place on the street.

Regardless of individual fitness levels, they took the stairs as a team. Tyree knew exactly how fast to run the stairs so they stayed together and no one was humiliated. When the group reached the basement, he led them into the classroom and they were all down on the mats pumping out pushups. Tyree did all 75, on his knuckles. Savage, Chen, and Mike Blocker were the only others that were able to do all 75. Most of the others ranged around 50 to 60 but determined to make 75 the next time. Wendy Sweet, one of the two females in the class impressively made it to 72.

As the movement on the mat came to a stop and everyone brought themselves to a standing position, Tyree popped up and said, "Ladies and Gentleman, shall we make some noise?"

This time, everyone, whether they had served in the military or not sounded off, "OOOAAH."

Logan Tyree marked each repetition on the line by shouting, "Allahu Akbar!" as was shouted by Hasan while the traitor killed his fellow soldiers at Fort Hood who were unarmed. Each shout was met by a volley of gun fire.

"Slow it down. Perfect practice makes perfect." shouted Tyree. "Like Wyatt Earp said about gun fighting, 'speed is fine, but accuracy is final,' and he knew a little somethin-somethin' about gun fighting. Some of you are jerking your weapons out of the holster and jerking the trigger. He also said you must learn how to be, 'slow in a hurry.' Remember, smooth is fast. Ready?"

John had trained often enough with Lt. Tyree. He concentrated on smoothly drawing his weapon, acquiring a lock solid grip over a balanced stance, and sending each round into Osama's brain. It was the brain that inspired the death of over 3000 on September 11. It was the brain that sent John Savage off to war. It was the brain which could never contemplate surrender until a Navy Seal's bullet found and scrambled Osama's brain. John wished it could have been his bullet that killed the monster...

After the range was cleaned and the group sat about the benches cleaning their weapons, Logan Tyree asked, "Let's talk about what we just did. Some in today's world would call that exercise insensitive or even racist. Anyone have an opinion one way or the other?"

"Politically correct bullshit," declared Wendy Sweet, whose blunt honesty always seemed to belie the pleasantness of her name. "The only insensitive thing about any of this is that the radical Jihadists kill men, women, children, Catholics, Jews, Protestants, and even Muslims who have never harmed them, nor intended to harm them. They would kill us all, if they could."

"We are in a shooting war, and some people can't even admit it. I read somewhere it's not a war anymore but an overseas contingency. Can you believe that?" Brady Gates incredulously proclaimed. Brady was a three-year veteran of the force and a four-year veteran of the United States Marine Corps. "Why don't they just say, please come over and kick our sissy asses? We surrender," Brady said in a mocking whimper. "I've heard that battle cry, and I think this exercise is a necessary reminder that our enemy is still alive and kicking and would love to come here and kill us. Hasan is an example that the enemy is even living among us."

John Savage then raised his hand.

"Go ahead, John, what do you think?" asked Tyree.

"I don't think it is an insult to Islam at all. The radical Jihadists truly believe they are pious and religious, but every single one of them in my view is going to hell the moment after a bullet stops them from killing innocents. I'll tell you why. It came to me in Iraq, when it was me or them. The third commandment is 'Thou shalt not take the name of the Lord thy God in vain.' I have come to believe that it doesn't refer to when you instinctively blurt out goddamn when you hit your thumb with a hammer. I think it means screaming 'Allahu Akbar,' as you are flying a plane full of innocent people into a building also full of innocent people." John paused and bit his lip, thinking better about saying anything else, counted to five, and then thought to hell with it. He continued, "It never crossed my mind, as we were doing the exercise, that we might offend someone. All I thought about was how the exercise might prepare our heads and our hearts to someday keep one of these maniacs from sending good people prematurely to heaven, by us sending those sons of the devil to their special place in hell."

CHAPTER THIRTEEN

Nikah al-Mut'ah

Her body sparkled in the bright lights of the stage from a combination of glitter and sweat after the four song set, during which she gradually as well as expertly disrobed. Her movement up, down, and around the pole was worthy of Caesar's Palace. Her light skin, long flowing blonde hair, tight body, dance skills, and small but alluring breasts were a perfect fit for the last song, Shakira's "Loca."

It was a Saturday Night at the Visions Night Club on East Washington Avenue in Madison, and Lara noticed Ahmed in the front row with his chest buttressed up against the stage. His brown eyes, wide with desire, seemed to be gathering in every inch of her nakedness.

Lara had never before been drawn to any patrons of Visions. She could not help but notice, however, the resemblance between this international looking man in the front row to a young Omar Sharif. Sharif was an Egyptian actor with international fame who played Yuri Zhivago in the movie "Doctor Zhivago." Lara's mother loved the movie and had named her daughter after the woman who fell in love with Yuri in the epic movie about a tempestuous love affair that spanned the Russian Revolution. Lara had seen the movie at least 100 times as a child, and she cried at the end of the movie 100 times along with her mother who would say, "That is what love is, little bits of joy floating on an ocean of tears."

Lara was a Sociology Major working for her Master's Degree. She had taken on the job of exotic dancer as part of her Master's Thesis project. She had read once about how activist and writer Gloria Steinem had done an article after she had become a Playboy Bunny. Lara was doing her thesis on the burgeoning sex industry and its impact on social mores. The dancing started as an attempt at a safe immersion into the sex industry, but in doing so she found it to be not only a bit of a rush but a way to make a great deal of money out of the reach of the federal government.

After her set, Lara changed into her lap dance ensemble and moved among the patrons. This is where the real money was made. She could make $40 or more in three to five minutes for a lap dance. Some of the other girls had told her that once in a while a big spender would come in with a huge wad of cash and, "If you can legally make them blow their wad on you, they might blow their wad on you." This oft told stripper joke never failed to cause the dancers to laugh like a bunch of giddy school girls.

Joke or not, Lara found it to be true. The big spenders were generous if Lara could make them feel desirable. Lara soon discovered another truth—rich or poor, they were all big spenders in a strip club.

As she made her rounds, she attempted to be nonchalant in her movement, but she was drawn first to the Zhivago look-alike and said, "Would you like a dance, handsome?" As she made the pitch, she slid her hand lightly across his shoulder and then gently caressed Ahmed's neck with a touch as light as the wings of a moth circling a flame. Ahmed was chilled and warmed at the same time by her touch, and was embarrassed by his instantaneous arousal.

"I wonder if, instead, I could buy you a cup of coffee when you finish working tonight?" he asked. "You see, in my culture dancers of your rare talents are some of the most respected of all performers. I would be honored and would even pay for the honor to buy you a cup of coffee. May I?" asked Ahmed.

"Your culture? Where are you from?" Lara asked curiously.

"I am from Saudi Arabia," answered Ahmed.

"Have you ever seen the movie Lawrence of Arabia?" Lara asked.

"Yes. My family fought alongside Lawrence against the Turks," answered Ahmed in an excited tone. This conversation was allowing for him to shift in his seat and reposition himself in an attempt to conceal his reaction to Lara.

"Wow! I was asking you because you look to me like Omar Sharif," said Lara, whose hand was still caressing Ahmed's neck, causing an incredible tingling that traveled from his neck to his heart to his groin. No woman had ever done this to Ahmed before, and he had experienced hundreds, having had sexual encounters on nearly every continent of the world.

"I must tell you that in my country there are many men who look like the actor Omar Sharif. So I shall ask you again, beautiful dancer. May I meet you and buy you coffee tonight after your dancing is completed?" Ahmed pleaded.

Lara looked at the man and asked, "What is your name?"

"Ahmed. I hope I am not making you nervous about your safety. I am most completely safe. I can wait for you here or meet you at…shall we say at Perkins on East Washington Avenue? Please do not say no." Ahmed pleaded.

Ahmed's eyes looked up into Lara's, and they had certain puppy dog innocence. That fact, coupled with Ahmed's resemblance to the handsome prince Lara conjured up in every romantic fantasy she had ever imagined made this offer irresistible. "Yes. I will meet you there after closing about 2:45," said Lara. She sounded as if she was being generous, but in reality she could not believe her good fortune.

After Lara left, Ahmed ignored the dancers on the stage and watched Lara as she worked the crowd. He watched from his seat as Lara would lead men to a couch in the corner and treat them to a lap dance that barely qualified as "simulated sex." Each customer returned not the least bit disappointed.

Ahmed knew he had to have her, but not in that way. He had to have her completely. Ahmed the Jihadist wanted to kill her for being an American whore, but Ahmed the man wanted her for being everything he had secretly desired in a woman. He had struggled with these desires on his first trip to the United States. He had managed to satisfy them with frequent trips to strip joints and by paying for prostitutes. Lara had added a new dimension to Ahmed's desire. He not only was drawn to her sexually, but this time his heart also cried out to be satisfied.

Unknown to Lara and Ahmed, they shared something in common. They were both prolific self-deceivers. Lara had convinced herself that dancing at Visions was a grand sociology experiment which she would someday translate into a thesis and possibly a best-selling book. It would be a unique part of her resume. Money was a convenient bi-product of the endeavor.

Ahmed was an even more prolific self-deceiver. What his peers would have considered an act of cowardice on Martyrs' Ridge, Ahmed had convinced himself was a clever ruse impeccably executed. He reasoned that his murder of Jorge was a necessary part of his plan. He believed that he had sent one more corrupt, western drug dealer to hell and yet, when he stole Jorge's drugs and sold them, this was a noble deed to finance his honorable jihad that ultimately would further weaken the resolve of his enemy. Even now he had rationalized his frequent trips to bars, strip clubs, and prostitutes as a camouflage no different than the desert mud Abdullah had smeared on his body to blend into his surroundings before he had set off the IED at the onset of the ambush at "Martyrs' Ridge." Ahmed saw himself merely engaged in a similar effort to blend into the decadent landscape of America by pretending to be as decadent as the "infidels."

As Lara was leading a fat balding man in dirty bib-overalls to the couch, Ahmed threw down what was left of his drink and made his was out of the club. Ahmed arrived at the Perkins early, took a rear booth and ordered tea. He fired up his laptop, connected to the internet, and began searching. During his search "Al-Qaeda in the United States?" he found an article that piqued his interest, "Al Qaeda at the border?"

With great interest, Ahmed read how confirmed intelligence indicated an undetermined number of Al Qaeda operatives had been using the unprotected Mexican Border to cross into the United States. The article mentioned the murder of a drug mule where an image of 9-11 was found, but it said, "Investigators have determined that it may not be authentic and may be a ruse to shift suspicion away from the actual perpetrators." One investigator was quoted as saying, "It may be the work of the Mexican Cartel."

Ahmed shook his head. He thought, *this has been a problem ever since Bin Laden declared war on the United States. The attacks of my fellow soldiers of Allah had been but flies buzzing around the tail of a lion basking lazily in the sun. The lazy lion has ignored them except for an occasional swish of his tail. After 9-11 the lion finally felt the pain and fear of war, stood up, and roared. The lion killed and scattered many of my fellow warriors.*

A lamb replaced the lion. Rage and fear was diluted by time to become complacency. Now war is not even called a war. It is an overseas contingency. They proclaim Al Qaeda to be "diminished," and seem to think that saying it makes it so. Camel Dung! That will soon change.

I will remind them that they are at war. Al Qaeda is at war and it will not be over until victory is ours. Ahmed shook his head as he looked up from his laptop and spotted Lara coming through the front door. Ahmed quickly closed his laptop, stood, and waved to Lara, who had transformed from a goddess of sex to a simple but still irresistibly attractive young college graduate student.

When she saw Ahmed, she smiled and joined him in the corner booth. "Let me formally introduce myself, I am Ahmed Wahabi and you are?"

"I am Lara Dickinson," said the dancer as she removed her jacket and laid it neatly in the booth next to her. She turned to the waitress who had followed up behind her and said, "I'll have what he is having. It smells good."

"Hot sweet tea, it will be then. Here is the menu, and I will be right back with your tea," said the waitress.

As the waitress turned and tripped back toward the kitchen, Ahmed took a breath and declared without hesitation, "I do not wish to offend, but I did not want to meet with Lara the dancer but Lara the person. I was very moved by something about you. In my country, men usually only see the eyes of a woman. That is all that is necessary because the eyes reveal her soul. Your eyes are beautiful and tell me your soul is beautiful. I would like to discover if I am right or wrong in this matter. Your eyes tell me that you are a woman that I could love."

Lara leaned back and her face reddened as if his words were a strong gust of cold arctic wind, but in fact she was experiencing a tsunami of warmth sweeping through every part of her body, so moved was she by these words. "In your culture are the men so open with their feelings on a first meeting?"

"Where I am from it has been a tradition that your wife often is chosen for you, and there is no need for small talk on your first meeting. The world is changing though, even in Saudi Arabia," said Ahmed.

"Do you have a wife, or someone who is already chosen for you?" asked Lara. "Will you be going back to them some day?"

"No. I have left all of that. My life is here now. I will live the rest of my life in America. I shall not return home," answered Ahmed truthfully. He sipped from his tea as the waitress returned with a steaming pot and poured a cup for Lara. Ahmed set his cup down, nodded to the waitress, and smiled at her as she refreshed his cup.

He has such a nice smile, Lara thought as she asked, "What about your family? I know I could not just leave my family."

"My father is a very wealthy man. We have different political views and we do not speak. He cares about nothing but his wealth and retaining it. He has many wives and many sons. He neither misses me nor needs me," said Ahmed.

Lara asked, "What about your mother?" Instantly Lara, saw a reaction from Ahmed. There was an undeniable sense of loss in his eyes, which Ahmed could not conceal. Lara instinctively placed her hand into his hand to comfort him and she did not yet know why. He accepted it.

"My mother?" Ahmed paused carefully considering what he should tell her about his mother. Strangely enough, except for his name everything he had said about his past so far was the truth. He continued, "Can you handle the truth? For the truth is not for someone I am having a cup of tea with. It is for someone I would like to see again and again. So I ask you once again, Can you handle the truth?" Ahmed's smile was gone and his face was somber as he added, "I do not share this truth lightly."

Lara was excited by it all. Even though she knew nothing of this man, she was excited at the prospect of seeing Ahmed again—her Zhivago. She was excited by the mystery and the privilege of this sensitive piece of personal history about to be shared with her. "Yes, I can handle it."

"Lara, I only tell you this now because I have never felt this way about a woman before, much less one that I have just met. I consider it a sign from Allah that we should be together. Do you feel the same?" he asked taking both of her hands in his.

"Yes, I do, it has to be some sort of Karmic connection. I have never felt this way before," said Lara truthfully. She had never fell so quickly and uncontrollably in love with someone she knew nothing about, but instead of being wary, she was thrilled that he felt the same.

"My mother was my father's first wife. I am the second son of this union. My father did not divorce her, but married other women, which is the way in my country. He could afford many wives and therefore he had many wives. As he grew closer to other wives, my mother found herself alone and became weak against… how should I put this? She succumbed to the temptations of the flesh. She took a lover and one day when she and her lover were… together, my father came into her chamber and found them. He killed them both without saying a word." With that Ahmed picked up Lara's hands and pressed his lips to them and then held them to his head as if they were a healing compress.

"What happened to your father? Did he…Is he in prison. Is that why you do not see him?" asked Lara.

"No, my father was forgiven. He did not go to prison because a wronged man can be forgiven for the murder of his wife and lover when the adultery takes place in his own home. So it is written in Sharia Law." He took her hands from his forehead, kissed them again, and set them back down on the table, as he continued to hold them.

"I am so sorry. That must have been hard on you. I can't imagine how that must have felt, or how it must still feel," said Lara looking into his brown, beautiful, but tragic eyes. She slid out from the table and sat down next to him. She placed her hands on either side of his face and turned his face toward her. She leaned forward and kissed him softly but with a rock hard passion on his quivering lips. She slid out and took him by the hand. She threw a $10.00 bill down on the table as she said, "Come. I hope you do not think badly of me or think that this is my way, but if you will have me I want to make love with you tonight."

Ahmed slid out of the booth and stood up and returned her kiss. As their lips reluctantly parted he answered, "Allah be praised. I have found you. You are to me *Nikah al-Mut'ah.*"

"What does that mean?" asked Lara.

"In my country, in Islam, if two people agree to become one and be together but can't marry, they can agree to be of one soul and one body. If they love each other they can choose to make love, live together, and share their lives together, and someday even marry." He kissed her again and said, "I choose you as my *Nikah al-Mut'ah.*"

Lara kissed Ahmed again, oblivious to the other patrons seated about them and the waitress beside them awkwardly holding her pad to take their order, frozen in place watching the love scene play out in front of her with her mouth agape.

Lara lips separated from Ahmed's only enough to repeat the phrase she thought so beautiful it belonged in a poem, "I also choose you as my *Nikah al-Mut'ah.*"

CHAPTER FOURTEEN

Emily Frickin' Dickinson

ven though the traffic flow was steady through town, the police radio was quiet. It was a Wednesday night in downtown La Crosse and the foot traffic on 3rd Street, the bar district, was ever present but subdued. They seemed more like tourists in a hurry to see the sights than drunks looking for fights. That could all change in a moment, and that was what John Savage loved about the job.

"That Toyota Camry rolled through the stop sign and it has no front plate on it," said Wendy Sweet, John's partner for the night. Wendy was a salty veteran street officer, 5'10" and an athletic 140 pounds. She was a long-time student of Logan Tyree and practitioner of Kei Satsu Jitsu. As far as cops were measured, she was tough as nails. Wendy was well liked by some and disliked by others because of her penchant for truthfulness. Except for her dealings with the public, where she could verbal judo most bad guys into cuffs without a fight, there was no filter between her brain and her mouth.

Women in law enforcement are placed in a tough position. They step into a male-dominated world, and wear clothing and carry equipment designed mainly for men by men. Much of their femininity has to be left in their locker when they hit the street. They strap on a gun belt and vest and are dispatched to deal with people who will hurt them or even worse if they sense weakness. Wendy was one woman who managed the transition well, and some would say "too well." To put it simply, Wendy was attractive but in a tough lady-cop sort of way. John Savage had made up his mind. He liked Wendy and liked working with her too.

As John and Wendy watched the Camry turn South onto 3rd Street from King Street, the tinted windows made a mystery of the occupant's identities. "I'll let it get out of the downtown area and then I'll stop it," answered John.

As the car reached Cass Street, the driver turned west and headed over the "Big Blue Bridge" crossing the Mississippi River's main channel. "I'll wait to get off the bridge. Do you think he saw us, before he turned toward Minnesota?"

"Hard to say whether he saw us or not with those tinted windows. A 30 point duck could be driving that car and you wouldn't know it," observed Wendy. "I hate tinted windows. They are like a death trap for cops, knock on wood," said Wendy rapping her knuckles on her baton.

"Did you mean 30 point buck, because you said 30 point duck," asked John.

"I was making a joke, John. You know duck, sounds like buck, but it would be more bizarre for a duck to drive a truck than a 30 point buck, but I guess duck instead of buck was not funny so, oh fuck! That was a poem, John. Did you like the poem better than my joke?" asked Wendy, as they gained ground on the car with no front plate.

"It was a fine poem," said John. "I now owe you one bad joke that needs to be explained and one poem. The kind that rhymes," answered John.

"Yeah," agreed Wendy, "Not one of those…. Iambic-pambic ones…you know the ones that don't rhyme," said Wendy watching the movements of the car they were about to stop. "But, don't strain your brain, Mark Twain. I like to write poems and limericks off duty."

"Really?" replied John, watching the movements of the vehicle they were following.

"Yeah, I'm a regular Emily Frickin' Dickinson when it comes to rhyming," claimed Wendy proudly. "Let's give this guy a fright and hit the lights," rhymed Wendy as the car reached the opposite side of the Mississippi River.

"10-4," said John as he hit the overhead lights. The driver of the Camry slowed immediately and pulled into the entrance of Pettibone Park where he parked against the curb.

John got on the public address system, from which his voice bellowed, "This is the La Crosse Police Department and I am Officer John Savage. Driver, please turn your interior lights on."

The driver turned the interior lights on.

"Thank you," said John over the speaker.

The driver was shaking his head in disgust, as John approached the driver's side. Wendy hung back a bit and then cautiously approached from the passenger side. John could see the driver was a middle-aged African American male in a suit and the passenger was a middle-aged African American female in a black gown. The driver was removing his license from his wallet, and as John reached him he thrust it out the window yelling, "Guilty as charged, Officer, take me to jail. How dare I? A pox upon me for the lout I am, because you have caught me driving while black again!"

John ignored the insult, took the license and said, "Good evening, sir, I'm Officer Savage of the La Crosse Police Department. The reason I stopped you tonight was you have no front plates and you rolled through the stop sign at King when you turned onto 3rd Street."

The driver fired back words as rapidly as rounds spitting from the barrel of Balduzzi's machine gun complaining, "No front plates, my ass. I'm black, I'm driving at night. You said to your partner, 'Look it's a new car with a black man driving. It must be stolen. He must be a drug dealer.' Admit it! Kiss my ass if I'm not tired of this. You stopped me because I'm black. If you can't admit it to me, at least go home tonight and look into the eyes of the man in the mirror and admit to him."

"John," called Wendy, motioning him over to her, "Let me handle this, please."

"Be my guest," acquiesced John, stepping back into the cover position. He could not help but notice the female in the passenger seat had her hand to her forehead and appeared deeply embarrassed.

Wendy walked up to the driver's side and said, "Professor Knox, sir. I am Officer Sweet of the La Crosse Police Department. It was me that asked my partner to stop your vehicle."

"Sweet and Savage. I will remember those names for the official complaint. What are your badge numbers?"

"Those will be on the warning citations, sir. I heard you questioning the grounds for our stop and I would like to point out to you, sir, that you have heavily tinted windows and we had no idea who was driving the vehicle prior to the stop because of the tint," explained Wendy.

"Tint my ass! Nice Try! Citation? You're giving me citation? I'm taking it to court!" Professor Knox barked.

"It's a warning, sir. There is no fine. You don't have to appear in…" said Wendy.

"I'll have your job! I am tired of this bullshit. Do you know who I am? I am Professor Henry Knox. I teach at the University, and I have heard about your department and its treatment of African Americans. I am telling you right here and now…"

"Henry, please," pleaded the passenger, who took hold of his arm and he pulled sharply away from her grasp.

"Wait right here, sir. We'll be up in a minute with your warning citations," said Wendy turning and watching the irate man over her shoulder spit and sputter out the front window like an out-of-control grease fire as she headed back to the car.

"Like trying to get a drink out of a fire hose," said Wendy.

"Gotcha," agreed John, "You know this guy, Knox?"

"Oh Yeah," answered Wendy as she slid into the passenger side of the squad. "We'll finish this stop and I'll explain. If we manage to keep him verbal only, we should be able to get out of this with only warnings. Don't engage him in an argument though. Stay calm and respectful. I'd say he was baiting us if I didn't know better. He believes his own bullshit and there will be no swaying him."

When the warnings were written Wendy returned to Knox's vehicle and the female passenger called Wendy over to the passenger window. "I am sorry, officers. My husband…"

"I was just trying," said Knox.

"Henry! Enough!" said the lady in a voice that was insistent in tone but subdued in volume. It silenced the flapping, but still gaping, hole in the face of the obnoxious professor. "I am sorry for the way my husband spoke to you. I will take those warnings. I did hear you say warnings, is that correct?" asked the woman.

"Yes, ma'am," said Wendy. "These are written warnings. There is no fine and no court date. They just give notice of the violations," said Wendy handing the woman the pink copies of the paperwork.

"Thank you for the warnings. After the way you were treated, if I were you, I would have written him a ticket. You know, the kind with fines," said the woman, who had the hint of a southern accent and the diplomatic genteelness of Condoleezza Rice. Her husband had resigned himself to the fact that his wife would have the last words. He looked straight ahead with his hands twisting on the steering wheel like a batter holding a bat, waiting for the next pitch on a three-two count.

"Thank you for your courtesy, ma'am," said Wendy. "If you'd like, later you can check it out for yourself. At night you really can't see anything inside your car from the outside. It's a very dangerous situation for police officers. Not everyone we stop is as nice as you. That is why we had your husband turn the interior lights on. Drive carefully and good night," answered Wendy. The professor ignored her and pulled away from the curb obviously undeterred and boiling in his indignity.

As the two partners returned to patrol John said, "Wendy, you surprised me on that stop."

"I did? Why?" she asked.

"When you asked to take over I thought maybe you had a special 'riot act' to read the guy for that set of circumstances," said John. "I figured being called a racist is so regular that you must have a way to deal with it."

"Yes, it's regular, but I deal with every potential confrontation individually as they come. There really is no cookie-cutter way to handle it other than to stay respectful, do your job, and don't be intimidated. If there is something you could say that would make you feel good, then absolutely don't say it. If it would feel good to say, it should not be said," Wendy said shaking a finger for emphasis.

She continued, "I asked to handle the stop because I had Professor Knox in college. I took a class with him on African American Studies as one of my Sociology requirements."

"Really? Is he a good teacher?" asked John.

"Some would proclaim him to be a great teacher, but as a human being he is a total bigot. He thinks he has justification for his bigotry and feels that only the majority can be racist because they have the power. He especially hates police officers," explained Wendy. "In his defense I must say that he is an equal opportunity bigot. He would have been yelling at us the same way even if we were two black officers."

"Were you a cop when you were in his class?" asked John.

"Yeah, I had a few credits to complete for my Bachelor's Degree when I got hired. I was a police officer when I was in his class and he knew it. Knox did nothing to hide his contempt for my profession in front of the class. In fact, having an officer in class allowed Knox to digress off onto many gleeful cop bashing tangents. At the end of the class, I earned an A and got a B instead," said Wendy tucking the warning citations into her easy rider clipboard.

"Did you let it go?" asked John.

"Me? Hell no! Have you ever known me to let someone shit in my sand box and get away with it?" asked Wendy, startled by the question.

"Not so much," agreed John shaking his head and laughing at the stupidity of the question.

"Hell no, I didn't let it go! I went in and talked to him about it. I had all my bucks in a row," said Wendy with a pause.

John laughed a polite, that's-not-that-funny-laugh and said, "Got it."

"Good. I just wanted to see if you were listening," and then Wendy continued, "So, anyway, I had all my ducks in a row, and I showed him the criteria on his syllabus for an A and my grades on all of my assignments. He shrugged his shoulders and that was that. He changed the grade to an A," said Wendy. "His only defense was a puzzled shrug." Wendy then demonstrated Knox's display of nonchalance.

"He acted like 'Big deal. So I got caught, so what.' I am quite certain the B was either a personal social experiment or an attempt to achieve some sort of social retribution against the woman who was 'the man' for centuries of unbridled oppression. I knew this contact was going to be difficult and thought it would be less likely that Knox would be able to talk his way into jail if I handled it. I had an advantage, because I knew his propensity toward cop hating and cop baiting. He boasted that he was a member of the Black Panthers in the 1970s. I spent an entire semester building up a tolerance to his racist bullshit."

"I'm glad you did," said John as he turned one more time onto 3rd Street from State. The pedestrian traffic still looked sparse and subdued. "His wife sure seemed nice."

"Yeah, you have the old, 'Beauty and the Beast,' or 'The Princess and the Frog,' syndrome going on there," observed Wendy, "except she can kiss that frog all she wants and he's still nothing but a big fat mouth with warts and nothing credible to say."

"Still, it's hard to be called a racist when you try so hard to be fair," opined John.

"Yeah, but I look at it this way. I don't care what color of skin the man has. I look at the content of a man's character not the color of his skin, and I don't care what color Professor Knox is. Assholes come in every race, creed, and color, and Professor Henry Knox is an asshole. He would be one even if he was green as a fat old bull frog sitting on a lily pad. If I was a princess and that old bullfrog said I could change him into a prince for a kiss, you know what I'd do?" asked Wendy.

"What?" John said, smiling in anticipation.

"I would bend over, drop my fancy princess dress, and say that he could kiss my lily-white ass and I would live happily ever after, but not with him. Even if he turned into a prince he would still be an asshole. You can paint it, plaster it, chrome it, gild it, or kiss it, but a prince that is an asshole is just another asshole, who happens to also be a prince," declared Wendy pulling up the collar of her uniform in disgust.

"Gild it?" John laughed.

"234," the dispatcher rudely interrupted John's laugh.

"234, we're at 4th and Jay, go ahead," answered Wendy.

"We have a complaint of a mother who wants her son removed from her home. They argued after his dog defecated on the living-room carpet. Additional information has been sent to your computer," said the dispatcher.

"We're 10-76 (en route)," answered Wendy as she clicked the call page up on the laptop screen.

"I have been here before," said Wendy. "The guy's name is Richard Poplinski and his mother's name is Ruth. She's nice and he's not. He's a 37 year old leach—no job, no ambition, no personality, no friends, no life—and has succeeded in everything he's ever tried, which is nothing. He's usually no problem, but she's never tried to kick him about before. I don't believe that is going to go over well."

"That's it. The brick one with the front light on," Wendy said to John as he pulled up short of the residence and shut the lights down.

Wendy cautiously approached and stood beside the front door as she knocked. John hung back and watched the front windows.

The door was opened by a tall, heavy, white-haired woman. She had a pair of glasses nestled in her hair on top of her head, which were attached by a gold cheater chain. "I'm glad you came so quickly. I want Richard out of here. He scared me tonight," Ruth reported. "Please come in."

"You said he scared you. How did he do that?" asked Wendy as she stepped past Mrs. Poplinski and scanned the rooms in the immediate vicinity. John moved around her and did a safety sweep of the immediate area. He moved through the vestibule. There was a line of coats hung on hooks with shoes below, mostly women's but also a pair of Nike running shoes. To the left there was a stairway and John pointed up as he passed, to alert Wendy to the danger area as he went right into the living room.

"Watch your step—dog shit," warned Ruth as John nearly stepped on a hefty steaming pile of freshly deposited, recently digested dump of a dog. "The dog is a Pit Bull and I locked it in the basement. It's mean," cautioned Ruth from the vestibule.

The house was built in a circle and John worked his way around to determine if Richard was either sulking or skulking on the first floor.

As John started the protective sweep, Wendy asked, "What happened tonight, Ruth?"

"Well Wendy, It's Wendy, right?" asked Ruth smiling and shaking her head.

"Yes, that's right. I have been here before," answered Wendy.

"I remember you. Well tonight the dog shit on the floor of the living room. It's not a puppy anymore, and I told him I didn't want a Pit Bull in my house in the first place. He got it anyway, and he never trained it right.

Tonight, I told him I wanted him and his dog out of here. He's in his room all the time and won't let me in there to even clean. He's perfectly healthy and could get a job if he wanted to. This is my house, and there comes a time when a son has to go out on his own. Don't you agree?"

"Where is Richard right now?" asked Wendy.

Before the question could be answered, Wendy heard a creek on the steps to the left of Ruth.

"Richard is right here," a voice came from the darkness above. Two bare feet appeared and trudged down the steps.

Wendy said, "Ruth, why don't you step into the kitchen, and I will talk to Richard."

As Wendy said this she took Ruth by the arm with her left hand and gently eased her out of the vestibule, directing her through the living-room toward the kitchen. As Wendy turned back to Richard she saw the Colt Model 1911 45 caliber semi-automatic pistol pointed at her with one hand and a machete in his other. At the end of that incredibly long second, the gun flashed with a dull bark. Wendy felt the round hit her hard in the chest as if a lumberjack and driven the end of his axe handle into her vest.

Wendy instinctively pivoted as she drew and avoided the second round, which punched through the window in the door behind her. Wendy had her gun out and fired three times hitting Richard in the chest staggering him, but he brought his weapon up again as he continued down the steps and fired again, hitting her in the right hand as well as smashing into her weapon. The pain was intense. It felt as if someone had slammed her hand in the door of a semi-tractor, and without so much as an apology slammed it once again. Her wounded hand failed her and Wendy dropped her weapon, but she managed to dash into the living room trying to get out of the line of fire.

Poplinski kept coming after her and took careful aim at the retreating officer. As Wendy cut into the living room, she stepped into the pile left by the Pit Bull, causing her to slide like a runner trying to take out the second baseman on a close double-play.

As Wendy went down Poplinski fired again, but he was unable to react to the sudden unplanned shit-induced directional change Wendy had made. The round passed over Wendy's head and harmlessly into the wall. No one involved could hear her, but Ruth Poplinski was screaming incoherently from the doorway between the kitchen and the living-room, and the pit bull with the loose bowels that started the whole trouble was howling in the basement.

John Savage had been making his way through the clutter of a long-unused sewing room just off the kitchen when he heard Poplinski coming down the steps. He moved two boxes away from a door which he figured opened up to the Vestibule. He hoped the door would be open, but he was not certain. He was setting the second box on top of the first when the shooting commenced.

John dropped the box and drew his weapon. John pulled the door open and saw the man on the second stair turned toward the living room taking aim with a Colt 45. John saw the Colt but never saw the machete. It did not matter. John brought his own weapon up as Poplinski fired and the round appeared to send Wendy sprawling across the living-room floor, out of John's field of vision.

John, frantic about his partner going down, quickly brought up his Glock and found his front sights naturally aligned on Poplinski's arm pit. He squeezed off two quick rounds, and Poplinski's only reaction was to turn toward John with a puzzled look on his face. The weapon began to swing toward John, but it was being handled by Poplinski as if it weighed about fifty pounds. John took a more careful aim; this time Poplinski's nose was balanced on the top of John's sights. John had prepared for this moment as long and as diligently as any gun fighter in history. Tyree's word's came to him as if Tyree was behind him giving him a little advice in the middle of this big problem, "Wyatt Earp once said, speed is fine, but accuracy is final. You must learn how to be slow, in a hurry." John saw his sights—saw them suspended in the air in the middle of Poplinski's face. He squeezed, "Bam!"

The round hit Poplinski square in the nose and then he was gone. There was no more puzzled look. There were no more shots. There was no more Richard Poplinski. The gunman dropped as if he was a marionette and someone had abruptly cut the strings.

John covered the gunman for a moment, then shouted, "Wendy, are you OK?"

"I'm a hurtin' unit, but I'll live. My vest stopped one, but I'm hit in the hand and it's all fucked up. What about you? Are you all right... and Poplinski?" shouted back Wendy.

John would not have to wait for a medical opinion replying, "Suspect is 10-100 (dead)," said John. John keyed his mic and breathlessly reported, "Shot's fired, officers involved. The suspect is 10-100. My partner needs an ambulance; she is down. She's shot, but doing OK. We need back-up to clear the upstairs. We'll need the sergeant, detectives, and a chaplain," John added thinking about the grief of Mrs. Poplinski, "and eventually animal control. I am OK," concluded John.

John moved over to his partner and was met by Ruth Poplinski, who was screaming, "My boy! You shot my boy. I did not want you to shoot my boy. He never hurt anyone in his whole life!"

John embraced her and pinned her arms, which were flailing about, sometimes in mid-air and sometimes striking John's chest. John calmed her, "Mrs. Poplinski. I am sorry, but your son shot my partner. I do not want to restrain you further, but my partner is hurt and I have to help her. Shhh," he said each word slower and quieter in an effort to calm the grieving mother.

Ruth put her hands at her side and sobbed, laying her head on John's shoulder. "I am sorry. I knew there was something wrong with him, but I never suspected this." Now she had her eyes closed and she just sobbed.

"Mrs. Poplinski, please, take a seat right here, while I take care of my partner," John suggested even as he firmly, physically directed her to a couch against the wall so that she did not have a view of her son lying dead on the steps.

As Mrs. Poplinski sat down, John moved swiftly, pulling out his wound packet from the side pocket of his tactical pants. He brought out a cling bandage and pressed the rolled up bandage into Wendy's wounded hand, which had locked into a claw-like formation. "This will help hold your hand in a natural position until the doctor gets a chance to see you. How are you doing Wendy? Are you hit anywhere else?"

"Yeah boy… Whew… hurts like hell," she wheezed, "… but I'm OK. He hit me center-mass, John, Woooo… but I already checked. My vest stopped it," Wendy blurted out haltingly, gasping for each breath sounding as if she was doing the post-fight interview in the ring after just going 15 rounds with the heavy-weight champ.

John covered the back side of her hand with three large bandages and pressed them firmly in place while he anchored another cling to the wrist and began to wrap the hand, holding all of the bandages in place.

"John! Are you all right?" shouted Lt. Tyree.

"Come on in. Suspect's down, but the upstairs is not clear, and there is an unfriendly Pit Bull locked up in the basement." shouted John.

Tyree entered and quickly checked Poplinski. He could see that he had gotten his ticket punched for a ride on the original Soul Train. Tyree pointed up the steps and then Ryan Chen appeared and the two of them headed up the stairs. After a few moments, the Lieutenant shouted, "Clear-up!"

As Ryan came down the steps, he carefully stepped around the crumpled body at the bottom. Poplinski's only cooperative act of the evening was to fall into a position which allowed officers to pass around him without visibly disturbing the scene.

Tyree was shocked to find Wendy standing on his return. "Should you be up?" asked the Lieutenant.

"I wouldn't have been down in the first place except I... slipped," answered Wendy indignantly wiping the bottom of her shoe on the carpet. "Oh the indignity of it all," lamented Wendy looking at the smear on the bottom of her $85 Herman Survivors.

"Ryan, can you assist Mrs. Poplinski. Please take her out the back door to the station for a statement," directed Tyree.

"Mrs. Poplinski, why don't we take you down to the station and get you a cup of coffee. One thing police stations have is the best coffee in the world, ma'am," said Ryan as he eased her up and she came along making only an occasional whimper, shocked now, but no longer surprised by what had happened. He led out the back way to avoid the resting place of her only son.

———>●<———

Three days later Stella and John knocked on the door frame of 3301 at Lutheran Hospital. They could see they had arrived in between what had been a deluge of visitors on the first day that visitors were allowed. Wendy had been through four separate surgical procedures to first save the hand, and then the specialist told her, "We will see to it that you will not only be able to play the harmonica again but also the guitar."

Wendy was told by her surgeon that the operations were a success after waking up from the fourth surgery. The surgeon was still in his scrubs and stood smiling with his mask hanging loosely around his neck, "The surgeries were all successful, and if you are patient you will be able to do everything you could do before the injury," said the doctor.

"Will I be able to shoot again?" she asked with concern.

"There may be some stiffness that might actually allow you to shoot better. There was a nerve damaged that sometimes causes a slight tremor in a hand as you age. That nerve was cut and that should help you to hold rock steady while you aim," said the doctor. "Don't rush it, though, because you may damage my masterpiece," he said smiling.

"Are you a shooter, Doc?" asked Wendy.

"Went to college on the G.I. Bill, and believe it or not, I was a range instructor when I was an active Marine. You'll shoot again as long as you do not do too much too fast and mess up my work," cautioned the doctor laying a caring hand on the protective cast around the wounded appendage.

"No worries, Doc," assured Wendy with a smile.

As John Savage knocked on the door frame, Wendy, who was sipping orange juice through a straw while she watching Sponge Bob Square Pants on the television, turned, smiled hugely and said, "Come on in, partner."

"How are you?" asked Stella.

"Getting better and better, thanks to your boyfriend," answered Wendy as John leaned down and gave her a hug. "I can't believe I didn't put him down at that distance. I must have missed him," said Wendy.

"You didn't miss him at all. Poplinski was wearing body armor," answered John.

"No shit?" Wendy asked in disbelief.

"No shit!" John answered. "When he went upstairs, he put on body armor and covered it with a shirt. Your rounds hit him in the X-ring, but the vest stopped them all. His room was an armory," said John. "DCI called today and confirmed that all the shots you fired hit him in the vest. They also confirmed the trajectory of the last round he fired at you. Well, if you hadn't fallen there probably would have been more damage," said John.

"So I would really have been in the shit, if I wasn't in the shit," observed Wendy shaking her head.

"That's no shit." agreed John.

"John, everyone always says you're the shit magnet, but I guess it turned out to be me—and lucky it did," said Wendy. "Anyway, I feel glad that I didn't miss the dirt bag. Not that I wanted him dead, but I always thought that if that ever happened to me, stress or not I wouldn't miss what I was shooting at," said Wendy.

"As it turns out, you were right," said John. "You didn't miss him."

Then Stella smiled and stepped forward, obviously concealing something behind her back. "We have something for you, Wendy," said Stella bringing the gift around slowly from behind her back as if she was responding to a slow drum roll. "We did not wrap it, because we thought you might have some trouble opening it." Stella then brought a framed portrait with some words written beside the portrait in an Old English font reminiscent of the Declaration of Independence. "John wrote the poem."

"I owed you a poem, so we're even on that," said John.

"You still owe me an un-funny joke," reminded Wendy. "Feel free to make it funny though. I'll still call us even," she added.

"Be patient. That will be easier than the poem," said John. He continued, "Stella did the portrait from the last police department yearbook, and she made the frame herself."

Wendy looked in amazement at the charcoal portrait etching of herself in her Class A uniform. With her good hand she lightly traced the detail of the patch, which included a steam boat, an eagle perched on the state of Wisconsin, and Grandad's Bluff, the most prominent of all the bluff's surrounding La Crosse. There was an American Flag atop Grandad's.

Since Wendy was a child she could never take a posed picture without blinking, and most of her photos either had her eyes closed or half open.

The yearbook photo had been taken with her eyes at quarter mast, which was the best she could do after many takes. Stella had fixed the photo and drawn Wendy with her eyes wide open. Stella had even improved upon the smile. Wendy was a bit cynical at times but loved being a cop. Before her surgeries, she had worried more about losing her career after being shot than losing her hand. The smile captured her sincere love and pride about the fact that she was a police officer. "It's beautiful. Stella, you're better than Picasso."

"I don't know about that," blushed Stella.

"I mean it. That guy would have painted me with one eye five times bigger than the other and my nose would have been where my ear should be. I'd probably have had three breasts. This looks just like me. Maybe even, a little better than me." Then she fell silent as she read the words, penned by John.

Ode to the Wounded Warrior

You raised your hand and stood there proud,
With fellow recruits you recited aloud.
With, "courageous calm in the face of danger"
You'd risk your life for a total stranger.

You picked up the gauntlet and served with pride
Brave men and women you stood beside.
Day in and day out you strapped on your gun,
Through dark of night and mid-day sun.

Then came that day, when came the test
You answered the call and gave your best.
With courageous calm you faced the danger
And you risked your life for a total stranger.

You faced knife, the gun, and flash of steel
You survived, and now it's time to heal.
The men and women that you serve beside
Will tell others they know you, with pride.

Your example will help them face their test,
Better prepared than before, to do their best.
With courageous calm they'll face the danger
As they risk their lives for a total stranger.

"It's...too cool. Thanks, John. Thanks, Stella. I love...it," and Wendy began to choke up. She took a deep breath and regained her composure and a veil came over her face. She was the old brash Wendy again and she said, "It could have been a lot shorter poem though and more accurate in its depiction of the events as they unfolded," explained Wendy, deliberately looking at John and Stella and not at the painting.

"How's that?" asked John.

Wendy thought for a second and looked up as if she was reading off the ceiling and recited,

> *"The nut had a gun*
> *It wasn't for fun*
> *I got shot*
> *It didn't feel so hot*
> *So I ran like hell*
> *And that's when I fell*
> *But thanks to the shit*
> *I didn't get hit."*

Wendy's gaze came back to eye level and smiled.

Stella covered her mouth and laughed while John commented, "Hey Sweets that's not too bad,"

Wendy answered, "Like I told you, John, I'm a poet... a regular Emily Frickin' Dickinson."

CHAPTER FIFTEEN

An Old Friend

Lara's breathing became deeper, longer, as they moved together. Ahmed whispered, "In you I have found heaven on earth."

Her eyes opened and locked into the Ahmed's gaze and her movement was slow at first and then faster. Her eyes held his tightly, growing wider with every breath they took. Their breathing became deeper then louder, and suddenly, as if on cue, they collapsed together holding on to each other until their breathing's natural rhythm returned. After; they lay side by side in the gradually brightening room as the sun rose to meet a new day.

Lara's head nestled in the crook of Ahmed's neck, and when she regained her energy, she kissed him on the earlobe and breathily whispered, "I love you, Ahmed."

Ahmed did not hesitate in his response, "I love you, Lara. You are my princess, my oasis in the desert. Allah has sent you to me to make my life complete."

Lara kissed him softly on the lips and said, "Now I have to go. I have an early class." She gave him one more kiss on the cheek and bounded, with great energy, out of bed and strode un-blushed across the room into the bathroom. Ahmed's eyes did not leave the beautiful nymph until the bathroom door closed behind her and he even watched the door in the event that there may be an encore of her magnificent morning performance, but Ahmed slipped back into a deep dreaming sleep.

In his dreams Ahmed found himself atop Martyrs' Ridge once again. He took careful aim, squeezed the trigger, and his rifle jammed. He tried desperately to clear the weapon, and suddenly there was the American Soldier with his muzzle ready to send Ahmed to Allah. Ahmed began to scream, "Please don't shoot. Don't shoot. I love America. Fuck Saddam!" Ahmed turned and spit at the mention of his name. "My name is Ahmed. I am not your enemy. God Bless America. God Bless You. You have Saved Me!" whimpered Ahmed. "Please don't shoot."

In the dream the American smiled, closed one eye to take careful aim, and fired. Ahmed screamed, "YEEIII!" and sat straight up in bed, sweating. He was in his bedroom. The apartment was quiet except for the pounding of his heart in his ears. He looked about taking a few moments to remember where he was and then he called out, "Lara. Are you here?" There was no answer. Ahmed breathed a heavy sigh of relief that no one had heard his scream and that he once again had not died at the moment without having the chance to redeem his honor. He wondered if Allah would have accepted him if killed while screaming "God bless America."

Allah would know my intent. Allah would know I said these things only so that I could live to continue to serve him, he thought to himself. I must be certain about this, for if I doubt my motives, Allah may doubt my motives.

After Ahmed showered and dressed, he prepared a breakfast of boiled eggs and olives and sat down to read the Capital Times newspaper. He popped half an egg into his mouth and began to chew as he unfolded the paper and was met with a familiar face, which caused him to immediately begin coughing and gagging on the egg. He ran over to the sink to continue to cough and hack until all of the particles of the egg had been cleared from his throat. He ran the faucet and took a drink of cold water and splashed some in his face. "It can't be," he said out loud.

He returned to the table, sat down, and slowly picked up the newspaper once again to read the headlines, "Iraq Vet Kills Fourth Suspect in La Crosse. Experts Troubled." He read with great interest the article about an officer named John Savage. Savage had shot a prowler in the back. He also had shot two armed robbers and now a son, whose mother complained, "I just wanted him out of the house. I didn't want my son killed."

The article continued, "Chief Ronald Sherman of the La Crosse Police Department said, 'Each one of these incidents was thoroughly investigated, and in each case Officer Savage was found acting, according to policy, within the scope of his employment and with total justification. Each shooting was ruled justified. In my personal assessment each shooting was not just defensible but reasonable."

The Associated Press Article reported that there had not been four fatal police shootings In La Crosse in the ten years prior to Officer Savage's arrival, and now one officer had shot and killed four suspects in one year. Ahmed sat straight up as he read, "John Savage received a silver star for single-handedly attacking a contingent of Republican Guards, and according to sources," claimed the reporter, "'he killed them all,'" high-lighting the words as if it was an indictment.

The article went on to say, "Civil Rights Attorney and former Police and Fire Commission Member Jane Thomason declared, 'this candidate actually raised many red flags for me. I wondered if the man may have developed a penchant for killing and might find it difficult to transition to the peace-keeping function of a police officer. I was overruled, however.' Thomason resigned from the commission over the controversy."

"He killed them all? I am afraid he did not kill them all, for there is one left. I think I will pay a visit to John Savage and let him know how much I appreciate what he has done for me," said Ahmed as he crumbled the paper up and threw it across the room. After he sat quietly letting his brain marinate the idea to kill John Savage for several minutes, Ahmed got up and opened a kitchen drawer. He removed scissors and then picked up the newspaper and flattened it out across the table, smoothing it out. He carefully cut the two photos of John Savage out. He pulled out the wallet from his pants, opened it, and slipped the photos of Savage—one photo of Savage in his police uniform and the other in his desert armor—behind one of the plastic photo compartments in the wallet.

He removed a piece of paper and a pen out of the same drawer and wrote, "I will be gone for a few days. I have left an envelope with some cash for you on the table. I will be back as soon as possible. I have to visit old friend."

Chapter Sixteen

They Spit on Heroes

ohn Savage had only accumulated two weeks of vacation time since coming to the La Crosse Police Department, but in the last year he had been off duty for over a month without using any of it. The time was from the mandatory suspensions he had to take after each shooting.

He had just completed his meeting with the psychiatrist, and this time she had not cleared him for return. Dejected, he went to the weight room at the police department to work out. He was happy to see Ryan Chen and Lieutenant Tyree were lifting.

"Hey, John, when you coming back to work?" asked Ryan.

"I don't know. I asked to come back, but the doctor wouldn't clear me," answered John as he did a warm-up set on the bench press.

"Why is that?" asked Ryan.

"She said she was concerned about the frequency as well as the fact that I did not appear, 'sufficiently reactive to the emotional trauma that must be attributed to the taking of four lives,'" explained John as he slammed another 45 pound plate on one end of the universal bar atop the bench press rack.

"What the fuck?" said Ryan, who stopped in the up position while in the middle of a bicep curl. "Are you supposed to be traumatized for saving Wendy's life? What the fuck is this doctor talking about?"

"She's a nice lady, but she seems to believe I am not outwardly messed up enough for someone who killed four people in La Crosse and more in war." John slammed another 45 pound plate on the other side of the Bench Press. He lay down on the bench, took five deep breaths, and lifted off the weight, bench pressing the 225 pounds eight times. As the weights clanged back onto the rack, John sat up and took a few recovery breaths and said, "She thinks I am in denial."

"Did you see the fucking paaa-" blurted out Ryan, stopping in mid-sentence when he saw Logan Tyree shake his head sternly without skipping a punch as he was making the speed bag sing its "thumpity, thumpity, thumpity," tune, which echoed throughout the basement of the P.D.

"The paper?" asked John speaking loud enough to be heard over the pounding of the bag. "What does the paper say?"

"Never-mind," said Ryan, feverishly finishing his curls. Then he set the curl bar down and went over to the pull-up bar in an attempt to act as if he had said nothing of significance.

"Come on. Now you have to tell me," said John as he sat at the end of the bench.

"The paper is suggesting that maybe some of these incidences may not have happened if you weren't a war vet. You know, if you weren't such a highly-trained killer. Jane Thomason even said that you being a veteran should have been some sort of red flag and she did not want to hire you," said Ryan. "That's just crazy. You serve your country and risk your life, and you come home and that's a red flag?"

John sat upright on the bench and his shoulders retained the rolled back position they had been in while benching. As Ryan's word and their meaning soaked in like a toxic spill into roll of paper toweling, his shoulders rolled forward and his head sagged.

Tyree slammed the speed bag one last time and in a caring tone explained, "Listen, John, you have been involved in the shooting of four people who sincerely needed to be shot. We have not had an officer killed in the line of duty here since Joe Donndelinger in 1937. I believe that string would have ended this year if not for you. Instead, there are four dead suspects who would have shot at someone else if you were not here. These criminals made poor decisions throughout their lives, right up to the bitter end, and when they had to decide on a their last victim they chose you and your partners. It's just a clear-cut case of one last bad decision—poor victim selection. They had choices and ultimately the choices they made left you with no choice." He hit the bag hard one more time for effect.

"Why are people, the newspapers, and the doctor having such a problem with that? I don't understand it," John asked this question with his head still slumped.

"John, there is not another way to explain it other than that's the way it is, and that's the way it always has been, and that's the way it always will be. The world is split into three groups of people: the predators, the prey, and the protectors. The problem is the prey trip through life with no ability of recognizing the difference between their protectors and predators. They seem to not even sense danger. They hear shots and say 'fire crackers.' They see a pedophile offering candy to a child and say 'What a nice man.' They see a police officer defending himself against a predator and about the predator they say 'that poor man' and about the protector they say 'brute!'

"I am telling you facts here. You shot four bad people and in the process saved good people, including yourself. Let's cut to the chase—that doesn't make you troubled, tightly wound, or any shade of bad. It makes you a protector. There are many cases of law men being treated badly no matter how courageously they protected the prey. Did you know they arrested Wyatt Earp and his brothers after the gun fight at the O.K. Corral?"

"Really?" said John snapping his head up and rolling his shoulders back again as if he was about to do another set of bench presses.

"Really, and Jane Thomason and her ilk spat on returning Viet Nam vets," said Tyree.

"She did?" asked John Savage incredulously.

"She did. I personally heard her bragging on one occasion about how she was still proud of it," said Tyree shaking his head. "John, you did not set out to be a hero, but you are. You have set yourself above many, not by your words, but by your deeds."

"I don't consider myself a hero. I did what I was trained to do and what I was paid to do. You would have done the same thing," reasoned John.

"Maybe, but it wasn't my turn. It was your turn. You experienced something that all cops daydream about and wonder about. They ask themselves, 'What will I do when it is my turn?' Make no mistake about it, John, what you did in Iraq, in Afghanistan, and what you have done here since you were hired makes you a hero by any definition. Hell, John, I may be your Lieutenant, but you're my hero," proclaimed Tyree.

"In the old days they called combat seeing the elephant. Well you have seen the elephant and survived, and now you have to prepare yourself to survive the Monday morning quarterbacking, the civil law suits, and the attacks in the media that go hand in hand with being the winner of a gun fight. I could give you example after example of heroes doing great things and then being misunderstood, discarded, or treated badly for it. But still, they keep returning to the fray and continue to protect the Jane Thomasons of the world, who rally around to sing "Kum bay yah" at the execution of cop killers, while they spit on heroes."

CHAPTER SEVENTEEN

Crazy

Ahmed had no trouble locating John Savage's home. Online he found the recent record of the land transfer for a home located at 858 Milson Court to John Savage. It had to be the same John Savage. "How many could there be?" he said after shutting down his computer.

Ahmed put a holster on his belt, slipped a loaded magazine into his 9mm Beretta, and then tucked the weapon into the holster. Ahmed slipped on his black jacket and slipped the Map Quest directions to John Savage's home inside the interior pocket of his coat. He took a spare magazine filled with ammo and slipped it into his left coat pocket. "What else?" he asked himself. "Keys!" He went back into the kitchen and slipped his keys from the wicker basket on the counter. "It is time to pay a visit to my old army buddy as they say in this country."

Two and one half hours later, Ahmed was driving down the ramp from Interstate 90 to Highway 16. He turned toward La Crosse and took Highway 16 to Bluff Pass and then turned onto Milson Court. The street ran right past John Savage's house, and it looked to Ahmed as if no one was home. Ahmed drove all the way back into Hixon Forest and confirmed that there was no exit on the road. He decided that if he parked in Hixon he would have to drive past Savage's house after he killed Savage. That would not be a problem if all went well, but if something went wrong he would be trapped.

He concluded that if he parked on Bluff Pass his car would look so out of place that it might be noticed. It would be best to park in the 900 block of Milson Court. It would be a short run for his escape and the car would blend into the neighborhood as long as he didn't stay long. If Ahmed parked the car facing north, he would be able to drive straight out quickly.

Ahmed looked at his watch. "2:30 PM. I can reconnoiter for my mission while I am here." La Crosse was one of the cities that "The Lamb" had visited during his last campaign, and he quite possibly would be coming again. Ahmed spent the rest of the day locating all of the possible locations that might be a venue for political events. He checked out the Civic Center, The Radisson Hotel, Memorial Field, Loggers Field, City Hall, and the County Building. When he entered the public entrance at the County Building he saw the scanner and screeners at the entrance.

Ahmed feigned receiving a phone call, "Hello. Yes… Oh, it's good to hear from you. Just a second, I am going to go outside. I am having bad reception in here." Ahmed then turned and walked out continuing as he exited, "Hello, can you hear me now?" He walked out the door and back out to the parking lot carrying on the mock conversation all the way to the car for best effect.

The day was well spent. Ahmed believed he had a great mind for strategy and could have been brilliant as a commander in a more conventional fight. If at all possible he hoped to complete his primary mission, to kill "the lamb," without becoming a casualty. It would be a difficult task, but not impossible.

As Ahmed scouted the potential sites, he took time to bathe his eyes in the beauty of the city that lay nestled between the great Mississippi River and the span of bluffs. He stood at the spot where the Mississippi, La Crosse, and the Black River converged. This was the point where their waters commingled to begin their combined journey to the Gulf of Mexico. As the native of desert country stood in amazement admiring the churning waters, he thought, *It is hard to believe this country is at war. It is so peaceful here. I hope "the lamb" comes here. I will remind the people of La Crosse, as well as this country, that they are at war.* Ahmed smiled. John Savage will be the first to fall here. The killing of John Savage should be easy. He will not be expecting an attack at his home. I will strike him and disappear.

Hours later, as John Savage turned off Bluff Pass onto Milson Court, he did not even notice the car parked on the East side of the street next to a large evergreen tree. After John passed, Ahmed sat up and looked at John's tail lights in Ahmed's rear view mirror. He smiled as the brake lights went on and the car turned into the driveway. "Good, it's him," Ahmed said with a smile.

It was dark as John pulled into his driveway. John climbed out of his car and popped the trunk with his remote, causing a flash and a beep. John gathered up two bags of groceries he had purchased. He planned on transforming at least some of the groceries into his four star veal parmigiana and spaghetti. As he reached the door he fumbled a bit trying to fit the key into the lock, but the stubborn dead bolt lock finally relented and John was inside.

John dropped the groceries onto the kitchen counter along with his keys, abandoned them, and went searching for Stella. He found her at her easel with a portrait coming to life on the canvas. It was amazing to John to see how fast she worked. John leaned down and kissed Stella, who put her arms around John's neck and kissed him back. As they separated and she opened her eyes, she laughed and said, "I'm sorry, I'm sorry."

"What are you sorry for? That's the nicest anyone has treated me all day," said John.

She grabbed a multi-colored, bad smelling rag and rubbed it vigorously on John's nose. "I painted you. I'm sorry," she rubbed for a while longer and said, "There. I got it."

As she gazed at John, her smile faded and was replaced with concern. "How are you doing today? I am guessing you saw the paper," said Stella.

"It hit me kind of hard at first, but I talked to Lt. Tyree today and he helped me put it into perspective. Besides, what am I going to do about it? It could be worse," said John shrugging his shoulders as he slipped his off-duty weapon and holster off his belt and tucked it away on the shelf in the closet. He re-buckled his belt.

Stella agreed, "Yes, it could be worse. You might not have been there when Wendy and I needed you and we could have been… I don't even want to think about that," said Stella grabbing John's hand and kissing it.

"Are you hungry?" asked John kissing the top of her head.

"What do you have in mind?" asked Stella.

"Veal Parmigiana. I stopped at Festival Foods and got all the fixings. It will take about an hour and a half to throw it together, so supper will be a little later than usual if you can wait," John said.

"I can wait. I would rather work a while anyway. I am on a roll here," said Stella taking her thumb and spreading a small glob of black paint and magically turning it into shadowing. "Did you get anything to drink?" asked Stella.

"The wine!" said John with a snap of his fingers. "Oops! I left it out in the car. Would you like a glass now?" asked John.

"I didn't mean for you to wait on me hand and foot. I don't want you to…"

"Be not distressed for I am at your service, my lady," said John with a mock High Brow British accent and an added bow for effect. "Why, even the Pope served an occasional glass to Michelangelo while he painted the Sistine Chapel."

"Really? The Pope?" asked Stella as she dabbed at the canvas with her brush.

"I've never read it in the historical record, but he must have. When a guy comes in and spends four years painting your ceiling, it would be rude to never offer the painter a drink, and you don't get to be the Pope by being rude," answered John.

"That makes excellent sense," said Stella with a nod.

"I'll be right back," and with that John threw his jacket back on and he headed out the door. As John reached the door, he flipped the driveway light on and jogged out to the car.

Ahmed was headed across the driveway toward the front door. It had been his plan to ring the doorbell and kill John when he answered the door. A simple plan, but he wanted Savage to know that it was Ahmed who was killing him. As Ahmed reached the car, the driveway light came on and Savage burst out of the front door and was running right at Ahmed.

Ahmed froze for a moment as this terrible warrior, who had killed all of his men on Martyrs' Ridge by launching a surprise counter-attack, seemed to be launching a surprise pre-emptive attack on Ahmed. How can this be? Ahmed had slipped his Berretta into his coat pocket, and now as he tried to pull it out he discovered the front sights were hooked on the fabric of the inner pocket. As Savage came face to face with Ahmed, ten feet from him, their eyes met and Savage said simply, "Ahmed?"

Ahmed jerked hard and the weapon was still hung up. He pushed hard, hoping to release the snag, and then pulled hard. There was a loud rip, but the Beretta came free. He aimed the Beretta at Savage. What was to be a smooth execution had now turned once again into a life or death proverbial cluster fuck.

John was caught surprised and unprepared. His mind could fathom neither how nor why Ahmed Abdullah Rahim, the Queen of Hearts, came to be in his driveway. John watched in disbelief as Ahmed began yanking at something that was stuck in his jacket and literally ripped a Beretta from his pocket and swung it up, bringing it to bear on John.

Ahmed squeezed the trigger and there was nothing but a metallic, "click."

John heard the click and instinctively reached for the weapon on his belt.

Just as John could not fathom why Ahmed was in his driveway trying to kill him, Ahmed could not understand why his weapon did not go bang. As Savage reached for his weapon, Ahmed turned and fled at a dead run. This time he did not disrobe, feign love for America, or convince himself that he was engaged in a clever ploy. He was simply fleeing from what he thought would be a premature, but certain death without purpose. His death would be a failure with nothing achieved. He, the only survivor of Martyrs' Ridge, had traveled all the way around the world at great sacrifice and expense only to be killed by the same man that had killed all of his comrades. He ran with the speed of an Olympic athlete.

As John reached where his weapon had been, he realized it was no longer there. While Ahmed fled, John, with the instinct of a beagle, took two long strides after Ahmed, but then wisdom prevailed. He pivoted and ran back into the house, slammed the door and hit the dead bolt. He ran into Stella's studio, slammed opened the closet, and retrieved his weapon.

"John, what's going on?!" asked Stella startled into a state of terror.

"Stay here. Someone just tried to kill me in the driveway. I'm calling 911."

Ahmed sprinted to his car and climbed in. He had disconnected the interior lights and left the keys in the ignition. He did not turn the lights on until he was turning north onto Highway 16. He drove the speed limit to I-90 and was turning onto Highway 90 heading to Madison before the first squad pulled up to John's house.

As the first officer arrived, John sat in a quandary. He knew he had to report what happened, because the truth is the truth even when that truth is too unreasonable to be believed. John realized that after he told his story there would be arguing and hand wringing by many outside of his presence, wondering whether or not John Savage might not be absolutely crazy.

CHAPTER EIGHTEEN

Drink From the Well

here was a long silence after John explained the history of his relationship with Ahmed Abdullah Rahim. The explanation ended with a description of Ahmed's attempt to kill John in his own driveway. Dr. Sistek found the story incredulous, but to tell John this would only hinder her ability to help this obviously troubled veteran. The doctor was certain the manifestation to be a result of post-traumatic stress syndrome. If she was correct, it would be the most serious case she had ever seen.

"John, did anyone else see this person?" asked the doctor.

"No, but I did. He tried to kill me. I saw him," said John.

"You said his gun did not go off, why do you think that was?" the doctor asked.

"He either did not charge the weapon, or when he tried to get it out of his pocket, he put the weapon out of battery. Either one of those would cause a malfunction. I heard a click, so I think he just hadn't charged the weapon," concluded John.

"What does that mean did not charge the weapon?" asked Sistek making a notation on her pad.

"When you load a Beretta, which was the weapon he was carrying, you push a magazine filled with bullets into the magazine port. It will lock in, but there is not a bullet in the chamber yet. You have to work the action on the weapon, which feeds a round into the chamber, and then it is ready to fire. A lot of forces in the Middle East, especially the Israeli's, do not carry a round in the chamber and they work the action, when they draw it to fire. I think I surprised him when I came out to get the wine, and he panicked and forgot to charge the weapon."

"Why do you think he didn't just charge the weapon?" asked the doctor.

"I instinctively reached for my weapon, and he reacted to that and fled. I was lucky, because I didn't have my weapon on. I had left it in the house," said John.

"Have you noticed any changes, small or large, in your behavior, emotions, patterns, or beliefs since all of these traumatic events?" asked the doctor.

John thought for a bit and then answered honestly, "only one."

"What is that?" The doctor asked with a curious demeanor on her face.

"I stopped chewing Bazooka Bubble Gum and felt compelled to sell my comic collection," answered John.

"Really, and why do you feel you did that, John?" asked the doctor in a now-we're-getting-somewhere tone.

"I don't know? I have been collecting them my whole life, and I just felt like… time to grow up," answered John with a shrug. "When Stella moved in, I was kind of… embarrassed to have them."

The doctor followed with, "How did that make you feel, when you disposed of your collection?"

"I haven't given it that much thought." said John.

"Getting back to your meeting with Ahmed, was there any physical evidence of this occurrence?" the doctor asked.

"I saw it. It happened. I can't lie and say it did not happen just so people like you will not think I'm crazy, because he may try it again. This man is dangerous, and he did not come here just to kill me. I believe he is here for a reason, saw the coverage on the shootings, and decided to come kill me to take revenge for the death of his friends. To answer your question though, no there was no physical evidence. Are we done here?" asked John with disgust.

"We can be," said the doctor.

"Are you going to authorize my return to work?" asked John.

"Let's give it a little more time. I would like to examine the root cause of this incident to make certain that this is not a symptom of a deeper problem, John," explained the doctor.

"You don't believe me," said John with his head cocked to the right.

"John, I believe that you may be suffering from post-traumatic stress disorder and your dreams, your disposal of your Bazooka Joe collection, and now the possible apparition from the battlefields of Iraq while you are awake may be examples of a kind of emotional bleeding. If so, we can't ignore the emotional wound. I am your doctor and must treat the wound. I do not feel you are ready to go back to work," Dr. Sistek summarized.

"You know, there is an old fable, doctor, which fits here. May I tell it to you?" asked John.

"Certainly," replied the doctor, while looking at her watch.

"Sorry, I will give you the short version. Once upon a time there was a wise old king, who lived in a castle on a mountain overlooking his loyal and loving subjects in the city below. There was an evil wizard who was jealous of the king, so he put a potion in the city well. Gradually as the loyal subjects drank the water it affected their reasoning and they all became crazy. The king saw the drastic change in his beloved subjects and tried to reason with them, but in a very short time they believed the king to be mad.

"The loving king learned of the wicked spell the evil wizard had cast upon the well, and he went once again to his subjects to explain what happened and reason with them, but the subjects in the midst of their insanity continued to think the king was the crazy one. The king returned to the castle and sat despondent all evening, having lost the love of his subjects. Finally, after much thoughtful deliberation, he saddled his horse and road down the mountain to the city's square, dipped a ladle into the well, and drank heartily from it.

"The next morning the citizens of the city were greeted by their king, who now shared in their insanity. They rejoiced at how wise their king had once again become. They all loved him.

"Doctor Sistek, it does not matter how many people do not believe the truth; their disbelief can't alter the truth. When you are ready to return me to work, contact my Assistant Chief, please, and let him know," said John.

"We may make another appointment for next week, and we will continue with this discussion," said Dr. Sistek.

John interrupted, "No, I will not come see you again unless I am ordered to. You see, Doctor Sistek, when you chose to believe that what really happened was my hallucination, the treatment you offer has become the water in the well. There is such a thing as post-traumatic stress disorder. I have seen it devastate others I went to war with, so I know I am not suffering from post-traumatic stress disorder.

"I only shot people who left me no other choice, and it was my sworn duty to do so. I have reconciled all of these events in my mind. These incidents have not created unmanageable stress for me. They have been easy to rationalize in my reasonable and healthy mind. Dr. Sistek, just because you can't grasp the reality of my life from your comfortable office does not make my reality unreal. Just because you believe a human being can't take the life of another without being emotionally unhealthy afterwards does not make me unhealthy.

"I was attacked in my driveway by Ahmed Abdullah Rahim, who in Iraq was known as 'The Queen of Hearts,' and that was not a hallucination. You are trying to make me drink from your well so that I will cease to believe what really happened, happened. That would be dangerous to me." As John Savage stood and turned to walk out, he added, "Doctor, I will not drink from the well!"

CHAPTER NINETEEN

Shit Storm

"John Savage. Your timing couldn't be better," said Detective Nate McPherson as he stuck his head inside the doorway of the weight room. "The shift commander said you were down here working out," continued Nate, an investigator assigned to the drug unit. "Can you come upstairs for a bit? There are some people who are very interested in talking to you."

John sat up from the bench press and said, "Mac, do I need to shower and change? I am sweating like a whore in church here."

"No. They'll understand. That won't be a problem. They will be happy you just happened to be here. They'll fill you in when we get upstairs." said McPherson.

As they rode the slowest elevator in the world to the second floor John asked, "What do you think of the Packers' picks in the draft?"

"I'm hoping they don't work out. I am a Bears fan," said McPherson.

"That must be tough," said John.

"You mean being surrounded by Packers fans? Yeah it is," answered Mac.

"No, being a Bears fan period. They suck. Why not just convert. There is no dishonor in abandoning the Bears for the Packers when you live in Wisconsin." John suggested sincerely.

"Yeah, I'm going to do that, right after I grow tits," answered McPherson as the elevator opened.

McPherson led John Savage into the conference room, and John was startled by the high power presence in the room. The room was occupied by Chief Ronald Sherman, the Assistant Chief Henry Mullins, Captain Jack Potter, who was in charge of the Detective Bureau, Lt. Tyree, and "a suit." John did not recognize the suit, but he stood as John entered the room.

The suit approached, shook John's hand, and said with a Midwestern smile, "John Savage, it is an honor to meet you. I am Special Agent Charles Martel of the Federal Bureau of Investigation, and I understand that you ran into someone I am trying like hell to locate."

"It is good to meet you sir. I am guessing you are talking about Ahmed Abdullah Rahim?" said John, who sat in the chair McPherson directed him to.

"Yes, I am. He has nine aliases that I am aware of, and for some reason he always uses his given name of Ahmed." Agent Martel then picked up a remote and hit a button, starting a Power Point that showed a line-up of Arabic men dressed like Soldiers of Allah, projected onto the smart board in the conference room. "Do you recognize anyone here?" asked Martel.

Without the slightest bit of hesitation, John said, "The third one from the left is Ahmed, except on the two occasions I have seen him he was not wearing the beard or the kufiya. He doesn't look much like that now."

Martel looked at the Chief and subtly nodded while Chief Sherman nodded back. Martel asked, "If he doesn't look like that now, how could you possibly be sure if it was him in your driveway?"

"When we met the first time it was... let's say intense. Our eyes were locked in on each other, and I do not know what the explanation is scientifically, but I do believe 50 years from now, if we meet and look into each other's eyes, I will be able to recognize him and he will know me," explained John.

"When a call from Lt. Tyree was referred to me about your incident, initially I wondered why one of the most deadly field operatives of Al-Qaeda would try to kill a La Crosse Wisconsin Cop in his driveway. We checked your file and discovered you killed a shit load of his friends back in Iraq. You know what Al Qaeda calls that engagement?" asked Martel.

"What's that?" asked John.

"They call it 'The Battle of Martyrs' Ridge.' The count was 1000 after that engagement, correct? 1000?" asked Martel.

"No, sir. We had three Humvees with twelve in my unit, and there was about a platoon-sized contingent of Republican Guard on the ridge," said John.

"No, not 1000 killed on the ridge. After you finished, Allah had to scrape up 72 virgins for each jihadist, and that adds up to about 1000 virgins to fill the order. Nice work. Ahmed may have been wearing the uniform of the Republican Guard that day, but he is Al-Qaeda. We have no pictures of him without the beard. Is there any other description you can give me?" asked Martel.

"His hair is neatly trimmed. He is clean shaven. He looks like he works out, and he is 5'10" and about 180 pounds. He was dressed in black in my driveway and was armed with a Beretta 9mm," answered John. "The man was definitely Ahmed. I even called him by name, and he did not say anything, but I know it was him. There was recognition when our eyes met."

"I am curious. Why didn't you shoot him on the ridge?" asked Martel.

"He was the only one on the ridge that surrendered… instantly and quite uniquely," answered John, who paused, looking up and to his right as if someone had distracted him.

"How's that?" Martel asked.

"Ahmed threw down his weapon then started ripping off his uniform, saying that we had liberated him. He said he hated Saddam, and then one of my guys fired a MK 19 in our direction. I hit the dirt because I knew a grenade was headed right at us. Anyone standing would be a dead man. It landed and exploded, and by the time I could lift my head up again, Ahmed was sprinting down the opposite side of the ridge in his underwear screaming 'God Bless America!' I could not bring myself to shoot a guy in his underwear screaming God Bless America," explained John.

Martel laughed, "No shit. This guy is slick."

"You said you have been looking for him?" John asked.

"The intelligence services alerted us that there was chatter that he crossed the border in Arizona, and they think he killed his guide." Martel hit the remote again and a mug shot appeared on the screen, "This is Jorge Sanchez. He is a Mexican guide and drug mule. He was found shot in the desert just north of the Juarez. This was tied to his leg." And the next slide showed a blood-stained scarf depicting a plane flying into the second tower on 9-11. "The inscription on the scarf in Arabic reads, 'To the hero of Martyrs' Ridge.' It wasn't left for you by the way," said Martel to John with a wry smile. "Our sources identify the hero of Martyrs' ridge to be our mutual friend Ahmed."

"We have information from the DEA that he may be a person who sold a large quantity of cocaine to a biker gang at a ridiculously low price, and then he disappeared off the map until he tried to kill you," said Martel nodding to John. "Can you give me the cliff-notes version of what happened?"

"Sure. I had just gotten home, taken off my weapon, and said 'Hi' to my girl. I had forgotten something in the car, so I threw my coat back on and ran out to the car. I am certain I surprised him by my sudden appearance, and he began yanking at the gun in his coat pocket. When he drew it, he pointed it at me and squeezed the trigger, but it didn't go off. I think he either didn't charge the weapon or he put it out of battery when he was trying to get it out of his pocket. I instinctively went for my gun, and that movement made him turn and run. I started after him, but realized I was unarmed and chasing an armed man with my girlfriend unprotected in an unlocked house. I ran back into the house, locked the door, got my gun, and called 911, in that order," emphasized John.

"I am guessing the press you've received on these recent officer-involved shootings alerted him to your presence here, nice work by the way," added Martel. "Every one of them was a righteous shoot."

"Thanks sir," answered John.

"As I was saying, the press you received on the shootings probably brought him here. I am sure you were a target of opportunity. Chatter indicates he is here for a larger purpose, however, but we do not know what that purpose is yet. What I do know is he must be within a day's drive of La Crosse, which is huge. This will help." Martel said.

"What would you like us to do?" asked Chief Sherman.

"You do not need to do anything right now. Officially he is not yet in this country. You have already answered this question, but I will ask it again, does this photo look much like him now?" Martel asked.

"I would have to say no. I don't think too many people would be able to pick him out from this photo. The beard and kufiya alter his looks considerably," answered John. "I would say the photo is over ten years old, too."

"We may need to borrow you at some time, John, since you are the only man in this country that can identify him. We have to keep this information classified right now," cautioned Martel.

"Why are we not releasing this photo and information to every police officer and news station in the country?" Chief Sherman asked.

"It's Homeland Security's call. I had to call in favors just to get authorization to come here and talk to you. There is some concern that putting out this information, when his presence is not confirmed, would cause a panic among citizens and in law enforcement. They believe on one hand it would create a situation where innocent Muslim men would be harassed all over the country," Special Agent Martel said unable to conceal his annoyance.

"I am going to be blunt here," said Chief Sherman, "That's absolute bullshit! This is a public safety issue. What kind of confirmation do they want? Officer Savage just saw the man and he tried to kill our officer." Chief Sherman pounded his fist on the table to emphasize "kill!"

"This is not my call, and I will do everything I can, but I can't release this information to anyone yet. It has to come through Homeland Security. My orders are direct and specific and authorization has to come down from much higher. Those are my orders. I may at some time need to borrow John for a bit to either talk to my superiors or identify possible suspects we might be watching."

"I would be happy to, but I am still on paid suspension because of the Poplinski shooting," said John Savage. "Doctor Sistek will not release me to come back to work. She thinks Ahmed is a flash back. She believes I'm suffering from post-traumatic stress and am in denial, which is causing this graphic hallucination. She calls Ahmed's assault on me 'emotional bleeding.' I can assure you, I am not suffering from post-traumatic stress, but I can't return to work until she approves my return," explained John.

Chief Sherman nodded toward Assistant Chief Mullins who said, "I will take care of this today. Do you feel ready to come back, John?" asked the Chief Mullins.

"Yes, sir," answered John without hesitation.

"Go finish your work out and thanks for your help, John," said Chief Sherman, who stood up and came around to shake John's hand.

John stood up and offered his hand in return and said, "Your welcome, sir, I am very happy that I did not have to live with Doctor Sistek's diagnosis too long or I probably would have really experienced emotional bleeding, whatever that is."

"Don't worry a bit about Dr. Sistek," said Chief Sherman.

All persons present in the room shook John's hand, and John accurately sensed the sudden silence meant that the minute he walked out of the room there was going to be one violent, administrative inter-agency shit storm.

CHAPTER TWENTY

The Asshole

ohn did not care what was said to Dr. Sistek. All that concerned him was he was back out on the street. John was working beat six tonight in the college area. As he did his squad check, he popped the trunk and took the Remington 870 shotgun out to check the less lethal rounds to make certain they were still in good repair. He checked the safety and saw it was on, checked the chamber and saw that it was empty and saw the "super sock" rounds were in place in the bandolier on the stock.

As John was conducting the check, he saw Sheriff's Deputy John Anderson cutting across the parking lot so John put the weapon at port arms to allow him to pass safely. The deputy stopped and put his hands in the air, "Don't shoot! I'm one of the good guys. You're supposed to wait until you get the car out of the lot before you start shooting people, Savage," then the deputy laughed. He pointed to the driveway and said, "Out there, John. Go get them. Hey, John, I have a new theme song for you," Anderson walked away singing, "Another one bites the dust. Another bites the dust. Another one bites the dust."

John just shook his head, finished his squad check and left the ramp, hitting the street. He tried to find the humor in Anderson's remarks, but no matter how he tried, he could not. Maybe someday that will be funny, but not tonight. Not yet, he thought.

Robert Booth sat sipping on a large glass of Korbel Brandy, straight with no ice. He loved Korbel like nothing else in his life. In his mind it was the only thing he had left worth living for, but as drunk as he was at the moment, finding a justification for continuing to live his life was beyond his comprehension. He sat drinking and reading the letter he had just finished. He named the document, "Suicide Attachment." He read off the screen of his laptop:

Dear Brenda,

By the time you read this letter I will be dead. Yes that's right, dead!

If you feel responsible, great, because you are, BITCH!

Tell Beth and Little Bobby I love them and that you are the reason they have to grow up without their Daddy.

If you want to know the details of my death, watch the news.

I want to be cremated and have my ashes secretly sprinkled into your chocolate ice cream. It will give me the opportunity to give YOU shit for a change.

Sincerely,

Robert

After reading the document one last time, Robert saved the document and then attached it to an e-mail that he had prepared for his wife. As he re-read the e-mail one more time, he picked up the phone and dialed the non-emergency number of the police department and waited for the answer.

"La Crosse Police Department," answered the female voice.

"Yes, I would like to see an officer about some threatening notes I have been receiving. I have them and have been careful not to handle them. Maybe you can get some prints off them," said Robert.

"We'll send an officer over to see you. I will need to get some information from you…"

After Robert finished with his call, he slipped one of his handguns into his belt and carefully covered the pistol with his sweat shirt. With that done, he picked up his second pistol and walked over to the front door of his three-bedroom home and set his second gun on the table next to the door.

He had purchased the guns especially for this night. He leaned over and pulled the cord for the drapes on the front picture window snapping them wide open and allowing him to watch for the officer's approach.

Robert sat back down and continued to enjoy his last drink, "Better slow down, Bobby Boy," he said out loud to himself, "You don't want to pass out before he gets here." Then he looked at the glass, tossed down another large drink and said to himself, "Fuck you!"

———————>●<———————

"236," said dispatch as John turned East onto La Crosse Street from West Avenue, having forgotten the deputy's little ditty.

John smiled at receiving his first call since the shooting of Poplinski. It had been a month and he was thrilled to be back. "236 go ahead. I am at 1300 La Crosse Street."

"I am sending you the address of a subject who would like to see you about some threatening letters. He states he thinks he knows who is sending them. He says he has been careful not to handle them so that we can get some prints," explained the dispatcher. "The complainant is Robert Booth."

John tapped on the call received icon on his laptop. He recognized the address as being a house which was right across the street from Myrick Park. John drove by the address and saw the lights on through a large front picture window. There was a man seated at a card table placed in the front room. John parked on the street north of the house and reached into his duty bag. He obtained some evidence envelopes and folded them up and put them in the side pocket of his tactical pants. This would allow him to be able to take the notes from the complainant and place them in evidence to be processed later.

As John walked cautiously up to the residence, he stopped by a large maple on the boulevard and looked across the front yard at the complainant. The man was seated calmly at the table behind a laptop computer, drinking heartily from a tumbler filled with a brown liquid that did not look like soda. Other than the fact the complainant was drinking, John could see no other reason to be overly alarmed, and he began his walk toward the front door.

As he stepped out from behind the tree, the man behind the computer smiled, waved, paused for a couple more key strokes, stood up and headed quickly to the front door.

As Robert saw the young police officer step out from behind the maple tree, Robert smiled and waved, "Good, he's cautious. That is all the better." Robert clicked send on the suicide email to his wife. "No turning back now," he said to himself. He stood as he smiled and waved again. Then he hurried to the front door.

As he reached the door, he picked up the handgun lying on the table next to the door and lifted his white Harley sweat shirt exposing the gun in his belt. Booth took two deep breaths and swung the door open wildly.

John had reached a spot halfway between the boulevard and the house when the front door flew open so quickly he reacted without forming a conscious thought by stepping to the side and drawing his weapon. The moment Booth appeared in the doorway, John saw the black handgun in the man's right hand thrust toward the spot John had been standing at a fraction of a second before. Booth growled, and without pause the growl turned into a shout of defiance.

John shouted, "Drop the gun! Drop the Gun! Drop the gun!" His repeated pleas were disregarded.

Booth continued his battle cry as he adjusted his aim to John's new position and reached into his belt to produce a second handgun, identical to the first, and began his advance down the steps toward John.

John was out of options and shouting was not working. He fired once, striking Booth in the neck tie area, and Booth dropped both guns as both hands instinctively reached for his throat. Booth stood for a moment then dropped to his knees, next to his guns.

John shouted, "Put your arms out palms up don't move," but Booth did not respond. Instead he coughed and hacked as he struggled unsuccessfully to breathe.

John covered Booth as he called in, "236, I have shots fired, the suspect is down. I'm OK, but I will need back-up, a commander, and an ambulance." The transmission's subtext was interpreted by all who heard the transmission. John clearly was saying, "Oh shit not again."

John approached the suspect slowly and kept him covered as he reached for the semi-automatic hand gun that was closest to Booth. As he closed the distance enough, his heart seemed to sink into his stomach. As he looked closely at the second hand gun, his heart left his stomach and sank further to his feet.

John now discovered he was having as much difficulty breathing as Booth. He checked the weapons again and confirmed his fears. Both guns were very realistic, but he could see they were non-firing replicas of the Colt 1911. He could see the headlines in his mind's eye. "John Savage Shoots Man Armed With Toy Guns."

"Why did you do this?" John asked angrily as he holstered his weapon and began putting pressure on the small hole just above the sternum.

Robert Booth looked at John and his eyes registered pain, fear, and finally regret as he struggled without success to take a last breath. John told him, "Hold on. The ambulance is on the way."

John tried to adjust Booth's head to open up his airway, but the bullet had granted at least part of Booth's wish. He had hoped for an instant painless death. Death would come, but not instantly and most certainly not painlessly. Booth lived long enough to realize he wanted to see his children again. He wanted to teach his son how to throw a spiral and bait a hook. He wanted to watch his daughter's spring ballet recital, and he wanted to apologize to his wife for the terrible things he said to her in his last letter. He even wanted to apologize to this officer, who was trying save him, for making him do something that Booth was too much of a coward to do himself.

Booth tried mightily to take one more breath, just one more. He had taken breathing for granted. He had taken everything for granted.

Robert Booth had spent his whole life blaming. He blamed his parents, his teachers, his bosses, and finally his wife for all of his problems, and then in the last moment of his life God granted Robert Booth a clear and honest perspective as he gave up his struggle to breathe. In his last thought he confessed to himself, Robert Booth, there is no one to blame for your problems but Robert Booth. They have all been your responsibility. Robert Booth, you are the asshole!

Chapter Twenty-one
"We're Done Here"

It had been four days since the "suicide by cop" orchestrated by Robert Booth had taken place. John found himself once again on administrative leave. Stella arrived home and found John staring out the window of Stella's studio into the woods that climbed steadily up into the bluffs beyond. She crossed the room and kissed him on the cheek, and when he turned towards her, she kissed him hard on the lips.

"How are you doing today, my heart?" she asked putting her hand over her heart.

"How do I answer that? For the first time in my life I understand what it means when someone says they're languishing," answered John looking back out into woods.

"I have a treatment for that," suggested Stella.

"What's that?" John asked.

"I suggest," she said in a playful tone as she placed her hands on John's cheeks and turned his head toward her; she continued, "that if you must languish, you languish in my arms for a while." She followed up on her offer by kissing him long and lovingly.

As their lips parted John declared, "I love you, Stella."

"I love you, John Savage," she answered kissing him once again.

"This is my kind of languishing. I could languish like this 24-7," observed John as he returned the kiss. "I suggest we try it and see how long we can go in a total state of this kind of languish. Maybe there's a world record we can break. I think I'll check…" and then John's phone began to vibrate and spin slowly on the table. He caught the phone, and looked at the display, which read, "Ryan Chen." John pressed the enter button and then answered, "Hello."

Ryan answered with a hint of agitation in his tone and a bit breathless as if he was calling from a tread-mill. "John. I'm glad I reached you. Turn on the television and go to CBN."

"What channel is that? I never watch that channel," said John as he snuck in another kiss from Stella and grabbed the remote for the television.

"Turn it to Channel 57. Diane Cruz is doing a piece on your shootings. It is the second story in. They are talking about a lady who had a face transplant right now, and after that they are going to run a story on your officer-involved shootings," said Ryan Chen. "The lead in made it sound like it might be a hit piece, and I debated whether I should call you or not, but I decided I'd better tell you and let you decide,"

"Thanks for that. I'll watch it. I think it is better to watch it than to have someone tell me about it. That might be worse," deduced John.

"That's your call. No matter what they say, you did what you had to do—what anyone else would have done."

"Thanks, buddy. I'll see you. Bye," said John. Setting the phone down, John pointed the remote at the big screen and lit up ESPN sports. Then John changed channels to 57, and the screen changed to show a split screen with a middle-aged woman smiling with her family on the left. On the right, another woman was saying, "What words do you use to thank someone for a gift like this? This woman, in death, has given me a chance at a normal life. There are no words. I didn't know her, but just the same I love her."

The scene then shifted to anchor woman Diane Cruz, who sat at a desk and behind her two images of John Savage. One was in his military uniform and in the second John was wearing his La Crosse Police uniform. Stella slid onto the couch next to John, her attention transfixed on the television.

Diane Cruz's smile left her face and she became deadly serious, "Tonight we are bringing you the story of an Iraq War Veteran who has returned home to become a police officer. Since he has become an officer for the bucolic City of La Crosse Wisconsin, he has shot and killed more people in one year than have been killed by the entire department twenty years prior to his arrival. Some speculate his shoot-first-ask-questions-later tendency may be attributed to his military combat experience and training. Stay with us, and after the break we will bring you the story of a soldier who has a license to kill."

John sat motionless in front the television through one commercial where babies were discussing stock trades. Stella looked at John and noticed that the commercial, which never failed to make John laugh or at least smile, had no impact on his granite-like pose. When Cruz returned, she outlined John's history. She reported how he had been an All-American kid who had competed in the martial arts, wrestled, played football, and graduated from Aquinas High School in La Crosse, which was a Catholic School. "But then he went to war," she said in an accusatory tone.

Cruz continued, "John was trained as an Airborne Ranger and served in Iraq and Afghanistan. Sergeant John Savage saw a great deal of action and received a number of decorations, including the Silver Star. With me tonight is CBN's Chief Investigative Correspondent William Barclay. Bill I understand that you have obtained a copy of the actual Silver Star citation, which was given to Savage in this incident, and from what I understand it is very telling."

The camera panned out to reveal a skinny weasel of a man seated, smiling, next to Cruz at the long desk. "Yes, Diane," agreed Barclay, as he proceeded to report his version of the Silver Star citation as if he had discovered a suspect standing over a body with a smoking gun. "The citation is very telling about the combat nature of this young man. The citation tells of an incident where John Savage was able to gain a flanking position on a number of Iraqi soldiers. I must explain that flanking means he was in a position where they were not aware of his presence. From this position he was able to single-handedly kill 14 of them." Then a smile formed on Barclay's face which gave the appearance that he had saved the best for last, "Diane, Sergeant Savage never ordered them to drop their weapons even though he came up from behind them. It is important to note that there were no prisoners and no wounded in this engagement."

"Is this unique?" Diane asked, reading the prepared question from the monitor.

"Yes, Diane. Usually in an engagement, under these conditions, you will have wounded. These were Iraqi troops who, as you know, have been known to surrender when given the opportunity," explained Barclay with a motion of his hand, suggesting it was a fact easy for anyone to deduce.

"Now, you have looked into the shootings this John Savage has been involved in as a police officer. What can you tell us about them?" Cruz asked with a scowl.

"Well, Diane, they have all been ruled justifiable, except the most recent one, which was a tragic event. It was a man who was, by those who knew him, at the end of his rope. He was having great difficulties and he called the police. When Savage arrived, he pulled out two toy pistols and waved them about and was shot dead by Officer Savage," Barclay emphasized the words "shot dead" by patting his hand over his chest twice.

"Shouldn't a man with his training and experience be able to tell a real gun from a toy gun in an instance such as this?" Cruz asked with a pained expression.

"This is a question that needs to be answered in the ongoing investigation. There is also the issue of the first of his police shootings. I have been able to determine that Officer Savage shot the first of his victims…"

"Victims?!" shouted John Savage angrily at the set.

Barclay continued after a pause for effect, "in the back. The man was a Peeping Tom. He ran and was shot in the back by Savage as he fled."

Diane Cruz then shook her head, passing her journalistic judgment, "Shooting a Peeping Tom in the back sounds a little excessive, but I am not an expert. We have brought in experts in the field. I would like to introduce Arthur Singleton," and a third screen popped into view with a man in his early forties. He had an artificially black, carefully coifed comb-over, was wearing a matching black shirt and a tightly tied pearl-colored tie. He possessed a dark tanning-booth tan with glasses hanging precariously low on his nose. "Mr. Singleton is currently the Director of the Law Enforcement Oversight Institute based out of Chicago. Mr. Singleton is the author of a book on rogue police shootings called *They Shoot Humans Don't They?* He served as a police officer for nearly ten years for a number of police agencies throughout the Midwest. Now he serves as an expert witness in cases where police officers have crossed the line. His agency serves as a watch dog and is highly respected in legal circles." Singleton smiled and nodded, causing one of the strands of the comb-over to dislodge and hang down the side of his face.

"Asshole! He worked for multiple agencies because he was a dill-rod and couldn't hold a job. He couldn't do the job so now he tries to sink the ones that can. That hair looks like a fast rope for his head lice," said John with a sincere disdain.

Stella turned to John to respond, but decided against it and turned her attention back to the television.

Diane Cruz sat straight up and the screen split into four screens. There in the fourth screen was a familiar face. The appearance of the fourth person hit John as if he had received a kick in the groin from a little old lady. It was Jane Thomason, who had been on the Police and Fire Commission when he was hired.

"One more chance to spit on a vet," said John grinding his teeth.

"What's that, John?" Stella asked.

"Never mind," answered John coldly.

Stella folded her arm tightly across her chest, hurt by John's sudden brusqueness, and she began to mope, but her sullenness went unnoticed by John.

Diane Cruz smiled as she made the introduction, "We have with us tonight Jane Thomason, former member of the Police and Fire Commission in La Crosse Wisconsin. Dr. Thomason has a PHD in Constitutional Law and has spent her career in the Wisconsin University System as a professor. We are happy to have you all here with us tonight, and I would like to start with Dr. Thomason. Doctor, is it correct that you were on the commission when Officer Savage was interviewed?"

"Yes, that is correct, and I had reservations about this gentleman," said Thomason, who pushed at the ear piece in her ear and registered annoyance on her face.

"Could you elaborate, Doctor?" asked Cruz.

"At the time of his interview, I wondered whether this soldier, or any soldier, who had seen such violence and was previously in a position where he had to kill so many of his fellow man in a war with questionable justification, could make a healthy transition into a career as a police officer which requires so much restraint and allows no excuses for collateral damage caused by hyper-vigilance.

"I expressed my concerns vociferously with my colleagues on the commission, but they disregarded my concerns, patted the man on the back, and everyone actually shouted their "Marine corpse Semper Fee's!" exclaimed the doctor flashing a mock Heil Hitler salute, "and the next thing I know he was hired."

"You mean Marine Corps and Semper Fi," said Singleton pushing the glasses up on his nose and smiling the smile of one of those guys who answers a question correctly out of turn in a trivia game when their opponent answers it incorrectly.

Somehow Thomason's face's look of annoyance appeared to have been dialed up a notch by Singleton's comment. "I was of the opinion and still am of the opinion that someone who has been so traumatized by war and damaged by their own participation in what is a sanctioned human depravity should not be expected to be able to make such a transition without undergoing extensive psychotherapy. John Savage, whose name also concerns me under the circumstances, had no such treatment, and I believe the circumstances give credence to my concerns. This many police-sanctioned murders in this period of time in the City of La Crosse is unprecedented," concluded Thomason.

"Murders?" shouted John, "What the fuck is she talking about?"

With a furrowed brow, Diane Cruz shook her head subtly in tacit agreement and turned the discussion to Singleton, who smiled at the opportunity to have such a high profile interview. This would beef up receipts for his business. There was money to be made being an expert witness in high liability law enforcement cases. Singleton had been nervous in the service as a police officer, so he exited stage left on that career and had made millions testifying in civil cases against police officers as an expert witness. He was the crucial witness against officers in hundreds of cases based on incidents from pursuits to use of force cases that he had not witnessed. Singleton had kidded friends over cocktails one evening, "It takes a genuine expert to be a witness in a case that happened 300 miles away when I was sound asleep." He had told his non-law enforcement friends, "What can I say? I'm good."

"Mr. Singleton, have you been able to look at these cases and draw any conclusions?" Cruz asked.

"I would not draw a conclusion as of yet, but I can certainly give you some observations for the sake of discussion," said Singleton, initially smiling, excitedly and visually composing himself to take on a professorial demeanor. "The suspect was armed and fired at Savage. If he fired while running away from Officer Savage, the return fire would quite naturally strike the suspect in the back, and this would still be a defensible shoot. In all of these cases, the shooting could be argued to be defensible. I have a different concern," said Singleton.

"What would that be?" asked Cruz, trying to make this carefully choreographed exchange look spontaneous.

"In every career, officers are afforded many opportunities where they could shoot someone, but choose to use other options and tactics to avoid the shoot. The numbers suggest that in Savage's case he shoots every time he gets an opportunity to do so. The shooting on one hand might be reasonable, but on the other it might not be necessary."

"For example, in the last shooting, where the suicidal man was armed with toy guns, clearly if Savage thought those guns were real then it would follow that it was reasonable to shoot. The problem I have with this particular incident is, no matter how you cut it, the shooting does not fit the officer's own Law Enforcement Code of Ethics that Savage raised his hand to. He said he would only use force when 'reasonable and necessary.' Clearly John Savage is familiar with weapons, and it is reasonable to believe he would know a toy firearm from a real one. Since this was a toy, it was not reasonable to shoot the man, and since it was a toy and could not harm him the shooting was not necessary," said Singleton suddenly feeling the hair hanging down on the side of his head tickling the side of his cheek. He tried to nonchalantly slip it back into place, hoping that his follicle faux pas might go undetected by the national viewing audience.

"I do not wish to speculate, but…" and Singleton stopped, waiting for a prompt.

"Please do. This is an open forum to investigate all sides of issues of the day," encouraged Diane with anticipation.

"All sides my ass," sputtered John angrily crossing his arms tightly across his chest.

"John Savage may be what I have found in Law Enforcement and like to call an aggressive opportunist," said Singleton. "This is my term, not something that was conjured up by any scientific behavioral study."

"This sounds interesting, please continue," said Diane.

"An aggressive opportunist is an officer who seeks out danger by aggressively pursuing the criminal. He is like a heat seeking missile, and these officers will find criminals more often than most officers. That aggression is good when all goes well, because the officers will clear the community streets of many of the worst of the worst," Singleton then paused and gazed up and to the left of camera, wondering himself if he should continue with a "theory" that he had just in the last three minutes pulled out of his ass.

After a brief moment, Singleton looked back into the camera and continued as if it was lecture he had given one hundred times before and a topic he had written a Master's Thesis on. "The aggressive opportunist is an officer who puts himself in bad positions with these criminals deliberately or subconsciously knowing that, when cornered, criminals will do what criminals do. Then he takes each and every opportunity to use deadly force to inflict the greatest amount of casualties on what they perceive as the enemy in the war on crime," and with that Singleton paused and added, "I am preparing a piece for publication on the topic." Singleton proudly smiled knowing that he had just given his theory credibility by lying about his piece for publication. I will start on it as soon as I leave the studio, he thought to himself.

"I would like to add," piped in Thomason, "that there is also a mental stability issue with this particular officer. Recently, there was an incident where John Savage reported that a terrorist he had met in Iraq or Afghanistan tried to kill him in the driveway of his home. There was no evidence of the assault and no other witnesses. This is a man in serious need of treatment, and I feel he is dangerous to the community. He is a highly trained killer who I firmly believe has reached the psychological breaking point. When he was hired against my wishes, he was given a badge which became his license to kill. I must say he is using it as casually as some people use a fishing license."

John Savage could take no more. He hit the power button on the remote, causing Thomason to get sucked into the blackness of the screen. He threw the remote down on the couch and shook his head slowly as he took deep breaths.

"John, are you OK?" asked Stella.

"There is nothing wrong with me. There never has been. I can handle the decisions I have made and I can deal with their consequences. It is not me it is them. The shoot decisions I have made have all been reasonable and defensible. This expert witness guy knows that the landmark Graham Versus Connor case ruled that force has to be objectively reasonable based on the officer's perception at the time of the use of force. Those guns were not toys. That prick Simpleton, or whatever his name was, knew what he was talking about and chose to use the term 'necessary,' which is no longer even a valid standard. The standard for use of force is that it has to be objectively reasonable."

John was now up and moving about the room gesturing like an adrenalized referee. "The guns were not toys, they were replicas. Simple-fucking-ton would be familiar with those also. Experts can't tell the difference between a replica and a real weapon at a distance in the dark. You would have to pick the weapon up and handle it to tell the difference.

"Aggressive opportunist, what the hell is that? Ryan and I were trying to get some lunch when the robbery at the Kwik Trip happened right in front of us. I went in there to find a bratwurst and stumbled into a gun fight. All of the other cases I was involved in I was dispatched to. What crock! What an asshole! Aggressive opportunist, my ass, I think he made that shit up. I've never heard the term before."

John covered his face with his hands and said, "This is crazy. I risked my life for these people and this is the thanks I get. This is how I get treated." John then fell back and let his weight just sink into the couch like a drowning man giving in to exhaustion after treading water for hours in the ocean. He sank until he just sat there perfectly still with his hands limp at his side.

"John. I am only saying this because I love you, but maybe you should see someone… um… ah about the trauma and everything. It was war, you know. You were there. You of all people know it's like nothing else in the world. Maybe it did take a toll," said Stella placing her hand on his arm. She held the secret to a magic pressure point that usually soothed him.

It did not work this time. John sat back up more animated than before, "Stella you need to listen to me now. I am going to try to explain this to you," said John turning her face towards his and picking up both of her hands. "From my point of view I have a proper perspective. I did what I had to do, what I was trained to do. I reacted properly, and if I would not have I would be in Arlington taking a dirt nap right now, not sitting here with you. The people who are screwed up are Dr. Sistek, Diane Cruz, William Barclay, and Jane Thomason. The only one up there not screwed up was Fuckington. He knew exactly what he was saying. He wants this case and every case," said John with pleading, almost puppy dog eyes. "Fuckington is a mercenary who has gone to the dark side for the almighty dollar."

"Please, John. Singleton is his name. That does not sound like you when you use language like that," said Stella, looking frightened.

John could not understand the fear but recognized it. He deliberately softened his delivery and continued, "OK Singleton. Singleton walks into courtrooms all over the nation and spouts his intelligent-sounding blather, and insurance companies with no testicular fortitude panic and pay out two million bucks before solid cases of self-defense are ever taken before a jury." John squeezed her hand and continued, "You see they're the ones who are crazy, not the officer that did the correct, but difficult thing.

"The problem is that society has never come to grips with the fact that some bad people need to be killed so that the good people they are about to do harm to, or worse, can go on with their lives in relative peace. There are people who are tortured by post-traumatic stress, but I am not one of them. Don't you see? If I seek out treatment when I am healthy, talking to people who are convinced I must be sick could actually make me unhealthy? Don't you see that, Stella?" John asked.

Stella's lip quivered as a tear ran down her cheek and she haltingly asked, "John, I understand what you are saying, but…what if you are mentally ill and the illness is giving you this perspective?" Stella bit her lip to stop the quivering, swallowed, and asked, "John, what about Ahmed? How could a terrorist attacking you in our driveway be anything but a hallucination?"

John was taken by surprise by a sudden emotional flank attack. His lungs were filled with a gulp of out-of-sequence air, and he swallowed it quickly. Stella's question hit him hard—a sucker punch with his guard down. He felt a tear barely escape from the corner of his eye but he managed to push it back in and wipe away the excess with his index finger, as he quickly stood up.

John's sudden departure caused Stella to tip over on the couch sideways, as she had been leaning against him. He turned and left the room, taking on the demeanor of John Savage, the warrior. His vocal delivery was reminiscent of the one used by him during the pre-mission briefings he conducted as a team leader in Iraq and Afghanistan. He had but one thing left to say to the person he loved the most, who in her effort to help him had unwittingly hurt him the most. John Savage, without so much as a backward glance toward Stella declared, "We're done here."

Chapter Twenty-two

Death to the Lamb

As Diane Cruz concluded the John Savage hit piece, she encouraged viewers, "If you want to weigh in on the issue, go to our website and answer the polling question, *Do you think soldiers returning from combat should receive comprehensive counseling and treatment before they are allowed to become police officers?* Tomorrow night we will take an intensive look at our troubled returning war vets in our story, 'The Silent Casualties. The War comes Home.' Thanks for watching, good night," and as the show ended Ahmed hit the power button.

"Is that the man? Is John Savage the man who killed our brothers?" asked Rashid, an Al-Qaeda operative and Ahmed's contact, who was paying him a business visit.

"That is the man. He is the one who killed our brothers on Martyrs' Ridge. How fortunate that this country, in its cultural deprivation, treats such a magnificent warrior with such disdain," said Ahmed, his voice bearing a twinge of sadness, for he thought at the same time, at least the Americans do not waste their warriors by strapping bombs on them and blowing them up to Allah.

"You sound as if this man is a brother of yours," said Rashid.

"I have faced this man on the battlefield. He is a worthy adversary, and I respect him more than the pigs that sent him to do their bidding. I want you to disregard my request for you to kill him. The fools think I am a figment of his imagination and he is crazy. That will serve us better than to kill him and place them on the alert," said Ahmed, taking a drink from his glass of Ouzo, a Greek Liquor, which was brought by Rashid for their meeting. "This is warm, smooth and sweet," said Ahmed licking his lips savoring the taste.

Rashid smiled widely at having pleased someone of Ahmed's status. "I discovered it in a restaurant that I was reconnoitering for targeting last year."

"What of the restaurant?" Ahmed asked.

"Before I could carry out the bombing, I was ordered to the United States. The bomb was to have sent me to Allah," said Rashid unintentionally registering relief.

"You are not despondent about having missed an opportunity to taste the sweet moistness of your virgins?" Ahmed laughed.

Rashid looked ashamed, having been discovered, and then recovered, his demeanor changing from shamed to defiant he boasted, "I would have gladly died for Allah if not for this assignment to assist you in your effort to strike at the heart of the Great Satan here in the United States."

Ahmed emptied his glass of Ouzo and motioned for Rashid to pour more. Rashid happily obliged. Both men's movements were becoming loose and poorly directed as if their limbs were being operated by a novice using joy stick that controlled them.

Ahmed patted the bottom of Rashid's arm as he poured the divine drink into his tall glass, urging his comrade to fill the glass. "You do not have to put on airs, Brother. I have always felt Allah saves the best of his eternal virgins for his warriors who live to fight again and again and again. I am certain that the fools and the mentally diminished who are convinced to blow themselves up for Allah land in the middle of 72 oft-used, barren, and poorly lubed camp followers from the time of Saladin," said Ahmed laughing at himself. "As they would say in the tire business, 'recycled factory second' virgins."

Rashid, who had begun taking a drink from the bottle, choked in mid-drink and spit Ouzo out his mouth and nose as he began to laugh uncontrollably. Rashid found the joke especially funny because he had taken a cover job selling tires at a Goodyear Store in Rockford, Illinois. When he could finally respond, he said, "Ahmed, Ahmed, Ahmed, shshsh," he said looking about as if Allah himself might be listening in on what he was about to say and whispered, still sputtering out Ouzo and laughter, "Is that not blasphemy?"

Without hesitation Ahmed replied, "No. I am a true warrior for Allah. I have killed the enemy on four continents. I have gained insight from my life, and I have noticed those who order so many to a young and glorious death never seek out such glory for themselves. They live in palaces, sleep on silk pillows, and bed real-life virgins. This I have seen. Why do they not strap on a vest and rush gloriously into the jaws of our enemies? Instead, when the enemy confronts them they flee and leave a trail of young Muslim heroes in their wake, giving their lives so that they can escape to another palace." Ahmed looked bitterly at Rashid, then took a long drink of Ouzo, which washed the bitterness from his face and replaced it with a mischievous grin. He beckoned Rashid closer.

Rashid, initially stunned by Ahmed's insight, began to laugh also as he leaned closer to hear what else Ahmed had to reveal. "Rashid," he whispered, "To strap bomb vests onto half-wits and send them out to have their entrails mixed up with the entrails of pizza-eating prepubescent's at bar mitzvahs is not only a waste, it is a poor military tactic. You said I was speaking blasphemy, well what they are doing is blast-phemy!"

Rashid, who was now well oiled by Ouzo, laughed at the clever play on English words. The laugh was also a laugh of relief. He had wondered often about the decisions of the Al-Qaeda leadership. After a good laugh, Ahmed became serious and said, "I am the only one left alive from my initial training in the camp in Afghanistan before our great leaders decided to poke the American Gorilla with the stick to encourage him to chase us all over the jungle." Ahmed took a long drink of Ouzo to drive out the smiling faces of the ghost-like apparitions of his dead friends as they hovered in his consciousness. "Every one of them died in a horrible way, killed by an army of John Savages that inundated the mountains of Afghanistan and the deserts of Iraq. Others were obliterated by the precision-guided missiles fired by stealth bombers and those cursed drones. One moment they were sipping tea and the next vaporized."

Ahmed sat up straight and defiantly said out loud, "Mohammed Atta, the leader of the 9-11 martyrs, was my friend. He was a brilliant leader. He would have made a great commander or even a fighter pilot to wage war against the Americans and the British. Now he is wasted, a martyr. We have too many martyrs. The Americans grow weary of war and could be easily defeated if we would not have wasted so many of our best blowing up markets and parking garages filled with our own people," said Ahmed bitterly.

"Ahmed, how can you carry on if you feel this way?" Rashid asked partially sobered by Ahmed's blunt honesty.

Ahmed held up his glass as a toast, "Because of my mission. I raise a toast to it and to Allah. May Allah grant me good fortune and success in this, my last mission. If I achieve success in this, I will gladly give my life. To success!"

As Ahmed's glass clinked against Rashid's bottle and Rashid shouted, "Succsheshh!" They drank until they both blacked out.

———>●<———

"Ahmed, Ahmed," whispered Lara as she shook him by the shoulder.

Ahmed woke up and opened his eyes, but they retreated back under cover of his tightly closed eyelids after first contact with the early morning sun. "What?" he asked with a tongue which had the texture of industrial sandpaper. His head throbbed and pounded as if it contained a marching band's drum-line in the midst of a lively performance.

"I came home late last night. I didn't get to meet your friend. Who is he?" Lara asked.

"That is my good friend Rashid. He surprised me last night with a knock at the door. We talked and had a few drinks," Ahmed looked about the room to orient himself. He was sprawled on the couch and Rashid was passed out, but his clothes did not appear even slightly disheveled as if he slept the sleep of the dead, or rather, the dead drunk.

"I have never seen him around. What does he do?" Lara asked.

"He is from out of town. He came to this country for its opportunities and now he holds a job working for Good Year Tires. He is a sales rep," answered Ahmed, hoping that would satisfy her.

He immediately changed the subject, "Rashid introduced me to a Greek drink called Ouza or Ouzee…" and Ahmed rubbed his forehead hard in a futile effort to rub the throbbing pain out of his head. The throbbing would have registered, if measured, at about 8.9 on the Richter scale.

"Ouzo?" Lara asked.

"Yes. That is the one, Ouzo," said Ahmed, who now was attempting to without success to squint the pain away.

Lara left the room and came back with a glass of water and four Advil and said, "Take these. It might help, but I can't guarantee anything." She shook her head and smiled as she handed him the tablets, which he tossed into his mouth, and then he took the water and drank it all. The water in itself was just what he needed for his parched and foul tasting tongue.

"I had Ouzo one time in my life," said Lara as she massaged his temples lightly.

"Yes and what was your result?" Ahmed asked, keeping his eyes closed, but abandoning the pained expression for the look of a condemned man who had been touched by an angel.

"I remember tipping back my head to drink from an authentic Greek goat skin flask at a party and that is the last thing I remember of that night. I woke up the next day in my bed with my clothes on and car keys in my hand. I had the worst headache of my life. I never drank it again. The thought of it just gave me a headache." With that she popped two Advil into her mouth and swallowed them dry.

"I concur, never again. This Greek concoction will never wet my lips even if I lie dying of thirst in the desert, miles from water," concluded Ahmed with a sigh.

Lara leaned down, and kissed Ahmed's pained forehead. "I have a class, so I gotta run." She kissed him again and added, "Have fun with your friend. Will he be here tonight, when I get home? Maybe I can bring home some Chinese."

"No, he will be gone, so bring home Chinese for two." He reached in his pocket and pulled out a $100 bill and handed it to Lara. "Remember, sweet and sour chicken, not pork," he cautioned.

"I'll remember," and she kissed him again as she snatched the money out of his hand and ran out the door leaving her fragrance dancing lightly in the air for a moment.

Her perfume combined with the body odor of his still sleeping house guest morphed into a rank bouquet. "What a foul combination," said Ahmed as the two competing odors compelled him to rise up from the couch to rush to the bathroom. When Ahmed reached the bathroom he was met by an even more overpowering concentration of Lara's perfume. The fragrance he once loved was like flame to butane and served to spontaneously ignite his already troubled stomach, "BARAAAAAAAKKK," a slight pause, "BARAAAAAAAKKK," and then he set his head down on the porcelain. "Ouzo. I hate the…" and then he was up again, "GREEEEEEEKS!"

———⟫●≪———

Three hours later the two Al-Qaeda operatives were scrubbed and as recovered as possible after their night of blending in to the decadent western society they were bent on destroying. Rashid had gone out to his car and returned with a bulky black hockey bag and dropped it in the middle of the living room floor. Ahmed pulled the shades, dead bolted and chained the door.

"You have everything I asked for?" Ahmed inquired.

"Yes I do. I am certain you will be quite satisfied," answered Rashid. Rashid pulled a bulky item from the bag, which was carefully encased in bubble wrap. "This was originally meant to conceal an explosive device, but our people modified it to carry a weapon the size of a Beretta 92F, Glock 17, or a Colt 1911. Obviously it would also hold a weapon with a smaller frame." Rashid un-wrapped the item and revealed what appeared to be a full-arm cast along with a sling. "It has been made to fit over your left arm so that, when you do unleash your attack, you will be able to shoot with your right hand."

"Excellent!" Ahmed said with excitement as he took possession of the only piece left of the puzzle. "Now all we need is to have my target wander into the kill zone," said Ahmed almost wistfully.

"You must see if it fits," said Rashid.

Ahmed carefully took the cast and realized it was sturdier than he had anticipated. He slid his hand and then his whole left arm into the cast. He cocked his head, "It fits as if it was measured and custom fitted for me. It is perfect," proclaimed Ahmed. "I am a little bit overwhelmed. I believe now I will be able to carry my plan into fruition."

Rashid pulled a folding file from the bag, opened it, and began to set paperwork down on the end table in front of the couch. "Here is your military identification. We used the picture you sent me, which you had taken while you were in your American uniform." Ahmed looked at the identification and nodded in approval at the official-looking identification.

"Also here is your driver's license. We have given you a western name so that you will arouse less suspicion," said Rashid.

"Robert Margolis? The name has a Mediterranean flavor, which fits my look. It does not really matter though. People in this country seem to trip over themselves trying to be nice to a Muslim in this country. They are more afraid of being called a racist than of dying a horrible death." Ahmed thought for a bit and then added, "That is because so few of them know how horrible dying in a ball of fire can be."

"If you are stopped by the police and asked, you are Robert Margolis. This name will come back on a computer check as having a clear record. We have stolen the identification of this person and forged the license so that if a policeman stops your car and runs a check everything will come back copasetic." Rashid paused, thought, and added, "It may help if you open a checking account and obtain a credit card in the name of Robert Margolis as well as rent your vehicle under this name also. The more types of things verifying that…"

"I have done this before, Rashid," said Ahmed tersely. "Please don't treat me like a child."

"I am so sorry, Ahmed. Of course you have. It should be you teaching and me listening. Do you know when and where?" Rashid asked as he tried to change the subject.

"No, but if I did I could not tell you. It will happen where it happens, when it happens," said Ahmed.

"Good. That makes sense. I have been told that all contacts will be made through me. It will add a layer of protection in the event someone comes looking for you. I will never betray you. I will die before I allow myself to be taken," declared Rashid. "Just in case I am about to be taken, my last act before I go to Allah will be to text you the message 1-5-5-1-4. The numbers on the phone spell…"

"Allah," answered Ahmed. "Hopefully we will never need it."

"Once again I will ask you, what of John Savage? If you have reconsidered I could make a trip to La Crosse and kill this crusader? I would consider it an honor to do so."

"No. He has been dishonored and discredited. He has been suspended and is not even allowed to work as a police officer. For John Savage, I have inflicted upon him a wound worse than death," and Ahmed simulated a dagger thrust to the heart of an imaginary adversary. "For this I am greatly satisfied," he added as he nodded to the adversary he imagined lying fallen before him.

"Savage poses no further threat to me. They believe my attempt to kill him was a hallucination and he is mentally ill. Whether or not another attempt fails or is successful, it would only give credence to his claims and cause the authorities to come looking for me. He is debunked and must stay debunked. My mission is too important to be jeopardized by a personal vendetta," explained Ahmed as he fitted the sling over his head and adjusted the strap for the proper positioning.

Ahmed popped open the door which had been cut into the cast, laid his Beretta into place, and closed it. He walked over to the mirror on the wall and positioned himself in front of it and practiced popping the door open, drawing his weapon, and pointing it at the mirror. He replaced it and repeated the drill. With each repetition his speed improved and his demeanor became more and more severe.

Rashid watched in admiration. After the tenth draw, Rashid proclaimed in a maniacal whisper, "The hero of Martyrs' Ridge shall strike again. Allahu Akbar! Death to the lamb!"

Ahmed paused in his practice and stared deeply into the eyes of the killer looking back at him from the mirror. In a pose reminiscent of De Niro in *Taxi Driver*, he seconded the sentiment, "Death to the lamb!"

Chapter Twenty-three

Fate

732 AD on a field near Tours.

Sir Savage halted his troop in the foothills just to the south of the Muslim encampment. "We shall sleep here in our armor. Pass the word," the warrior chieftain whispered to Marcwulf, his lieutenant. The whisper spread quickly down the line, and each standing knight slowly lowered himself to the ground, where he knelt, upon hearing the command. The movement gave the line the appearance of a row of dominos toppling, except every tenth man stepped forward to the tree line to stand first watch. There would be no fire tonight, for they were within hailing distance of the enemy.

Savage would not sleep tonight. He and his men had either been moving toward battle or in battle for seven days. He should be exhausted except the anticipation of this next engagement was a potion that energized him body and soul. Savage was a Frankish warrior who had earned his name because of his stubborn refusal to allow the marauding bands of loosely aligned armed men to rape and pillage at will. He delivered a savage kind of justice to those armed warriors who threatened unarmed farmers and villagers under his protection. Sir Savage was feared by some enemies and respected by those who would not acknowledge fear.

Savage's people loved him, and when they bowed upon his approach, Sir Savage would shout, "Good man, lift your head and greet me as your equal. You are a free man and I am but the humble servant of free men.

While I carry this shield and sword, my people shall bow to no one, but God and our king."

The current threat was much more ominous then any faced by the Franks before in Savage's lifetime, and because of it, Savage left his family in the north a year earlier and rode to join the fight with his 100 Comitatus. The Comitatus were mounted knights under his command. Word had spread that Umayyad (Arab) armies had driven across North Africa and had jumped continents at Gibraltar. The invading army of mounted warriors swept through and conquered Spain, creating "the Caliphate of Cordoba." The Crosses of Christian Churches were torn down and replaced with spires topped by crescents. The Umayyad put to the sword anyone who would refuse to bow before the crescent.

Savage would rather die than renounce his God, his faith, or his freedom, and he decided he would never take a knee before the crescent, even at the point of a sword. Savage, true to his name, delivered many of these warriors a savage passage to their god, Allah. Savage did adopt one innovation of the Umayyad. He supplied all of his Comitatus with captured Umayyad saddles, which were equipped with stirrups, allowing for more control of the horse. It also allowed the warrior to more readily fight mounted. His knights took to fighting on horseback like a robin takes to flight.

Savage and his Comitatus rode to join the youthful Germanic Prince, Charles Martel. Charles welcomed them into his army and, because of their skill, asked them to help train his army into a professional fighting force. Charles knew that warfare was as much a part of the Umayyad life as suckling was to a baby. The Umayyad would not fall before a disorganized rabble. Charles would need a well-trained, professional army to defeat them.

The army was an interesting coalition of Franks, Liberians, Visigoths, Romans, Spanish, and Germans. There were even some Turks and Greeks, who had fought the Muslims until the fight was lost and fled west rather than capitulate. Their dream was to live and fight another day, and Charles would bring those dreams into fruition.

The training ended when messengers brought news that the Umayyad army was on the march and had crossed the Pyrenees. Messengers carried sad tidings of the crushing defeat suffered by the Aquitanians at Garonne and the subsequent ruthless sacking of Bordeaux. Estimates of the size of the Umayyad army numbered from between 60,000 and 400,000, depending on which breathless messenger one chose to believe. Numbers mattered not to Charles, for he would fight them if they were a million.

This would not be Charles Martel's first battle against overwhelming odds. He said, "Choose the right ground and the right tactics, and the smaller army has the advantage." He had proved this theory time and time again. Charles told his assembled forces, "We must fight them and defeat them here and now or the Umayyad will conquer and Christianity and the Frankish way of life will go the way of the Pharaohs. We fight strengthened by the love of family, the love of country, and the love of God. I promise if you fight with me, I will bring you victory, and victory will bring you freedom! Will you fight?" The army roared sounding like thunder rolling across the plains.

Charles chose to delay the battle and parallel the Muslim march until they arrived at the battlefield of his choosing. It would be ground that offered his army a superior position. Patience paid off, for the opportunity presented itself when the army of Abdul Rahman Al Ghafiqi set up camp between Tours and Poitiers. Charles positioned his army directly to front of the Umayyad Army, effectively blocking their path of advance. Charles determined the stretch of high ground between Tours and Poitiers was the ideal position to give battle and end the harsh religious conversions by fire and sword of these ruthless Islamic missionaries. The Muslim's having a large number of mounted cavalry would not be an advantage because the heavy wood line on both flanks of his army would funnel their cavalry into a compact formation of manageable numbers.

When Rahman's army moved, they found 40,000 soldiers trained to fight as one formed up in phalanx upon phalanx on a plain above them. They were armed with swords, and the exterior of the rectangle shaped formations bristled with long lances. The Christian army looked determined, but Rahman was delighted they chose to fight. Infantry had never before been able to stand against a mounted cavalry charge, and he was certain his army would destroy this last feeble impediment to a Muslim Europe in one swift charge. "Have the cavalry attack," he bellowed.

"Allahu Akbar," was shouted from the throats of thousands of horseman waving their long swords or carrying their lances. Upon reaching the enemies formations, however, most horses heeled back and skidded to a stop while others crashed and tumbled against the phalanxes which held against charge after charge. As the Muslim army retreated, their badly wounded left lying behind were treated to the only mercy of the day, a swift death by the *misericorde*. The long narrow knife was thrust quickly into the heart of the wounded Saracen warriors, preventing a long and agonizing death.

Savage had lost count of the Umayyad charges as well as the days this battle had gone on. It was days for some and an eternity for others. During a lull in the fighting, Sir Savage had been called before Charles Martel, "Savage, you and your Comitatus have fought bravely, and I have summoned you to give you a great honor," said Charles.

Savage bowed and started to kneel, but Charles objected, "None of that, sir. We chose to stand and fight together when it would have been easier to kneel together. I would not have you kneel before me any more than before Rahman." Charles then handed a cup of wine to Savage, "Tonight we shall drink together."

The wine was both bitter and sweet. It warmed his body, which had been lying under the stars upon the battlefield moments earlier on this cold October evening in the year of the Lord 732.

"How can I serve you, My Lord," asked Savage.

"I have called you because some of our men were cut off by today's fighting. They are being held in the camp of Rahman. His army will strike us again on the morrow, and we will throw him back again, but without you and your 100," said Charles, who sat down heavily in his camp chair, obviously weary from the day's relentless fighting. "Sit and drink with me," said Charles motioning to the chair to the right of him.

"Thank you, My Lord," said Savage as he adjusted his sword and sat beside the revered leader, who the men called The Hammer.

"I have called you, for I want you to leave from here immediately and ride around the Saracen army, conceal yourselves and your horses, and wait. When the Umayyad ride from their camp on the attack, I want you to launch your own attack on the camp. Destroy what you can, and kill whom you are able, but do it quickly. Your real purpose is to rescue our men who have been taken prisoner. You might also create enough confusion to cause a split in their army and offer us an opportunity for complete victory," He paused to drink from his cup.

After taking on a more serious tone Charles continued more slowly, "I feel that if our men who are prisoners are left to the mercies of Rahman, they will suffer the worst of degradations and torture. Move silently, strike swiftly, mercilessly, and may God go with you and your men, Savage," said the Hammer, who set aside his cup, removed his gauntlet and extended his ungloved hand to his friend.

"Thank you for this honor, My Lord. While God is with us, how can we fail?" Savage said finding that if Charles' arm was a hammer, his grip was a vice. Savage was confident that with such a warrior-prince as this in command, the army could not lose the battle.

Savage knew the terrain well. He had led his soldiers during a night ride to within 100 yards of the Umayyad tents. They could hear the shouts, murmurings, and laughter of the Umayyad warriors. It could have been their own camp except for the vastly superior number of tents and the strange music of the invading enemy.

As the night moon took its lazy journey across the sky, the voices and rhythms drifted slowly away as if muffled by the blanket of stars. The entire camp seemed to roll over at once and lie its head down to sleep. Savage leaned over and whispered, "Marcwulf, are you sleeping?"

"Not yet, My Lord. I am anxious for tomorrow to come," answered Marcwulf. His name, which meant the border wolf, was given to him to describe the vicious, wolf-like defense he would mount to protect his hearth and home any time threats loomed.

"If I had 1000 instead of 100, we could charge into that camp right now and put them to the sword in their sleep," said Savage shaking his head in disappointment. "We could scatter their army to the winds."

"Yes but 100 is not 1000, My Lord. Tomorrow though, when we attack, we will make such a noise they will think us to be one thousand," answered Sir Marcwulf.

As the sun came up, the 100 lay still while the camp awoke and with great excitement horses were saddled and mounted. The large camp was all but abandoned as the aggressive Umayyad army was urged forward by their leader Abdul Rahman, who hung back astride a majestic chocolate Andalusian with a jet-black mane. The horse was said to be from the lineage of Bucephalus, the war horse of Alexander the Great. The horse stood as calm as if he was mounted on a great Roman Relief amidst the organized chaos of an army on the advance. Rahman hoped to match the conquests of Alexander the Great. "Allahu Akbar!" Rahman shouted.

The response "Allahu Akbar!" turned into a chant, which spread like a wave through the warriors willing to kill or die for Allah.

Mounted and formed, Savage road in front of his men and called out, "When I move, you will move. We will be silent on the advance. We will shout like angels of death when we are upon them. Kill all targets of opportunity and let those who flee out of reach, escape. Scouts report, our prisoners are held directly to our front. When we locate them, we will each take one up behind us, and we shall escape through the same door from whence we came. God be with you all."

Savage turned his horse and spurred it whispering in a rasp, "On Equus," and he moved forward at a walk followed by a canter and then a trot. As the tents came into view, Savage's line broke into a thunderous gallop.

The Comitatus came rolling down upon the camp as sudden and as deadly as a desert sirocco. The surprise was complete. Few were left behind to guard the camp, the spoils of war, and the prisoners. Savage and his men slashed and cut down everyone as the few left behind made hopeless attempts to fight or flee. Some merely froze in place with eyes and mouth open as they were sent to Allah. The prisoners were exactly where the scouts had said they would be. Their smiles flashed gleaming white in contrast with their bloody, grimy faces. They were housed in a corral-like structure considerably less accommodating than those for the animals.

As their liberators swarmed into the camp, the captives that could do so climbed up on the back of their rescuers' horses. This was done, however, only after those that could not make the climb themselves, due to the severity of their wounds from battle or torture, were helped to mount.

One prisoner had died during the night. The deceased's brother knelt beside him to say a quiet, reverent prayer. The offering was much abbreviated by the circumstances, and he quickly crossed himself, kissed his brother's forehead and, with respects paid for a brother lost, the survivor was instantly up from his knees. He turned, ran, and rolled up on the back of one of the horses which was swirling about in front of the gates of their foul confines.

The rescue unfolded even better than Savage could have prayed for. While the rescue was in progress, Marcwulf road up to Savage shouting,

"My Lord, it is Rahman," as he pointed his sword to the north. "We can gobble him up or strike him down but a short ride from here."

Savage gestured to Boniface, Grimoald, and Hermann as he shouted, "Join me and follow Sir Marcwulf." He turned to Sir Henry and shouted, "Continue with the rescue. If we do not return escape out the door we came in," and Savage rode after Marcwulf.

Marcwulf led them through a line of tents and, when they reached a vast opening, Savage was astounded to discover before them the crowned jewel of the battlefield ripe for the picking. There, sitting upon his horse, oblivious to any danger behind him, was Rahman. His steed was majestic. His colorful banners flapped in the wind next to him, held by an unarmed horseman. Rahman's personal guard formed a line between Rahman and his own advancing troops but had not positioned a single guard to the rear of Rahman.

Savage, with but a few gestures, assigned each to a target and after a nod Marcwulf, Boniface, Grimoald, and Hermann along with Savage spurred their mounts forward with their swords ready to strike a blow for God, country, and Charles. Their horses, who seemed psychically connected to their riders, rode with the same excitement and abandon toward the prize. Rahman's personal guard looked unconcerned, watching the advance of the army as each secretly wished to be among those on the advance. The glorious ride seemed to last forever, but the unwelcome intruders to the camp of Rahman covered the distance in mere seconds. Savage's sword struck a blow that changed the history of the world. Abdul Rahman Al Ghafiqi was as dead when he hit the ground, as was his dream of conquering Europe for Allah.

The guards seemed confused by the turn of events. So sudden was the attack, the guards were paralyzed by it. Savage and his knights spun, slashed, and parried until the two guards who did react joined Rahman lying ingloriously on the field. Then Savage and his small band turned and rejoined the rescue. The last of the prisoners were holding tightly to the waists of their rescuers as some were sobbing in joyful disbelief.

Savage spurred Equus, who rose up on his back legs as the general shouted in a booming voice, "Comitatus, victory is ours! Now, out the door we came in. Comitatus ride!"

"OOOOOAAAH!" was the shout of 156 strong acknowledging that they had done what some would have thought impossible.

Savage had ridden into the camp with 100 and rode out with 156. Those Umayyad left in the camp who heard their battle cry on the advance were not alive to hear the shout of victory and sheer joy as the 156 rode out of the camp.

When reports of the attack on the camp reached the attacking Umayyad army, many abandoned the battlefield. This was not done out of fear for their safety but out of concern for their plunder. Many were made rich beyond their imagination because of the plunder they had taken in this campaign, and the enemy raiding the camp posed a serious threat to their financial future. The Umayyad army fractured as half of their number streamed to the rear.

Charles' plan had worked better than he imagined possible. Seeing the reaction to the raid, he ordered a charge which slammed into the diminished, confused, and leaderless Umayyad. Those remaining on the field fought but found themselves suddenly leaderless and outnumbered.

The fight was desperate, but word that Rahman had been killed spread like Greek fire through the Muslim Army. The partial retreat turned into a route.

Charles was as shocked by his sudden victory as the Umayyad army was stunned by its defeat. He could hardly believe his victory was as complete as it appeared to be, so he regrouped, held his ground, and waited for another charge which never came.

The remainder of the Umayyad warriors of Allah retreated through the mountain passes of the Pyrenees. With new leadership, the would-be conquerors of Europe returned with their plunder to Spain and settled for maintaining their much smaller dominion at the Caliphate of Cordoba.

The crosses would remain atop the churches in Europe, and the words of Christ would be passed on for generations to come.

Three days after the victory, Savage was summoned once again to the camp of Charles Martel, who would forever be called by the world "The Hammer of Tours."

A surprisingly boyish smile flashed broadly across the bearded face of Charles who, flushed with victory loudly proclaimed, his voice hoarse after days of shouting commands on the battlefield, "Come drink, my friend, and on this occasion I shall not let you rush off so rudely with tales of deeds to be done more important than assuring our friendship as you did the last time whence we drank." He pointed at two cups of wine already set upon his camp table.

"I am afraid that, on that occasion, the real weight of my rudeness fell upon the shoulders of Rahman," said Savage with a smile as he took his wine and the seat next to Charles.

"From what I understand, when you ended your rude visit to Rahman, the weight came not upon his shoulders but off his shoulders," laughed Charles.

"I must confess, My Lord, that my blow did not cut as surely as that, but it did the job and never will he threaten our homes and our faith again." Savage squirmed a bit, uncomfortable with his pride for fear of being thought to boast, even though it was indeed a boast he was proud to share.

Then Charles became somber. "Do you know why I, Charles, son of Pippen, born in Belgium came to fight with the Franks against the Umayyad Army?"

"Why, My Lord?" asked Savage, surprised that this man who possessed the power of kings should share his most intimate thoughts and motivations with a lowly knight.

"I must confess I knew if the battle was waged and won by me, there may be a crown in my future." Charles took his cup from the table and drank heartily, spilling a bit, but he wiped his face with his sleeve and continued, "I now see that there was much more at stake than a crown in this battle. These Soldiers of Allah planned on forcing every man, woman, and child to take a knee before the crescent or take a knee before the blade of their executioner. They call it their Jihad," said Charles.

"Jihad, My Lord?" Savage asked.

"It means struggle. Our enemy believes that if they are killed in the struggle against non-believers—that would be us, Savage...Christians— they will escape judgment in heaven." Charles paused for an impromptu toast and raised his cup, "To us!"

Charles raised his cup higher and continued his toast, "Today we rejoice in victory, but I believe this struggle will continue for 1000 years, possibly 10,000 years. May God always send warriors such as yourself, Savage, to defend his people against the terror wrought by this unholy Jihad."

After that toast Savage lifted his cup and returned the toast, "May my children's children, who are called upon to fight this Jihad, be led by a man with wisdom and courage such as yours, My Lord."

The king-to-be and the knight drank heartily to seal their toast. It was a toast that would be forgotten by history, but remembered by fate.

Chapter Twenty-four

Dear John

"This is Dr. Sistek," said the voice on the phone. "How can I help you today?"

"Hello, Dr. Sistek, this is Special Agent Charles Martel of the Federal Bureau of Investigation. I am calling you today about Officer John Savage," said Martel.

"The department said you were going to call, so as I said, how can I help you?" The doctor repeated, sounding pressed for time.

"You sound rushed, so I will get to the point. The FBI and Department of Homeland Security would like you to clear John Savage immediately for duty," declared Martel.

"I have my concerns. He is resistant to treatment and claims he needs none even though there is one major unresolved issue," explain the doctor, attempting to keep it vague.

"I sent your office the medical release form signed by John Savage, so we should be able to talk frankly. The issue you have is the fact that he says he was attacked in his driveway by a terrorist named Ahmed, who he remembered from a battle in Iraq. Well, I have classified information that I am cleared to give to you as long as you do not release this information to anyone. This is a Doctor-Patient issue as well as a national security issue. Are you agreeable to that, Doctor?" asked Martel.

"Of course! I should let you know my office was contacted by Diane Cruz of CBN and I declined to return her calls and will continue to do so.

I thought you should know, though, that they have called me," shared the doctor.

"I appreciate you telling me that. If I would give you no further information would you release John Savage for duty just upon my request?" Martel asked.

"No. I am concerned about the possibility that he is seeing post-traumatic stress induced manifestations. That can be dangerous for most people and even more so for an armed police officer," said the doctor with deep concern.

"Well then. This is not for public release, and beyond that, it is highly classified. John Savage was attacked by a man named Ahmed Abdullah Rahim. We believe he is in this country, and John is the only one who knows what he looks like now. We know where he has been, but we do not know where he is or what he is up to. It appears that he took a little vacation from his duties to try to kill an old adversary but hiccupped on the attempt," explained Martel.

The doctor paused before asking, "Why isn't there some sort of national alert on this man?"

"We are doing everything we can, but to put this out nationally would make this man move out of reach. He has the ability to move rapidly and change his appearance drastically. John is the only person we know that can pick him out on the street. We need him available again. Ahmed was not a manifestation. Ahmed is real and we believe he constitutes a national threat," said Martel.

"I will release John for full duty, but now I have another concern. I am concerned about the long-term psychological damage to John after all he has been through to be treated like he is being treated in the media coverage. For his sake shouldn't you contact this Diane Cruz and ask her…"

"Sorry, Doctor. There was a time that you could call a reporter and sincerely say 'National Security,' and it would be like gold. They would hold the story. But those are the bygone days of yesteryear, Doc. Now if they get a chance to print national secrets that would bring down this country in a week, they would consider it a journalistic coup and claim it was their First Amendment Right to do so. That's not me being cynical, it is a fact. Can't do it, Doc." answered Martel. "So what's the verdict? Is he back?"

"Absolutely," answered Sistek as she scribbled the words "Clear Savage Immediately!!!" on the pad on her desk.

"Hey, Doctor, one other thing," said Martel.

"What's that?" asked the doctor.

"Don't worry about John Savage's psyche. He's cut from tough timber—a lot tougher than the kindling that has been trying to burn him down. I hate to interfere, but you didn't encourage confidence in him either, Doc. He needed someone to believe him, especially you," said Martel. There was a long silence on the phone and Martel said, "Doctor?"

The doctor said, "I am here. Your words were true and they hit me pretty hard. I do not think I am going to see Officer Savage again, so can you tell him how truly sorry I am that I questioned his veracity. It sounded so…."

"Crazy?" Martel said filling in the blank.

"I didn't want to use the word. You think a psychiatrist could come up with a better word than that, but it did. It just sounded absolutely crazy," explained the doctor.

"One thing I have discovered after my years in law enforcement. The truth is stranger than fiction. Well, thank you, Doctor. I will pass along your message to John, and I am certain you will be back in his good graces if you were ever out of them," said Martel. "Do you need anything else from me?"

"No, thank you. I will get the release out today. John should be back on the streets by tomorrow."

———————

John Savage and Ryan Chen sprinted the last 100 yards to John's driveway after their run through Hixon Forest and up the bluff. As they crossed the imaginary finish line, they high-fived and began the process of bringing their heart rates and breathing back to normal. John's legs felt like logs, and the sweat was rolling off his nose.

"Hey, Ryan, how about a cold Gatorade?" asked John.

"You got it, buddy. Sounds great," answered Ryan. "So, when are you coming back to work?" Ryan asked hesitantly.

"I just got the call from the Assistant Chief today. I am officially back, but it just so happens I am on my days off. That means I will actually be back on shift Tuesday," said John as he unlocked the door with a key from a chain around his neck.

As John swung the door open and entered the kitchen, he noticed an envelope on the table with "John" written plainly in Stella's hand. There were no hearts, flowers, or art work typical of every written communication she had ever left for him. He stopped dead in his tracks as the dread swept over him. He picked it up and set it on top of the refrigerator, trying to hide any physical reaction to what he was feeling. "All I have is original lime. I have water, too, if you'd prefer. I also have Bud Light if that's your preference?" John asked leaning on the refrigerator door as he scanned the interior for the available options, "I have wine, Pepsi, and Mountain Dew in here—oh yeah—and milk," offered John.

"Bud Light sounds good, but not after a run. I'll take the Gatorade," decided Ryan as John handed him the cold drink, Ryan wasted no time unscrewing the cap and taking a huge first drink. "How are you doing with all that Diane Cruz bullshit?" asked Ryan after downing the bottle in his hand.

"What can I do? At least I'm here to put up with the bullshit. If I was the perfect cop in their eyes, you guys would have buried me a long time ago. I'd like to kick that Art Singleton's ass, though. I wonder what kind of cop he was?" pondered John.

"Chicken shit mother," declared Ryan with conviction. "Lt. Tyree said he had heard from guys who worked with him across the state that when there was a hot call he was down at the gas pumps or laying low on some back road having 'radio problems.' Every department he's been with has allowed him to 'resign,' if you know what I mean. Then he becomes some national fucking expert because he has a few years' experience and the degrees. He has the BA, the MS, PHD, and most importantly, his BS. It really pisses me off!" Ryan tried to wipe the sweat from his face, but there was nothing dry enough on him to absorb any amount of perspiration, "You got a towel? I'm dripping all over your kitchen floor here."

John left the room to get a towel, and as he passed Stella's studio, he could not help but notice her easel and paints were gone. His legs, already fatigued from the run, became weaker still. *Can't think about that right now*, he thought. He recovered and went quickly to the bathroom, grabbed two towels and paused to slowly open the medicine cabinet. He saw empty spaces where Stella had stored her things. "Later!" John said to himself in a whisper.

John returned to the kitchen and tossed Ryan the towel. They dried themselves and sat down at the kitchen table. John opened his Gatorade and took a drink trying to wash away the desperation he felt. It did not help. He shifted his focus to Ryan, as Ryan said, "What did they expect us to do, John? I listened to that bullshit, and I am wondering, what did they expect us to do?"

John found the shift in focus a welcome reprieve from the emotionally crushing thought of Stella's absence. He could not help but notice that Ryan sounded angrier than John about the CBN coverage. John realized the piece done by Cruz criticized all of John's shootings. By association, they would have to be questioning Ryan's shoot, because Ryan was involved in the Kwik Trip shooting. He had also delivered rounds into one of the suspects. The report had obviously impacted Ryan personally, maybe even more so than John. It was Ryan's first life or death encounter. "Sticks and stones, Ryan. We did what we were trained to do. They're the ones who are messed up, not us. How are you handling it all, buddy?"

"I don't know. It bothers me because I know that we were right to do what we did. We weren't looking for trouble, we were looking for a Bratwurst, remember? Bratwurst! Then those two bastards came in and the next thing I knew we were shittin' and gittin' while we were shootin' and scootin'. Then that rapist, what's his name?"

"Smythe," answered John.

"Smythe, yeah, that's right. He was shooting at you, man. He was pulling a gun on us. He was a rapist and a killer. He would have killed us both if you had let him, and they say you shot him in the back? That's just bullshit, man!" Ryan almost sounded as if he was on the edge of tears.

"Hey, Ryan, it don't mean nothin'! Let 'em say what they wanna say. Someone told me once that a lie will die of a common cold, but the truth can get run over by a train and survive. Cruz is the engine and Singleton is the caboose, you know. He's the train's asshole. They just ran over the truth, and we're still here and the truth is still the truth," said John in a soothing voice.

"What about that Jane Thomason? She's a police and fire commissioner," asked Ryan. "She's got juice. People believe someone who has 'Dr.' in front of their name."

"Thomason is an ex-commissioner. She is worse than nothin'. She spit on troops coming home from Vietnam. I mean this sincerely. She is dog shit on the sidewalk of humanity to me. If I see her, I'll walk around her; maybe I'll even hold my nose." John said with disdain. "Sometimes you can't help but step in it, but you scrape as much of it off as possible and then you keep on walking. Sooner or later you walk it off. She is nothing."

John took a drink of Gatorade, wiped his forehead and continued, "Ryan, this stuff could make you crazy if you let it. We know we did the right thing, and that's what matters. We're here to allow those people the opportunity to second-guess us. I would rather have those two guys lying on the floor at the Kwik Trip with Cruz second guessing us, than us lying on the floor with our own people second guessing us. Don't you think?" John waited for a response to see if anything he was throwing out was sticking to the wall.

There was a thoughtful silence as Ryan wiped his face with the towel and held the towel covering his face for a few moments. Ryan, dropped the towel from his face and with enthusiasm replied, "You're right, man. If you aren't going to let them get to you, I can't let them get to me. We're partners, man. I got your six!"

"Got your six, Ryan," agreed John, and they shared a buddy hand shake and a fist bump in confirmation.

"So, now that we got that settled, do you think Diane Cruz is hot?" Ryan asked.

"I'd watch her take a shower, but I wouldn't get in with her," said John.

"If she wanted to show me how sorry she was by scrubbing my back... and stuff I'd get in," said Ryan. I wouldn't let her use one of those shower brushes though, She'd have to scrub ever so vigorously with her hand," he added.

"Yeah, I suppose you would insist that she not stop until everything was real clean," said John.

"Exceptionally clean—you know so that she could eat off it," said Ryan with a wink and a smile.

"I know exactly what you mean," nodded John.

"How're things with you and Stella?" asked Ryan.

John hesitated, "I actually think Diane Cruz created problems between Stella and I."

"Between you and Stella? How could that be?" Ryan asked.

John stood up and retrieved the envelope from the top of the refrigerator then sat back down at the table and just stared at the envelope. "She listened to that story the other night, and she put two and two together. She thinks I imagined Ahmed and must be deeply disturbed."

"How can she think that? She knows you. You two are great together," said Ryan stunned.

John turned the envelope slowly in his hand and shuddered at the plainness of it. He picked it up and smelled it, but all he could detect was the bland smell of standard stock paper. There was not a hint of lilacs and peaches. "Doesn't matter, they painted the picture of a troubled vet on the edge. That's the same old bullshit they laid on all the Vietnam vets."

John continued, "I have met Vietnam vets who said they changed out of their uniforms in the airport after returning from the Nam. They never wore their uniforms again and didn't talk about the war because the media painted them as psychologically damaged from all the horrors and atrocities of war. Some of the folks back home called them Baby killers. It was all bullshit just like this, but what could they do? People believed the bullshit and now Stella believes the bullshit. After her close call with Smythe, she has been a little gun-shy about the world in general."

"Are you going to open it?" asked Ryan.

"I don't want to dump this on you," said John waving the envelope at Ryan. "I think it's bad, because her envelopes are usually a work of art and smell like spring-time. Look at this thing. Bland, plain, blasé, it has to be bad news. Besides I checked, her stuff is moved out."

"Did she say anything about moving out?" Ryan asked.

"No. Nothing at all, but I don't need to read this to know. Her stuff is gone and..." John's voice trailed off.

"Why don't you open that right now and read it to yourself, but I'll stay here in case you need someone, you know, a buddy," said Ryan.

John sat staring, smelling, flipping it about, sliding it away and pulling it back and he finally took a deep breath, grabbed it, ripped open the envelope and read it to himself.

Dear John,

This is the hardest letter I have ever had to write. If love alone could sustain us, I would lock the door, crawl into bed with you, and never leave that place. This is not the way it is in the world. I have a life outside of "us" that is normal and peaceful. Your life is so violent, and I am afraid to be around it, much less be a part of it.

I wondered if I was cut out to be with a police officer. It seemed so unlike me, but I was blinded by love. Then all of these tragic things happened, and at first I thought I could handle it, but after watching it all laid out on the television, I realized I can't handle it. I do not have what it takes to give you what you need.

I am sorry I couldn't face you with this, but I am not strong like you. I have moved my things. Please don't try to reach me. I need some time away from you to sort out my feelings and my fears.

You need help John. "A terrorist tried to kill me in our driveway." Do you know how that sounds to people? My professor and my friends are afraid for me. They can't believe that you can't see this aberration is a sign that you need help.

This is all the harder because I still love you and think I always will.

Please get some help John.

Stella

John placed the letter back in the envelope and got up. He walked over to the garbage and dropped it in.

"Wow, that bad?" Ryan asked.

"That bad. You know I have seen my buddies in the service get "Dear John" letters and it just tore them apart. I always wondered how it felt, and now and I know. It feels like... I had this good buddy Chase in my unit. We were friends like you and I. We got into this ambush and, during the fight, I just happened to be looking at him when he got hit. He slumped to the ground and died. That was the worst feeling I ever had in my life. It felt like something died inside of me with him. That's how it feels right now," explained John.

"Are you going to be all right, buddy?" Ryan asked not knowing what else to say.

"I remember thinking when Chase got hit that I had to keep going. People needed me. I didn't quit then, and I'm not going to quit now," he said with pretend determination. That would have to do until he could manage to conjure up the real thing. "When Chase went down, he never got up again. Stella's just on the other side of town somewhere. I'll give her some time. She'll come around. Anyway, it might be best if I am by myself right now."

"Hey, you're not by yourself. What am I, a blow up doll?" Ryan asked indignantly.

John looked Ryan up and down slowly and said, "If you are I'm hitting deflate and you're going right back in the box cuz I want my money back," said John.

"Hey that was unnecessarily unkind. By the way, since we are both off tonight and I am now properly hydrated, I'll take that beer," said Ryan holding his hand out urgently hand like a baby demanding its bottle.

"Now you're talking." John got up and went to the refrigerator, opened two bottles, and took a drink out of one. He handed the other to Ryan who wiped the top with his shirt and took a swig. "Hey, shut the door to the fridge, John. I want to make sure you keep his friends cold for me," barked Ryan with sincere concern.

Laughing, John shut the door to the fridge, and they sauntered their way into the living room swigging their drinks. While John dropped into the couch, putting his feet up on the coffee table, Ryan sat in the recliner and leaned back to pop up the foot rest. "This is the life: feet up, beer in my hand, and no women, sitting with my buddy with nothing to do. Who else has it so good? No one has it better," concluded Ryan.

"I disagree, what about firemen?" answered John. "Granted, they can't drink beer when they are sitting in recliners with their buddies, no women, with nothing to do, but they are generously compensated for not being allowed to drink beer," explained John.

"So that's why firemen get paid. They get paid to not drink beer. I did not know that," said Ryan sounding enlightened. "Do you know the fireman's credo?" Ryan asked.

"No, tell me," said John.

'We sleep 'til we're hungry and eat 'til we're tired.' Here's to firemen." said Ryan, as he lifted his bottle to offer a toast.

"May they never suffer from chronic tennis elbow from excessively polishing their own poles," added John.

"Nor carpal tunnel syndrome," added Ryan. With that, they drank and laughed at the expense of every cop's arch-rival, the firemen.

When John went to the kitchen to get Ryan another beer, he returned with Stella's letter. He handed Ryan the beer, sat back on the couch, put his feet up, and opened the letter, "You know, Stella's upset because she believed a lie. The truth got run over by a train, but it's still the truth."

Ryan took a drink of his beer and added, "She's confused now and she will be back when she learns the truth."

"It does sound a little crazy you know," said John.

"What's that?" Ryan asked reading the contents on the label of his beer.

"That a guy named Ahmed from Iraq would try to kill me in my driveway in La Crosse, Wisconsin. How could I have expected her to believe such a thing? It doesn't compute hardly to me, but I know what I saw and I know it was him," said John.

"If he'd have done it, it would have been the perfect crime, because no one would have figured it out," said Ryan.

"Two things I am sure of," said John.

"What's that?" Ryan asked as he took a drink.

"Number one thing I am sure of is when the truth comes out I will get Stella back. The second thing I am sure of is I am going to meet that son of a bitch Ahmed again," declared John.

"You think so?" Ryan asked.

"I know so. I can feel it in my bones. The next time we meet no one is running off in their underwear," said John seriously.

Ryan said, "You wanna know something? I don't know what that means, and I do not know if I want to ask," puzzled Ryan.

Then John, who was three beers ahead of Ryan, smiled boyishly and held up the letter, "Lookee here."

"What's that, Johnny?" said Ryan matching his smile, without knowing why.

"It says she loves me, and do you know what else she said?"

"What's that?" Ryan asked.

"See," he said pointing and tapping repeatedly at the letter, "It says it right here. I'm still her Dear John."

CHAPTER TWENTY-FIVE

Matter of Time

It had been a quiet first night so far. It was just what John needed to get his rhythm back. He had made some stops, wrote a couple of traffic tickets, and handed out a couple of warnings. He had pulled the doors on his beat and found an open door at the Freight House restaurant. It was a nineteenth century railroad station turned into a restaurant, and he had eaten the best steak of his life there the week before Stella left.

Everything checked out, and after seeing the condition of the kitchen, he decided he would eat there again. The food and service was great and the kitchen was as clean and shiny as a glacier after a snow fall. Nothing smelled better to John than a great steak restaurant two hours after closing time.

The rest of the night drifted along as if every criminal, drug dealer, and wife beater just took the night off. Finally, "234," said the dispatcher.

"Go ahead," said John. He looked at the time. He thought, *it is ten minutes before quitting time so this call must be really hot or really not hot to give it to me.*

"Check Riverside Park for a white male in his 50s running his dog without a leash," the dispatcher said without an ounce of emotion.

"Not hot," said John out loud to himself and then he keyed the mic, "10-4 dispatch, is there a named complainant?" asked John.

"The complainant is anonymous. He says it's a small white hairy dog that looks like Benji," said the dispatcher, this time with a hint of "can you believe this bullshit?" in the subtext.

"10-4. I am 10-23," said John over the mic.

As John turned into the park, he gazed once again, amazed, at the huge wrought iron eagle at the park's entrance. John circled the park and saw a man running on the sidewalk paralleling the Mississippi River. He had the slim but muscular build of a man training for the iron man rather than the anorexic look of a marathon devotee. The dog was a small ball of fur that did not have a leash, but he ran along-side the runner as if he was leashed. Parking the squad strategically so the runner would have to pass him, John got out and waited. As the runner approached, John asked, "Good morning, sir. Can I speak to you a minute?"

Smiling, the man, who had a good sweat going, stopped and said, "Certainly, Officer, but this is going to mess up a world-record time for me," he said pushing a button on his watch.

"Ark, Ark!" agreed the little white mutt.

"Leave it, Tigger!" said the runner, and the dog sat.

"What kind of dog is that? John asked.

"It's a Schnoodle. That's half Schnauser and half Poodle. They used to call that a mutt, and you would get them from a kid with a boxful of them down on some corner for free. Now they call them a hybrid and charge you $400. What a racket." The runner looked at the dog and said, "Right, Tigger?"

"Ark!" replied Tigger on cue.

"Cute as heck," said John, "Can I pet him?"

"Sure. He'd probably get into the squad car and go home with you, if I let him. He loves everyone."

John crouched down to pat the dog's head, and Tigger jumped up putting his front white paws on John's shoulder and licked his face. The dog's coat had a soothing effect on John as he petted the dog, for it felt like an old comfortable sweater. "Boy, look at those cute eyes."

"Yeah I call him my little black eyed pee-er," said the runner.

John laughed and stood up. "That's good."

"Thanks, I try," said the runner.

"Well, the reason I stopped you today—we actually got a complaint about you running the dog without a leash, sir," said John.

"Well, technically, that's not true, Officer," said the runner with a smile.

"How is that?" said John, returning the smile but not knowing exactly why.

"Well if I was running the dog, I would need to have a leash on him, but you see, the dog is running me and that's the truth, and I am not required to have a leash on me," said the runner, whose smile held fast on his face.

"The dog is running you?" asked John.

"Yes. You see, it barks in the morning, and I have to get up and it takes me for a run. I pick up its dog crap and it doesn't even flush for me. I have to feed it when it tells me to and get it water when it tells me to. Whenever we go somewhere, I always have to drive and it never even offers. So, Officer, I do not take this dog anywhere. You see it takes me and I am not required to have a leash. Right, Tigger?" asked the runner.

"Ark!" agreed Tigger.

John laughed and shook his head. "You should take this show on the road."

"You think?" the runner asked.

"Yes, indeed. I am going to get a legal opinion on this, and in the meantime I am going to give you a verbal warning and let you go on your way," said John.

"Did you hear that, Tigger? He bought it."

"Ark!" Tigger approved in disbelief.

"We dodged a bullet—no leash and no ticket. Are you happy?" asked the runner, who turned and faced Tigger who began jumping and barking each time the runner repeated, "Are you Happy? Are You Happy? Are you Happy?" The dog easily reached a height of five feet on each bounce, and after the dog finished its show, the runner hit the button on his watch and was running again. He shouted back at John, "and that's why we named him Tigger."

"I understand. I am telling you, all you need is a circus, a big tent, and a clown car and you'd have yourself a show," John called to the runner.

"Ark, Ark!" agreed Tigger.

"He says he can't talk now he has to take me for my run," answered the runner.

As John turned from 4th Street into the parking lot of the police department, he keyed the mic and said, "Dispatch, I am 10-8 with a verbal warning and will be 10-42 (ending tour of duty)."

Thirty minutes later as John lay down in his bed, he said a silent prayer to himself, "Dear God, thank you for this night. This was just what I hoped for and just what I needed. It was perfect. There was nothing hot, nothing heavy, I was just back; that's all. Thank you, Dear Lord. Oh yeah, and if you can see your way to sending Stella back in my direction, I'd appreciate it. Amen. Now I'm ready for anything. Bring it on!"

He closed his eyes and then looked up and said, "That last part wasn't a part of the prayer, Lord. That was just a little bit of military OOAHH. You don't have to feel obliged to bring it on." He then closed his eyes and was asleep in sixty seconds.

———◦○◦———

The ringing phone shook John out of a deep sleep. He turned to look at the clock. Although it said 10:00 AM, it was actually his 3:00 AM night-worker sleep time. John fumbled the phone, dropped it, picked it up, and answered with a raspy, "Hello."

"Did I wake you up?" asked the voice on the other end.

"No. I was just um. Uh…"

"Liar! I hope you don't do that under oath. Good morning, John, this is Chief Sherman," said the hurried-sounding voice on the other end, which caused John to sit straight up in bed and wake up instantaneously.

"Yes sir, Chief. I mean, no sir, Chief Sherman. I was sleeping. I just was…" and John's mind went blank. He had nothing.

The chief rescued John by picking up the conversational ball and running straight up the middle with it. "I am re-assigning you to assist Special

Agent Martel on his investigation. This is classified. You will have full powers as long as you are working under his direction. It will be plain clothes until further notice. You are the only one in this country who has seen this Ahmed character, and I do not know what he is planning, but the FBI want him pretty badly.

"You will be on duty eight hours a day, and if you accumulate overtime send it through my office. My secretary will do your payroll, and I will approve your overtime. How does that sound? Is that agreeable to you? This is voluntary duty even though it sounds like an order. You can turn it down." After the pitch was completed, Chief paused for an answer, knowing full well what the answer would be.

"No, sir, I mean, yes sir, I do want the assignment. When should I...," but John failed to complete the sentence, before the Chief was running again.

"Don't worry about that. Martel will probably call you before you get a chance to shit, shower, and shave, so go ahead and try. I dare you," said the Chief.

"Yes, sir," said John.

"How are you weathering the storm?" asked the Chief with sincerity.

"It was great to get back to work last night. As far as all the negative reporting, I am hanging in there," said John, who sounded weathered.

"Well, son, you can't change a baby's diapers without getting a little poop on your fingers once in a while. The media are like a baby. Not just any baby, though. They are like a colicky baby. You ever had a colicky baby?" the chief asked.

"No sir. I don't have any children, someday I hope..." was all the chief had time to listen to if he listened at all.

"Don't wish that on yourself, John. You don't want a colicky baby. They do six things for almost three straight months. It's terrible," said the Chief. "They poop, they pee, they eat, rarely sleep, but mostly they whine, they cry, and they scream. Damn, I think that's seven. The only thing that shuts them up is to feed them something, and when you feed them something inevitably it disagrees with them and then they whine, they cry, and they scream. My point is, John, it is my job to satisfy the screaming and crying baby. The Bible says, 'this too shall pass.' Pay no attention to the screaming of the media. I'll handle them. The truth will come out, and when it does, the shit the colicky baby media are shitting is going to get shoved right back up their asses. I can't wait!" the chief said with almost gleeful anticipation.

John stayed silent through the pause, a bit troubled by the picture conjured up by the chief's analogy.

The chief continued, "We are proud of you, son. You will get through and beyond this. Trust me," assured the chief.

"Thank you, sir. That means a lot," said John.

"Don't mention it. When one of my officers is in the right, I will back them up all the way to hell and back. This time, damn it to hell, John, you are in the right!

"Now back to your assignment. Special Agent Martel believes this Ahmed is up to something very big. He thinks you can help them, and I believe you will. While you are at it, take some notes from Martel. I hear he's good at what he does. Now go out and get that son of a bitch," the chief challenged and hung up.

John was wide awake and shot with adrenaline. He snatched the remote phone and tried to shit, shower, and shave before Martel called, but halfway through his shave the phone rang, "Hello."

"Is this John Savage?" The voice asked.

"Yes it is," answered John, "Special Agent Martel?"

"You guessed it. Call me Charlie since we are going to be working together. Did the chief fill you in?" Martel asked, already knowing the answer.

"Yes, sir, he did," answered John.

"You can leave out the sir. My father was sir. Like I said, call me Charlie. Do you know where the FBI office is downtown?" asked Martel.

"Yes I do," answered John.

"Do you have a plain clothes rig for your weapon, handcuffs, and such?" Martel asked.

"Yes I do."

"Gear up with your vest and dress like you're going to a ball game or something. Wear something that allows you to blend in, but you can still run and fight in," said Martel. "Pack a bag for a few days. Are you able to do that?"

"I can do that," answered John genuinely excited.

"Can you be down here in an hour?"

"Yes, sir, I mean, sure, Charlie," said John.

"See you then. Do you have any questions?" Martel asked.

"No. I'll be there in an hour."

It was summer, so John dressed exactly like he was going to a ball game. The hard thing was choosing the right jersey. He grabbed an old Cubby's Jersey that he had for years. His dad got it for him when Sammy Sosa and Mark McGwire were chasing the home run record, and it was much too big for him then, but now it fit him just right. He put a Cubs hat on, and the Sosa shirt served to conceal his vest, Glock, spare magazines, and handcuffs. He grabbed a stinger flashlight pen and pocket notebook and dropped them into the side pockets of his pants. He looked at himself in the mirror for a quick assessment. Then he turned his hat backwards. "There."

John gazed upon the crucifix he had hanging on his bedroom wall, then turned his head to the heavens and said out loud, "I guess I better be careful what I pray for. This is my fault for saying bring it on!" As John headed out to his car, he smiled thinking, *This is a good sign the big guy upstairs was listening. Now I know I'm getting Stella back. It's just a matter of time.*

CHAPTER TWENTY-SIX

Allah

As John walked into the office, Charles Martel was waiting and greeted John with, "Good, let's go. I will fill you in on the way."

As the two hit Interstate 90 heading east, Martel said, "Well, John, here's the deal. We absolutely want to take this guy alive if possible. Do you think that's possible?"

"I believe so. When I first met him, he could have gone to Allah if he wanted, but instead he gave this bull shit story about hating Saddam and loving America. He ripped off his clothes and ran away in his underwear. He did that all to stay alive. He is not a suicidal jihadist. He is a homicidal jihadist. I found out later the weapon he had in his hand had just killed the best friend I ever had."

"I do not mean to be critical, but tell me once again how he got away, if you don't mind my asking?" Martel asked.

"My unit didn't know I had taken the position and fired a volley from a grenade launcher, and I decided to hit the dirt rather than die from friendly fire. After the grenade hit and I was able to call for a cease fire, Ahmed was gone," explained John. "I'll never know if I would have shot him running away in his underwear or not. The grenade made that a moot point."

"Son of bitch, that bastard is lucky…. and in your driveway? How did he manage to survive that night?"

"I had just put my weapon away and remembered I had left something in the car. I got out into the driveway and surprised him. When he tried to shoot me his weapon malfunctioned. I am thinking he was carrying Israeli style, with the chamber empty, and squeezed the trigger on an empty chamber. The funny part was I reacted by reaching for my gun but realized it was not there. He reacted to my drawing movement, panicked, and ran for his life like a frightened doe. Ahmed has a healthy fear of death. I could see it in his eyes. I believe he can be taken alive if we surprise him and have a superior tactical position," said John assertively. "Do you know where he is?" John asked.

"We know where somebody is. We received intelligence about the location of a man believed to be an Al-Qaeda operative. Intelligence gurus think he may be Ahmed. There is a combined local and FBI SWAT team ready to move. They have some shots of him coming and going. I have you for two reasons. Number one, you can confirm it without us having to go through all the DNA bullshit. Number two, we are very limited in what we can do to insure cooperation. We think just seeing you will loosen his lips," explained Martel.

"You think?" John asked.

"Yeah, his bowels too I think. I am certain of it. At the very least we can threaten to put together a press release about how he ran away from you in his underwear screaming... what was he was saying?"

"He was screaming God Bless America," answered John.

"A threat to release that story to the Arab World would work better than water-boarding," supposed Martel. "By the way, water-boarding isn't an option anymore, just so you know."

"I will just take that tool right out of my tool box," said John sarcastically.

On the ride, John and got to know each other. Martel was married to his work. He was a rabid Green Bay Packer fan and tepid Milwaukee Brewers fan, but he liked watching the games at Miller Park. He was not military but was a long-time veteran of the Federal Bureau of Investigation and a former member of the Hostage Rescue Team. He had experienced the thrill of victory at the Talladega Prison siege but was still processing the agony of defeat at the Waco siege. "Some experts believed if we pressured Koresh he would surrender. There were other experts that adamantly felt a move would trigger a local apocalypse. There was political pressure from the very top to choose to believe the former, and history says the latter experts were right. You never get the smell of burning flesh out of your nose. It haunts my dreams," said Martel, obviously troubled.

"Has anyone ever told you how to tame your dreams?" John asked.

"Tame my dreams? No," asked Martel with interest.

"Yeah tame your dreams. In Iraq I had this buddy named Balduzzi..." and the skill of dream taming was passed once again from warrior to warrior as it had been for centuries.

The rest of the trip flew by—a ride shared no longer by an FBI Special Agent and La Crosse Police Officer. It was shared by two men who became, quite instantaneously, friends. Unknown to Charlie and John, their ancestors had bonded after a battle toast over a fire over 1000 years earlier. Fate set them on a collision course with history long before either of them were born.

Martel and Savage arrived at the command post at 6:30 PM. The captain began, "I'm Captain Hartwig, officer in charge of the team. The suspect is at the residence. We do not believe there is anyone in there with him right now. The perimeter is sealed, and we have a no-knock warrant. The entry team is on the move right as we speak, so stand-by,"

"I'm Special Agent Martel. On the move now? Got it," said Martel and he slipped his hands into his raid jacket pocket, crossed his fingers and took a deep breath.

The entry team was stacked in a line, and with the tap up they were on the move. When they reached the door of the single dwelling, the breacher quietly moved forward and aimed his breaching gun at the door between the door handle and the jamb and fired, "Bam Chick-Chack Bam, Chick-Chack," blowing the lock out with the two shots of frangible rounds. Without hesitation, the door was kicked open and the breacher spun out of the way as the entry team streamed through the door and flowed into the apartment shouting in unison, "Police Search Warrant! Don't Move."

As a team member moved into a hallway, he turned left and saw an athletically built Arab male seated, stunned on a couch, watching CBN News. He was barefoot, wearing tan slacks and a white T-shirt with no sleeves. He stood up and put his hands up for a moment, then spun and ran toward the rear of the home.

"Contact! He's moving toward the bedroom!" The team leader shouted as he moved after the suspect. The leader, who was armed with a Benelli M-I Tactical Shotgun, focused on the hands and saw the suspect had a cell phone in his hand and his thumb was moving in what appeared to be a practiced manner, like a professional stenographer taking a letter from the boss.

The suspect ran into the bedroom and dropped the cell phone. *Bomb,* thought the team leader as he followed the suspect.

As the Arab man reached the bureau on the opposite wall of the bedroom, his movements seemed to slow down dramatically. The team leader's vision focused, as if suddenly he was looking through a peep hole in the door. The Arab man pulled the top drawer of the dresser open and the team leader shouted, "Gun!"

The suspect had a black semi automatic handgun in his right hand and he spun as he shouted, "Allahu Akbar!"

"Boom, Boom, Boom, Boom!"

"Shots fired! Shots fired!" crackled the transmission followed by an eerie white noise.

"What? Who?" said Captain Hartwig asked, hoping for clarification.

"Suspect's down. We are all OK. This is an officer involved shooting scene. Lock it down. Ambulance is not needed. The suspect is 10-100." (Deceased).

An hour after the shooting, John was taken into the apartment. He was wearing booties, a face mask, and gloves as he was led to the body of the suspect. John found that all four 12 gauge slugs of the team leader had taken out the heart and both lungs of the suspect, whose gun was still lying next to the body. The suspect's eyes were locked open.

The investigator at the scene said, "The look on his face looks like he's saying, 'What do you mean no virgins?' Get it?" The investigator laughed, but received no reaction. It was the seventh time he had told the joke and he complained, "Come on, that's funny. Why am I the only one who sees that is fucking hilarious?"

John missed the joke and ignored the question because he was intensely concentrating on the suspect's face. Death had distorted the features of the man lying below him, but even so, John only needed a few seconds to be certain and he turned to Martel saying, "That's not him."

"Damn!" Martel said.

"Do we know who he is?" Martel asked Captain Hartwig.

"We know who he said he was. He said he was a tire salesman named Rashid, but I'm certain that is not who he was. We have a team cordoning off a storage unit a mile from here, and they have called for the bomb unit. A guy named Felix is here, says he's with you and has taken the cell phone. Our man saw the suspect frantically punching in a text message, and after it was sent Rashid went for the gun," said Hartwig.

"Felix will mine the phone and get the gold for us. There has to be something there for us to use. It was his last act in life, before he chose death. If there is anything there that we can follow-up on, Felix will find it," said Martel.

"Who is Felix?" John asked.

"Felix is… that is difficult to explain. There will come a time, possibly, that you may get the opportunity to meet Felix. He's easier to explain once you meet him and even more so after you experience his capabilities. Roughly, he is a techno-geek that hits the recovered technology hard and fast, so information is immediately available at scenes. Felix is the magician assigned to work with me on my cases."

"With one piece of technology, Felix can take a dead case and give you more leads than you have time to follow up on in a lifetime. Felix can do that and more. He will look at 1000 possibilities and whittle them down to one or two that are the most viable. He has… talents. I think Rashid knew Ahmed and was in contact with him. They are placed too close together not to be working together. I think that phone in the hands of Felix will lead us to Ahmed," said Martel.

"So you think we will find out where he is." said John.

"No. We will find out where he was, not where is. I am sure that as we speak Ahmed knows something is up and is on the move," said Martel. "When Felix contacted me, he said the last message this suspect sent was

1-5-5-1-4. That's it. It has to be a code to run, abort, shit and get off the pot. Felix will figure out what it means, where it was sent, and where the phone is that it was sent to," said Martel.

"How long will that take?" Hartwig asked.

"It will trickle back to us, but I am guessing it will be 12 hours at the most," said Martel.

"You need to find a hotel in Rockford for the night?" Hartwig wondered.

"Yeah, I think so. If we don't hear back in the next hour I will get with you about that. Thanks," said Martel.

"I think I can decode your message for you," said John. He had his phone out and was looking curiously at the touch pad.

"Really? I'd like to see that. What does it mean, Sherlock?" Martel asked skeptically.

"1-5-5-1-4?" John said with certainty. "He just told someone who his next contact would be."

"Yeah. That would be very helpful. Who would that be?" Martel asked registering skepticism.

John looked up from his phone and soberly said, "Allah."

CHAPTER TWENTY-SEVEN

Coyotes and the Crows

Ahmed sat down to a candlelight dinner prepared by Lara. The table was set, the candles were flickering invitingly, and the aroma of Lara's special meal permeated throughout the house, making it feel like a home. "What is this surprise dish that you have prepared for us tonight?" asked Ahmed.

"It is a new recipe I got from one of my friends at school. I hope you like it. It is vegetarian lasagna," she said as she set the dish down on the table. "It needs to set for a few minutes, though. I just took it out of the oven."

Just as the dish touched the table, Ahmed's phone vibrated. Lara noticed that his demeanor turned immediately from delighted, to dour, then ominously to fearful. Ahmed knew only one person had the number for this phone. The call had to be from Rashid.

Ahmed stood up, quickly, knocking his chair over backward and nearly toppling the candles as he went into the bedroom. He tugged the phone desperately out of his pocket and checked the screen. The message was 1-5-5-1-4, Allah. His stomach felt as if a booming firework had gone off in it.

Ahmed was stunned for a moment, but after he recovered he was the picture of frenetic movement. He unlocked the bedroom closet and pulled out the black Hockey duffel. He unzipped the side pocket and pulled out the holstered Glock 17 and attached the holster to his belt. He threw on his Badger Hockey hooded sweatshirt and pulled the sweatshirt over his handgun. Then he began turning off lights throughout the house. "What is going on?" Lara asked, but no response was forthcoming.

When all the lights were out, Ahmed went to each window and carefully lifted each curtain while he peered outside and scanned the area for police. There was nothing out of sorts up and down Mifflin Street. The scene looked serene on all sides, in all directions. "I still have time," he said out loud, but to himself.

"Time for what; what is going on?" asked Lara near tears, "You're scaring me."

Ahmed suddenly became aware of Lara's presence again. "Do you love me?" Ahmed asked.

"Yes. Of course I love you. What is going on?" she asked again.

"If you really love me, then you must trust me and do what I ask. I will tell you everything, but we must leave this place before I can take the time to explain," said Ahmed while still on the move. He figured he had time to do some things. If they had known about Ahmed also, he would already be in custody or dead. That meant they only knew of Rashid. Eventually they would find him if he stayed here. He had to assume that, but he still had time.

"I want you to get some water and Mr. Clean. I want you to scrub, quickly, every surface we have touched. Wear gloves. What you need is prepared under the kitchen sink. I want you to dust every wooden surface with Pledge. Do it quickly, thoroughly, and do it now. I will pack," Ahmed was moving again. "Lara move!" Lara immediately began to move as if the house was ablaze and she needed to clean it up before the firemen arrived.

Ahmed pulled out two empty hockey bags, and in a matter of minutes they were packed and he carried them immediately out to the car. When he came back in, he was gratified to see that Lara was moving with the same urgency. He watched for a moment and observed that Lara's efforts were thorough enough that it would be difficult to pick up comparable prints. "Get all the hair out of the drains and around the toilets. This place must be beyond spotless," shouted Ahmed. *Keep her busy*, he thought.

He then unzipped the hockey bag and made certain the uniform, cast, plastic explosives, ammo, and identification were there. He pulled out the identification for Robert Margolis and slipped it into his wallet. He removed everything out of his wallet that showed his current Ahmed alias and placed them in the identification packet. He would destroy it later. Then he zipped everything back up and hauled the heavy bag out to the car and set it carefully in the trunk.

It was ten minutes since Rashid had warned him. He wondered if Rashid was with the police, talking, or if he was with Allah. "Allah, please grant Rashid a martyr's death. Accept him into your bosom." Ahmed grabbed Lara's purse, and with a gloved hand removed the wallet and set it on the bureau next to the bed.

Ahmed then called into the bathroom, "Lara that is good enough. You have done well. We must go. Come with me and I will tell you everything. You can get your things later if you choose to go with me," he called to her as he took her jacket from the closet, holding it in the hand which held her purse. He then hurried into the bathroom.

Lara looked up from the tub and said, "But what is going on Ahmed?"

"Come with me, my dear, and I will explain everything. We do not have time, though. We must go," and Ahmed took her by her yellow, rubber-gloved hand and helped her up. She took off her gloves and dropped them in the pail. Ahmed placed her jacket over her shoulders and kissed her on the cheek as he handed her the purse.

"There is no time to explain now. We must go. They are coming." She melted. It was as if she was Lara to his Zhivago and they were fleeing the Bolsheviks. She had been programmed as a child to follow this man. Ahmed was in every way her beautiful, loving Zhivago. He swept her out of the bathroom, turned and, after wiping the phone vigorously, placed it down on the top of the toilet and followed Lara out of the house.

In minutes they were on East Washington Avenue with the State Capitol Building looming in their rearview mirror. Ahmed drove silently for over an hour. He left Madison Westbound on Interstate 90 and turned North on Interstate 39. The roads from there were a blur to Lara. Her mind was racing, and it was all headlights, bucolic towns with strange Indian names, and an occasional darting deer or waddling raccoon crossing the highways in front of her. Finally, Ahmed took an exit marked Endeavor.

"Endeavor?" asked Lara.

"Trust me, my love," was Ahmed's answer.

The highway he turned onto seemed to lead to nowhere, when, suddenly, Ahmed turned off the road onto a dirt path formed and rutted by farm equipment. The car bounced wildly as Ahmed shut down his headlights and seemed to navigate by radar, because Lara could see nothing. Her special evening had turned into a headlong flight to nowhere. The love she felt was replaced with fear. As the car came to a sudden stop, fear was quickly replaced by sheer terror. "What is happening?" cried Lara.

"Do not be afraid, my darling. I have stopped to explain all this to you. We are safe now," Ahmed said in a soothing voice, which served to alleviate her fears ever so slightly.

"You are scaring me," Lara said.

"There is nothing for you to be afraid of, my darling. I am the one they are after, not you. You deserve an explanation, and I will tell you everything as I promised." Ahmed opened the door and stepped out of the car and said, "Come, Lara. I will explain all this to you."

Lara sat for a moment then reluctantly opened the door and got out. Ahmed walked to the front of the car and sat on the hood. He motioned for her to sit beside him.

Lara climbed up next to him, and Ahmed kissed her. "You see, Lara. I love you. This is not about you. This is about me. I, Lara… am a warrior of Allah who has fallen in love with a daughter of my enemy."

"Warrior of Allah? What does that mean?" Lara asked relieved by the kiss and his blatant honesty.

"In your country you would call me a terrorist or a radical jihadist. In my country I am a warrior. I am a hero. They sing songs about me and paint murals to my exploits. Warriors in your country who have served your Uncle Sam as I have served Allah would receive medals for such exploits, but in my country I must wait for my just rewards, which I will receive in the next life. I have been sent here on a very important mission. My friend Rashid has contacted me and warned me to meet him here. He will be here shortly, and I want you to come with me. It will be a dangerous but exciting life. Eventually we will return to my country and we will live there for all of our lives."

"My name is not Ahmed Wahabi. I am Ahmed Abdullah Rahim. My father is a rich man, and I have given up riches to fight. You are the love of my life. I was not supposed to find you here, but I have. I have taken you as my Nikah al-Mutʻah. I want you to become my wife, but this must be your choice. I must ask you now. Will you come with me, share the dangers and the rewards of this life, and be my wife, or will you choose to leave now?" asked Ahmed.

"I can leave now? How can I leave you?" Lara asked, while her lips quivered as if the temperature had dropped suddenly to freezing.

"As I said, Rashid will be meeting me here in a very short time. I will unload the car here and give you the keys and you may leave. Rashid will pick me up and you may return home. If you choose to stay, we will wait for Rashid and leave with him when he comes. This must be your choice. I will not force you to come with me," said Ahmed.

Lara searched Ahmed's handsome brown eyes looking for some hint of betrayal and she only saw love. Finally she gave her answer, "Ahmed, I love you, but this is all too much for me. I can't live like this," she answered.

"I understand," said Ahmed. He jumped down from the hood and circled the car, unlocked the trunk and unloaded it. "You may take the car, Lara," said Ahmed. He opened the back door, pulled the hockey duffels out and carried them to the front of the car.

"Are you sure Rashid will find you here? This is pretty remote," said Lara.

"Yes. This was pre-arranged and he has a GPS. He will find me. Please do not call the police. By the time they contact you, I will be far away. They eventually will come to you," said Ahmed.

"What shall I tell them?" asked Lara.

"Tell them the truth. They will already know who I am, but they will not know who I will be. I will be impossible for them to find. You cannot hurt me by telling the truth, but you will hurt yourself by trying to lie. I can't bear to have my beloved Nikah al-Mutʻah hurt in any way." He then brushed her hair from her eyes and kissed her warmly.

The kiss was long and sweet and chased all the needless fear from Lara's heart. This man loved her. He would never harm her. She knew that now. *I hope I have made the right decision*, she thought.

"Good-bye, my dear Ahmed," said Lara. "Be safe. I will never forget you."

"Good-bye, my dearest Lara. We will be together again someday. I feel it," he reached into his pocket, fumbled about and said, "Now leave quickly. This is too painful. Here are the keys." He pulled the keys out of his pocket and the ring of keys slipped from his hands and twirled to the ground, "Oh I am so sorry."

Lara tried to catch them but missed and bent down to pick them up.

The draw was cat-like, practiced. Ahmed pulled his Glock from his holster and moved it quickly to within one inch of her ear. Lara sensed the movement and began to turn.

"Bam!" The noise was swallowed by the indifferent night sky as Ahmed's Nikah al-Mut'ah crumpled lifelessly to the ground.

Ahmed stood over his beloved Lara for a moment, to grieve for the loss of the love of his life. "I loved you, Lara. I wanted you to have a choice. I offered you a life with me and you rejected it. You must understand at that point you became dangerous to the success of my mission. I could not let you leave. This mission is more important than two insignificant people, even if they share a significant love. I pray that you are in Allah's hands. I pray to Allah that when my journey on Earth ends and I join him that you will be my reward for my life of service. What I have done I have done for Allah. Allahu Akbar!"

Ahmed lowered himself to a knee and brushed Lara's blonde hair from her face. Her face gave no hint of her violent death. Her persona bore the essence of the beautiful dreamer. Ahmed sighed, feeling deeply for his loss. He checked for a pulse and found none. "Good, a second shot would have been even more difficult for me," he said out loud to himself. He snatched the keys lying beside her. *Perfect diversion*, he thought. *She never saw it coming. It was all I could do for her.*

With the keys recovered, Ahmed quickly carried the bags back to the car and loaded them into the trunk refusing to look again on the lifeless form of the one who dared to love him with all her heart.

Ultimately Lara's mother was proved, wrong. She had said, "Love is, little bits of joy floating on an ocean of tears." Lara's love brought her great joy from the moment she met Ahmed until that love and her life were extinguished in an unseen flash in the darkness. Her remarkable love inspired no ocean of tears. In fact, it ended without a single tear shed for her lost love…her lost life.

Ahmed's eyes were dry as he drove away, with the beautiful, tender Lara left alone to the un-tender mercies of the coyotes and the crows.

CHAPTER TWENTY-EIGHT

Proceed with Caution

Martel and Savage were having breakfast in the hotel restaurant when Martel reached for his phone, looked at the caller ID, and answered, "Martel here."

John finished sopping up his last bit of egg yolk and popped the toast into his mouth. He sensed they would be leaving.

"No shit," said Martel. "Hold on, let me get a pen." He began fumbling for a pen as John laid one down in front of him and slipped opened his notebook in front of Martel. Martel picked up the pen and said, "Go ahead."

Martel wrote feverishly as he chirped, "Got it... hm-hm...yeah...that sounds good...yeah. Have Hartwig notify Madison P.D. and tell them we're on the way. Give them this number and tell them when they assign a commander to have him call me immediately. Thanks."

Martel motioned to the waitress as he threw cash down on the table. He took one last sip of his coffee and said, "We're out of here."

John was already heading for the door.

Once in the car John asked, "I am guessing we have a lead?"

"Yup. That was Felix. Working on the cell phone and the registration plate on Rashid's car, he was able to get a location for us. A parking ticket was issued in the same spot as the GPS location of the Allah-phone in Madison," said Martel.

"Wow. You can do that?" asked John.

"Not me. Felix. This investigation has top priority," said Martel as he drove through an I-Pass lane on the toll-way.

"Why have they still not released the photo of Ahmed?" asked John.

"That's Homeland Security's call. Since you are my partner now, I am going to tell it to you straight. The political influences in law enforcement are like a rat. When you are doing your job in a municipal agency, you know you have rats, but you rarely see them. So you go about your daily business unperturbed. In a sheriff's department, the rat makes itself visible every once in a while, and you find it disconcerting when it shows up in the kitchen and scares your wife and kids. At the state level, the rats are crawling around at the table every time you come home at the end of the day and they are hesitant to leave even when you run around yelling and waving your arms. At the federal level the rats are chewing constantly on your left arm, and if you want to survive you have to learn how to work and make do with your right arm while the rat is dangling from your left. Rats being rats, they think they are the most important part of the operation. They don't even see themselves as obstructions much less the pariahs they are." He then turned toward John and asked, "You with me so far?"

"I'm with you," replied John, "Rats."

"Well as bad as it was in the FBI, it has somehow become worse... wait, you have to agree that this is between me and my partner. It goes nowhere else. Do you agree?"

"Yes. I agree. It's just between you and me. It goes in one ear and not even out the other, because I will take to the grave with me," promised John.

"Good. I believe you. As bad as it was in the FBI, somehow it has gotten worse since Homeland Security joined the fray. They see threats differently than you and I. They seem to me to be more about protecting a political power base than protecting the lives and lifestyles of the American people. This case is an example," explained Martel.

"How is that?" asked John.

"You have asked why haven't we released Ahmed's photo nation-wide. There is one reason. The rat chewing on my arm will not allow me to do so. The rat calls the shots. The rat is…" the answer stuck in Martel's throat, fearful of the consequences if John was to ever tell anyone he said it.

"In Homeland Security," said John.

"You said it. I didn't," said Martel.

"I said it, you didn't," agreed John.

"The prearranged answer, if the decision is ever questioned, will be that Ahmed's appearance has changed so much it would not have been helpful," said Martel. "Therefore, releasing the photo would only serve notice to Ahmed and he would have burrowed out of sight."

"The eyes have not changed," said John.

"It doesn't matter. The truth is that the people calling the shots are listening to the people above them. These are the same people who have declared that the war on terror must never be called a war. Our enemy can never be identified in terms that would in any way injure, harm, offend, disenfranchise, or cause minor indigestion in anyone who is Muslim. If we release a picture of this person before we have DNA to prove that he is actually in this country, it might cause someone to call the police on someone else. They are concerned someone who looks like Ahmed will be needlessly harassed. To them that is more dangerous than injury Ahmed might inflict," explained Martel.

"That is the thinking of people who have never had someone try to shoot, stab, or blow them up," said John.

"Yeah, and they are the same people who go ballistic if the maid does not put the right brand of chocolates on their pillow at their four star hotel. Or is it five star, which one is the best?" asked Martel.

"I don't know. I've never been to a five star hotel," said John with a shrug, "I did stay a few nights in one of Saddam's palaces in 2003," said John.

"You did? Awesome," said Martel, "Now, Where was I?"

"Chocolate on pillows," said John.

"Oh yeah, they can take their God Damn chocolates with the cream-filled centers and shove them up their asses because they can't homeland security their way out of a fucking paper bag. Do you know what that would make them? You know if they shoved the candy up their asses, do you know what that would make them?" Martel asked.

"What?" John asked, knowing the answer, but preferring to hear Martel say it.

"Not just dumb asses, but candy asses. That would make them candy asses and that's what they are anyway. It just pisses me off," said Martel.

"I can see that," answered John. "I think if they released Ahmed's picture and said how dangerous he was we would have him in 48 hours. This is Wisconsin," said John as they passed the "Welcome to Wisconsin" sign on Interstate 90 leaving the Illinois Toll-way behind. "For the most part, people like the police in Wisconsin and dislike terrorists a whole lot. They want to help," said John.

"Yeah," agreed Martel and his face suddenly lit up with a smile, "That's for sure. Listen to this. I was in Wal-Mart last week and I was in a hurry. I wanted to get some pictures developed. I don't usually use Wal-Mart, so I got turned around and must have looked like I needed some help. A lady says, 'Sir, may I help you?' I said was looking for the photo-shop. She says, 'Just go down four aisles and take a left. It will be on the far end of the store.' Then I noticed she had a cart and she was shopping. I was a little amazed and asked her if she worked for Wal-Mart and she said, 'No you just looked like you needed help and I'm glad that I could help.' Can you believe that? She didn't even work there," said Martel in disbelief.

"That's Wisconsin," agreed John. "I'm telling you, if they gave Ahmed's information to the media outlets, we would have him."

Martel paused to change lanes and pass a truck, and then he added, "In contrast there are parts of this country where a neighbor can get gunned down right in front of everyone in the neighborhood, and when the cops get there all you get is, 'I didn't see nuttin.'"

"Have you personally talked to the people at Homeland Security?" John asked.

"Some HUAS calling the shots is saying no, and it's got to be a big shot, because no means no," explained Martel.

"HUAS? What is HUAS? I've never heard of it," said John.

"HUAS stands for Head Up Ass Syndrome. It's totally curable. All the patient suffering from this syndrome has to do is pull their head out of their ass, abracadabra, just like magic they're cured," enlightened Martel.

"HUAS. I'll have to remember that," said John, "HUAS."

"You're saying it wrong. It's not WHO-AS; it's WHO-AZZZZ. It's spelled H-U-A-S, but pronounced WHO-AZZZZ, kind of like pizzazz with an attitude."

"Got it! WHO-AZZZZZ," said John nodding and smiling. "I know some people who are chronic sufferers," said John.

As Martel passed the Janesville exit, his phone began to vibrate. He grabbed it and hit a button without his eyes leaving the road. "Martel here," he said. He listened for a bit and then responded, "That sounds great. I'll punch the address into my GPS. Is there a command post that you want me to head to?" There was a long pause. "I believe I am about 30 minutes out now. If you have to go without us, don't worry about it; just go. If you locate him I have someone with me that can identify him on sight…. Thanks. Good luck."

Martel set the phone down and filled John in immediately, "Hartwig contacted the Madison Police Department and they got on it right away. They sent plain clothes investigators over to the address on Mifflin Street where the phone was located and the parking ticket was received. One of them has contacts in the neighborhood—friends, family or such—and they were able to find out that a suspect was living at an address right where the parking ticket was placed on Rashid's car."

"They contacted the landlord, and the guy living there is actually using the name Ahmed, last name Wahabi. He rooms with a good looking blonde named Lara Dickinson. Madison Police Department is set up outside, and they do not see any movement in the house. They will only move if Ahmed tries to leave, otherwise they are going to wait until we get there and it will be our call. They have called out their SWAT Team, who were being briefed as I was on the phone." Martel took a deep breath and slapped his hand down on the steering wheel and said, "I'm pumped."

"Do you think he is going to be there?" John asked.

"Are you kidding? Not a chance! He got that text, dropped the phone, and ran like hell, but the deal is he had to leave fast. I'm pumped because this is the closest we've ever been to getting this guy since you let him run down the hill in your underwear," said Martel.

"He was in his own underwear, and I didn't let him go there was a grenade coming... never mind," said John realizing that Martel was pulling his chain.

Martel laughed, "Gotcha."

When Martel turned into a Goodyear dealership less than two blocks from the target house, he pulled up to a group of SWAT officers. As he did, a serious looking muscular man with a shaved head and a graying mustache stepped out of the group and approached them. Martel parked the car and he and John stepped out of the vehicle. The SWAT Officer shook Martel's hand and said, "You must be Special Agent Martel. It is good to meet you. I am Captain Art Boland of the Madison Police Department. I am commander of the team."

He turned to John and said, "You need no introduction. It is an honor to meet you, Savage," and he shook John's hand considerably more vigorously than he had Martel's.

"The honor is mine, Captain," said John.

"Don't call me Captain, my friends call me Bull," said the commander.

"Bull it is," replied John with a nod.

"What do you have now, Bull?" asked Martel.

"One of our officer's sons has an apartment across the street from Ahmed's place. He was the one who was able to tell us the information about Ahmed, and he let a sniper/observer team set up and watch the place. They have optics on the house, and they report no sign of movement. Nothing coming, going, or driving past that looks even a little bit interesting. It is our sense that the coop has been flown, considering the information we received from Rockford. We have a no-knock warrant in hand. What's your next move?" asked Bull.

"I'm guessing that he is gone. The last thing the suspect in Rockford did, before he departed to the beyond, was to send a text message to a phone that is still inside the residence here. The message was "ALLAH." We think that's probably an abort or a flee code, but I would advise caution going in." Martel paused and turned to address the whole team, which had gathered around its captain, "This suspect, Ahmed, is as dangerous as they come. He is a weapons and explosives expert. I want him arrested or neutralized if he is in there. If he's not I would like the place cleared as soon as possible and locked down as a crime scene, and we will want an evidence team in there."

"Well then we'll go," said the captain. "We formulated an entry plan. We will wait for the Dane County Bomb Squad," and just as the words left his mouth a large brown truck pulled into the lot bearing the logo of the Dane County Sheriff's Department Bomb Unit. Captain Boland added, "And here they are, Bachman!"

"Yes, Captain," said a team leader standing behind the Captain to his left.

"I want Reynolds from the bomb team behind the shield and the M4's. Take it slow, and if Reynolds sees anything that might look, smell, sound, or feel like an IED, back out. Damn, I wish we had a robot," said Bull.

Within minutes the entry team was on the running board of the armored personnel carrier, the Bear Cat, and on the move toward Ahmed's. Martel and Savage waited on edge in the command post. After grueling minutes of quiet came the transmission, "The house is clear. It looks like they left in a hurry."

Martel drove over to the residence on Mifflin Street, just off Blair. It was an area a few blocks from the capitol and heavily populated by college students. "Ahmed would have blended right in here," said Martel to John.

The house was well kept except for the signs of the sudden exodus. A pan of cold, hardened lasagna sat on the table on top of a fresh white table cloth. Candles were neatly positioned on either side of a centerpiece. Two places were set with what appeared to be the best china and flatware, displayed as if laid out by the maitre-de at a fine French restaurant.

Martel took a walk-about through the apartment and narrated for John's sake, "The woman must be nuts about the guy to go through this much trouble," said Martel. He walked past open closets and drawers, "She's gone, but all the she-stuff is still here, and all the he-stuff is gone. That's a bad sign," said Martel.

"You think he forced her?" asked John.

"No. I think she left willingly. So, if he's on the run, trying to keep a low profile, why do you suppose he takes along a beautiful blonde, but she doesn't pack so much as an overnight bag?" he asked rhetorically as he pointed to the women's luggage left in the bedroom closet. "Look, all of her clothes are still hanging here too."

Martel strolled into the bathroom and noticed the bucket, mop, and yellow rubber gloves lying in the bucket next to the tub. He glanced around the bathroom, seeing the curling iron, hair dryer, and other lady's sundries still lying about. "Ahmed gets the Allah-text and knows he has to flee. He tells her to start cleaning. Probably gives her a half truth and keeps her busy cleaning while he is packing."

"Why cleaning?" asked John.

"He wants to get rid of fingerprints, DNA, anything that we might be able to identify him with. He figures it is a matter of time before we find this place, so he leaves the phone on and drops it here," says Martel, pointing to the phone which was sitting on top of the toilet tank.

"If he knows we can find him here, why does he leave the phone?" asked John.

"Ahmed is smart. He knows that we are getting close because he got the message from Rashid in Rockford. He leaves the phone where he isn't, giving him time to get where he is right now," said Martel.

"The girl?" asked John as they walked back into the bedroom.

Martel picked up a wallet left lying on the bed stand and flipped it open to a driver's license bearing the photo of a long-haired blonde whose smiling face belonged in a model's portfolio rather than on a driver's license. "Wow. Not what I picture when I think of cheesehead," said Martel.

"Pretty lady," agreed John, missing Stella for a moment.

"He left this here for us to find, for a reason," said Martel shaking the wallet for emphasis.

"Why would he do that?" asked John registering curiosity rather than disbelief.

"He left this here because now we are looking for Lara, lovely Lara. A missing pretty blonde college student will keep the police busy here. It's like, have you ever been in a foot pursuit where a piece of shit dumps garbage in your path to slow you down?" Martel asked.

"Yeah, as a matter of fact one time…" answered John.

Martel cut off the war story in mid-air and continued, "Well that's what Ahmed has done here. We were hot on his trail and he felt it. He leads us here, where he isn't, and dumps a load of garbage in our path to slow us down. He is not worried about being tried and convicted. He just needs some time and distance," surmised Martel.

"So Lara?" asked John.

"If I were a betting man, she is dead right now," said Martel as he set the wallet back down, turned to the evidence tech and said, "I handled this to check out the ID. I picked it up and moved it." The technician, who was busy taking notes, nodded and made a notation, without commenting.

"Why didn't he just kill her here?" John asked, feeling like a three-year-old kid asking Dad, "Why," and then after receiving answer, asking again, "Why," and so on. He was hungry to learn. John Savage was new to this, and he clearly was with someone who had done this sort of thing many times before. He had the opportunity to learn from a master and he was going to take advantage of it.

"Ahmed brought her along to be as much help as possible. She cleans up for him and helps haul out his gear. If he kills her here, it becomes messy. She might run, scream, a neighbor might hear a shot and call the police. So he gets her on board and convinces her to come along without a fuss, maybe using half lies and half-truths. He plays her big time. Hell the girl obviously cares for him. Look at that spread on the table. That's a girlfriend hoping for a ring," observed Martel. "He leads her on, strings her along, and when he is far enough away he kills her and leaves her somewhere,"

"Do you think we will ever find her body?" John asked.

"Most certainly we will find it if my guess is right. We will find the body. He does not want it found in minutes or hours; that would be too soon. He does not want it found in weeks or months because that would be too far off. He wants her found in a day or two at the most. It will give him some time to get beyond her but will slow down anyone looking for him," said the agent as he walked slowly through the house. "Man he cleaned out everything," added Martel.

"Is it possible she may have joined him?" asked John.

"She may have, but I doubt it. She has nothing to add to the partnership. Ahmed will be changing his appearance soon, but it's hard to hide a drop dead gorgeous blonde like Lara. Even if he wanted her to be with him, she brings nothing to the table but enhances the odds of his capture. She served him to a point alive and now she will serve him dead," said Martel. "He works better alone."

John followed Martel as he walked outside, "Here's Felix," said Martel.

A diminutive balding man with glasses in a Bucky Badger jacket carrying a small duffle bag was showing identification to a female patrol officer, who was enforcing the cordon. Martel picked up his pace and called to the officer, "He's with me," and the officer nodded, handing the identification back to the man.

Martel met the man and directed him away from the scene and the three began to meander up Mifflin toward the state capitol building.

"Do you have anything for me?" Felix asked. John Savage thought the choice of the Bucky Badger jacket made him somehow look even more like a computer geek than he already did. To look at the man, no one would guess that he aided in some of the most high-powered investigations in the nation. He looked like an accountant's assistant.

"First, I have to ask, do you have a jacket from every Big Ten team and pro-football team in the United States? It seems that no matter where I see you, you are a fan of the local team," observed Martel.

"I have apparel from every Big Ten team, Pac Eight team, and most pro baseball and football teams. They are camouflage and tax deductible, too. It helps me walk unnoticed through the environment I am working in and still remain reasonably fashionable," said Felix as he belatedly looked around to make certain that no one was close enough to hear him. "I started heading this way when I picked up what was going on," said Felix.

"Did someone call you?" Martel asked, "Because I was just about to."

Felix rolled his eyes and gave Martel a look that said, "How good would I be if I didn't know when I was needed."

"This was Ahmed. I can't prove it, but I'm sure," said Martel.

"You can trust your instincts," said Felix. "I am also sure that this was Ahmed."

"I am…," said John Savage extending his hand.

Felix interrupted John and recited a rapid, but dispassionate monologue, "John Savage, an only child. You were born and raised in La Crosse, Wisconsin, and I shall fast forward to adulthood. You were attending a law enforcement academy, but left it and enlisted after September 11, 2001, to join the fight against terrorism so moved were you by the events of that tragic day. You excelled in combat in Iraq and Afghanistan. While stationed in Iraq you met Ahmed, who was commander of a group of Iraqi Republican Guards, who ambushed your unit. You single handedly wiped out every one in Ahmed's command and spared Ahmed, which resulted in your winning of the Silver Star. There was some talk of a Congressional Medal of Honor, but it was downgraded considerably because you missed an opportunity to kill or capture Ahmed," revealed Felix with a slight hint of disappointment at the end. "Certain people were actually pissed."

"Sorry," acknowledged John instinctively.

"It is neither for me to condemn nor forgive," answered Felix. "Continuing, you returned home and were hired by the La Crosse Police Department and to make a long story short, killed more criminals in the less than two years you have been there than have been killed by the department in modern history. This mathematical oddity has caused the media to release an outpouring of sympathy for the fallen dirt bags as well as a psychic dismembering of returning veterans reminiscent of Vietnam. You like country music, working out, and Italian food. You are enough of a threat to Ahmed that he decided to make you a personal project, but he failed. You have been called in on this case because no matter how Ahmed changes his appearance, you have the ability to look into his eyes and make instantaneous positive identification, according to Special Agent Martel. You may call me Felix," and the frail looking knock-off Badger fan extended his hand.

"Wow. How did you…?" John said shaking the hand of Felix, which Felix retracted after completing this necessary social amenity.

"Felix is one of only a few people who have a condition called Hypermessiness," said Martel.

"That's Hyperthymesia," corrected Felix.

"Come on, Felix. I was close; cut me some slack. He has total autobiographical memory of everything he does, sees, or reads in his life. He is a phenomenon of the greatest magnitude. It's like a super power, and we should get the man a colored cape, matching tights, and a mask. This power coupled with his technological capability and his brilliant deduction makes him invaluable. You need to know that I am on this case and Felix is on this case because someone has decided Ahmed needs to be seriously caught," explained Martel.

"I understand why you need Felix, but why am I here?" asked John. "You can always call me when you find him."

"To be honest, I have always worked better alone. The FBI has come to understand this and lets me work alone, but I know when I need help. John Savage, I asked for you for several reasons. Number one, you are someone that has a connection with Ahmed. You have proved it. He knows you and fears you. Let's say he changes his appearance so much so that not even you can recognize him. I believe if I come into an area inhabited by Ahmed and he sees you, he will react. He will react big or react small, and I am hoping the reaction will be something I can pick up on," said Martel.

"The second thing is, I am a fair shot, but I have never shot anything but paper targets. I am 0 for 0. I have trained but have not yet got 'in the game' so to speak. I believe this guy is dangerous and will not come along peacefully. You are a known quantity. In both the military and law enforcement you have faced the enemy under the worst of conditions and you are undefeated. What are you, like 32 and 0?" asked Martel.

"I have never kept," John hesitated, "score."

"47 confirmed kills," answered Felix. "That is military and law enforcement combined."

"See what I mean," answered Martel. "Now I am going to tell you something that makes Ahmed very valuable."

"Yes?" asked John.

"He is the only person in this country that has met the current top dog of Al-Qaeda," said Martel, "and I am talking about recently. He knows the entire chain of command and has trained or worked with most active unit members on four continents."

"You mean he is an intelligence treasure trove if taken alive," John reasoned.

"Yes. I wanted you, because I figure that as good as you are at winning gun fights under stress, you may be even good enough so that if we come into a situation where we have to shoot this cold blooded killer, you might just be able to... How do I say it?" Martel asked.

"Knock him down, but not out?" answered John.

"Exactly," said Martel. "Now I do not want to end up dead, and I don't want you to end up dead, but I also don't want Ahmed to end up dead. I think you are the best guy for that job right now. With you as my partner, I am confident we're going to get this fucker or we're coming home on our shield," growled Martel talking through gritted teeth.

"If you are finished with the macho posturing, I will ask you again, what do you have for me?" asked Felix.

"There is a cell phone that guided us here. I don't think you will find anything of help that leads us anywhere but back to Rockford," said Martel as they crossed the street on Capitol Square and began to walk leisurely on the sidewalk that circumvented the State Capitol building.

"I am certain you are correct," answered Felix.

Just then a small balding man with glasses carrying a computer case passed them wearing a Bucky Badger jacket, and Martel commented in amazement, "Damn, Felix, you do blend in."

"That is what I was saying," said Felix dispassionately.

"If you were to take all that you know about Al-Qaeda and Ahmed, what can you tell me about his next move?" asked Martel.

"It is not based on hard intelligence, because hard intelligence only tells us Ahmed is here for something big. Ahmed is a people killer, not a suicide bomber, so he is here to kill a person or persons," said Felix.

"I agree, but who and why? They didn't send him here just to kill John Savage," said Martel.

"No. I think that he was already here and you were a target of opportunity. Your attack occurred after the press coverage of one of your shootings. In checking, I discovered the coverage prior to his failed attack did not extend outside of the immediate Midwest, and I believe he was here in Madison, saw the very visible coverage on the front page of the local newspaper, and was inspired to take a road trip," said Felix.

"I agree with you on that," said Martel.

"Of course you do. By now, after our many pairings, it is only reasonable for you to agree on what I say," said Felix.

"Did anyone ever tell you that you sound like Spock from Star Trek?" John asked.

"No, you are the first," said Felix.

"He's being sarcastic," said Martel. "He gets that all the time when people first meet him."

"Shall I continue Special Agent Martel?"

"Go ahead," said Martell.

"Sorry," said John.

"I believe he is waiting for his target to come to him. I believe he has positioned himself in a central location, which allows him to move about freely, while he waits until that happens. I believe he will relocate to another major town with a tolerant population whose suspicions will not be aroused by a foreign person with a middle-eastern dialect," said Felix.

"He speaks very good English," interjected John.

"All the better for him," acknowledged Felix. "He is waiting for his target to come to him. I believe he will run to Minneapolis and move in to the University of Minnesota Campus area. Another possibility is that he might move to Rochester, Minnesota, and move into the neighborhoods near Rochester Mayo. No one will notice a quiet middle-eastern gentleman who appears to be minding his own business. That is where I would expend my efforts."

"Sounds about right," answered Martel. "You said he is waiting for the target to come to him. Do you have any idea about the target?" asked Martel.

"Of this I am certain as I can be without any hard intelligence directing me to this conclusion. He is here to kill one man and one man only. I think you already know who it is, Charles," said Felix.

"I have been afraid to say it because it is the kind of thing that, when you say it without hard facts, you get called paranoid and get pulled from cases," said Martel.

"Then we are of one mind and I can feel free to pass along this reasonable deduction based on analysis of all factors available to me?" Felix asked.

"The Commander in Chief?" asked Martel.

"The Commander in Chief," answered Felix. "You must find Ahmed, Charles…and stop him."

As they paused at the cross-walk, Special Agent Charles Martel noticed a large circular planter that was filled with red and white petunias. The exterior of the planter was a memorial covered with names. "What is this?" asked Martel.

"It is the memorial to Wisconsin Officers who have been killed in the line of duty," replied John.

"I hope this isn't a bad omen," worried Martel.

John answered with conviction, "Felix, you have your technology and your intuition; Charlie, you have your power of deduction. I believe the big guy upstairs brought us together on this search for a reason. I do believe this is a sign. I have found in my life I have survived a lot of tight situations because I have not ignored the hints the big guy upstairs has left for me. I have always been given a subtle heads up when the shit is about to hit the fan. This is one of those heads ups. God is saying loud and clear, 'John, Charlie, and Felix, you are going to find Ahmed and when you do proceed with caution.'"

CHAPTER TWENTY-NINE

Head Shot

artel and Savage had been Westbound on Interstate-90 a short time when Martel's phone vibrated. "Martel here," was all Martel said and followed by a long silence as he listened intently.

As Martel listened, he turned smoothly off Interstate 90 and headed North onto the ramp toward Interstate 39 and continued to listen. Merging onto 39 from the ramp, he answered, "It's your scene. Just don't move her until I get there. That is all I ask. I will punch in the coordinates. I'll find you. Tell your perimeter people I am coming and have them lead me to wherever you want me to park. Thirty minutes, maybe 45 at the most," and then Martel pushed end and set his phone in the charger on the dash.

"Lara?" asked John.

"Lara," said Martel. "I knew she'd be found, but this is even sooner than I thought."

Martel added the coordinates into his GPS and continued North on 39. After a quiet ride, the sexy female voice of the GPS said, "Turn right here."

Martel answered, "Thank you, dear."

Martel took the Endeavor exit and traveled down the ramp. At the bottom of the ramp the sexy voice in an almost breathy, suggestive tone said, "You need to turn right here, Charlie."

"Thank you, my darling," replied Martel.

"You're welcome, Charlie," said the computer-generated female.

"Ain't she a babe?" Martel asked.

"I think you have been on the road too long, Charlie," John observed.

"Yeah, the Garmin Nuvi 5000 is not just a GPS it's also my babe-ometer," said Martel.

"Babe-ometer?" asked John.

"Babe-ometer. I know when I start making unscheduled turns just to hear my GPS-lady's voice it's time to take some personal time.

"What do you do for personal time?" asked John.

"Kind of personal, John," said Martel, "that's why they call it personal time."

"Why? I was just wondering, do you fish? Hunt? Golf? That's all I was asking," explained John.

"Oh. Well the answer to that is no, yes, and never," said Martel.

"What do you hunt?" John asked.

"Bad guys," answered Martel matter-of-factly. "They are always in season and I have an unlimited license to hunt them until I retire."

"What else do you do for recreation?" John wondered.

"If you must know, I find short term but intensely enjoyable relationships with beautiful women. It is a challenging sport because my time is limited, and I must meet, greet, mate, and then skate all in about four to six hours, when time permits," said Martel. "Sometimes I get skunked, but most often I do quite well."

"How often do you…" and John's question was interrupted by the appearance of a squad car with its lights flashing up ahead. As they approached, it was obvious the squad was blocking a dirt path which ran between two harvest-ready fields of corn.

Martel pulled his car up to the officer near the squad and showed him his badge and identification stating, "Special Agent Charles Martel of the FBI."

The officer in his twenties had an all-business look on his face and it remained. He looked unimpressed but responded, "I was told to expect you. The road has already been chewed up by a tractor, so just drive down the path a little ways and I will radio ahead that you are coming."

"Thanks," said Martel folding his badge and identification. He drove about 100 yards and parked behind the Department of Justice evidence van. As he got out, he popped the trunk and grabbed a raid jacket that said FBI across the back while John pulled up his jersey, exposing the badge and gun on his belt.

A plain clothes detective approached. "I'm Sergeant Bill Plesho of the Marquette County Sheriff's Department. I am pleased to meet you," he said extending his hand, and then paused to take his glove off. With that done he shook both Martel and Savage's hands.

"Special Agent Charles Martel," said Martel.

"John Savage," said John.

"Heard of you," said Plesho. "You're all over the news. I hope you find the bastard that did this and add him to your tally," said Plesho, looking back toward what appeared to be some discarded laundry with a clump of blonde hair sticking out of it. "I'd prefer to have the pleasure myself though."

Appreciating the sentiment, but unable to conjure up a better reply John nodded and said, "Pleased to meet you."

"Follow me," said Plesho. "I will show you what we have." Plesho was young for a detective. He was about 6'2" and slim. John decided that he must be good to have made detective at such a young age.

A Division of Criminal Investigation Agent was taping the scene. He ignored the arrival of Martel and Savage, thoroughly engrossed in what he was doing. "We haven't moved anything yet. We received your 'attempt to locate' on Lara, and I gave you a call as soon as I got on the scene. I think this must be her, considering the time and location."

Martel carefully approached the clump of clothes and squatted beside it. He canted his head to achieve the proper perspective on the once-pretty face of the victim. "It's her," said Martel definitively.

Martel then did a quick scan of the victim and stood up to narrate his conclusion, "He brought her here. It looks like she didn't know this was how it was going to end for her. There is no evidence of force or a struggle." Martel looked about the scene. "Here is where they parked the car. If you need a tire-wear impression, here is where they parked," said the agent pointing out a distinct impression in the dirt not yet destroyed by the tractor driven in by the young farmer who discovered the body. "They got out and she walked to this spot where he distracted her. It was close, but not a contact wound. He intentionally put the bullet where she wouldn't know what hit her. Bang, lights out. Nothing says I love you to an assassin like an unanticipated, instantaneous and painless death," said Martel.

"Who are we dealing with?" Plesho asked. "Is this a domestic?"

"Yes and no. They were living together, but it is much more complicated than that. When we find the man that we are looking for, we will also have your killer," said Martel.

"Who is that?" Plesho asked. "Who are you looking for?"

"I will be contacting my superiors to authorize a release of information to the public, but right now, for law enforcement only, we are looking for a Saudi-born member of Al Qaeda named Ahmed. I will send the information to you for your agency, but unless I receive authorization it can't be released. Work this scene like the homicide it is, but I definitely want a rape kit done."

"Do you think she was raped?" asked Plesho.

"No. I am certain he has had sex with her, but it has been consensual. I believe she was living with the suspect. She probably thought they had a future together. She went along with him all the way to this spot, which was literally and figuratively the end of the road. Their relationship was such that I believe his DNA has to be on her. We were at their home and she was on the pill, so it is possible he was not using a condom when they had sex."

Plesho looked again at the young woman lying abandoned, wasted. "This woman loved the guy and she was treated worse by this son of a bitch than a county worker would treat a road-kill skunk,"

Martel continued, "No argument here. Ahmed is a heartless killer. He is foreign born, and I want to have some DNA on file. Have her clothing and body checked for sperm, body hair that is black in color, and anything that we can confirm DNA on the suspect. It may come down to having to use that to identify this son of a bitch in the event of..." Then Martel stopped and bit his lip.

"In the event of what?" Plesho asked.

Then Martel, still biting his lip as the anger welled up in him. He turned toward John Savage, looked him in the eye and said, "In the event of a head shot."

Chapter Thirty

Looking Forward to Alzheimer's

"Where to from here?" asked John as Martel turned west onto Interstate 90 after leaving the Marquette County crime scene.

"Minneapolis. Have you ever been to Dinky Town?" asked Martel.

"Yes, are you kidding? I graduated from the University of Minnesota. What will we do there?" John asked.

"Great! It will help with you knowing the city an all," said Martel. "I am going to make another pitch to have Ahmed's photo released. We can argue that we have two homicides and an attempt to murder a police officer on him. It clearly is a public safety issue. If I can make that case, we will be able to have the release of this guy's photo along with the computer-generated likeness we have based on your description. That might shake Ahmed out of the tree that he is hanging in. Regardless of all that, I agree with Felix's assessment. He relocated to Minneapolis."

"Sounds like a plan to me. I hope they agree with you. It makes perfect sense," said John. "The press release that Ahmed is real would help me with my girl too."

"Why's that?" Martel asked.

"She thinks my post-traumatic stress caused me to conjure up Ahmed. She already was worried about living with a cop, but the final straw was when Diane Cruz decided, during my 15 minutes of national fame, she would tell the nation that all combat veterans are dangerous, especially John Savage. 'He conjures up imaginary terrorists who attack him in his driveway and, by the way, it seems as though he shoots dead nearly everyone he meets.' Damn!" exclaimed John in frustration. After a pause he reasoned, "When the world finds out that Ahmed really exists it won't guarantee she will come back, but at least I will have a fighting chance at getting her back."

"Is she worth it?" Martel asked.

"She's worth it. She's smart, funny, talented, and gorgeous. I have met many women in my life, and I truly believe she's the one," said John.

"The one what?" asked Martel.

"The one I want to spend the rest of my life with," answered John. "Have you ever... sorry. That's pretty personal."

"Nah, that's OK. I have found 'the one' a hundred times. I don't see myself finding one that I want to settle down with anytime soon. One reason is I can't imagine someone living with me. I have the best and worst job in the FBI. The good part is I get one case at a time. My mission is to find the worst guy at the time in the country and bring him to justice.

"As soon as I am assigned, I am like a hound after the fox, running in circles until I catch the sneaky bastard. I get so into the hunt that I forget to go home. My foxes take me all over the country, sometimes the world. I have a home where I have to pay someone to cut the grass. I sleep there 20 days a year. What woman would stay with a husband who asked her to share a life like mine? Even if one agreed to do it, she would bid me adieu before our first anniversary."

"Or ask you to give it up," added John.

"Yeah or give it up, and I have not met anyone yet I would be inclined to give this up for. I love it," exclaimed Martel. "It wouldn't be fair to the woman and wouldn't be fair to me, because any wife in her right mind would insist I quit doing what I love doing. Let's say I did find someone that could talk me into quitting. If I quit for her, I would be miserable and I would hate her for it." Martel explained.

"You mentioned one reason. What's the other reason?" asked John.

"Hey, kid, that's good," said Martel.

"What's good?" asked John.

"You are a listener. You pay attention and you pick up on subtle inferences. That will serve you well in this profession. It's the most important skill a good interviewer needs to have," Martel observed. "You get the text and the subtext. I'm truly impressed."

Martel then changed lanes and passed a semi-trailer painted with black and white spots like a cow. It had a sign in the back that said If you like my driving call 1-800…. "I wonder if anyone ever calls those numbers?"

"Nice dodge," said John. "You don't want to tell me the other reason."

"You're persistent, too. Like I said, you are going to be a good interrogator. OK, OK, I'll tell you if it goes nowhere else," agreed Martel.

"You have my word as God as my witness. May the Packers never win again if I reveal to another human being what you are about to tell me," said John.

"You swear on the Packers? That sounds good enough to me. The problem with me settling down with one woman is I enjoy the firsts too much," said Martel taking his right hand off the steering wheel and using it to trace the hourglass figure of a beautiful woman in mid-air."

"The firsts?" asked John.

"Yeah, you know that first time when you are with a beautiful woman. You've wined her and dined her and made her laugh the first time. You look deep into each other's eyes the first time and kiss the first time. She takes your hand and leads you to the couch, the bed, the kitchen table, or wherever and then it happens, the first time. Firsts are the most exciting part of a relationship, and to me it's like crack cocaine. I'm hooked on firsts. There can only be one first of anything," said Martel. "If there is a woman so interesting to me that I would give all the firsts for the rest of my life, I have not met her yet," said Martel.

"Stella," said John.

"Stella?" Martel asked.

"I agree with you about the excitement of the first time, but I would give up all my firsts for the rest of my life to be with her," said John with a sigh.

"With Ahmed paying attention to your situation as he seems to be, it may be best if you are perceived to have no romantic connections. It makes us more effective and keeps this Stella safe while you are away," reasoned Martel.

"Now that you mention it, you are right there," agreed John, comforted greatly by the thought.

"Anyway, John, if she is the one meant for you, and worth having, she will still be there when the truth about Ahmed comes out. If she isn't, then it was not meant to be. That much I am sure of," said Martel with conviction.

"When will that be?" John asked, "You said that's classified information."

"So was the recipe for the Atomic bomb, and the Russians stole and copied it by 1947.... or 1948, I forget. Today it's even harder to keep a secret. We have been sending out classified bolos (be on the lookout) for Ahmed to agencies in areas where he has appeared. Nothing has been leaked because most cops know the media is not their friend."

"Tell me about it," said John.

"Exactly! That's what I'm talking about," Martel said with such emphasis the car swerved a bit within his lane. "Unfortunately, until someone finds it necessary to release this information to a Congressman, Senator, or any politician who thinks he can manipulate the information to make another one of their fellow swamp rats look bad, it will likely stay classified," explained Martel.

"They leak classified information just to make each other look bad?" said John.

"John, you have a naiveté which is precious," said Martel. "But no, that is not the only reason they leak secrets. They also will leak information because they are drunk or because it will get them a string of condos in Boca Raton. They might leak it because they want to impress friends by showing that they know secrets and, therefore, they are important. The reason this group goes to the press is because they believe the press are their friends or they think that giving them a little bit of information will secure a friendship. There is a saying in the CIA. If you want information leaked, telegraph, telephone or tell-a-congressman," said Martel, who chuckled. "That still makes me laugh because it is so absolutely true."

After his self-induced chuckle, Martel continued, "The point is, the information will eventually come out, and Stella will feel like crap about the way she treated you and you'll get her back. If she doesn't come back, she was not worth having and you should move on," said Martel with the conviction of a mathematician declaring the one plus one does actually equal two.

"What if she finds someone else in the meantime?" John asks.

"She clearly left someone she still loves. How does she hook up with someone else when she is still nuts about you? Once again if she does, she ain't worth fussing over," said Martel.

"I hope you're right," said John with little conviction.

"Oh, I'm right, all right. Trust me on that. I could feed the data to Felix, and he would come to the same conclusion. Hey! It's Kwik Trip. Well, there's a little bit of home away from home for you," said Martel. "How about we stop here? I have to drain the main vein, and acquire a supply of fresh coffee to start the whole process over again."

"Sounds good, I could use a Dew," said John.

Later the two were shuffling their drinks around in the two available drink-holders when Martel's phone vibrated, "Martel here," answered the agent.

Martel was quiet for several minutes, breaking the silence with an occasional "Hmm" and a "You don't say." After five minutes Martel said, "Thanks for calling. That will give us a place to start. Call this number again if you find out anything else." Martel hung up and said, "Sweet."

"That sounded promising," said John.

"It seems that Lara Dickinson is a graduate student in Sociology. As a part of her program, she was doing a paper related to the sex industry and decided to experience it firsthand while making some money at the same time. She became an exotic dancer at a place called Visions in Madison. That's where she met Ahmed. She quit dancing shortly after the two met. The owner remembers Ahmed real well. They are going through security tapes at the place to see if they can find one with a good shot of Ahmed. If we can lock Ahmed in with Lara, then I might be able to convince the HUAS to allow a press release of Ahmed's photo," said

Martel. "More importantly, we know he needs a new squeeze, and now we also know he doesn't pick them up at the campus student union."

"Strip clubs?" asked John.

"Yes, John, strip clubs," said Martel, "and I'm guessing that gauging his tastes after Lara he doesn't chase after skanks or pretty, shy middle-eastern women in a burka types either. He apparently likes the high-end, blonde, and blue-eyed daughters of western devils. Yes indeed, John, we have a place to start."

Martel drove quietly for a while and then said, "I might get married under one condition."

"What condition would that be?" John asked with his curiosity sincerely piqued.

"If I ever get diagnosed with Alzheimer's," Martel proclaimed thoughtfully.

"Alzheimer's? Why would that induce you to get married?" John asked.

"Well, for one thing, as the disease progressed I would not lose my sex drive but I might forget some of my great pick-up lines," explained Martel.

"That makes sense," agreed John.

"The other great thing about it, the loss of memory would create an ideal situation where it would be like the first time over and over and over again," Martel said with an enthusiasm that bordered on mildly disturbing.

"Whoa, Charlie, settle down. Remember you're driving," cautioned John.

"It's OK, John, nothing to worry about; I have everything under control," said Martel giving John a thumbs up. "I tell you this though all of a sudden I am looking forward to Alzheimer's."

Chapter Thirty-one

God's Country

Ahmed had taken a disjointed route to get to Minneapolis. It had been two days since he had killed Lara, and he followed the news carefully to determine if he had been identified yet. He hovered about the Canadian Border in the event he had to make an emergency crossing. When it appeared that he was in the clear and there was no nation-wide man-hunt in progress as of yet, he turned his car toward Minneapolis where he would attempt to lay low again until his opportunity to strike his target presented itself.

After he arrived in Minneapolis, he found the campus of the University of Minnesota "Gophers" and circled the campus perimeter trying to find a nesting place. Ahmed had grown complacent with Lara. He had not spent that much time in one place with one person since he took on the mantle of a soldier for Allah. "It was very pleasant while it lasted; in another way it was most unpleasant. At any rate it shall not happen again," he said to himself. "I must stay out of reach for a month at the most. The target will come to me or I will go to the target."

Ahmed drove out of the campus area and followed University Avenue until he found a dingy looking motel that advertised the fact that the rooms had television. "That looks about right."

Ahmed parked his car in the lot, avoiding the front door as he scanned the area. "No security cameras," he said to himself. "Good." Ahmed got out and found a matronly woman with a Lucille Ball, red bouffant hair-do, seated on a tall, spindly chair behind the front desk. There was a coffee pot with a stagnant-looking, brown-colored liquid set on a small table with a box of "honor shop" snacks next to it—the closest thing to a continental breakfast.

"Do you want to pay with a credit card?" asked Lucy.

"No, I prefer cash," said Ahmed with a smile.

"Cash works, but we will need cash in advance to hold the room without a card," said Lucy.

"No problem. How much for the week?" Ahmed asked.

"$382.50, including tax," said Lucy.

"Tell the cleaning lady I will not need her services," said Ahmed.

"You're looking at her and that just warms my heart, sweetie. We just met and I like you already," said Lucille. "If you need new towels just bring them here to the desk and I will change them for you.

"Thank you," said Ahmed.

"What brings you to town?" asked Lucille.

Ahmed just turned and left without answering.

When Ahmed left the room, the redhead muttered, "Well, a regular Mr. Fucking Congeniality."

As Ahmed parked his car directly outside the door to his room, he paused, deciding whether it would be best to leave his gear in the car or bring it into the room. Finally, he concluded he would rather be caught with it than caught without it, and carried everything into the room.

After unloading, Ahmed checked the Beretta he had slipped into a pancake holster in the small of his back, made certain he had a round in the chamber, and then slipped the weapon back into the holster. He turned around and checked himself in the mirror to verify that his untucked shirt covered it. It did.

Ahmed checked his hair and shook his head, "It must all go," he said out loud. "It is the only way," and then he left his room, jumped into his car, and went out to forage.

He hopped on to I-35 and just drove until he saw a Wal-Mart and quickly took the exit. Inside the Wal-Mart he grabbed a cart and rolled about the store. He was always amazed at the abundance at the finger-tips of every American. "I wonder if we hate them for their decadence or for their affluence," he whispered to himself.

As he rolled through the store, he gathered some oranges, apples, bananas, and a supply of wine. Ahmed worked his way to the opposite side of the store following the sign for "Health and Beauty Aids," and there he found shaving cream and razors. The most difficult item to find on his mental list was the scissors. He circled the store twice before he located them. Once he found them, he wheeled his cart to the lines at the check-out.

He fell into the shortest line behind a young mother who had two small children in a cart shaped like a red racecar. One of the children held a box of Fruit Loops cereal, and when the pretty blonde mother leaned over to get the box of cereal to check the item out, the little boy wrapped his arms tightly around the box and refused to give it up. The fight was on.

Ahmed was delighted to discover that the young mother's white-flowered top was designed to be generously revealing under normal, everyday conditions. Now that she was bent forward in a furious struggle with her four-year-old over the Fruit Loops, her abundant, maternal breasts were barely encased by her top. Ahmed found himself embarrassingly aroused by the spectacle and was loath to look away.

Lara. Why did you not choose to come with me? Ahmed thought to himself, grieving for what was lost to him rather than what was taken from her. *I must find relief*, he thought as he unsuccessfully tried to direct his eyes away from the scuffle and gazed hungrily at the woman's breasts as they heaved one last time while she wrested control of the Fruit Loops from the screaming four-year-old.

Just before he reached the checkout, he saw the Minneapolis *Star Tribune* displayed on a rack next to the counter. The headlines read, "The President to Visit God's Country." Ahmed could hardly contain his excitement. He grabbed a newspaper and laid it on the counter with the rest of his purchases, barely feigning nonchalance.

As he threw his bags into the back seat of his car, he removed the newspaper and read and re-read the headline. He could not believe his luck. It was as if Allah was guiding him toward this, the greatest moment of his life. He thought to himself as he read the details of the planned visit to La Crosse. He had very little time to make ready his final plans. He threw the newspaper into the car and sat down, motionless behind the wheel for several minutes. He started the car and said to himself out loud, "How ironic this shall be. What may very well be my final mission for Allah will be in a place these infidels call God's Country."

Chapter Thirty-two

Déjà vu

Martel and Savage got off the elevator on the third floor of the Minneapolis Police Department. "This way," said Martel, "I have known this guy for years. His name is Siggurd Olsen. How's that for a Norwegian name? Everyone calls him Sig, but it's not short for Siggurd."

"OK, I'll bite. What's it short for?" John asked.

"Sig Sauer. He has four or maybe five, I forget, officer-involved shootings, and they have all been with a Sig Sauer," answered Martel. "He's an amateur compared to you, though, because some of them have lived."

"Gee, thanks," said John in a dead pan voice.

"He has comparable quantity but not the quality," added Martel.

"Thanks again," said John. "Your high praise has almost moved me to tears."

As they reached a door with sign that read, "Captain S. Olsen, Special Crimes Unit," Martel said, "This is it," and knocked.

"Come in," came a deep voice whose tone seemed to be really saying, "Get the fuck out of here."

The two entered and seated at a desk across the cluttered office was a tightly-muscled man wearing a white shirt with a loosened tie around his neck. John could tell that this captain was not a desk-bound administrative captain because of the tell-tale line of a well-fitted bullet-resistant vest under his shirt.

Above the desk were signed and framed glossy photos of the two best quarterbacks to ever play for the Vikings, Fran Tarkenton and Brett Favre. Hanging crookedly below those pictures was a smaller picture of his family. As they entered the room, the large Nordic man, who looked to be the descendant of Viking raiders, looked up from the computer and a smile instantly broke across his face. He stood up quickly, bumping his thighs hard on his desk, and proclaimed in his rich booming voice, "Chuck-wagon!"

"Sig-Sauer, it's been too long," Martel replied as Olsen rounded his desk and they shook with one hand and man-hugged with the other. The friendship was obvious as well as genuine.

"What brings you to the Twin Cities? Pleasure, not business, I hope," said Sig Sauer, knowing better.

"It's always a pleasure, doing business with you Sig," proclaimed Martel.

"Go ahead, Martel, and lay it on me, but remember you can't bullshit a bullshitter," as he extended his hand to John, "You are John Savage, right?" asked Olsen.

"Yes sir," said John.

"Trust me. There are no sirs here. You call me Sig," said the tall captain shaking John's hand with a strong grip, which managed to find the perfect balance between firm and "you're hurting my hand you son of a bitch."

"I have been following your situation in the news. Sounds like good police work in my professional opinion. If you ever decide to change locations, contact me. We'll find a place for you here," said Sig making a no bullshit recruiting move.

"Thanks, Captain," said John.

"Sit down," said Sig, removing a bullet-dinged Kevlar helmet and his personal tactical vest from one of the two chairs in his office and setting them in the corner. "How can I help you?"

"We are looking for a man we suspect of two murders." Martel said.

"I am sorry, my friend, you are going to have to do better than that if you want my unit to drop what they are doing and give you a hand. That would be way down on the priority list for us," opined Olsen.

"There is more to it, but it has to stay confidential. It is classified," explained Martel.

"Shoot. It doesn't go any further than my unit on a need to know basis," assured Olsen as he turned over the note pad on his desk in an unconscious, but not so subtle, gesture of confidentiality.

"We are looking for this man," and he set the photo on the pad in front of Sig. "Ahmed Abdullah Rahim. This is the only photo we have of him. He is a member of Al-Qaeda and one of their top killers. We know he is here to hit a major target, but nothing specific has been picked up in the chatter," said Martel.

"Why do you think he is in Minneapolis?" Sig asked.

"Felix and I have a hunch," said Martel.

"Kid, I want to tell you something. When this guy and Felix get a hunch, believe it. I can say without qualification their hunches are more reliable than eye-witness sightings." Sig made a mid-air quotation gesture to highlight eye-witness.

"What do you need from us?" asked the captain.

"Felix and I believe he is in Minneapolis, and if he is he will be as horny as a three-peckered pimp on a Viagra over-dose. He will most probably start looking to satisfy his itch at one of your local strip clubs. I would like you to give me what manpower you can to sit on as many strip clubs for the next two days as possible," said Martel.

"Why would you want us for only the two days if you don't mind me asking?" Sig asked.

"I believe he will be moving on his target after two days," said Martel.

"And that is…" asked Martel.

"It's a hunch, so I dare not say. If Felix and I are right, then it's huge and we have to stop it," said Martel.

"If it was just you, Martel, I would tell you to piss up a rope, but since Felix says, I will see who I can shake free to help. Where did that guy come from? I swear he's an alien. Did I ever tell you about my Roswell theory? You know that supposed alien crash, back in the 50s?" asked Sig.

"No, what's that?" Martel asked.

"It was Felix. He flew here from a galaxy far, far away and his premium teridium tank was low so he tried to land here to fill up. Well, he found out earthlings were so far behind his home planet that we had no teridium stations here, so he had to crash land. After the crash, the government made the space ship disappear and they did an assessment of Felix. When they found out about his powers of deduction, they offered him a job. He agreed and works for hot dogs and an unlimited supply of Big Ten sweat-shirts," said Sig with excitement. "I'm right, aren't I?" Sig's smile lit up his face. "He's an Alf."

"What's an ALF?" asked Martel.

"An Alien Life Form," said Sig Sauer.

"That's right. Felix is an ALF. You are dead on, but keep it under your hat," said Martel.

"I knew it," said Sig. "I can probably cut loose four of my people to help you, starting tomorrow, but that's all I have to give you. Is that going to help you?" asked Sig.

"It'll have to do. How about we have the briefing here tomorrow at 5:00 PM? The shift will run from 5:00 PM to closing. John and I will go check out the clubs and decide which one we will target. What is your recommendation?" Martel asked.

"Top-end strippers he would find at Sheik's Palace Royale, and naughty but still nice you would find at Déjà Vu on North Washington. I'd guess he'll find his way to one or both of those," said Sig.

"Thanks. That's where we'll head then," said Martel.

"Do you need directions?" Sig asked with a smile.

"No I have a GPS and a working long-term memory. I've been there before, remember?" Martel asked wryly.

"Are you sure, because if not I can personally give you a police escort. Nothing is going to bleed to death on my desk, if I take a break..." and then the phone rang, "Olsen here...hold a second," Sig covered the speaker on the phone and said, "Got to run. 5:00 PM tomorrow. I'll have four of my guy's meet you in the conference room two doors down on the left," said Sig who waved and returned to his call.

———>●●<———

Martel had been to Déjà vu in the past and decided to go there first, once again on a hunch. It was nestled on North Washington Street in a neighborhood that also housed "Sex World," offering a variety of personal home recreational accoutrements. It was 4:15 PM and traffic in downtown Minneapolis was moving, but just barely.

As they walked from their car toward Déjà vu, John asked, "You told Sig Sauer two days. Why not run the detail for five days or three?" John asked.

"Nice catch. The reason for that number is because we are going back home to La Crosse if we don't find him here," said Martel.

"Why? Are you planning on setting me up as a target?" asked John.

"Not quite yet. That's plan C, though," said Martel. "Can you handle it?"

"Bring it on," said John sincerely. "At least I would know where and when. Why are we going back to La Crosse?"

"The president is kicking off his re-election campaign by having a rally in La Crosse. He liked the fact that it is one of the only 1000 places in the United States that is called 'God's Country.' If we don't locate Ahmed by then, we will be following him from city to city with one mission. Stop Ahmed," explained Martel.

"You think the president is the target?" asked John, looking about to make certain no one had heard him once he remembered they were speaking on a busy Minneapolis street. He was relieved to see that no one was close enough to have heard.

"Yes, I would bet my right nut that the president is the target. I would not just move on my hunch alone, but Felix believes it also. I have grown to take Felix's hunches as gospel. He can even sort through hard and soft intelligence to pick out the truth from the lies and distracters. He is so accurate I have wondered myself about the origin of Felix," said Martel.

As they reached the door, Martel said, "Pay the cover charge. Put it on your expense account. We don't want to badge them here," said Martel.

"You want me to put Déjà vu on my expense account? That is something that could haunt a local cop," said John sincerely concerned.

"I understand. I will cover you," said Martel. As they entered, both of the cops looked about for the location of security cameras. There was one looking down at them as they entered the door.

Martel paid both cover charges and turned to John, "This one's on me buddy."

As John looked about the room he was surprised that at 4:15 PM in the afternoon there would be such a large crowd at a strip club. There were two blondes occupying two of the three stripper poles on stage. Their performance was choreographed and had a Cirque du Soleil meets Hustler Magazine look about it. John reluctantly pulled his focus away from the entertainment and scanned the room. His gaze went from face to face, and he saw truck drivers, attorneys, drug dealers, college kids, and even one bearded Amish gentleman wearing a black hat, suspenders and a big smile. There were no Al-Qaeda assassins, however.

Martel and John circled the room. After one complete circuit, Martel led John downstairs, where there were about a dozen couches. Over half of them were occupied with men leaning back, their hands gripping the couch. A Baskin-Robbins variety of strippers were indulging the paying customers. Once again, there was no Ahmed.

"We'll be inside and we will position our four MPD guys outside," said Martel.

"What about FBI?" John asked.

"I am going to set them up at Sheiks Palace Royale. I think he is coming here and we can only be in one place at a time and only have enough people to loosely cover two places," explained Martel. "I have to take a leak," said Martel. "When I finish I'll meet you upstairs and then we'll go get something to eat."

"Sounds good," said John. "I'll be upstairs.

As John walked up the steps to the first floor he looked about the room and saw nothing had changed on the floor. The stage now was occupied by a tall and tanned redhead, dressed in a revealing black one piece and high-heeled boots twirling rhythmically about the stage. The heads of the patrons seemed to be wired to the woman, because every head in the room was swiveling like a magnetic bobble head figure on the dash board of a 1960 Oldsmobile maneuvering through sharp curves.

John watched, mesmerized for a few minutes, and then he heard the words of his field training officer who caught him looking straight ahead on one occasion as he patrolled shortly after arriving in La Crosse. His field training officer said, "Remember you are on patrol. You are not on a Sunday drive. Pay attention. You should always be scanning and processing."

John found it difficult to pull his eyes from the stage because the red-headed dancer cracked open the one piece black outfit like a lobster cracking open its own shell. In doing so she revealed two medically perfected breasts, whose unannounced release so startled the Amish man it caused him to snap his head back abruptly. This sudden movement flipped his flat straw hat backward off his head. John laughed and finally was able to tear his eyes away from the stage.

John turned about and scanned the room once again and there at the door, handing the bouncer a twenty dollar bill, was Ahmed. Before John could react, Ahmed looked up from his transaction and his eyes turned toward the redhead on the stage. As fate would have it, John served as the mid-point on a straight line that ran between Ahmed and the redhead.

Ahmed and John's eyes locked in, and there was absolutely no hesitation. Ahmed turned and hit the door on a run. John instinctively reached for his radio but had none. He looked about the room, and Martel was nowhere to be found. John worked his way through and around the tables and made his way to the door. As he reached the door, a bachelor's party was arriving and bullying their way drunkenly through the entrance.

As John attempted to press his way through the group, one of the drunks pushed John and yelled, "Hey, dick head. Who do you think you're pushing?" John ignored him and continued to push his way through to daylight. As John finally reached the sidewalk, he frantically tried to find Ahmed. He scanned up and down the busy street filled with the buzz of a big city, but Ahmed had disappeared into the crowd. John ran back and forth on the sidewalk trying to reacquire his adversary, but for the third time Ahmed had caught John Savage off guard. Ahmed was gone.

John went back into Déjà vu and motioned frantically to Martel, who was looking about the room. The agent worked his way through the bachelor's party, who had in mere moments forgotten their encounter with John, and one asked, "Come on in buddy. We'll buy you a drink."

As Martel reached John at the door, John went outside on the sidewalk and continued to try to get his bearings on where Ahmed could have disappeared to as he said to Martel, "Ahmed was just here. He no sooner got inside the place when he saw me and bolted," explained John looking up and down the street.

"Damn it!" Martel got on his phone, immediately.

"Sig. Yeah it's me. We are at Déjà vu. Ahmed was here and he ran. We have no direction of travel. Can you put out a bolo for a suspect of the description that I gave you? He uses the name Ahmed and a variety of last names. He does not look like that picture; he is…," then Martel looked toward John.

"Clean shaven, medium length black hair, wearing brown and beige dress shirt and beige Dockers with brown half boots," said John.

Martel repeated the information as he hustled to their car. "Thanks Sig. We will be circling the area here."

When Martel and Savage reached their parked car, it was clear that their odds of relocating Ahmed in the heavy rush-hour traffic were somewhere between slim and none, but they made a hearty effort. After circling the area for thirty minutes, Martel asked, "Are you sure it was Ahmed?"

"Positive," said John. "If it wasn't why would he have run? What about the security camera at Déjà vu? At least we can get a current image of him," suggested John.

"Let's do that. No sense in coming up empty handed," said Martel. "I can't believe he was there and I was on the shitter."

"Don't beat yourself up too bad, it's the third time he has slipped away from me," said John.

"Did you get that strange feeling, when it happened?" asked Martel.

"What feeling is that," asked John.

"You know the feeling that something familiar was going on like you have been in that very place before doing the same thing. You know that feeling."

"Yeah, I know the feeling," acknowledged John. "We couldn't have picked a better place to have it—Déjà vu."

CHAPTER THIRTY-THREE

Allahu Akbar

Ahmed circled his vehicle around the area of Déjà vu looking for the best spot, and as a car left the perfect parking spot on the street he was on, he pulled in. He preferred on-street parking because there was no record of his being there. Most ramps were filled with cameras, and some had attendants. They were all permanent possible witnesses. He felt boxed in when he parked in ramps, so he avoided them like a platoon of U.S. Marines.

This spot was perfect. It was the last spot on the end of the block allowing for a rapid departure. He got out, plugged the meter, and began walking toward Déjà vu. If things went as planned, this would be the last time he would get a chance to engage in worldly pleasures before taking on his mission.

Ahmed walked up North Washington and noticed the traffic had slowed to a speed varying between a walk and a slow jog. It never ceased to amaze him how so many in this country had so much. Once again his brain began its incessant questioning of the tenets of this violent Jihad he had embarked on, "Do I hate these people because they are decadent or do I hate them because I have been told to hate them by my Imam since I was a young boy in the Madrassa?"

Ahmed wondered, *Do my leaders want to kill them because the Americans are evil or because they are jealous of their wealth and covet their power? The leaders who direct us seem to want for nothing and risk nothing.* He shook his head, trying to shake out the doubts he found himself thinking too often, *These thoughts make me feel more guilty*

227

about having them than I have ever felt about killing Americans, so they must be the temptations of the devil, Ahmed concluded.

As he reached the door at the Déjà Vu, a beautiful blonde with lips as red as the desert floor at sunset beckoned him from the marquee. The pouting lips caused a churning of excitement instantly in his groin that could hardly be contained. With great anticipation he removed a twenty dollar bill from his wallet from the stack of twenties within. He opened the door and stepped in squinting, allowing his eyes to adjust from sunshine to the low light of the club.

As he entered, he raised his hand over his brow to block the view of any security cameras and handed the cashier at the door his money. Ahmed looked up just as a tall red-head released two unnaturally perfect breasts from her outfit. Ahmed's subconscious brain struggled to direct the focus between two of Ahmed's needs: satisfy his libido or survive. Ahmed's subconscious finally chose survival, and in that moment he saw, standing between himself and the beautiful breasts, John Savage.

Instantly, the fear he felt on Martyrs' Ridge returned and covered him like a snow avalanche overtaking a lone alpine skier. Ahmed turned and hit the exit at a run. He cut left and saw a rowdy group of drunken men occupying the entire sidewalk stumbling toward him. A large brown UPS truck was passing in front of him at jogging speed, and Ahmed bolted towards it. Cutting behind it, he dodged right and kept pace along-side the length of the truck, keeping it between him and the entrance to Déjà vu.

Ahmed ran, staying in the blind spot created by the truck for entire block. He continually glanced behind, waiting for the pursuit, but John Savage never came. After a block Ahmed peeled away from the truck and ran down a side street, ignored by the occupants of the large metropolis who had grown accustomed to absurdities. They all had more serious matters to concern themselves with than a strange man racing a UPS Truck.

Ahmed made his way cautiously from doorway, to alleyway, to cul-de-sac, to doorway, until he was back in his car. He started it and took a circuitous route back toward his hotel to make certain he was not followed. He began to wonder, *Am I as crazy as they think John Savage is? Did I really see him? What would he be doing here? If it was John Savage, why did he not pursue me?*

The only way to be certain is to return to Déjà Vu, and I will never go back to that place, he concluded. Ahmed continued to drive toward his hotel, checking his rearview mirror repeatedly, and he said out loud to no one, "It is time to leave this place."

Ahmed's head was never stationery on the way back to the hotel. He watched every vehicle behind him to determine if it might be a tail. He assessed every occupant of every vehicle to the right and left of him to make certain the children were not decoys, a potential ruse of the CIA. A thought came to him, and he turned quickly into a parking lot. Grabbing a small flash light from the glove compartment, he climbed out of the car and dropped to the pavement to check the under-carriage of his car for a tracking device. "Nothing," Ahmed said as he reached the front of the vehicle and pushed himself up with a grunt.

Climbing back into the car, he hurriedly drove back to his hotel. After he bolted the door and checked the window, he set two Berettas on top of the dresser, ensuring both were loaded and charged. He lined up four loaded magazines next to them and then gathered what he needed. "Even if that was Savage, and I do not believe it was, he does not know where I am or they would already be upon me."

Ahmed took the newspaper heralding the coming of "The Lamb" and slipped the critical sections of the paper containing details about the presidential visit into his hockey bag. He took the sections of the paper he did not need into the bathroom. Ahmed laid the papers over the sink and took out his scissors. He took one last moment to vainly admire his wavy black hair and said to his reflection, "Lara said I looked like Omar Shariff. I must say there is a resemblance, but it is I who is the much better looking of the two of us."

With that Ahmed began cutting vigorously, letting the locks of hair drop onto the newspapers below. When he had cut his hair down to the nub-line, he covered his head with the white foam of the shaving cream and took out his razor. Ever so carefully, he shaved his head, inch by inch and section by section. He desperately wanted to avoid rushing and cutting himself. Ahmed knew that multiple cuts on a bald head would make security wary of a recent appearance change.

Once Ahmed finished, he carefully cleaned up the loose clumps of hair before showering and bagging his towels and bed sheets. He then scrubbed down the sink and every surface he had touched.

After the room was cleaned, Ahmed laid out his uniform, preparing to dress himself as if for a military inspection. Ahmed put on his jump boots and gave them a quick buffing before slipping the military jacket over his shirt and tie and buttoning it according to Class A regulation. Finally, he carefully set the beret upon his head.

As he looked at himself in the uniform standing at attention in front of the mirror, he thought, *I do envy the Americans so many things. A warrior should feel a part of something: a platoon, a company, an army of their fellows to share the glory and horrors with. I have no uniform, no flag, and no country to die for. I wonder if anyone will mourn me when I am gone?* Ahmed found himself sinking suddenly in a pit of despair and saw the evidence of this on the face in the mirror. "Enough of this," he stubbornly declared in a cautious but throaty whisper. "These distractions are once again the work of the Devil. I am a soldier of Allah and my army is a heavenly host. Allahu Akbar!"

Ahmed recovered from his reverie and checked his wallet to make certain he had all the proper identification, including the forged leave papers. He was Sergeant Robert Margolis, wounded in Afghanistan and on medical leave, approved for extended visit to his large and scattered family in Iowa, Illinois, Wisconsin, and Minnesota.

After Ahmed had packed everything he needed to take with him, he put on the cast. He slipped one of the Berettas into his gear bag with the extra magazines. The second Beretta he nestled into the compartment carved into his cast and he popped the hinged lid back into place. *If I set off a metal detector I will tell them it must be the screws holding the shattered bones in place. I will use the word 'shattered.' It sounds much more wounded*, he thought.

Ahmed covered the weapon compartment of the cast with his sling and checked himself again in the mirror. In the uniform, with the shaved head and cast, Ahmed could not recognize himself. He smiled, "The Commander and Chief will not pass up the opportunity to shake hands with a so obviously wounded soldier such as myself. The crowd will most certainly allow me to move unmolested to the front. The opportunity will present itself. I am certain of this. This is a perfect plan."

Ahmed smiled into the mirror and extended his right hand as he said, "It is an honor to serve my country, Mr. President," and then with lightning speed he slipped his hand under the sling, hit the release on the door, and drew the Beretta out into a firing position, "Bam!"

Ahmed smiled as he said, "John Wilkes Booth, Lee Harvey Oswald, and Ahmed Abdullah Rahim. We all have three names but one destiny. The difference, however, is none of them escaped. I will escape. I must escape."

Ahmed slipped his Beretta back into its compartment and looked out the window. The lot was clear. *It could not have been John Savage I saw*, he thought. *Savage would have pursued me to the ends of the earth.*

Ahmed popped the trunk of his car with the remote and carried his bags to the trunk. He took the garbage bag and tossed it into the backseat of the car. He was moving a little bit awkwardly. The sling would take some getting used to. "I should have worn it more, but now that makes no difference."

Ahmed took one last walk around his room to make certain he had scoured the place of all evidence of his presence. The room was cleaner than when he had moved in. After he reached the door and scanned the area one last time, Sergeant Robert Margolis walked nonchalantly to his vehicle, climbed in, and drove carefully out onto University Avenue.

Ahmed maneuvered his way through the Twin Cities until he left them behind, heading South on Highway 52. After driving over an hour, he took a sharp left from Highway 52 onto Interstate 90, and he could see no one was around to follow him. He felt exhilarated.

He said to himself, "If I should die then so be it. This mission is worth dying for."

Feeling his energy revitalized and his spirit renewed, Ahmed—AKA Sergeant Robert Margolis—merged into traffic onto Interstate 90 as he shouted loudly to the heavens, "Allahu Akbar! Allahu Akbar! Allahu Akbar!"

CHAPTER THIRTY-FOUR

A Sign from Allah

artel listened on the phone as the HUAS clarified the big picture as if Martel were a confused child. "Let me explain this to you again. We at Homeland Security are concerned about creating an unwarranted panic which might cause law enforcement to initiate a campaign of harassment of innocent immigrants and citizens. Sounding a false alarm such as this could be as dangerous to our country as a legitimate foreign threat. One can be as devastating as the other for our nation."

"But, Ma'am," said Martel.

But the word "Ma'am," was Martel's final word on the subject. This was neither a dialog nor a discussion. This was a monologue…a lecture.

"But nothing! All you have is a dead drug mule on a border littered with dead drug mules. That's hardly news. Let's see what else do you have? You have a dead Yemeni National on a legal work visa shot down by a SWAT Team. The numbers he pressed on his phone allegedly spell the word Allah. You have a dead stripper, killed by a live-in boy-friend, who has since disappeared. Sadly this also is all too common."

"Last and certainly not least, you have a police officer, who may or may not be suffering from post-traumatic stress, who is seeing a terrorist that he met in Iraq and it just so happens no one else has seen this terrorist, including you. Special Agent Martel, I am told by your superiors that they have a great deal of confidence in your abilities to do whatever it is that you do, but we are not authorizing the general release of the information on Ahmed Abdullah Rahim until we have hard evidence that he is in this country." After she finished, the HUAS added, "Do we have an understanding?"

"Ma'am…" Martel began.

"Do not call me Ma'am. That conjures up the picture of a matronly spinster, which I am not. You can call me Assistant Director, Special Agent Martel. I prefer to keep our relationship formal," said the HUAS with a voice oozing with detestation.

"Madam Assistant Director, he was just seen in Minneapolis," said Martel.

"Don't call me madam either. Did you see him?" the HUAS asked.

"No, Assistant Director. Officer Savage saw him and I believe…"

"You believe a man who some say is suffering from post-traumatic stress, which may be causing a state of hyper-vigilance. I would like it if you would cease this outlandish partnership that you have established."

"Now, Ma'am, we are through talking. You have no authority over my investigation other than the release of that photo. When this plays out, I am advising you right now, respectfully, that this decision you have made will bite us all in the ass if we fail before Ahmed succeeds. Ahmed exists. He is here to kill someone important. If we could release that information, I am certain we would have him in 24 hours. I have asked you repeatedly for this authorization, and you have denied me this simple request. I will not have you hinder my investigation further by blinding me after you have tied my hands. Do you have anything else to say that is within your circle of control, Ma'am?" asked Martel. "If not I will bid you good day."

"Don't call me Ma'am!" The HUAS snapped.

"Good day, Ma'am," answered Martel as he cut off the call.

"What a mindless, bureaucratic, politically-appointed HUAS!" Martel growled. John brought their order over to the picnic table on the patio of the Taco Bell.

"I'm guessing they are not releasing the photo to the public, right?" John asked.

"You are correct, sir," answered Martel.

"I'm also guessing that my sightings of Ahmed are not hard evidence of anything. Am I Right?" John posed.

"Correct once again," said Martel as he opened his burrito and took a bite, then he threw the burrito down on the table, "Damn it! They put refried beans on my burrito. I'd rather have had them send out a dirty diaper. I may have been able to eat that."

Martel then picked up his phone and called Sig, "Yeah, Sig, this is Martel. Thanks for the help, but cancel the detail," he said.

There was a pause and then Martel said, "No. By 5:00 PM tomorrow he will be in another city and probably in another state. Thanks though. If we'd been set up a day earlier we would have had him. We were a day late and a dollar short. Thanks for the offer to help. Next time, Sig."

After he slipped his phone back onto his belt, Martel looked at his burrito with disgust and tossed it back into the bag and griped, "Refried Beans. I hate refried beans."

John took the cue and bagged what was left of his burrito and tossed it into his bag, and within two minutes they were on the road again. After a long silence John asked, "La Crosse?"

"La Crosse," answered Martel.

"Are we still partners?" John wondered.

"Absolutely! We're going to get this son of a bitch," declared Martel. "I am certain he will alter his appearance again, but even if he does you are going to spook him. If we proved nothing else in Minneapolis, we proved that," said Martel.

"We also proved Felix knows what he is talking about," said John.

"Something I already knew, which reminds me…" Martel pulled out his phone and hit two numbers. "Felix. Ahmed showed up in Minneapolis. He ran when he spotted John at a strip joint called Déjà vu and disappeared in rush hour traffic. Where do we go to next, Felix?" Then Martel hit the speaker on the phone and slipped it into the holder on the dash.

John sat up. The importance of the gesture of letting him listen in to a call to Felix did not escape him. *We are partners*, he thought with a smile.

"Unless you have any hard intelligence I would follow the president as he swings through the Midwest. I am certain that he is Ahmed's target. I am surmising that you have not gained any headway with Homeland Security on the release of his photo. Am I correct?" Felix asked.

"Yes, Felix. Does that surprise you?" asked Martel.

"Sadly no; turning on a light will not aid in a blind woman's effort to see. Charles, I believe that this man is so much of a threat that his image should be on the front page of every newspaper and on every newscast in the nation. Even if I am wrong in my assessment of the target, the nation is in grave peril." said Felix.

"Do you have any specific alternatives?" asked Martel.

"No. I would say given the lack of cooperation by Homeland Security, follow the president. You know he is speaking in La Crosse. He is arriving Monday night and speaking on Tuesday at 11:00 AM at a local stadium called Logger's Field. I believe Ahmed will be in town," said Felix. "I believe he will attempt to Americanize his appearance."

"What about his concern that John Savage is a cop in that town?" asked Martel.

"I believe he will be in such an altered state that he will not concern himself with that. Besides, the press believes Savage is still on administrative leave. If he saw him at Déjà vu in Minneapolis and he was not hotly pursued, that will either reinforce that point of view or lead him to question whether or not he actually saw Savage. Regardless, you must shadow the president until hard evidence surfaces about his location," reasoned Felix.

"We are driving to La Crosse as we speak," agreed Martel. "Where do you go from here?"

"The Special Agents from the Minneapolis Office are attempting to get me a clean copy of the security footage of Ahmed at Déjà vu. I will let you know if it is something we can use. I am cutting through and analyzing the chatter. Hopefully Ahmed will come up for air somewhere, but if we are right about his target, he will maintain his lone wolf approach to the target and contact no one. Obviously you are planning on making the necessary contacts in La Crosse," said Felix.

"We will be contacting the advance team as soon as we arrive. They will be there now prepping for the visit," said Martel.

"I will send you the contact number and name of the Secret Service advance team commander. You should be receiving it...now. I will contact you again if I have anything at all. John, I would use caution in town. It is not reasonable for him to attempt to kill you again, but I believe Ahmed has a fixation on you. He may rationalize that killing you will clear the way for whatever his mission is here. As you folks would say, watch your six," cautioned Felix.

"Thank you for your concern," said John, leaning up to the phone. "I will be careful."

"That is all I have for you," said Felix.

"Good bye," said Martel and he tapped the phone.

"La Crosse. I sense that this will be our O.K. Corral with this Al-Qaeda son of a bitch," said Martel.

As Martel came up on the exit for St. Charles, he turned to John and asked, "Hey, John, could you drive? I want to make contact with our Secret Service counterparts in La Crosse and tell them of our concerns," said Martel glancing over his right shoulder and swinging the car onto and down the ramp.

"Sure, I'll drive," and John turned and smiled at Special Agent Martel. If his being able to listen in on a phone call with Felix didn't mean they were partners, "you drive," certainly sealed the deal.

When Martel saw John smiling at him like a bum finding a wrapped burger in a McDonald's dumpster, he asked, "What?"

"Nothing, I just got a feeling Ahmed is toast," said John.

"Let's hope," said Martel, pulling over into a gas station with an Amish restaurant attached. "We'll switch here."

After John took over the driving, Martel made a series of phone calls gathering information and arranging meetings. He made it clear to everyone he talked to that although it was classified and speculation, he strongly felt Ahmed would be shadowing the president on his swing through the Midwest.

As John was crossing the Mississippi River Bridge, entering Wisconsin, Martel turned to John and said, "Head home and grab whatever you need for a stay at the hotel. The president will be staying at The Radisson Hotel and so will we."

"Got it," acknowledged John.

"It sure is pretty here," said Martel, pausing to take in the unbroken line of bluffs to the east and west of the city, as well as the Mississippi and Black Rivers flowing through the lush green valley that John called home.

"I have lived here my whole life, and I still am often awed to silence by the beauty of this place. I have been all over the world and have seen places as beautiful, but none more beautiful to me," answered John.

The sun was setting, and as it slipped down behind the Minnesota Bluffs, the sky exploded in colors so awe inspiring it would have caused Claude Monet to blush at his vain attempt to capture its beauty on canvass. Martel admired the display and proclaimed, "No wonder they call this God's Country."

———>➤●ᗤ———

Ahmed did his reconnaissance by car around the area of Logger's Field. The Black River blocked an escape to the west. The area was wide open to the north by Copeland Park, making it difficult to disappear in that direction unless he followed the river bank.

Ahmed drove to the dead end at Copeland Park, which stopped at a turnaround that abutted up to the Clinton Street Bridge. He parked and got out. He walked down to the river and thought, *a boat?* Ahmed continued walking north along the river passing under the Clinton Street Bridge and saw a boat landing on the opposite side of the bridge. *The river will be covered. It is too small to disappear on that river*, he reasoned.

The only place to escape will be if I make it to the east or south. There are alleyways, railroad tracks and places to run and fade away into. The possibility of succeeding in this mission is high. The probability of my escape is low, thought Ahmed as he scanned the entire area.

Ahmed parked again. As he exited his car, an older couple walking in the road holding hands waved to him, "Thank you for your service."

Ahmed paused, smiled, and responded, "You're welcome."

He walked down the embankment realizing that to anyone looking he appeared to be a wounded soldier returned home from the war, taking a moment in thoughtful remembrance of a youth raised in the river town. No one would have suspected Ahmed to be an Al-Qaeda warrior. Ahmed scanned the river and saw an opportunity offered by a line of boat houses on both sides of the river. If *I made it to the river, I could hide indefinitely under the boat houses and swim out after dark*, he thought. Then he looked to his left and saw a huge culvert. *The culvert is an option, but I believe those will be covered... too predictable. I could make it appear that I used the culvert and then hit the water and duck under the boat houses if I had to*, thought Ahmed. *The best avenue though is to the south and east. If I make it beyond Copeland Avenue, I will have a chance of escape.*

Ahmed's gaze and attention focused quite suddenly on the sunset directly across the Black River to the west. The sky was ablaze in color. The scattered clouds were in motion, absorbing and reflecting the colors which gave the appearance of a vast heavenly kaleidoscope. Ahmed, overcome by the natural exquisiteness of the display gasped and proclaimed out loud, "My success is pre-ordained. This must be a sign from Allah."

Chapter Thirty-five

Bragg

After John crossed into Wisconsin, Martel asked, "Can we drive by Logger's Field?"

"You Betcha," answered John using his most fluent Wisconsin/Kanuch dialect. The exit came up fast and within minutes John took the ramp taking him south on Highway 53.

As John rolled down Rose Street, paralleling the Black River, Martel said, "Rose Street. My mother's name is Rose."

"Really? My grandmother's name is Rose," said John.

As they reached a large nineteenth-century Steam Engine parked at an intersection, John said, "This is Copeland Park. At the far end of the park is Logger's Field. You will see it on the right," said John.

"I love those boat houses down on the river. If I built one could I put it down there?" Martel asked.

"No. The ones that are there can stay, but no more can be added. I think they have been declared a historical spot. A buddy of mine owns the third one from the Clinton Street bridge, and we used to sleep-over in the summer. I lost my virginity there on the night of my graduation," said John.

"The best night of your life?" asked Martel.

"More like the best two and half minutes of my life," laughed John. "That's classified," cautioned John.

"The Iranian Secret Police could not get it out of me," assured Martel.

As the light changed to green, John pulled out and trolled along in the right lane, allowing Martel to take a good look at the park. As they reached the park, Martel said, "Whoa. This place is wide open from the east. I am certain the Secret Service will have to construct a barricade."

"I was here for another rally once, and they lined the area to the east with dump trucks, preventing a sniper shot from the east," said John.

"That works," said Martel.

As John started the turn into Copeland Park, he caught sight of a driver turning right out of the park. John said, "Airborne!"

"What's that?" Martel asked.

"There was an airborne soldier in the car that just turned onto Copeland. He must just be back on a medical leave. He had his left arm in a cast and sling. I wonder if it was someone I know. I didn't see his face," said John still rubber-necking in a futile attempt to identify the soldier.

After John completed the circuit, Martel said, "Let's get your fresh gear and get checked in at the Radisson."

John reached the turnaround at Copeland Park and noticed four reprobates sitting on top of two picnic tables under the large shelter next to the turnaround. As the car made the turn one of the beer-bellied quartet smiled and shouted, "Yoh Sa-VAAAGE!" The long haired, bearded man smiled showing off a gap, where his front teeth should be.

John waved and shouted, "Yoh Grizzly!"

"Savage, have you shot anyone yet today," shouted the drunken bear/human, and then he laughed until he lost his balance and nearly fell of the picnic table he was perched upon.

"No, Grizzly, but it's still early," answered John," So behave yourself."

"Friend?" asked Martel.

"One of my law enforcement contacts. His name fits him. He got it because he looks like Grizzly Adams. Grizzly wakes up in the morning with his blood alcohol level at about point two zero. He drinks until he either goes into hibernation or gets angry and fights. When he fights, he growls like a grizzly, but in truth he fights like a bear cub," said John, "Hence the missing teeth." John continued his drive out of the park and through town to his home.

As John pulled into his driveway, he scanned the area carefully, unfastened his seat belt and quickly exited with his hand in a position to draw. The area appeared safe, but the woodline of Hixon Forest would allow for the perfect sniper's nest. "Care to come inside, while I pack?" asked John.

"Sure," said Martel, exiting much less warily than John. "I don't think he is going to try anything on you, with the president coming. I think Felix is wrong on that point," said Martel.

John took out his flashlight and took one quick turn around the house and found all the doors and windows intact. He let himself quietly in the back door and worked his way through the house and then let Martel in the front door. "Wine, beer, or soda?" asked John.

"Nah. I'll wait until we get back to the hotel," said Martel.

As John headed for his bedroom to get some fresh clothes, his home phone rang. John checked the caller identification and it said "PRIVATE CALLER."

"Hello," said John.

"Hey, Johnny, guess who?" said the good-natured voice on the opposite end.

"Balduzzi!?" asked John in disbelief.

"Good guess, Johnny. I have been calling for days. I couldn't leave a message because I have to ask you something that has to remain between us for now. Can you do that my friend?" asked Balduzzi.

"I can keep it confidential unless you are conspiring to commit a felony. I am a cop now, you know," said John in a cautionary tone.

"No shit. You are all over the news, all over the place. I check the paper every day to see if you killed anyone else. Hey, Johnny, fuck them! I read everything there was to read. I would have shot every one of those sons of bitches and their fucking pet monkeys too," said Balduzzi with great sincerity. "That's not why I called, though. I have a proposition for you. Interested?"

"I have a career and a home here, but I'll listen to anything you have to say," said John.

"That's all I ask. This is the deal. I am now Captain Balduzzi," said the captain.

"No shit? Congratulations," said John.

"Thanks. I have been ordered to recruit and train a special Hostage Rescue Unit. There are more hostage takers in the middle-east than there are goat-herders. I am supposed to find them and rescue their hostages with a team trained to deal with as many hostage takers as possible and eliminate their threat with extreme prejudice. I was given total authority to choose and train the members of the team. John, you are still a reserve. I checked. If you want to climb aboard I can have you activated and assigned to my team. You will be able to answer your country's call once again and rid the world of some really bad dudes. At the same time you bring some nice people home to their families. Some of them have been held for years. Since it will be a reserve call-up, your job there in La Crosse will be waiting for you when you return. What do you say buddy? Are we going to be together again?" Balduzzi made his pitch as if it was well practiced.

"When do I have to be where?" John asked. "I am right in the middle of something I can't quit."

"You will need to report to Fort Bragg on November 10," said Balduzzi.

"It sounds pretty good to me, but like I said, I can't quit what I am doing until I have finished. When do you need to know by?" John asked.

"You have until November 9 if you can hop a plane and be here by November 10, 0800 hours, I will have a place reserved for you," promised Balduzzi. "I will be the Officer in Charge, and I want you for my Team Leader."

"I will think hard about it. To tell you the truth, it sounds pretty good to me right about now. Between you and me, I feel pretty God damn unappreciated here," opined John. "I'll get back to you with an answer as soon as possible. Good-bye, my friend."

"I am counting on you to cover my six, buddy," said Balduzzi. "I am not even going to say 'goodbye.' I'm going to say see you at Fort Bragg."

Chapter Thirty-six

Robert

Ahmed parked his car in the Radisson lot and scanned the area. He'll enter through the south door. He will be bracketed by the Radisson and the Civic Center, he thought, making a mental note. He grabbed his black bag, set it down on the ground with his free arm, and shut the trunk.

As Ahmed was about to pick the bag up when a smiling attendant with a wheeled cart came rushing up and said, "I'll get your bag, Sergeant," and the man wrested the bag away from Ahmed and hoisted the bag to the cart. "Is this all you have, sir?" The man in the black and gold uniform asked.

"That's everything," said Ahmed with a smile. "I have to check in though."

"Certainly. I will take it to the front desk and then, when you are ready, I can take it up to your room," said the attendant.

Ahmed crossed the spacious, beige, and heavily planted lobby to the check-in desk. The manager was strikingly beautiful with long blonde tresses falling lazily about her shoulders. Her smile was accented by dimples and her warmth triggered a feeling in Ahmed as if a rock was slowly sinking in the void that was left when he put the bullet into the head of Lara, whose only crime was to love him.

"Can I help you, Sergeant?" the manager asked. Ahmed just stood standing with mouth and eyes opened as his mind punished him by replaying the moment he dropped his keys and his beautiful, loving Lara bent down to pick them up and then...

"Sergeant, are you all right?" the manager asked.

"Yes. Yes, I am all right. I just remembered I forgot my credit card. Can I pay in cash?" the phony Sergeant asked.

"Yes, you may. We need to have it in advance, though," she said crinkling her brow, "I hope that is all right."

"I want to pay for four days in advance," said Ahmed.

Ahmed struggled a bit, pulling his wallet out of his pocket and then painstakingly picking the cash out with one hand. As Ahmed slowly counted out the twenties, the manager sheepishly asked, "Were you in Iraq or Afghanistan?"

"Both," said Ahmed truthfully.

"Wow! Thank you for your service," and she said turning her head to read the name on Ahmed's uniform, "Sergeant Margolis."

Ahmed replied, "You're welcome…," and he turned his head and leaned forward to read the manager's name tag, "Bree. From now on every time I hear the song 'America the Beautiful' play it will be impossible not to think of you," he said as he handed the carefully counted out pile of twenties to Bree.

"Why, thank you," Bree answered visibly blushing. "Here is your room key," and she slid an envelope with the number of the room written on it. "You will have a view of the bluff, and here is your change, sir."

As Bree handed the change to Ahmed, he reached for her hand and held it gently closed as he said, "No thank you. That will not be necessary. Please give it to this good man, who is helping me with my bag." Then he whispered, "Please, Bree, call me if you feel something between us. I would love to spend some time to get to know you better."

She allowed her hand to linger in his, and as he released it she tucked her hair behind her right ear as she cast her eyes shyly down and slowly brought her eyes up to his. His brown eyes look so innocent and beckoning, she thought. "Just call the desk if you need that taken care of," she said, trying to be business-like.

Ahmed smiled and nodded as he headed to the elevator. The attendant followed with the bag on a wheeled cart. As they reached the elevator the attendant turned to Ahmed and asked, "Were you injured in Iraq or Afghanistan?"

"We call it wounded, and I was wounded in Afghanistan," said Ahmed. This was also true, since he had been hit with shrapnel in the defense of Tora Bora.

The comment caught the attention of a man approaching the elevator who was thoroughly occupied by a rather detailed, multi-paged itinerary. He looked up and was surprised to see Ahmed approaching. A smile burst onto his face and he said, "You say, Sergeant, that you were wounded in Afghanistan?"

"Yes, sir, I was," said Ahmed without hesitation.

"Great! … I'm sorry, I mean, not great that you were wounded, but great that you happen to be here. Are you aware that the president is coming to town tomorrow?" asked the man.

"Well, yes, I think I saw a paper somewhere that mentioned that," said Ahmed with feigned uncertainty.

"Well, I am Mark Greenburg. I am Assistant to the President's Press Secretary. How would you like to meet the president?" Mark asked shaking Ahmed's free hand.

"Who wouldn't like to meet the president?" said Ahmed.

"Great. I would like to have you meet him as he arrives tomorrow for some photos, and if possible, I would like to put you in the gallery behind him the next day, while he is speaking. Is that doable for you Sergeant…,"

"Margolis, Sergeant Robert Margolis," said Ahmed wincing and re-adjusting his sling as if his wound was bothering him. "I would be honored."

"The president loves meeting wounded soldiers. Here is my card. Call me at this number sometime after 10:00 AM tomorrow, and I will tell you when and where to be. I will have everything you need to get inside the cordon. I'll clear you myself," said Greenburg.

"As I said, I am truly honored, sir," said Ahmed feeling a rush.

"No, we are honored," said Greenburg, shaking Ahmed's hand one last time as he continued on to the hotel restaurant, the Three River's Lodge, re-burying his head in his itinerary as he pulled out a pen and wrote the name Margolis in large letters on the second page.

When Ahmed reached his room, he thanked the smiling attendant and as he closed the door his phone rang. He smiled, picked it up, and said, "Sgt. Margolis."

"Hello, Sergeant. I only have a few moments, but well...I am engaged to be married....and...I get off at 10:00 PM. I will come to your room unless I am ah...being too forward and maybe I shouldn't..."

"I will be anxiously waiting for 10:00 PM to arrive. You are not married yet, and the old saying 'All is fair in love and war' after meeting you, has become my credo."

Love? Bree thought hopefully.

"I felt something very strong pulling us together, Bree. I do not propose a meeting to every beautiful woman I meet. There was something between us, strong and beautiful. Did you feel it?" Ahmed asked carefully, playing her like fisherman trying to land a trophy musky. He needed this, one last time before his glory day, and she was gorgeous.

"Yes I did. I did feel it. I will be there at about 10:15 PM. Do you drink white wine?" she asked.

"I will drink it too your beauty," Ahmed said.

———➤●◄———

Ahmed woke early. The warmth of her exquisite body next to him would be something he would miss if he did not survive this mission. "Allah, may you allow me to enjoy the fruits of the flesh in heaven after I have served you so well." Ahmed slipped silently out of bed, walked to the window, opened the drapes, and sat next to the window. He looked below as a policeman walked along the street, pulling the doors of each business to make certain they were locked.

He looked out across the city. Rising above the collection of three story buildings that made up downtown La Crosse was the cross of Christ atop St Joseph the Workman's Cathedral. Ironically, beyond that, the sun was peeking over Grandad's Bluff. Even at a distance of miles, Ahmed could see what must have been a huge American Flag silhouetted by the rising sun unfurled and flapping furiously in the summer breeze.

He looked down at the policeman, who was stopped and talking to a man on the sidewalk. Ahmed, try as he might, could not resist the temptation to conjure up portends of future successes as well as failures in this everyday occurrence. The police officer stood in a direct line between Ahmed, the cross, and the American Flag.

Allah is telling me to use caution. My attack on these Christian Americans will not go uncontested. I wonder why Allah would tell me something I already know? thought Ahmed.

His attention was drawn to the sweet music of Bree taking in a deep breath as she stirred. He left the drapes open and crossed the room. He marveled at her beauty in the orange glow of the sunrise. Her ring on her finger, pledging her betrothal to another man, somehow aroused him. He picked up the sheet, slowly, and drank in the image of her perfect soft and natural breasts uncorrupted by the surgeon's knife as so many American breasts he had seen. Her stomach was delectably flat and lay motionless as her breathing caused her breasts to rise and fall gently like the wings of a nested dove settling down to sleep. She was irresistible.

As he slid into bed and onto Bree, she accepted him immediately with a gasp and a kiss. Bree gazed into Ahmed's eyes as the two lovers became one and brought her hands up to caress his face. She caught the glint of her engagement ring in the morning light and Bree slid it off her finger in the midst of their love making and showed it to Ahmed. Bree laughed gleefully as she threw the ring across the room and it chinked off the window, chipping the glass. With that gesture completed, she gave in to her passion and gasped; swimming in the lake of her new found love, she cried out, "Oh God, Robert!"

CHAPTER THIRTY-SEVEN

Last Meal

As Martel pulled into the rear parking lot at the Sparta Campus of the Western Technical College, he was put in awe at the panorama of preparation taking place before his eyes. Cars were spinning about on the driving track practicing emergency pursuit immobilization maneuvers. Secret Service snipers were prone on the far end of the 300 yard rifle range taking their cold bore shots, maintaining their finely honed skills.

Brian Noble, one of the police trainers, had his academy students lined up for shadow fighting in the summer sun. They were punching and kicking at imaginary suspects aligned on all sides of them. Brian saw John and yelled to his students, "Keep fighting. Never give up. Pace yourselves. Back-up is three minutes away. While you're at it, give our friend John Savage a shout out."

The class shouted in unison, "OOO-AAH!"

Brian then ran over to John while the class kept step sliding, kicking, and punching with an admirable intensity. "John, do you have a second?"

John looked at Martel, who glanced at his watch and nodded.

"Sure, Brian," said John.

"I wouldn't trouble you if it wasn't important," said Brian, sweating, but barely winded. "Did you hear about the guy who went to the dentist, sat down in his chair, and said 'Doctor, Doctor I think I'm going crazy. I keep thinking I'm a moth.' The dentist says, 'Well if you think you're going crazy, why did you come to me? I'm a dentist.' The guy looks

248

around the room," then Brian Noble took on the persona of a paranoid schizophrenic and flapped his arms wildly, then stopped as suddenly as he started and said, "Your light was on."

Brian, John, and Martel laughed. John said, "As usual, that was a good one. Are there any good candidates in this group?"

Brian shook John's hand and said, "They're all good, they don't become great until they show they can perform on the street, like John Savage. I brag about you every time your name comes up," Brian got a smug look on his face, shook his head and said, "Yeah, you know that John Savage guy. I trained him," as he pointed both his thumbs at his own chest. "See you in the funny papers, buddy. I gotta run." The intensity returned to his face and he ran back to his sweating, kicking, and punching charges.

"Sorry, Charlie, I should have introduced you. That was Brian Noble. He was one of my instructors at the academy. He is a great guy, great instructor. Somehow he keeps you laughing, while he is keeping it serious."

"What would we do without guys like that?" Martel asked.

Martel and Savage made their way to room 130 at the campus, which was a state of the art public safety training facility. The Secret Service had arranged for the final coordination meeting before the presidential visit. Every agency which had anything to do with the presidential visit was present. There were representatives from the Wisconsin and Minnesota State Patrol, the La Crosse County Sheriff's Department, Houston County Sheriff's Department on the opposite side of the Mississippi, as well as the Secret Service, which was handling coordination.

William Roberts, who was Special Agent in charge, started the meeting by having everyone introduce themselves and explain what piece of the presidential-visit puzzle they represented. When it was John's turn he introduced himself as he had been directed to do by Martel, "I am Officer John Savage of the La Crosse Police Department. I am currently on special assignment with FBI Special Agent Charles Martel.

The reaction in the room was instantaneous. There had been blasé reception for each introduction up until this, but John's introduction quashed the indifference. Feet were shuffling and heads were turning when everyone in the room turned to see the local officer turned national celebrity. John Savage was semi-famous as the poster-child for Unjustifiable-Media-Cop-Bashing.

One of the State Troopers, decked out in full regalia, still wearing his hat, spontaneously started clapping and was followed by every other person in the room. If John was a prone to tears he would have shed some at that moment. Instead he nodded his head, shying away from the attention, and then saluted and sat down, visibly moved.

After the introductions Secret Service Agent Roberts handed out a small booklet, containing plans, codes, protocols, procedures, dates, times, locations, and assignments. He explained that the sub-groups would break off and meet so that each member of each team would know their assignments. Roberts explained, "The president will be arriving at the La Crosse Airport on Air Force One at 5:12 PM. He will be shuttled from the tarmac to the Radisson Hotel, and a security cordon described on page 23-2 will be set up for his arrival at the Radisson." Roberts paused while pages were shuffled by everyone to 23-2.

"The president will be arriving via motorcade at 5:45 PM at the Radisson Hotel. We will secure an exit on the south-side of the building between the Civic Center and the hotel. He will be speaking to a group at the Civic Center at 8:00 PM, and he will spend the night at the Radisson."

"The president will proceed to Logger's Field for a rally at 10:00 AM tomorrow, and the motorcade will transport him to the airport. We are expecting to be wheels up by 11:32 AM," explained Roberts. "Are there any questions?" No one raised their hand, and some looked about the room to see if any others did. Roberts continued, "Special Agent Charles Martel would like to share a security concern with the group. Agent Martel," and with that Roberts stepped aside and sat down.

Martel slipped his thumb drive into the computer at the front of the room and the word classified appeared on the screen. "I am Special Agent Charles Martel, ladies and gentlemen, and I would like to make you aware of the fact that we have no hard intelligence of the whereabouts of the following person, but it is my educated… guess that he may be showing his face at presidential rallies. The problem is this face," and Martel advanced the slide to the bearded Ahmed in his kufiya , "will undoubtedly be altered. We have updated to a computer generated Ahmed," and Martel advanced to new image.

John looked at the photo. The hair was current, the shape of the head was correct, but there was something drastically different in the eyes. He could not identify what was missing, but the eyes were wrong.

Martel continued, "We suspect him in a murder on the border and also the murder of a Madison woman. This man is dangerous. This is a photo generated from a security camera in Minneapolis," Martel advanced to a photo shot from overhead. John recognized the doorway as the front door at Déjà vu. Ahmed had his hand up, scratching his eyebrow, which caused his face to be hidden from the view of the camera, making the grainy image worthless in any effort to identify Ahmed. "This is what he looked like days ago, but I can't say what he looks like today. John Savage can identify him, and if you have any concerns use caution and do not hesitate to call us."

After the large group briefing, the teams split up. The airport team went in one direction, the motorcade officers another, and the on-sight tactical teams still another. John and Martel left. "John, you drive. You know the city best. Let's just do some old-fashioned patrolling and see what we can see."

"Sweet," John replied.

━━━━━➤●◄━━━━━

Ahmed kissed Bree at the door, and as their lips separated she held onto him and asked, "Will I hear from you again?"

Ahmed reached into his pocket and handed her the ring she had tossed during their love making and responded, "You should have this. Whether you put it on again will be up to you, but you should have it."

"Does this mean the answer is no?" Bree asked again in disbelief.

"I am a soldier. I have known nothing but war my whole adult life. I want to see you again, but I must be honest with you. My life is what it is, but most women can't handle it and ask me to change what I have no power to change in my life. If I am able to, I will call you tonight at the desk. Do you work again until 10:00?" he asked.

"Yes. Please call me though. I must see you again," Bree said desperately. She kissed him again.

"If I can I will," Ahmed said as he kissed one last time and opened the door for her.

Bree cautiously looked both ways in the hallway and ran quickly to the exit stairwell, down and out, avoiding the lobby.

Ahmed shut the door and checked the clock. It was 10:06 AM and he used the hotel phone to call Greenburg's number. Greenburg answered before the phone rang, "Greenburg."

"Mr. Greenburg, this is Sergeant Robert Margolis. You asked that I call you after 10:00. Is this a bad time?" Ahmed queried.

"There is never a good time. Meet me in the Three River's Lodge at 11:00. Wear the uniform," said Greenburg in demanding tone that made Margolis decide that if it were possible he would put a bullet or two into Greenburg when the opportunity presented itself.

"I'll be there, is there any…" and Greenburg was gone. "Swine," Ahmed said out loud.

Ahmed entered the Three Rivers Lodge and saw Greenburg at a window seat, which allowed for a panoramic view of the Mississippi River. A tug pushing a barge chugged lazily down the Mississippi, but the scenic beauty was wasted on Greenburg. The government employee in the Armani suit sat navigating a laptop and blackberry while he talked incessantly on another cell-phone. Ahmed walked up to the table and stood silently for a minute before Greenburg noticed him. When Greenburg saw Ahmed, he motioned quickly toward the seat opposite his and Ahmed sat down.

"I'll call you back. My meeting is just getting started. This shouldn't take long," and Greenburg set the phone down on the table.

"Sgt. Margolis, it is so good to see you. I will make this quick, because I have to run. Here is your clearance to be allowed inside the presidential cordon. He handed him the necessary identifiers and directed him on how to use them. The process was over in less than three minutes and Greenburg was packing up.

"I am pressed for time so I have to run. Order whatever you want, lunch is on me. I want you to report to the south door of the hotel by 5:00 PM. They will be expecting you. You will shake hands with the president, and we will get some shots. Then tomorrow, report to Logger's Field by 9:00 AM, and they will get you situated on stage. We have placed you in a place of prominence, behind the president. Call your parents and tell them you will be on television." Greenburg was hastily packing his technology as he spoke.

"Don't forget to call your parents and have them watch for you," Greenburg repeated as he walked away but abruptly turned to add, "I almost forgot. I will need a little personal history. The press will want to know and the president might work you into the speech. I would like to know, for example, where you're from and the circumstances of your wounding and such. It should be kind of like a résumé. Please write something up for me, put it in an envelope and drop it at the desk. I will pick it up later. Thanks, Sergeant. Bye. Gotta run," said Greenburg, who was on the phone again. "Yeah, sorry I had to cut you off, my life is organized insanity. I had a quick meeting; now as I was saying...." and Greenburg was gone.

"Résumé?" Ahmed said out loud with a smile. "I think not."

"Good morning, sir, what can I get for you today?" asked the waiter, who suddenly appeared over Ahmed's right shoulder, startling Ahmed.

Ahmed's smile left and then returned to his face as he said, "I'll take the salmon with rice pilaf and an ice tea. Charge it to Mr. Greenburg, please."

"That has already been arranged, sir," said the waiter picking up the menu as he poured Ahmed a glass of water.

As the waiter spun and walked away, Ahmed pondered, *I hope the salmon, rice pilaf and ice tea is very good here. This may be my last meal.*

Chapter Thirty-eight

Wheels Down

Ahmed circled the area around the hotel planning, planning, planning. He did not need to plan the assassination. He was ready for that. Greenburg would say, "Mr. President this is Sergeant Robert Margolis, wounded in Afghanistan," and as the president extended his hand, Ahmed would pop the door in his cast, draw, and fire.

It was his escape that he needed to plan. *I will need to shoot my way out of the cordon. I will have a short run into the parking ramp on Jay Street. I will cut through the ramp. In and out, quick so they will swarm the ramp, but I will cut across Jay Street to my car at the far side of the lot, across the street.*

When I am in my car, I only need to take a left, a right, and another right, and I will be in Minnesota before they have the parking ramp closed off, if all goes well that is. If not, I will be lying next to the President of the United States. My name will be sung by Muslim children in every Madrassa in the world, he thought with a sigh. *This thought holds little solace for me. I prefer life, but death may be the only path to success.*

Ahmed pulled into the lot and found a spot on the opposite end of the parking lot. He locked the car instinctively, and then unlocked it again. "It must be ready to go immediately." As Ahmed turned to walk away, he weighed the possibility of having his car stolen against the possible advantage of having his keys already in the ignition of his car. "I think it is best to leave the keys in the car."

He returned to the car and slipped the key into the ignition. "I am ready."

The day went fast for Martel and Savage, as it often does, even though it might have seemed like nothing was accomplished. When a hunter enters the woods just before sunrise and stalks his prey until sunset then comes home empty handed, some would think it a boring day. Those are the foolish words of someone who has never lived the life of a predator, or the prey. The discovery of every track, the sound of every cracking twig, the rustle in the brush; all senses are stimulated in the thrill of the hunt.

The sands of a day on the hunt flow too quickly through the hour glass. Every inch of the route, every angle of the stadium, and every street around every location the president would be was covered by Savage and Martel. They hoped their path would cross Ahmed's. Martel said, "He will be scouting as well." Both men sensed the urgency as the time of the president's arrival approached.

As John Savage wheeled his way around the perimeter of the airport, he noticed a familiar face seated along the perimeter fence. It was Stella. She sat beside an easel and she was sketching the panorama of the airport. Stella had saved a spot in the middle for Air Force One.

"Stella," said John sadly to himself but loud enough for Martel to hear.

"That's her, with the easel?" Martel asked.

"Yes," answered John quietly.

"She's beautiful," said Martel, who seemed to share John's sense of loss. "Go talk to her, man."

"She didn't want…" said John.

"No. Time's up on that deal. This is just a chance meeting, that's all. You are working a security detail and decided to stop and say 'Hi.' Check it out, John. You will be able to see how she feels without asking her how she feels. I'm telling you, talk to her," insisted Martel.

John turned about, parked the car near Stella and slowly walked toward her and stopped. As he turned back toward the car, Martel gave him a stern look and shook his head, "No."

John continued his tentative approach as if treading thin ice. She did not see him until he was standing next to her. "Hello, Stella," said John.

There was an ever so slight jerk, showing he had startled her.

"I'm sorry. I didn't mean to…"

"Oh that's all right, John. Hello. It's been a long, I mean I haven't seen you…Hello, John," said Stella.

"That's very good," said John as he gestured to her sketch.

"I hope to paint it and make a print that I can sell in this area. Local prints do pretty well when you have something major inserted like Air Force One," she said. "What brings you here?" Stella asked.

"I am working security for the president, and I saw you here. I thought you might not mind me just stopping to say 'Hi.' I know you said you didn't want me to…well I just thought it would be friendly just to stop. I hope you don't mind," said John.

"No. I'm glad you did. It is good to see you and…," but she was unable to complete the sentence.

John was overwhelmed suddenly by an incredible urge to hold her and kiss her but knew that he could not. "I am sorry, Stella. I have to go. I can't do this. I thought I could, but I can't. I can't bear to be by you without being with you. I love you and I will always love you, no matter what. Good-bye." He turned and walked away and did not look back. He walked past Martel saying, "Let's go."

Stella put her hand up about to call him back but nothing came out. She crumpled forward, covered her face and cried quietly.

As John steered the car away, refusing to cast his eyes upon her again, Martel determined, "That girl still loves you, a lot, John."

"Where to now?" asked John looking straight ahead. He appeared as if absolutely nothing had happened, as if it didn't feel like his heart had been torn from his chest just moments earlier.

"Hotel," said Martel, respecting his friend's decision to ignore what Martel had just witnessed. "There is nothing planned at the airport. He will be able to get into the limousine without much opportunity for an assassin. The perimeter is too heavily covered," deduced Martel.

"The hotel it is," said John, wheeling the car away from his past into his future.

The drive toward the hotel was so quiet you could almost hear the tinnitus in the ears of both cops. As they pulled into the east lot of the Radisson, the buzz of activity was visible immediately. Men and women in suits, wearing pins and ear pieces were traveling in and out the sliding doors making a constant swish swoosh sound from the entrances and exits.

As John turned the lot he said, "Damn it looks like an SUV dealership."

"Yeah, their sales pitch would be, 'Come on down to Secret Service Sales! We have thousands of high quality SUVs for you to choose from. You can get any color SUV you want as long as you want black,'" said Martel.

As John hit the auto lock on the car, he stretched and looked up and down 2nd Street. He recognized the wounded soldier from the night before just coming into the lot. "Say, Charlie, I am going to talk with this guy. He's airborne. I'll see you at the cordon in just a few minutes," John said.

"Got ya," replied Martel heading into the hotel.

John jogged over toward the soldier, who appeared to be pre-occupied. John slowed wondering if he should say anything because the soldier looked like he might be late for an appointment, but as John looked closer he thought, Damn. I don't know this guy, but he looks familiar. I think I served with him.

John smiled and shouted, "Yo, Airborne, OOO-AAH!"

The soldier jumped as if John had shouted "Incoming," and turned toward John. John smiled and shouted to the soldier, "Hey, buddy, I'm John Sav..." and their eyes met. The smile left John's face and the pre-occupation in the face of the airborne soldier turned to fear. John drew his weapon and shouted, "Police! Get down! Do it now!" but Ahmed was already running.

John pursued him out of the lot across 2nd Street. "Damn. I've got no radio, no back up."

Martel heard the shout just as the door to the hotel swooshed open for him and he turned to see John sprinting out of the lot after the wounded soldier, who was fleeing. Martel's feet were already breaking into a run when he heard John yell as loud as he could to anyone who was listening, "IT'S AHMED!"

As Ahmed cut across the street and took his planned route of escape, he thought, *If I can make it to the car I can try again, another time—another place.*

Reaching into his sling, he removed his Beretta on the run, but the sling and cast were slowing him down. He ripped the sling off, slid his arm out of the cast, and tossed it aside as he crossed 2nd Street, heading into the ramp.

John had gained ground on Ahmed. He brought his gun up to take a shot at the fleeing terrorist, but the headline played out in his mind, "Savage Shoots Illegal Immigrant in Back!" During the media-inspired hesitation, the cast came off and it was as if Ahmed hit the hyper-drive on the Millennium Falcon.

John was in good shape, but fast does not catch faster in any race, when both athletes are in top condition. "Damn. I'm not going to lose him again." John holstered his weapon and concentrated on speed.

Ahmed cut into the Jay Street parking ramp, and John was at least 100 feet back. As John passed from the light into the darkness of the ramp, his eyes tried to adjust. He barely caught the figure of Ahmed leaping over the wall of the parking ramp running south, across Jay Street. John turned back and quickly cut out of the ramp and ran south on the sidewalk and paralleling Ahmed, who was cutting into the parking lot across the street. Ahmed looked behind him and in his current tunnel vision he saw no one in pursuit from the ramp. *I lost him*, he thought. He did not see John, who was beyond Ahmed's fear-induced tunnel vision, farther to his right on Second Street.

As Ahmed reached the parking lot, he looked over his shoulder and still saw no one behind him. "Good. I must get to the car." Upon reaching the lot, Ahmed dropped to the ground and moved as quickly as a snake on the attack through the lot. Still no one followed. *I am going to make it*, he thought.

John stayed on the sidewalk alongside the lot and paralleled Ahmed, occasionally dropping down to get his bearings on his prey by looking under and between the parked cars. John gained ground and cut off Ahmed's escape. *My cell phone*, thought John and he reached into his pocket and as he ran punched in 9-1-1.

The voice on the other end answered, "911 dispatch, what is your emergency?"

"This is John Savage. I have Ahmed in the parking lot at 2nd and Jay, south of the parking ramp. He is dressed like an American Soldier. He is 10-32 (armed). I need back up immediately," John shouted.

Ahmed stopped crawling. He heard Savage shouting. Somehow he had gotten ahead of him.

As John was making the call, he saw Martel approaching up the sidewalk. Martel shouted, "Where is he, John?"

"He's in the lot on his belly. You get yourself some cover on the northeast corner of the lot, there!" John motioned to the corner of the lot like an Atlanta Braves fan doing the tomahawk. "I will cover the southwest corner and we will have him boxed in. Use cover; he is armed with a handgun," said John, who now had his own weapon in hand again. He kept the phone to his cheek so his communications would be heard by dispatch.

Instantly, Martel was at a dead run with his weapon drawn. John sprinted to his corner and hunkered down next to the tire of a red Ford F-150. John flattened out to reacquire the location of his adversary and thought, this is it. As he calmed his breath, he could hear the scritch-scratch of movement heading his direction two lanes over. Suddenly, there were footsteps and he heard Martel yell from across the lot, "He's running right at you, John!"

John looked up just as Ahmed appeared from behind the car parked in the next lane over. Ahmed was much more startled to see John than John was to see him. John stepped and slid to the front of the parked truck as Ahmed fired. The shot was on the run, and John heard the tinkle of the tail-light glass and the "thunk" of the round burying itself into the frame of the truck.

John leaned out and fired quickly, causing Ahmed to abandon his immediate plans of escape and duck for cover behind his car. "Damn you, Savage!" Ahmed shouted.

He stood up to acquire a fix on Savage and saw nothing but cars. Martel fired from the far corner of the lot, but shattered the back rear window of Ahmed's car. Ahmed fired wildly toward Martel with no hope of hitting him at such a great distance and dropped to the ground at a crouch.

John went prone and could see Ahmed crouching behind his vehicle. John moved into a roll-over prone position where he had a shot—not a great shot, but a shot. All he could see was the foot, shin, and ankles of the crouching terrorist. John steadied his Glock on the pavement and aligned his sights. They balanced delicately in the middle of Ahmed's ankle. John took a breath, let half of it out and gradually, and smoothly squeeeeezed, "Bam!"

Ahmed had heard the sirens coming and could not decide whether to make a break for the car or flee the lot, hoping he could lose the uniform, steal a car, make a run for it, and live to kill another day. He froze in a moment of indecision. "Allah, what should I do?" Ahmed prayed. Suddenly it came, the shot, the fall, and as he fell, Ahmed's Beretta flew out of his hand and skidded across the ground under his vehicle.

John watched Ahmed collapse to the ground while the gun clattered to the pavement under the car. Ahmed felt the pressure of the bullet smashing into his ankle bone immediately, but no pain. As he hit the ground, Ahmed sensed he had lost his gun and looked about frantically for it, spotting it under his car lying in the middle of a dried stain from a long gone leaking oil pan. The wounded but still dangerous killer stretched for his Beretta, but it was just out of reach.

Without thinking, Ahmed braced the foot of his smashed ankle to push off, and there it was waiting in the wings for its cue… the pain. "AAAIEEEEEEE!" screamed Ahmed as he rolled back and forth. He could no longer think of his Beretta. He could not think of Savage, he could not think of the president, he could not think of Allah, virgins, death or glory. Every one of his conscious senses was occupied with feeling this all-encompassing pain. All he could feel, hear, see, taste and smell was the **PAIN!**

Ahmed was rolling about writhing and screaming in pain, no longer concerning himself with the gun, which appeared to have slid out of reach. John picked up his phone, which was still connected to dispatch and said, "I have shots fired; the suspect is down. Keep back-up coming. I'll need a shift commander, investigators, and an ambulance. Martel and I are on scene and uninjured."

John cautiously approached at a crouch in a tactical Groucho-walk still covering the suspect from under the car. When he reached the would-be assassin, he could see Ahmed had prepared himself to inflict suffering, but was not prepared to endure suffering. The pain was so intense he was crying like a child calling, "Omy… Omy… Omy," meaning 'mother' in Arabic. Martel was close by now, "Cover me, Charlie," said John.

Ahmed was holding his shattered ankle with both hands and rolled on his back. John grabbed the crying man's wrist, placed it in a lock and rolled Ahmed to his belly, "Put your left hand in the small of your back and we will get you to a hospital. Do it NOW!"

Ahmed managed to pull his hand away and put the bloody hand into his back, and John swung his right back with it, pulled his handcuffs out and clicked them into place on Ahmed. As John conducted a search of Ahmed, he advised him, "Ahmed Abdullah Rahim. You, sir, are the enemy, wearing the uniform of an American Soldier in a time of war. You, sir, are a prisoner of war! Do you understand?" John asked.

"Fuck you, John Savage. May you die and suffer the wrath of Allah," said Ahmed and then he spit.

John's anger surged. He wanted to rip the uniform of the United States off this enemy who had sworn to bring the country down. John wanted to bring swift and final justice to the man who had killed his friend Chase. He wanted to send to hell the man who had used Lara Dickinson and then killed and discarded the lovely young woman like a banana peel. Instead, John took a deep breath through his nose, blew it out slowly through his mouth, and re-focused, saying to himself, "John, the man who angers you conquers you."

John stepped out of the momentary white rage and shifted gears. John did a quick triage and saw that the blood flowing freely from the wound on Ahmed's ankle would be life threatening if not stopped. We need him alive, thought John. John had been in this position before. He knew what to do. He ripped off his Packer Jersey and fashioned a makeshift bandage. He tightened it around Ahmed's wound, staving off the bleeding. He saw Martel standing next to him and said, "I think I may have nicked an artery here," said John working as feverishly as if it was one of his buddies in his platoon.

Ahmed became quiet, puzzled by the kind treatment of his enemy. Treatment he would never give if in John Savage's position. Ahmed pleaded, "Let it bleed. Let me die. I would kill you if you were in my place."

"Well, I am not in your place, am I? And I am not you. Consider yourself a guest in my country and chances are you will be for a very long time, so tough luck, buddy; you will see Allah some day, but not today," said John Savage.

John tied his Jersey tightly in place and held pressure on the wound. He moved his hand about until he found the pulse and pressed the artery against the tibia, which immediately stemmed the flow. John held pressure there until he was relieved by the arrival of the two firemen, who were the first rescue personnel to arrive on the scene.

As John looked about, he noticed that he had been joined at the scene by three suits, two brown shirted deputies, a state trooper, and three city cops. He had not even noticed their arrival. Crouched right beside him was Special Agent Charles Martel.

As the firemen took over, John and Charlie stood up and stepped back to watch. "I am glad you saved his life. He will be a treasure trove of information for us, but that jersey was number 12. You used your Aaron Rodgers jersey, man, to save the life of a terrorist. In Wisconsin isn't that almost like desecrating the flag?" Martel wondered.

"If you think about it, it might financially pay off. I'm figuring if I can get it back someday and get it signed by Rodgers, it might be worth some serious change when I auction it off on e-Bay," reasoned John.

"Shrewd." Martel said as he nodded in agreement.

Martel watched as the firemen carefully placed a tourniquet above the wound and then secured the ankle with an air splint. That finished, Martel walked over to Ahmed and crouched down next to him. The wounded man was grimacing simultaneously in pain as well as anger. He had regained the persona of the dangerous Al-Qaeda killer that he was. Martel laid his hand on Ahmed's shoulder and said, "Ahmed Abdullah Rahim, I am Special Agent Charles Martel. I believe you have met my partner John Savage before. I am very pleased to finally meet you."

John Savage, with a phone to his ear crouched down next to Martel and said, "We made it. I just heard from the dispatcher; Air Force One is wheels down."

CHAPTER THIRTY-NINE

I'm In

It had been three days since Ahmed had been shot by John Savage, and Martel was on the couch of John's living room waiting for the press conference to take place. Hours after the shooting, John and Martel were gently eased out of the loop. John's report was stamped classified, and the release of information was placed in hands of Homeland Security. John entered the room and set a tray in front of Martel. Piled high were Doritos topped with melted cheese, slightly browned after being cooked under the broiler. John set down a cold glass of La Crosse Beer in front of him.

"Why aren't you a part of this?" asked John.

"It was our job to find him, and when that happened, I handed off the ball. That's what I do. Now Ahmed is someone else's concern," said Martel.

"What has taken them so long to have a press conference?" asked John.

"They were able to take their time because every eye in La Crosse was looking at the Air Force One landing when we shot it out with Ahmed in that parking lot," said Martel.

"What about the radio transmissions?" John asked.

"All of the transmissions around the hotel were on a secure channel, so scanner land didn't hear anything. You didn't use a radio, so your 'shots fired,' transmission wasn't heard by anyone except the dispatcher," said Martel. "That gives them some time to shape the information in this press release to best serve their needs," said Martel.

"You mean they won't tell the truth?" asked John.

"Yeah, they'll tell the truth but not the whole truth. This is a sensitive situation. We have Ahmed in custody alive. That is a major intelligence coup. There is no telling, when Ahmed realizes how truly fucked he is, how much actionable intelligence they can glean off him. He knows locations of camps, contacts, communication, and supply lines. He can draw out the names of commanders, right up the chain of command and even possibly right up to the top echelon of Al-Qaeda. You did well by not killing this guy." Martel took a swig of beer, grabbed a chip and slowly pulled it away from the plate marveling at how the authentic Wisconsin cheese created a thin wiggly bridge between the chip and the plate. "This stuff is awesome."

"Thanks," said John as he shoved a cheese covered chip into his mouth.

"John, I've meant to ask you. Did you deliberately shoot him in the ankle so that we could take him alive?" asked Martel.

"No. Gun fights don't work like that. I could not get a good shot at him, so I shot at the only target that he presented. The rest was luck. He fell and dropped the gun out of reach; otherwise, I am certain Ahmed would not have killed himself, but he would have gone down fighting," said John.

Just then the press conference started as a tall man, who looked a little bit like a young Robert Redford, stepped up to the podium and read from a teleprompter in a deep radio announcer voice, "Good afternoon, ladies and gentleman. I am Greg Pepin of the Federal Bureau of Investigation. I am happy to announce that a suspect was taken into custody three days ago after a short gun fight with federal and local officers. He was being sought after having been identified as a prime suspect in the murder of his girlfriend and also a drug-related homicide in Arizona."

The suspect is currently listed as John Doe because he refuses to identify himself and he has used many aliases in the past. He has been treated and released into federal custody. Investigators have been able to match the weapon he was carrying to at least one homicide, and his DNA has been found at the scene of two homicides. This is an ongoing federal investigation, and we will release further information as we receive it. Thank you." Pepin then turned and walked away.

"Was the president ever in danger?"

"Can you verify reports that he was an American Soldier?"

"Can you give us the aliases he used?"

"How did the officers know he was here?'

"Can you verify reports that his target was the president?"

"Who was the La Crosse officer that was involved in the shooting? There are unconfirmed reports that Officer John Savage was the officer involved once again. Is that true?"

The shouted questions were urgently asked, but they fell on an empty high gloss but uncaring podium.

"Damn! They didn't even release his name," said John dropping into his recliner.

"That is classified. If it leaks out to Al Qaeda that we have Ahmed in custody, then the opportunities presented by the actionable intelligence they get from him evaporates. That's why Ahmed's name can't be released yet," explained Martel. "Now they have a legitimate reason not to release the name. Sorry, buddy. They are right on this decision John"

"But that means… Stella won't know… shit," said John dropping his face into his hands.

"It will either leak out eventually, or it will be released all at once, after they have capitalized on the information they glean out of Ahmed," said Martel.

"How long will that take," asked John lifting his head from his hands.

"That depends. The media will pursue it because they do not like unanswered questions. Bits and pieces will leak, but I am guessing that it will be at least six months and possibly as long as a year before they can properly move on everything they get from Ahmed," said Martel.

"What if he doesn't talk?" John asked.

"He'll talk," said Martel confidently.

"Water boarding?" asked John.

"No. We are kinder and gentler now. He will talk because he will find himself in unpleasant conditions for the rest of his life, and the only way he can improve his condition is by cooperating. It's amazing that when

Destiny of Heroes by Lt. Dan Marcou

you give someone three hots and a cot, and they know someone else is getting strawberry short cake, a queen sized bed, and television with the soft porn channel, even a guy like Ahmed asks, "What do I do to get that?" Martel reasoned. "Ahmed will discover he's fucked for life, and it's a matter of time before he bargains for some Vaseline. I guarantee it," Martel assured John as he crunched into another chip. "Besides, we have some secret information that will induce him to talk."

"What's that?" asked John.

"I am going to tell the investigators to threaten that they will release the truth about him running from Martyrs' Ridge in his underwear to Al Jazeera unless he cooperates. I think he will talk."

"I think he'd rather be water boarded," said John.

"Ain't that the truth? It should be a year tops, maybe sooner, before they can release his name," said Martel.

"That doesn't help me in the short term," said John. "That doesn't help me with Thomason and Diane Cruz."

"Just think how sweet it will be for you when it does come out though," said Martel.

"I don't care so much about them; the main thing is it doesn't help me with Stella," said John.

"Call her," urged Martel.

"Can I tell her about Ahmed and what happened if I tell her not to tell anyone?" John asked.

"No, John. That's classified," said Martel. "I don't think you have to tell her. That girl is nuts about you. I could see it in her eyes. Call her now, John."

"I can't. The only thing that has changed from her point of view is I just shot another guy. That won't help me. Besides, she said don't call, so I won't call," John said. "It's her move."

John leaned back in the recliner and stared out the window into Hixon Forest as the shadows of the setting sun grew longer. He stayed alone in his thoughts while Martel flipped channels until he found ESPN. He looked back at John and almost spoke, but realized there was nothing left to say that could possibly help his friend.

As the pretty blonde ESPN reporter interviewed a multi-millionaire dressed in a Yankee's uniform about the possibility of the Yankees winning yet another World Series, John Savage reached for his phone on the table next to him. His thumb danced with great certainty across the phone pad, and then he held the phone to his ear. After a few moments of silence he said, "Hey, Balduzzi. Make the arrangements. I'll see you at Bragg. I'm in."

CHAPTER FORTY

The Destiny of Heroes

18 Months Later
0330 Hours in a mountainous region inside "one of the Stans"

Savage dropped to a knee and his team came to a halt. The village was laid out exactly as it had appeared in the dry runs. They had come off the trail forty yards from the target house. The dark in the mountainous regions of Afghanistan and Pakistan, was a dark not found anywhere back home. Back home at night, there where street lights, headlights, taillights, flashlights, nightlights, refrigerator lights, and all kinds of technology preventing the total blanket of darkness offered by a cloudy night. There were none of these in the mountains of the Stans.

Back home there were harvest moons, quarter moons, winter moons, autumn moons, but in the Stans there were nights in which, thanks to clouds and tall mountains, the light of the silvery moon was as difficult to find for an American soldier as a kind word. However, American soldiers did what American soldiers have done since Washington crossed the Delaware. They took an environmental adversary and made it their ally.

Darkness was their friend. The "thermals" took the temperature variations of rock, dirt, metal, and human beings and then created contrast. The world looked like a black and white television that was a little out of focus, but the contrasts were sharp tonight. John spotted the sentry seated in a chair in front of the target house. He held up one finger for all to see and then laid his hand against the side of his face and tipped his head slightly as if he was a child sleeping peacefully on a pillow, meaning "one sentry and he's asleep."

The sentry had done what so many sentries in every army throughout history have done following night after night of staring into bland nothingness. He relaxed and fell asleep at his post. John pumped his fist once and his team was moving as one toward the target. Their weapons were up and they were in the squat, doing the "Groucho," as they moved quickly, smoothly, and quietly across the 40 yards.

John had his sights dead on the chest of the sentry, and as he got closer he moved his sights half way between the bottom of his nose and the area right between the eyes. John's team moved like a whisper on the wind in an empty meadow. "FFFUMMP," was all that was heard as the suppressor silenced the shot that took "Ahmed One" out. They were all Ahmed's to John, now, when he did not know their names. They were his enemy. Neither a dog barked nor a cat meowed. Ahmed One's passing went unnoticed to all but the team.

The breacher moved up and deftly placed the charges on the door in less than a second, stepped away, and everyone crouched to wait. "BOOOM!"

They were in. John moved in and left, Balduzzi moved in and button-hooked right as Haldane entered and cut down the middle. "FFFUMMP, FFFUMMP," one rising left went down fast, "FFUMMP, FFFUMMP," one down to the right never to rise again. The doorway in the middle of the room had just ragged drapes hung over it. Haldane was through it and then "FFFUMMP, FFFUMMP." Haldane whispered over the radio for all to hear, "Target is clear. We have the golden ring; he's shining," said Haldane.

The target house was built into the side of the mountain, so they did not have to worry about being flanked. They could hear the shouts and the rushing of feet, so Balduzzi and Savage kicked open the shutters on the front windows and readied for battle. Savage looked at his watch. If everything was going as planned, they only had to hold off resistance for three minutes before the rest of the Ahmeds would be meeting Allah if they ventured outside into the hell that awaited them.

Balduzzi saw one man running toward the target, shouting in Farsi, "What's happening? "FFFUMP," He skidded into the harsh earth, forever stilled, his question unanswered.

Savage said, "Movement to the north," but before they could lay down any fire the location was pulverized by countless fifty caliber rounds. To the south John saw three men just stand up from behind cover to run.

He opened fire on them, and it appeared that his weapon had magically transformed to a fifty caliber Gatling Gun, because the area the group was running from, the area they were running to, and the area they currently were in suddenly came alive with a terrible swirling, churning dust storm of deadly rounds. They were no more.

John turned to Balduzzi and observed with relief, "Good, they're early."

Haldane came out assisting the weak but uninjured golden ring. He was a CBN reporter that came to the Stans after receiving an assurance of a dream interview. He wanted to find the current "Number One" and was promised a meeting, but the pundit became a pawn. He did not realize that hostages had been the currency of these peoples since their ancestors fought with Alexander the Great.

The black helicopters appeared in the clearing out front as gunners hung out the doors hoping for something to appear without a marker. Whump, Whump, Whump, Whump, the blades spun sending dust, gravel, and small creatures of the mountains flying. Every human being left alive in the village lay flat on the floor of their homes and prayed to Allah they would make it through this night.

Balduzzi shouted "Move!" and John covered, followed by Haldane, the golden ring, then the rest of the team with Balduzzi bringing up the rear. When they reached the chopper, John took one arm of the weak hostage and Haldane the other. After one smooth movement the golden ring found himself lying on the opposite side of the chopper. The already thin man had been reduced by being fed the meager portions of the barely digestible fare served to hostages in the Stans.

The chopper was up and out, while the second chopper fired a missile into the target and succeeded in making it disappear. It was a message from the United States of America. "This is the only ransom we will pay for hostages. If you harbor these people, you lose your home."

The message was lost in translation to Americans, who would call it excessive unnecessary collateral damage, but it was understood loud and clear without interpretation by the people of the Stans.

Once back in the debriefing area, the golden ring tearfully shook hands with each one of his rescuers, thanking them profusely. As the rescued newsman reached John, he read his name on his uniform, "Savage," and asked, "Where have I heard that name before?"

"You did an exposé on me once, Mr. Barclay. Don't you remember? You reported that in my encounters with hostile enemies there were never any wounded, and you wondered why. Well now you know. If we would have wounded any of your captors or missed even one of them, you would not be here right now. Now do you understand?" John asked.

"Yes I do, son. I am so sorry," said Barclay.

"I accept your apology, but do not call me, son. I am not your son. You see, I have a father, but I am quite certain he would not want you calling me son because he will never forgive you, sir," said John.

⟹⟫●⟪⟸

Later in the barracks, the beer and the bullshit were flowing. John reached next to his bunk into the package sent by Dr. Sistek, pulled out a Bazooka Bubble Gum and carefully ripped it open. He unfolded the comic and read what Bazooka Joe had to say, smiled, and put it in his pocket while he began to chew.

Balduzzi sat on the bunk next to him and said, "How did that feel? You know, with Barclay."

"I can't lie, Balduzzi, it was awesome! All the hell you have put me through in the last year and a half was worth it for that moment. The golden ring was a perfect code word for that target, because it was truly golden," said John.

"God loves you, man," said Balduzzi. "You are better than a rabbit's foot."

"We don't need a rabbit's foot; we make our own luck," said John, "most of it anyway."

After an awkward pause Balduzzi said insistently, "Now, John. Read it now!" said Balduzzi.

John looked over at the pillow on his bunk and sat staring for a long moment.

"Read it!!" Balduzzi barked. "That's an order!"

John leaned over and slid his hand under the pillow. It was an envelope penned in the hand of Stella. He had neither seen nor heard from her since their chance meeting at the airport. He had hesitated to open it before the mission, because no matter what it said he did not want that weighing on his mind during what looked to be his last foray in the Stans. There was talk that their work was done here, and they wanted Balduzzi back in the states to train other units to be as successful as his was.

John stared at the envelope and then smelled it. Lilacs and peaches, John thought to himself. The pleasant stomach ache inspired by love rumbled below. His buddies, the missions, and the ancient mountains, the birthplace of so many wars and the grave of so many warriors, had made him forget… for a time. Now love was a possibility again, back on his plate and its aroma was lilacs and peaches…maybe.

John, ever so slowly and carefully, ripped open the envelope. He unfolded it and read it to himself, while Balduzzi watched for a hint of its contents.

My Dear John,

I will start this letter asking you to be once again, "My Dear John."

You have been all over the news of late. I do not know if you are aware of it all, where you are at, but I guess that doesn't matter because what is news to us was never news to you.

The whole world knows now about Ahmed. They know now how he stalked you, stalked the president, and may have succeeded if not for you and your friend. You are a hero here, John. The chief said how hard it was on the department, watching Thomason and the media malign you, when they knew the truth but couldn't say anything.

Right after the information was released, I was visited by Charles Martel your friend from the FBI. He told me the visit was not official, but he had to speak with me as your friend. He told me everything and even said that you still loved me. I can't imagine how after the way I treated you.

I was frightened then, John. I know now that I will never be frightened again if you come back to me and be forever at my side.

Please say yes and I will wait for you to come home to me.

I know now we were meant to be.

All my love is your love,

Stella

At the bottom of the letter Stella had pressed her lips and left a rose-colored impression. John became lost in Stella's words and forgot where he was for the moment. John brought the letter to his lips, closed his eyes, and kissed her softly, 12,000 miles from home.

By now the entire barracks had grown quiet along with Balduzzi. His buddies were wondering whether it was a yes or a no for John and Stella. As John kissed the letter softly, an unrehearsed shout exploded throughout the barracks as if it was occupied by 16 Stanley Kowalski's from *Streetcar named Desire,* "STELLA!"

They all jumped him, scuffed his hair, rolled him out of his bunk, and roughed him up. It was their way of telling him they loved him too. Then they all laughed together, a laugh that only buddies at war have shared.

Later after lights out, John lay in his bunk, longing for his return to home, the police department, and, mostly, Stella. He had not felt so homesick since boot camp. The trip home would come soon, but it could not come soon enough. He ached to be home instead of in the rank, cramped quarters. Even though he was surrounded by a snoring bunch of buddies who, although they were worthy of the moniker "best friends a guy could ever have," were a poor replacement for Stella at his side.

"PSSST, Johnny, are you awake?" Balduzzi asked from the next bunk.

"Yeah," said John. "I can't sleep."

"Thinking about home?" Balduzzi asked.

"Yeah, pretty much," understated John.

"Me too," said Balduzzi. "I bet you this is the way it has always been."

"How's that?" asked John.

"You know. Soldiers lying awake at night next to clean weapons and dirty boots, surrounded by a smelly bunch of snoring guys, and all they can think about is the most beautiful woman in the world. You wonder why you left her behind for this. I wonder and wonder and wonder why, but never can come up with an answer," Balduzzi pondered.

"I can't answer the question for myself, so I sure can't answer it for you," said John.

Balduzzi let out a long philosophical sigh and concluded, "I think... I think it's just *the destiny of heroes.*"

About the Author

Lt. Dan Marcou retired after 33 years as a highly decorated police officer in 2006. In 2007 his first novel *The Calling, The Making of a Veteran Cop,* was published. It is still being used in police academies and criminal justice programs as an exciting and accurate portrayal of law enforcement. He followed this novel with *SWAT: Blue Knights and Black Armor,* and *Nobody's Heroes,* to complete the well-received "McCarthy-Compton Trilogy."

"Lt. Dan" remains active as an internationally-recognized law enforcement trainer. He has also had hundreds of articles published on-line and in print and is a featured columnist for PoliceOne (www. policeone.com).